ODYSSEUS AWAKENING

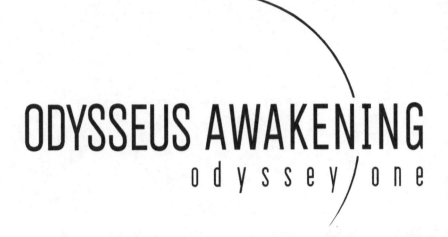

ODYSSEUS AWAKENING

odyssey one

(Book 6)

E V A N C U R R I E

47N⬤RTH

Text copyright © 2017 by Cleigh Currie
All rights reserved.

Published by 47North, Seattle

www.apub.com

Amazon, the Amazon logo, and 47North are trademarks of Amazon.com, Inc., or its affiliates.

ISBN-13: 9781542048477
ISBN-10: 1542048478

Cover design by Adam Hall

Printed in the United States of America

ODYSSEUS AWAKENING

PROLOGUE

Imperial Systems

▶ Navarch Misrem glowered at the darkness beyond her command, ignoring the specks of light as she focused on the abyss.

Her defeat at the hands of the anomalous species they'd encountered had been . . . galling, and also expensive, both in terms of the weight of metal in the skies and her own personal standing within the Empire. She had survived the resulting inquiry, of course. It would take more than one failed mission to topple her, particularly given the clearly faulty intelligence available to her beforehand.

And that is without mentioning the apparent sabotage we suffered in the very midst of battle.

Imperial Intelligence Services (IIS) had yet to determine how those nuclear weapons had been smuggled on board her vessels, but if anything, they were more infuriated than she was over the incident. There were plenty of potential suspects, of course. The Empire had enemies, both within and beyond its borders.

What was driving IIS mad was that the enemies who might desire to do such a thing, had the capability and opportunity *and* would use atomic fusion weapons, occupied a rather short list.

A list with no entries, to be precise.

If not for the few of her ships that survived to return with records and damage for IIS to examine, Misrem had no doubt they would have accused her of falsifying a data entry. With the evidence clearly in their face, however, the intelligence services were understandably perturbed and defensive over their apparent lapse.

So, with blame spread more or less evenly around, Misrem was still in her position and more eager than ever to move her forces back into the void and reclaim any lost standing with alacrity.

Thankfully, that opportunity was rapidly approaching.

Ships had been arriving for weeks, replacing her losses at first and then reinforcing and expanding her divisions.

The Oathers had become an unacceptable thorn in the side of the Imperial Council, one that had existed too long and become too painful to leave be. The Drasin probes had failed, not that it would have taken much mental acuity to predict that, Misrem supposed. Letting those beasts out into the galaxy had been a mark of *insanity*, no matter the supposed safeguards, and she expected the Empire would pay for that act of unmitigated foolishness eventually.

That payment wasn't due just yet, however, and she was now tasked with extracting a similar payment from the Oathers on behalf of the Empire.

Footsteps behind her gave Misrem cause to half turn until she caught sight of their source.

"Captain Aymes," she greeted the man cordially.

"Navarch," he replied with a bow of his head. "The *Piar Cohn* is fully repaired, all systems certified."

"Excellent," she told him, honestly pleased.

The *Cohn*, her crew, and her captain had been under a deep shadow with the Imperial Command since their first interactions with the anomalous species. They still were, in fact, but *not* with Misrem.

The ships the *Cohn* had encountered appeared to match both Imperial and Oather configurations at a glance, but she had seen them in action. They were neither.

Between that revelation and the fact that Aymes had risked his own ship to save her and what few of her crew could be pulled off the doomed wreck of her flagship, Aymes had more than earned his way out from under that shadow—in her eyes, at least.

The Empire was likely to require a great deal more, but the Empire always required more.

"The *Cohn*'s return to full duties brings our experienced vessels back to full strength," she said, "and the new vessels assigned to us replace our lost power and more besides. I expect that we will receive orders to break orbit soon."

"Back to the Oather territory, Navarch?"

"Indeed." She nodded. "This time, with teeth and will."

And a guiding mission, she continued in thought. They knew the Oather sector would be a tougher battle than expected, and they now had an idea *why*. What was needed, then, was to determine just how much tougher it would be.

They needed information, especially whatever they could learn about the new anomalous group that had made themselves heard and felt. With that, the Empire itself could move.

▶▶▶

Allied Earth Vessel (AEV) *Odysseus,* Earth Orbit

▶ Eric Stanton Weston stood alone on the open observation deck of the *Odysseus,* looking out at the stars that filled the black around him. A few, very few by relative measure, were moving, and it was those he watched in silence.

They weren't stars, of course. They were much smaller, much closer, and far more interesting to his mind.

He was watching the lights of the Construction Swarm, a new development from Earth's Technical Research Division. Self-replicating robots, built with some human technology, some Priminae tech, and just a hint of Drasin capabilities.

That last bit worried a lot of people, him included, but Eric had long recognized that technology was a tool. Even the tech that created the Drasin. One didn't get angry at a tool. One did not fear a tool. Emotions were reserved for the person handling the tool. Since the people handling this particular tool were Terrans and not some ethereal Empire, he would reserve judgment on the technology.

For the moment, Eric was more concerned with what they were doing than how they were doing it.

The Swarm was part of the Solar Reconstruction Effort and had started out as a relatively small piece of the whole, soon growing to unbelievable scales. Using the material left in the former orbit of Mars—that being trillions of dead Drasin along with a pair of now-aimless moons—the Swarm, at first simply self-replicating, was now in the process of building the beginnings of Earth's first Kardashev-scale construction.

It was a small thing, by such scales, but no less impressive for all that. The first of the new Kardashev satellites were already in solar orbit, downwell near the orbit of Mercury. They were purely power collectors, capturing solar radiation and storing it for use by other SRE projects. Mostly, for now, they were being used to power the Swarm, but that percentage was dropping off rapidly as more and more power stations were brought online.

Eric had seen the plans for the future of the system, and despite his misgivings concerning the source of some of the technological advancements, he couldn't fault either the vision or the sheer ambition of the designers.

Those plans, however, were for the future. In the present, he still had a job to do.

Eric took one last look at the lights moving through the black, remembering those lost on Mars, and said a silent prayer before he turned on his heel and strode off the observation deck.

▶▶▶

Ranquil

▶ Admiral Rael Tanner found himself staring at the night sky as it loomed over the planet Ranquil. The flickering light of the stars as seen through the thick atmosphere of the planet had once calmed him in his deliberations, back when his work had been merely ceremonial and of no particular import.

He had been promoted to his position largely because no one of higher importance wanted the job, and many considered it a pointless and thankless task that would end any hope of advancement within the merchant fleet. Taking his position among the admiralty had been a day of mixed feelings for him. Pride and honest satisfaction, because Tanner had never disdained those who desired to defend his people, but there had been a melancholy as well. Every man and woman who joined the fleet wanted a ship and the freedom to fly her as they wanted, and Tanner was no exception to that rule.

In his position, he would have neither.

In those early days, the stars had been a source of wonder and joy to him. That had been replaced by the foreboding terror the Drasin brought with them and left behind when they were destroyed. Wonder was for children, perhaps. But Tanner missed it terribly and wished deeply for its return.

A wish, it seems, I will be denied.

Since the initial Drasin attack on the Colonies of the Priminae, the universe had grown darker. The lights of those distant stars no longer housed the wonder of the unknown but instead its terror. Exploration had never been a primary interest of the people, yet in any society, there were those who longed for the frontier. In his youth, Tanner had been one of those folk, but he had grown out of his yearning with time, much as his family assured him he would.

He valued the secure and quiet culture of Ranquil in ways his young self would never have understood, but Tanner was well aware that many, even in Priminae culture, wanted something . . . different.

In prior years, those people had often been seen as hindrances by the society that birthed them. They were never happy with the way things were, always wanting something new, different. For those satisfied with the traditional life of a citizen of the Colonies, that mindset was more than merely baffling; it could even be considered insulting.

Now, those same people who had been considered nuisances by the Colonies were forming the backbone of the new fleet.

For Tanner, who had long straddled the middle line between the two camps, the changing winds of the stars were pushing him into the younger contingent. The Priminae had enjoyed a long peace. That was at an end.

It was time to raise the blood and look to the uncertain future with both a wary eye and a heart full of hope. War was coming, of that Tanner was certain. The reports from Captain—now Commodore—Weston, his friend, made that eminently clear.

Whether the conservative adherents of the traditional ways liked it or not, the times were changing.

CHAPTER 1

Station Unity One

▶ "Enter."

Commodore Weston stepped into the office calmly, trying to mask the shiver that passed down his spine. It was a different office, a different place entirely, but somehow he knew that wouldn't matter. Every conversation he had in this spiritual place seemingly ended with him and his crew fighting for their lives.

"Admiral." He nodded politely as Amanda Gracen gestured for him to take a seat.

"Welcome, Commodore," Gracen said as he sat down, taking a moment to look out the observation bubble behind her desk before she too took a seat. "Are your crew all back from leave?"

"For the most part," Weston confirmed. "Still a few unaccounted for, but they have a couple more hours. There's always someone who's late on a ship the size of the *Odysseus*, as I'm sure you're aware."

Gracen tipped her head with a hint of a smile. She hadn't ever commanded a starship, aside from her own incredibly brief stint on the *Odysseus*, but she had come up through the Canadian Navy and, later, the Confederate Blue Navy. A ship with the crew numbers the *Odysseus* boasted could normally be counted on to leave port light one or two sailors in wartime.

Such lapses were rarer in peacetime, of course, partially because the departure times could often be pushed a bit and few of the AWOL sailors were ever intentionally missing. Most often it turned out someone had partied a little too hard the night before and either passed out or, just as likely, got arrested, tossed in a drunk tank, and was forgotten about by the local police.

The need for warm hands was such that punishments were generally light, unless the sailor in question was an officer.

"Well, you shouldn't have to leave light this time," she said after a moment. "The *Odysseus* and your squadron have been slated for a patrol mission, but the exact schedule is largely left to you. We have a list of sectors we want checked into, however."

She pulled a data plaque from the pile on her desk and held it out to Weston.

"More take from Prometheus?" he asked as he accepted the screen and looked it over.

"Some," she admitted. "Passer has whipped the Rogues into a frenzy, and they've been tearing through every WTF-class star we have in our records. Most of them have natural explanations, of course, but there are enough traces of a previous high-technology race—or more than one—that we've been considering forming an official archeological division."

"We likely need one," Weston said, glancing down the list.

"No question there. The big problem is that we don't have ships to spare right now," Gracen said before scowling slightly. "Which hasn't stopped some people from going for it anyway."

That made Weston pause his skimming to look up in shock. *"How?"*

In order to do what she was suggesting, people would need access to an FTL-capable vessel, and he had no ever-loving *clue* how that was possible. There was no chance in hell that the Confederacy had released transition technology, so only . . . He groaned, cringing.

"The Block?" he asked, knowing the answer.

"They're selling drive tech to fund their own buildup," she confirmed with a curt dip of her head.

"Jesus. I hope they're locking down the safeties on those things." Weston winced.

The Block FTL drive was based on the mathematical calculations that had originally been the source for the Alcubierre Warp Drive. It *was* a perfectly functional faster-than-light drive, infinitely more comfortable than the transition drive, though nearly infinitely slower as well. The problem was that it relied on creating a gravity well for the ship to constantly "fall" into. The well trapped all manner of things besides the ship, including high-energy radiation. So if the ship's safeties were to fail, those particles would be released at multiples of the speed of light when the ship decelerated. The resulting burst of gamma, Hawking, and Cerenkov radiation was enough to irradiate a planet beyond the capability of sustaining life, and it would be aimed right at whatever the ship was traveling toward.

During the invasion of the Drasin, the Block's premier captain, Sun Ang Wen of the PLA star cruiser *Wei Fang*, had used that very design flaw as a weapon of mass destruction. The Chinese captain's actions had likely saved the Earth by utterly decimating the invasion fleet before it could even approach the planet, but the idea of that technology flitting around the galaxy in the hands of civilians whose maintenance schedules would likely be hit or miss at *best* frankly terrified him.

"If I might make a suggestion, ma'am," Weston said after a moment.

"Please," Gracen said, gesturing airily. "Anything that puts a shine on this turd is welcome."

He laughed a little, unable to hold back, but went on. "Get the Priminae to help with the drive designs. Maybe they have ways to foolproof it. They've had similar drives for centuries, remember."

"I'll do that."

Actually, now that it had been brought up, Gracen was surprised no one had suggested that option already. She supposed few people had really wrapped their heads around the notion that the world was about to enter an era of true faster-than-light travel for the masses, and those few that had were too caught up with their heads in the stars to think about the consequences.

"Well, if that works out," she said, "then possibly we'll be able to safely leave exo-archeology to archeologists while we focus on defense."

"That would be the ideal," Weston said, chuckling, "though I honestly have to say that the idea of commanding a Federation starship is one of the things that caused me to put my name into the *Odyssey* project for consideration."

"You would hardly be the only one, Commodore," Gracen assured him with a hint of a smile.

"We should be exploring and discovering," Weston said seriously, "rather than planning to fight another war that will kill hundreds of thousands—if we're lucky."

Gracen shrugged. It wasn't that she disagreed with the commodore; she'd just given up on her utopian dreams a long time earlier. Three wars, an alien invasion, and countless lives lost had burned those dreams from her brain. If such a future ever came about, she would happily retire to live out her remaining years with the satisfaction that she'd done her job well.

Until then, there were things to break and people to kill.

"Someday, perhaps," she said aloud.

"But not today," Weston said firmly. "What are our orders concerning Imperial contact?"

"If they'll talk, talk to them," Gracen ordered. "Not that we expect you'll be able to talk them down. Things have gone too far for that anyway, but any further intelligence you can gather would be of inestimable value. When talking fails, teach them they should have given talking more of a chance."

"Yes ma'am." Weston stood, saluting. "With your permission, Admiral?"

"Go on," Gracen said, turning her seat away from him as he retreated from the office.

She looked out into the abyss beyond her office, eyes picking out the moving stars she knew to be part of the Swarm Constellation working tirelessly on her personal pet project. She hoped it wouldn't be necessary, but Gracen had long since figured out she hadn't been born under a lucky star.

"Good luck, Commodore," she whispered after her retreating officer. "We are all going to need it, I fear."

Everything she knew told her that hell was coming.

Most thought they'd already been through hell during the Drasin onslaught, but as much as Gracen wished otherwise, she had a bad feeling those invaders were just the opening act. During her time in the service, Gracen had learned weapons were not to be feared.

The hand behind them, however? Well, that was another story, wasn't it.

▶▶▶

▶ Commander Stephen Michaels, known as Steph or Stephanos to his friends, walked across the flight deck of Unity Station, ignoring the big delta-wing shuttles as he focused on the ready squadron position where the new-generation Vorpal Space Superiority Fighters were resting.

Unlike his Double A fighter, the Vorpals had been designed primarily for space combat rather than adapted from an air superiority design. Ignoring aerodynamics in favor of pure design efficiency gave them an ungainly look, but having seen them in their natural element—or lack thereof, he supposed—Steph was comfortable saying he was impressed with their capabilities.

Still nothing on his Archangel, of course, but impressive all the same.

"Commander?"

Steph half turned, then grinned as he recognized the woman approaching him. "Chief!"

"Good to see you again, sir." Chief Corrin grinned back at him.

"I haven't seen you since . . . Hell, I think we were in the Forge."

"I was assigned to the *Bell* for a few months," she answered, "but it wasn't for me, so when a slot opened up on the *Big E*, I took it."

Steph was only mildly surprised. Most people in the current Black Navy would consider being reassigned from a Heroic to the only carrier in the fleet to be something of a demotion, but even he'd considered it in some of his weaker moments. Piloting the *King* was a thrill sometimes, but most of the time it was sheer drudgery. He was a fighter jock at heart, so the Vorpals called to him, and only the *Big E* carried Vorpals.

"They're lucky to have you," Steph told her honestly.

Corrin sighed. "Probably not for long. Scuttlebutt says the *E* is already being considered obsolete. We haven't had an assignment out of the system since the invasion."

Steph nodded thoughtfully as he considered that.

It wasn't surprising, since the *Enterprise* was the second—and last—ship of the Odyssey Class. There had been three other hulls laid out, with more planned, but those three had been *eaten* by the Drasin during the invasion. Now there was no point in building more ships of a class that didn't seem to have much purpose in the new Navy.

Without the singularity core of the Heroics or the stripped-down efficiency of the Rogues, the Odyssey Class just didn't have a role.

"Well, hang in there," he said finally. "Sooner or later, they'll remember how much they need people like us. They always do."

He chuckled and looked to the nearest Vorpal. "You know, I have to confess. I thought about requesting a transfer myself, just to get some time with one of these strapped to my back."

She smirked a little smugly. "I understand that. They're pretty hot rides."

"I've seen the specs. They're good," Steph said with an amused look. "But I'm Double A, so anything else is like standing still."

"Those sound like fighting words, Commander."

Steph and Corrin turned, surprised by the new voice.

The source was a tall woman with medium-length black hair hanging loose around her shoulders. She had sharp features and a muscular build, neither of which detracted in the least from the glare she was sending Steph's direction.

"Lieutenant Commander Black." Corrin nodded, smothering another grin. "Meet Commander Michaels. Commander, this is Alexandra Black. Wing Commander, Excalibur Squadron."

"Lieutenant Commander." Steph nodded to the woman, observing her for a moment before deciding that she was only half-serious in her ire.

It was sometimes hard to tell. Tormenting other units was one of the primary pastimes of any military group—the more elite the group, the better—but a lot of people took it too seriously. They were fun to troll, but Steph wasn't really in the mood at the moment.

A little honest ribbing, however, was just what the doctor ordered.

"You fly these toys, I assume?" he asked, smirking openly.

"Watch it, hotshot," she countered. "Last I heard, you were pretending to fly that barge you call a ship."

"Oh." Steph mock winced. "That would really hurt if, you know, I hadn't gotten a chance to make the '*Disseus* dance in a real furball already. How many combat hours do *you* have?"

"We got plenty during the invasion and the Liberation battle," Alexandra said, a little defensively.

With the *Enterprise* basically being system bound since the Liberation, Steph knew that her squadron hadn't had as many combat hours as any of them would have preferred. With a real live star war going on, she and the rest of her squadron must be chomping at the figurative bit to get out there and mix it up with ET.

It was something civilians and even a lot of military just didn't get about fighter jocks, pretty much all the Special Forces teams, and any group of dedicated specialists. Unlike your regular Joe, she and hers had spent a significant portion of their lives preparing for just this moment. Any unit that maintained that sort of dedication *wanted* to be in the middle of things with every fiber of their beings. Being told they couldn't get out there and do what they'd dreamed of, trained for . . . it had to be infuriating.

Steph, for his part, just nodded in clearly mocking sympathy at her statement.

"Nothing wrong with notching some Drasin decals up on the side of your hull," he told her. "My Double A still has all my decals painted on her."

"Under all the *dust*, I suppose?" Alexandra countered swiftly.

She noted with some pleasure the brief but clearly pained look that passed over his face. She'd struck home with that one at least.

"Children, please!" Chief Corrin stepped between them, rolling her eyes. "No slap fights on my flight deck."

Both officers shot the senior NCO dark looks promising retribution, but Corrin brushed them off with casual ease. She'd dealt with fighter jocks most of her career, every one of them outranking her in every way except the one that mattered. They knew better than to piss off the woman in charge of maintaining their rides.

Oh, she wouldn't do anything to reduce the combat effectiveness of the wing, of course. That was just *not* on, but she could damn well make a pilot's life a living hell in every other way if she chose, and Steph knew it too.

He recovered first from her jab, laughing openly. "Never change, Chief, but do keep in mind you're not maintaining *my* plane anymore."

"You really think I can't reach out and mess with you on that big beast-ship of yours?" she asked.

Steph gave her a long look before sighing and putting his hands up in surrender. "Yeah, I don't think I'll take you up on that."

Corrin nodded, managing to be completely professional while still exuding a smug satisfaction that would have been worthy of censure had an officer been able to point to any related, concrete action. Steph had sometimes wondered if there was some senior NCO course covering that particular skill, but he figured she'd have to kill him if she told him, and so he didn't ask.

"And from that exchange, I suppose that the Chief was much the same on the *Odyssey*?" Alexandra asked dryly.

"Hell," Steph responded in kind, "I think she may have mellowed."

If looks could kill, the one Corrin shot him would have had her up for a firing squad. Steph shrugged it off. If NCOs had a course on being smug to officers without getting censured, officers had a counter-course on pissing NCOs off by saying things other people on the planet might take as a compliment.

"If you two *children* are done," she said, "I have work to do."

Alexandra lifted her hands, palms out, not saying a word, while Steph half bowed with a flourish. Corrin rolled her eyes and stalked off, grumbling about "children" the whole way.

Steph waited until the Chief was well out of earshot before looking over at Alexandra and saying, "You're lucky to have her."

She snorted. "We know. Not going to tell *her* that, mind you."

Steph chuckled, knowing exactly what she meant.

"Of course not," he agreed. "That's just not how things are done."

The younger pilot smiled genuinely at that. "So what brings you slumming down here, hero?"

Steph let his eyes drift to the sleek, if not aerodynamic, hulls of the Vorpal fighters for a moment before he responded. "Just looking over the latest toys, Lieutenant. Ugly beasts, in the best possible military meaning of the words, of course."

Alexandra understood what he meant. Sometimes military designs veered to the ugly side so much that they attained a practical beauty, and the Vorpals treaded on that territory with an unholy glee.

Not needing to be overly concerned with atmospheric lift, the Vorpals had long spars that mounted weapon hardpoints, fuel tanks, and modular scanner gear out and away from the main body for maximum efficiency.

It was a look only a person in the military could love.

"I heard the *Odysseus* is shipping out," Alexandra said suddenly, bringing Steph's attention fully to her again. "True?"

"Yeah, we have a few more hours before everyone is supposed to be on board. Probably twelve after that before everyone is *actually* boarded, but you know how that goes."

Alexandra nodded, thinking for a moment before she grinned. "Since you're slumming here with us anyway, AA-boy, feel like getting some space time in?"

Steph looked at her sharply. "Think you can swing that?"

"Please," she scoffed, waving to someone across the deck.

Steph watched as Alexandra strode across the deck to accost an officer at least two grades her superior.

"CAG," she said, calling the man closer as Steph followed her. "Commander, this is CAG, our CSG."

"Pleased to meet you, CAG," Steph said, shaking the man's hand.

CAG was a throwback to the Blue Navy carriers, where the lead officer of an air group held the official title of Commander: Air Group. In the Black Navy, the title was officially Commander: Space Group, but even on the *Odyssey*, everyone had just called Steph CAG.

"Likewise, Commander Michaels," the CAG said. "Your reputation most certainly precedes you."

"Got most of it just following Raze where mere Angels feared to tread," Steph said with a wave. "Dumb luck I lived through it all."

"That's usually how it goes," the CAG said before looking at Alexandra. "What is it, Black?"

"We have a trainer ready to go? Figured I could give wing-boy here a taste of how the other side lives."

The CAG stared at her for several long seconds, then finally gestured down the deck. "Trainer Three is tanked. We were scheduled for some puke runs, but the civilians missed their shuttle. You can sign that one out."

"Thanks, CAG," Alexandra said.

Steph nodded his own thanks as he followed along in the lieutenant's wake. He, for one, had no intention of missing a chance to fly a fighter again. Shuttles and ships just didn't quite count, unfortunately.

Shuttle Bay

▶ Eric met his first officer, Commander Miram Heath, at the designated shuttle bay to transit back over to the *Odysseus*. The statuesque blonde commander had beaten him there by several minutes and was locking down the shuttle as he walked up the ramp.

"Sir, we're locked down and ready to depart," Heath said as Eric nodded to the loadmaster. The man hit the switch to bring up the ramp and seal the interior.

"Thank you, Commander," Eric said, walking past the rows of men and women settling in for the short hop across the black. "Get yourself strapped in, and we'll be on our way."

"Sir," Heath said, taking one of the front jumper seats.

Eric made his way up to the open accessway to the cockpit and stuck his head in.

"Ready to go, sir?" the Marine lieutenant at the controls asked.

"That we are, Hadrian," Eric said. "No one in the LEO seat?"

"Running light, sir," Lieutenant Hadrian responded. "Still a lot of people not back from leave."

"You mind?" Eric gestured to the LIDAR-and-executive-officer position.

"Have at it, sir," Hadrian said as casually as he could manage.

He'd not have turned down any officer, commander or above, who asked, but Hadrian would have been a lot more formal with most. With Eric Weston, however, that almost felt like sacrilege. The man had been a Marine before the Block War and was one of the liberators of Iwo Jima. Everyone involved in that battle was a pure-blooded Marine legend, even the Navy pukes. Hell, even the Japanese Self-Defense Forces (JSDF) walked tall in Marine tales of the second siege of Iwo, though that certainly had a touch of irony to it, he supposed.

Hadrian ran through his preflight as the commodore settled into the right-hand seat and strapped himself in, trying not to be too obvious as he shot glances out of the corner of his eyes at the man.

Apparently, he failed miserably, since Eric sighed.

"If I'm bothering you, Lieutenant, I can sit in the back."

"No sir!" Hadrian shook his head. "Sorry, sir. It's just . . . My dad was on Iwo, sir."

Eric looked over at the young officer for a long moment before he spoke again. "Hadrian? Marshal Hadrian?"

"Yes sir." The lieutenant was shocked that, just based on family name, the commodore remembered his dad, who hadn't been an officer or even one of the survivors.

"Gunnery Sergeant Hadrian made one hell of an accounting of himself, according to a friend of mine," Eric said seriously. "It's a pleasure to see his blood run true, Lieutenant."

"Never wanted anything else," Lieutenant Hadrian admitted as he finished the preflight and casually flipped a bank of switches to bring all the shuttle's systems to power. "Dad's buddies didn't talk much about most of the war, but they all talked about Iwo, sir."

"Mostly lies, no doubt." Eric chuckled. "I didn't have much to do with it. I just came in on the last day. People like Gunny Hadrian, they were the legends. Your dad and his unit and what was left of the JSDF held that island for three weeks before we fought our way to them. Turning point in the war, I firmly believe."

"Most people say that was Tokyo," Hadrian said as the shuttle vibrated under them, powering up.

"Tokyo was a more strategically valuable battle," Eric admitted. "Iwo was a worthless hunk of rock in the middle of nowhere. No strategic value at all, unlike what it had been back in the midtwentieth. There was no damn reason for all that fighting there, but the line had to be drawn somewhere."

"Holy ground," Hadrian said softly.

Eric just nodded, remembering what things had been like back then. The Block offensive had taken them by surprise, decimating the Fifth Fleet and driving American and Japanese military forces right out of Japanese waters. The JSDF had been *mauled* in the initial engagements, and being forced to fall back from their home island had destroyed their morale.

Not that anyone was doing much better in those days.

People had been war weary after decades of fighting one terrorist organization after another, and no one wanted yet another police action, to say nothing of a real war. The swift beating the Block Mantis fighters had unleashed on the old F-35s the Marines had still been running at the time had taken everyone by surprise. With air superiority, Block forces steamrolled every hint of resistance, driving the Navy, Marines, and JSDF before them like so much debris in a tidal surge.

At Iwo, the Marine commander had decided he'd had enough. Major Gib had written in his journal that he envisioned them running with their tails between their legs all the way to Pearl—maybe to the West Coast—if they didn't do something.

Iwo was as good a place to make a stand as any.

So they dug in. Marines, Navy, and JSDF spent the two days' lead they had on the Block offensive turning Iwo Jima into a fortress.

It made no Goddamn sense. The Block could have, no, *should* have just blown their ships and sailed around them, but Gib got on the radio and told the Block commander that Iwo was holy ground, and if he wanted it, he'd have to take it from their cold, dead hands. He taunted that admiral every minute for *hours*, days according to some stories, doing everything he could to rile the man up.

Damned if the Block commander didn't take the bait.

The biggest battle of the war was fought over an island that no one but a Marine gave two shits about.

For three weeks, the defenders held off wave after wave of landing forces, fighting under a steel sky . . . and for three weeks, those same defenders stalled the Block offensive in its tracks.

Iwo Jima was twice blessed or, as some said, twice cursed. The sands of that forsaken ground had soaked up the blood of Marines and Japanese twice. Once while killing each other, once while fighting shoulder to shoulder.

After the war, the island had largely been forgotten again, but Gib had been right about one thing.

It was holy ground.

"Yeah," Eric said aloud as the shuttle taxied out to the launch position. "Yeah, it was. Sanctified in blood."

Hadrian nodded as he settled the engines into standby and waited for clearance. "I went once. It's nothing official, but graduating classes from the depot bribed Navy pilots to fly us out there."

"Yeah, I know." Eric smiled. "The pilots still making a show of not wanting to fly out to a worthless rock for a bunch of green Marines?"

"Making a show?" Hadrian looked over at him curiously, almost missing the clearance to take off. "That was a show?"

Eric laughed softly. "Lot of Navy boys left their blood to soak those sands too, Lieutenant. They run a quiet raffle to see who gets to let the

Marines pay them to visit. Fleet authorizes the fuel every year using a discretionary account."

"I did not know that," Hadrian admitted as he engaged the engines, throwing white-hot plasma at the blast plates that had been raised behind the shuttle.

"You're not supposed to," Eric said as the shuttle leapt forward, pushing him down into the seat cushion. "It's better if you think you're risking something to pay your respects. That's why the Marines plant someone every year to 'suggest' it, usually a guest speaker who quietly reminisces about his own off-the-books trip."

"Son of a . . ." Hadrian just managed to keep from cursing as they left the station and blasted out into the black. "He was a plant?"

Eric laughed openly as he settled back and let the comforting thrust of the shuttle flow through him. "The Corps is populated by sneaky officers, Lieutenant, and even sneakier NCOs. Don't ever forget it, because you have to live up to it yourself."

The lieutenant shook his head, a chagrined look on his face as he used thrusters to pivot and glide the shuttle around the bulk of the space station. In the distance, he and the commodore could see the *Odysseus* rising over the station habitat, the big ship gleaming white in the reflected light of the sun.

With the ship in sight, Hadrian brought the main power plant up and sent them rocketing forward as they cleared the station.

"I can hardly believe that, sir," he admitted after a moment. "Are you sure?"

Eric just smiled. "Do something to get the generals' recognition and find out when they ask you to visit and give the new guys a talk. In the meantime—watch the road, son!"

"What?" Hadrian looked forward and let out a yelp, jerking the stick hard to the left as a blur flashed past *far* closer than he was comfortable with. "What the hell was that?!"

"That," Eric said, twisting his head and leaning forward to keep the object in sight, "was a showoff in one of the new Black Navy fighters. Probably figured buzzing a Marine shuttle was good for a laugh."

He sat back, chuckling. "What can I say? He was right."

The lieutenant managed to not *quite* send a death glare at his commanding officer, but it was a close call.

▶▶▶

▶ "Did you enjoy giving that Marine reason to change his underwear?" Alexandra asked dryly from the rear of the trainer, easing her hands back from where she'd *almost* taken control of the fighter from the man in the front seat.

Steph just chuckled softly.

"You know what," he said after a moment. "I'll give you this much: these Vorpals of yours are hot rides, Lieutenant. Faster and more responsive than even my Archangel."

"They're the best fighters ever developed," Alexandra said, smug pride making its way into her voice.

"Don't get cocky, Lieutenant. I said they're faster and more responsive, and they are, but they're nowhere near as precise in their responsiveness. One-on-one, I'd still favor the Double A platform. NICS is one hell of a force multiplier."

Alexandra was glad he was ahead of her and couldn't see the scowl on her face. NICS, the Neural Interface Connection System, was the technology that made the Archangels so damn deadly—not their weapons, not their engines. From what she knew, during the war with the Block, the enemy Mantis fighters actually edged the Archangels out in pure performance in several categories.

The neural interface allowed by NICS, however, turned the plane into a literal extension of the pilot. It made dodging an incoming missile by *inches* not only possible but standard operating procedure. Flying right into the teeth of your enemy, dancing between the bullets and missiles like something out of myth, was one hell of a way to catch even the best pilot flat-footed.

Unfortunately, the number of people both willing and, more importantly, capable of properly interfacing with NICS had always been extremely low. A lot of people had issues with shoving needles into their necks, and more couldn't reach the level of inner Zen needed to allow the computer to properly read user intent through the normal noise of being alive.

Over the years, computers had gotten better and the system a little less intrusive, but NICS had always been a high-cost, relatively low-payout program. With most of the Double A pilots now assigned to starship helms, it was pretty much a dead aviation program.

What galled Alexandra most, however, was that she had only *just* become NICS qualified before the invasion.

"Yeah, well," she said after a moment, "the Vorpals still *exist*."

She was both pleased and a little angry with herself when the commander had no comeback for that.

CHAPTER 2

Priminae Space

▶ Drey Marina, captain of the Priminae battle cruiser *Tetanna*, stood quietly at the observation portal and looked out over the system they had just transitioned into.

The captain, like every sane person he had ever heard of, despised the Terran transition technology. The method of transport was incredibly disturbing, but no one could deny the utility of near-instantaneous travel between stars. The faint odor of vomit that lingered for hours after a transition was so very off-putting, however, and his sensibilities were rather offended that his ship was put through such a process.

The times were changing, and unfortunately or not, he had no say in the changes. It was a matter of adapting or dying, and while he might personally have chosen to fade away while clinging to the old, Drey would not demand the same of his culture. Extinction was not preferable to change, however distasteful the change was.

That his vessel *bristled* with weapons was one of the more distasteful of those changes. To his knowledge, the Priminae had *never* had a class of ship that could be termed a "battle cruiser," but the *Tetanna* could assume no other name. Normal vessels carried weapons, of course, but they were primarily multipurpose tools, their ability to inflict harm a distant secondary concern.

Carrying lasers well beyond the old class design that had been disgorged by Central at the peak of the Drasin threat, the *Tetanna* could slag a continent with little trouble. Drey snorted to himself at the thought. Given a bit of time to plan, he could annihilate a continent with far less than the total output of the *Tetanna*'s lasers. As a former mining chief, he was well aware of the dangers of supervolcanos and tectonic stress fractures.

Unlike the designs that had originated from Central, however, the lasers were not the only teeth the *Tetanna* mounted. Terran transition cannons could deposit gigaton-level nuclear devices anywhere within three light-minutes in an instant, and the massive kinetic-kill missiles loaded into the ship's magazines were capable of destabilizing the orbit of a small moon.

Worse than all that, even, was the fact that sometimes, just sometimes, Drey found himself looking out into the abyss of the black and wishing he had more weaponry loaded into his ship.

The Drasin had been a nightmare, but they were almost a natural disaster. In many ways, there was no real point fearing them. They would come when they came, and you would live or not based almost entirely on the Fates themselves. The legends of those things were like stories of black holes and gamma-ray bursts coming out of the void.

If it happened, you were dead. No point in panicking about it.

The Terrans changed that, and while Drey was grateful, he was still adjusting to the state of his universe.

"Captain, system is clear. Transponders from all mining vessels have been checked. No unexpected signals."

Drey turned to his second, who was approaching from the main command deck.

"Thank you, Hara," he said. "Schedule our departure according to protocol. We will need to check the new colony systems next."

"Yes Captain," Hara Kanith said, tapping a few commands into her personal system. "The Lenata System next?"

Drey considered the question briefly and nodded. "That is fine."

Since the Drasin assault on Ranquil had torn through the major population center, there had been a significant upsurge of interest in colonial programs. Normally the programs saw a steady but slow trickle that served primarily as a safety valve for those less than satisfied with life on the core worlds and all the restrictions needed when billions of people lived within a few hundred kilometers of one another.

Now, the demand was probably a hundred times the norm as people had a sudden desire to spread out.

It wasn't the most logical of urges in his mind. The Colonies faced with the Drasin had all vanished into the abyss of time and space, while Ranquil had not. On the other hand, everyone knew it was almost entirely the intervention of the Terrans that had prevented Ranquil from vanishing as well.

The Priminae High Council were all rather happy with the current situation, particularly given the loss of several major food-production colonies. If people wanted to move to a rougher life—granted, one that provided many more personal freedoms—that was perfectly fine with them. Drey was personally happy that the fleet had seen a similar increase in recruiting, since clearly the old system of patrols would no longer be acceptable.

That didn't, however, take away from the very real dangers that had abruptly emerged from the black.

First the Drasin and now this Empire had been seen encroaching on Priminae territories, even engaging the Terrans in an all-out battle in one Priminae system.

It was as if some higher power had decided the Priminae had enjoyed peace for far too long and was intent on making up for lost time.

Even the Terrans, for all they have done for us, would have been considered a plague if they would have appeared just five years earlier.

Drey was under no illusions about that.

The Terrans were the most terrifying of the monsters inflicted on the Priminae. With technical development far below that of the Colonies, they barely had faster-than-light communication. Their ships were slow and had practically no power to speak of. And yet they were clearly the deadliest species when measured against the Priminae *and* the Drasin.

The attitude among the Priminae traditionalists—by far the most powerful political entity even now, during the waning days of their power—was clear. The Terrans might be allies, but they were no less monstrous than the things they had defeated.

For Drey, who had been a traditionalist most of his career but now considered himself too much of a realist to continue that path, the Terrans were clearly monsters, but they were *Allied* monsters.

Better the beast at your side than the one at your throat.

"Course has been calculated, Captain," Hara announced as she returned. "We await your final command."

"Jump us."

▶▶▶

Imperial Task Group

▶ Captain Aymes looked over the stars dotting the dark tapestry ahead of his ship, barely noting the drive flares of the other ships in the division as he buried himself in his thoughts.

The navarch was now a woman on a quest.

Her defeat in the Oather star system had been a bloody mark against her, one that would never *quite* be wiped from her record. He knew how the Imperial court worked, though he'd not made it that high in his own career—and most likely never would now—but he'd been forced to navigate the pale shadow of court that was the military officers' circles.

No matter what she accomplished from this time forward, her enemies would snidely refer back to her defeat whenever the opportunity arose. It was in the nature of the cutthroat politicking of the court. So the navarch was intent now on blunting those future slashes with the most one-sided victory she could possibly muster.

He well understood her desires, even her obsession. He'd been in the same position himself—still was, really. The unknowns, however, bothered him.

Aymes wished they had better information. A war was won or lost on three things: power, logistics, and information.

They had power aplenty. Ships, strategists, tacticians—all those were the cream of the Imperial crop. Few places in the known galaxy could match the division the navarch had gathered to her, and none could significantly exceed it.

Logistics too were unparalleled. With the Empire behind them, they would want for nothing in the pursuit of this war.

It was the third leg of the tripod that worried him. They knew *nothing* about these anomalies except that they existed. Initially they seemed to use incredibly inferior technology, though some things indicated that was a mask of sorts. Certainly, their effectiveness in battle was a blatant sign their supposed technical inferiority was, in fact, a false front.

Now, however, it seemed the anomalies had thrown off their mask and bared their teeth fully. The ships encountered at the battle in which the Empire had lost so many vessels had not been inferior in any fashion. They matched expected Oather and Imperial signatures in every measurable metric.

Aside from their weapons.

The weapons wielded were enough to leave the Empire drooling. The lasers, while no more powerful than their Imperial counterparts, had managed to tear through ship armor in *seconds*. Armor that—occasionally, at least—had shrugged off the most powerful of strikes.

Just too many questions. Questions Aymes knew the navarch was asking as well, but questions that had no answers yet.

"Orders just came through, Captain," his second said quietly from his station. "The navarch has directed us to join the division and make course for Oather territory."

"By all means," Aymes said softly in response. "Take us to formation and accelerate past light-speed on the navarch's signal."

"Yes Captain."

Information.

Aymes looked out into space as the universe wavered and the whites of the stars ahead of them tinted slightly blue as the *Cohn* accelerated past the speed of light. The background radiation of the universe itself shifted, not becoming visible precisely, but altering just enough that the view felt different, less real.

Or, considering how much of his life Aymes had spent plying the void, perhaps he should say that the universe had just become *more* real. It was a return home for a man who lived in the deep void, as he did.

▶▶▶

AEV *Odysseus*

▶ Eric stood, as he had quite a lot of late, overlooking the command deck and the spectacular view beyond to where the Earth floated in the black, a blue-and-white marble whose beauty now vexed as much as entranced him.

The Empire, this unknown galactic polity, was certainly his highest-priority problem at the moment, but the Earth *herself* was near the top. Since he had taken command of the *Odyssey*—it seemed so long ago now—Eric had found himself thrown into the very center of the struggle for the future of humanity in one conflict after another . . .

or perhaps they were all the same conflict. He didn't know about that, really.

Still, the conflicts were straightforward and solvable. Help the Priminae or run? His military tradition and honor made that choice for him. Face the Drasin head-on or lose Earth? Wasn't even a choice.

One problem he had encountered, however, had no apparent solution, and unlike the others, he seemed doomed to face it alone. He certainly couldn't go around telling people that Earth and Ranquil were both haunted by what he could only imagine as deities. Central and Gaia presented a problem Eric didn't know how to solve, one that left him with no access to resources that might offer a solution.

Central, in particular, was a security breach the likes of which he had never imagined in his worst nightmares. A mind-reading alien intelligence that couldn't be controlled in any way was a night terror for most intelligence officials. The fact that it was operating as a computer core for their allies was just . . . Well, honestly, he didn't know if it was good or bad. Central was one breach he could at least reduce. The Confederation *knew* about Central, even if they were convinced it was a supercomputer of some type. Limiting the classified knowledge available to those assigned to Ranquil was entirely feasible, and Eric had strongly suggested it be done.

His planet's own counterpart, Gaia, was another story. That entity had full access to the minds of everyone on Earth. The fact that she—if it was a she—was Terran made that breach only slightly better. Eric was reasonably confident Gaia wouldn't do anything to risk the security of the planet she was bound to, but he had no idea how firm her binding to Earth was.

Because of that, and his own personal issues with the knowledge he held, Eric had avoided returning to Earth this time around. He'd overseen the *Odysseus* refit, and he'd relaxed at Unity Station, even going so far as to schedule his debrief there under the guise of having shipboard business that was keeping him in orbit.

As best he could tell, Gaia was beneficent, but Eric didn't trust what he couldn't reliably see, and an immortal, incorporeal entity that could read the mind of every living being within the magnetic field of a world was . . . well, "discomforting" was so ludicrously understating the feeling as to be ridiculous.

Eric turned away from the rail over the command deck and refocused his attention on the computer display that held his research. Everything he could find, from legends and myths to the hypotheses of the most brilliant minds in quantum physics—none of it was much use to him.

The new assignment was honestly a relief.

A straightforward combat patrol, while more dangerous, was going to be downright tranquil compared to the growing tension he'd felt sitting this close to Earth's magnetic field, knowing what was waiting within.

Eric closed all the files and saved the research to the *Odysseus'* computers under his personal authority, then turned back to look down at the command deck below as his officers went about the business of getting the ship ready to depart Sol space.

The room available on a Priminae-designed vessel was practically obscene compared to any terrestrial example he could imagine, save perhaps the old Orion designs of the midtwentieth century, and even those were smaller than the *Odysseus* by a couple of orders of magnitude.

Outmassing any four supercarriers combined, the *Odysseus* could be crewed by thousands fewer than the aforementioned Blue Navy ships. Much of the internal space was dedicated to singularity containment, of course, but that still left a luxurious amount of open space for the men and women stationed aboard the ship. And unlike most Navies, the Priminae saw no reason not to provide extreme comforts for the crew.

Some of them were . . . odd comforts, of course. The Priminae didn't have showers or baths in the strictest sense of the words, and neither of those were good ideas on a starship even if you had reliable artificial gravity. The sheer mess possible if you lost gravity for any reason boggled Eric's mind. Still, the Priminae replacement did the job efficiently (though Eric honestly wasn't sure how) and managed to be nearly as relaxing as a hot soak or as energizing as a morning shower, if that was what you needed.

Similar oddities abounded on the Forge-built vessel, and while Eric insisted on military discipline, he was more than willing to extend some leeway to his crew so long as they didn't slack off. And if they did? Cutting access to those luxuries was one more stick to hold.

All that extra space had other effects, however, and one was the sheer size of some areas. The command deck was three or four times larger than the Confederate Op Center at Cheyenne Mountain, if his memories were correct, and his private office overlooking the deck was easily five times the size of the *Odyssey*'s entire bridge.

Getting used to that opulent space had taken time, but certainly hadn't been unpleasant. During his first tour on the *Odysseus*, however, Eric had spent almost all his time on the command deck proper. He'd still be there, in fact, except he needed the office to properly deal with the new responsibilities that came with his promotion to commodore.

Not quite an admiral but more than a captain, and with very nearly the same responsibilities as the former, Eric had been all but buried in desk work since he'd returned. His squadron was small, three Heroics: the *Odysseus*, the *Bellerophon*, and the *Boudicca*, with two Rogues apiece for a total of six. They'd also been assigned another half dozen logistics vessels, mostly carrying munitions that were to remain safely in Sol space until called for. Thank God for the transition drive.

Fifteen ships built up a frankly *stupid* degree of desk work even while they were sitting still—hell, *especially* while sitting still. Eric just wanted to be back out in the deep black as soon as possible.

Careful what you wish for, I suppose.

He reached out and lightly touched a comm link, buzzing down to Commander Heath's station.

"Skipper?"

"Has everyone reported on board, Commander?" Eric asked.

"Yes sir. All ships report crews accounted for. Commander Michaels was the last on board the *Odysseus*."

That surprised Eric. "Really? Did he say why?"

Heath laughed lightly. "I don't believe he did, sir, but I expect that his mode of arrival had something to do with it."

Eric frowned, puzzled. *Mode of arrival?* "I'm sorry, Commander, I'm afraid I don't understand."

"The commander arrived in one of the new fighters, sir," Heath told him. "I believe that he managed to secure a familiarizing flight, and knowing the commander . . ."

"He didn't want to end it any more quickly than he had to." Eric rolled his eyes, honestly jealous of his friend for a moment. "Understood. Are we on schedule, Commander?"

"Yes sir. The squadron will be departing Sol space at zero nine hundred hours, precisely on schedule."

"Excellent. Thank you, Commander."

"You are welcome, Skipper," Heath said in her slightly prim voice just before the connection closed.

Eric looked over the command deck and large observation dome with satisfaction.

It was odd, really. He'd only been a . . . a spacer? Was that the word he wanted? Eric wasn't sure. Some of the nomenclature just hadn't been set yet. Whatever word they eventually settled on, Eric hadn't been in the space service for long, but he was beginning to feel like he'd been born to spend his time in the black between the stars.

Earth was a battlefield to him, just one big battlefield, as much as he loved it. Too many memories in every blood-soaked corner. The black, for everything that had happened to him there, for everything he'd seen in the short time he'd been plying his trade between the stars, was somehow *clean*. Comfortable.

It was time. Time for the simple perfection of the abyss, time for the *Odysseus*—and her captain—to be back where they belonged.

It was time to go home.

▶▶▶

▶ Lieutenant Milla Chans, on an extended detached assignment from the Priminae Colonial Fleet to the Confederate Black Navy, looked confused when Steph happened upon her as he was making his way to his quarters. He shifted his grip on the flight helmet under his arm and cocked his head to one side.

"Are you alright?" he asked, watching as she looked up the empty corridor, seemingly completely absorbed in what she was doing.

"What?" she asked, her accent soft as she continued staring.

Steph walked up behind her, looking over the shorter woman's head in the same direction. "What are we looking at?"

Milla shook her head. "I don't know. I thought I heard something. Maybe the power conduits are out of alignment."

"Sounds like a job for system maintenance, not the ship's tactical officer."

Milla scowled. "I know. I made a report. It just—what is the word I want?—frustrates me."

Steph was unsurprised. From what he'd seen, in the Colonial Fleet, the jobs tended to be much more hands-on, particularly for someone in Milla's position. From some of her stories, he could tell that as a ship's weapons officer, Milla hadn't always trusted her subordinates to properly maintain the systems.

Weapons were, even now, unpopular with a large portion of the Priminae people. Even those who willingly picked them up considered them a necessary evil more than anything else.

From what Steph had heard from the trainers they'd dropped off on Ranquil, this reluctance made the trainees extremely safe with their weapons, but their shoot/no shoot instincts were heavy on the no shoot side of the equation, and training had to be adjusted accordingly.

It wasn't a bad thing, in general. Just different from how the trainers were used to teaching.

"Well, unless it's critical," Steph said with a guiding hand on her back to turn her away from the empty corridor, "leave it to maintenance. Have you eaten yet?"

The slightly guilty look on the young Priminae's face was enough to tell him the answer to that question. Steph sighed. "Damn it, Milla. We've talked about this."

Chans was something of a workaholic. No problem. So was he, if he were honest about it. As was the captain, the commander, and most of the people he could think of on board. Steph was sure that the *Odysseus* had its share of slackers, but the *Odyssey* certainly had not. Such dedication had a lot of good aspects, no question, but there had to be a line somewhere, and that line was certainly somewhere before starving yourself.

"Come on," he said. "We'll drop my kit off in my quarters, then go grab some food. You can tell me about your leave time. Did you visit Paris this time?"

She nodded, smiling widely. "I did, *oui*. It was both strange and . . . familiar."

That didn't surprise him in the slightest, given how similar the Priminae language sounded to French and other so-called Romance languages.

"Well, tell me all about it," he said as they headed for the lifts.

▶ ▶ ▶

Station Unity One

▶ With all on board and readying themselves for a new mission, the *Odysseus* signalled Unity One for permission to depart and was given both clearance and a flight vector. The big ship moved with a grace and speed that seemed in pure defiance of its bulk, pivoting in place without the telltale puffs of maneuvering rockets and then accelerating out of Cislunar space at speeds that would have hard pressed even full counter-mass vessels.

Flying in close formation, the rest of the *Odysseus* Task Force followed suit.

On Unity Station, many eyes watched the big ships as they broke orbit and headed back out into the deep black. One set of eyes watched, alone in her office, pondering the current state of affairs. Most people hadn't gotten it fully into their heads just how precarious Earth's position in the galaxy was at the moment.

Civilians mostly believed that the immediate danger had passed, but Admiral Gracen knew better. The real danger was looming on the horizon. She could *almost* see it from where she stood.

For the moment, they were riding the righteous fury that the Drasin invasion had generated. Politicians were jumping all over it, getting as much as eighty percent approval ratings for more and more expanded spending in space. That was great while it lasted, but she had absolutely no illusions that it would last.

The first rumblings about wasted money were already forming and, what was worse, they weren't wrong.

She'd been stomping on people left and right over just that, both within her command chain and in the civilian companies that supplied them. The supplying corporations figured it was government money, so who cared if they stuck the taxpayer for a few extra percentage points to add to their bottom line, and procurement agents in the military and government figured it wasn't their money, so what did they care?

Bribes were subtly thrown back and forth, which was par for the course and something that Gracen had mostly come to ignore as long as they got the job done.

When they didn't, she had to break out her steel-capped boots and leave people bloody in her wake.

Those idiots don't realize how close to treason they're really walking, she thought as the *Odysseus* Task Force vanished into the black.

She wanted to literally start shooting some of the idiots involved, because they were undermining the defense of her world in a very real way. It wasn't about the money, though that was bad enough. Losing a trillion dollars that could have gone to real defense instead of some rich bastard's bank account was a bad deal all around, but the world could suck that up and soldier on. They'd all fought through worse in the past and would again in the future.

No, the problem was that they were destroying confidence in the government and military among the people.

That was going to bite them on the ass if she didn't figure something out.

So far, she had a three-pronged plan, the best she could manage, given her limitations. The Swarm was her first ace in the hole while she did what she could to stem the bleeding of money and confidence, but it all hinged on the small group of ships that had just left Cislunar space and the man commanding them.

Buy us as much time as you can, Commodore, Gracen thought grimly.

The Empire was coming and, even if they weren't, the Drasin were *not* as gone as people wanted to believe. There was no way they'd accounted for all of them, and those beasts were a threat to every world in the galaxy as far as she was concerned.

It was a big, dangerous universe.

One world didn't stand a chance, especially if it was a world divided.

If only they could see what I've seen, she thought as she turned away from the stars that beamed seemingly just beyond her office. *Maybe they wouldn't be so quick to cheat our future for a few ill-gotten dollars.*

A nice thought, but Gracen supposed that they would do it anyway.

There was no such thing as a perfect system—she knew that too well—and in any imperfect system, the people who got ahead with the most consistency were the ones willing to twist the imperfections to their advantage.

A slightly more jaded individual might wonder why they were even trying to preserve such people, but Gracen wasn't *that* far gone. She smiled slightly, looking at photos resting on her desk. Most people in any organization were good people. Some forgot that it wasn't only the cream that rose to the top but rather, far too often, garbage gyres did also. But she would not forget.

She had her war, and the commodore had his.

Despite his war being the more dangerous by far, Gracen really couldn't help but envy Weston. At least he could shoot his enemies.

CHAPTER 3

AEV *Odysseus*

▶ Eric stood on the admiralty deck of the *Odysseus*, overlooking the command deck where Commander Heath was overseeing ship's operations.

Behind him were the holographic displays that linked him in real time to the other vessels of the task group as well as the primary communications suites intended to coordinate them. He missed the hands-on control of handling a single ship, though he supposed that he still got a fair share of that in reality.

Eric turned his back on the command deck and nodded to Captain Roberts, who was looking back at him through the holographic display while sitting at his command station on the *Bellerophon*.

"Our systems check out completely, Commodore," Roberts said. "All systems are perfectly within operational parameters."

"Same here, Commodore," Captain Hyatt of the *Boudicca* said. "No variations beyond the normal."

Eric nodded. "That's good news. The *Odysseus* has been experiencing spikes in various control systems that we're still tracking down. Nothing dangerous, but keep an eye on your systems in case they show up there as well. There could be an issue with the interface applications that's just showing up here first."

The two captains nodded, both promising to stay on top of it.

Eric gestured, opening the circuit to the Rogue Class captains of the task force. The display shifted, the projected figures changing in scale as more people were added.

"I'll assume you've all read our brief," Eric said, not bothering to wait for confirmation. The idea that any of them *hadn't* read it was ridiculous. "Officially, this is a standard deep-space patrol, but I don't think anyone really expects it to play out that way. We're hunting Imperials this time, and we have to assume that they're hunting us right back. For the moment, we have the Priminae worlds between them and us, and the goal is to keep it that way. That means blunting any advances they've made in any way possible. If I can pull that off by talking them to death, that's just what I'll do."

He paused to let the chuckles die out, smiling a bit himself.

"Unfortunately, I doubt we'll be that lucky." Eric took a breath. "The Priminae have expanded their patrols significantly, so we're going to let them take that weight. After a quick stop at Ranquil, hopefully we can hook up with the *Autolycus* to see if they've got anything new for us. We're going to be operating as a fast-response group. That's going to mean a lot of loitering, waiting for someone to scream for help. It *will* happen, but the timing is, as always, on the enemy's schedule."

That was an unpopular statement, not that he didn't understand the reason. Leaving initiative to the enemy was a dangerous way to conduct a war, but they just didn't have the resources or strong enough intelligence to take a more active stance.

Prisoners taken from the Imperial ships were reasonably talkative, but their access to information was limited compared to the Priminae or humans. The few officers saved from crippled and doomed ships were considerably less inclined to chatting, and what little they did say currently had to be treated with extreme skepticism.

"So keep your crews alert, but don't wear them out," Eric told his captains. "This could easily turn into a long, difficult slog. You all know the drill. Weeks of boredom, minutes of terror."

They all nodded, some with rueful grins as they remembered how often reality fit that mold.

"Okay, then I'll leave you to it," he finished up. "We'll transition to Ranquil by"—he glanced at their course and speed—"zero nine hundred, ship's time. I'll see you all on the other side."

▶▶▶

Imperial Task Group

▶ Navarch Misrem looked over her command center with something akin to satisfaction. From this location, she could control and command every ship in her battle group, from the largest down to the very smallest. All was as it should be.

The group was moving at maximum cruise toward the Oather territories, a bittersweet thought. The defeat she had suffered—and it was a defeat, though she knew that the enemy had taken significant damage as well—plagued her constantly. She knew that some of the captains believed she was concerned about her position in Imperial politics, and to a degree that was true.

If she had wanted to be deeply involved in such things, however, she would long since have given up her ship and moved to the capital. Even now, she had more than enough leverage to make that happen, and the Imperials owed her a few quiet favors that she could confidently be assured they would repay without question.

But she loved what she did. For all the trials of the deep void, it was the best place in the universe for someone like her.

Rules, laws—they were *hers* to shape when she entered a system with her battle group.

The Imperials only had the power gifted to them by people like *her*, and Misrem reveled in that knowledge.

Her face twisted into a scowl as she turned to look at a screen that was replaying the battle in Oather territory on an infinite loop. She had been studying it since they escaped the system, her ship a smoldering wreck, and her life owed to a minor captain who showed depressingly little interest in advancement.

She pushed those thoughts away and examined the scene on the displays again, watching as her ships were rocked by explosions from nowhere.

How did dissidents sneak old-style nuclear weapons on board my ships?

She'd asked herself that question a thousand times, if not more, but no answers were forthcoming. Such a confusing mess, and no one had any answers. Imperial Intelligence was tearing apart the last ten ports she had put her ships into for resupply before the battle, but nothing had come up before she had received orders to ship out.

Worse, the placement didn't make much more sense.

One or two weapons had been placed properly, but most of the explosions had been centered around bizarrely random locations on the targeted ships. The only theory that made sense was that somehow dissidents had managed to slip the weapons onto the ships disguised as items that the crew took to their quarters, workspaces, and such. That theory only opened up more questions than it solved, however, because those sorts of weapons weren't the easiest things to disguise.

Internal Imperial politics were ugly as a rule but generally stopped short of employing nuclear weapons to resolve problems.

Then there were the weapons used by the Oathers and the anomalies.

Oather technology had been assessed as being comparable to Imperial levels just a short two years earlier. In fact, Imperials had a tactical edge according to *every* analysis at that time, due to the Oather disdain for using dedicated weapons technology on their vessels. Even giving the impetus that the Drasin would certainly have forced upon them, however, the new weapons capabilities simply did not match up.

The weapons must be from the ones that Aymes refers to as the anomalies.

She gestured and another display shifted focus, showing one of the smaller ships that fit the general mass and configuration of the anomaly that had plagued the original Drasin incursion. It was, as the reports indicated, devastatingly difficult to locate on scanners if you weren't looking right at it, and in space, that was a rare event indeed.

The power curve of the smaller ships was effectively zero, at least as best they could detect at the ranges they'd engaged the ships. They would likely be able to register the curve more accurately if they got in closer, but to do that they'd have to be near perhaps the most terrifying thing she'd ever encountered.

Another gesture froze the image as white points of energy spat forth from the ship.

Antimatter, used as a *projectile weapon.*

That meant that either they had to generate the material on demand, which she refused to believe that a ship with such a nonexistent power curve could do, or they *stored it!*

Misrem shivered, a chill running down her spine at the very idea of having material that volatile stored within the same ship she depended on for life support. Sheer insanity, no matter how effective their containment techniques were.

So we are facing lunatics, then, she extrapolated, with mixed feelings.

Another Empire that she would revel in the opportunity to match wits against. A professional fleet to strike and counter, the sort of thing dynasties were born from. Tangling with insane people, however, was at best picking on the crippled and helpless. No matter how well one did, there was not much advancement to be had.

But that was the best-case scenario. The worst-case scenario was that they were *functionally* insane. The sort of people who, despite every possible sign otherwise, somehow actually managed to operate and function within the universe. Those sorts of people were not the type any professional fleet woman wanted to face, because no matter how good you were at your job, they would find ways to outthink you by doing the stupidest possible thing and somehow making it work in their favor.

Ultimately, however, it should not matter.

The Empire had faced all kinds and would face them all again. Insanity was no true key to victory; it just slowed the inevitable defeat. A disciplined and professional fleet would always win out in the end.

She just wasn't looking forward to learning the full nature of the cost her disciplined and professional fleet was going to pay to make that happen.

▶ ▶ ▶

▶ Captain Aymes sat at his station, silently letting his people do their jobs as he examined the combat records from the last times he had ventured into Oather space.

Something had changed with the Oathers, and he was betting that the anomaly ships were key. The original split between Oather and Imperial had been a long time in the past, long enough that it was just legend by this point, with an institutional hatred for the arrogance of the Oathers bred into Imperial children from the youngest of ages via bedtime stories and the propaganda machine that passed for an entertainment industry.

They may have been arrogant, but Aymes had access to original records—as original as any, he supposed. The Oathers had been firmly tied to their principles, the Oaths that had been sworn for reasons no record still listed. The split had come when the Imperial forbears had argued that the Oaths were obsolete, but the Oathers refused to listen to reason.

When the split happened, the Oathers considered the Imperials to be forsworn and fighting broke out. Again, no records existed to show who struck first. Given what he knew of the Oathers, he suspected it was the Imperial faction, but that no longer mattered. What did matter was the Oather faction either lost and was driven out or refused to fight and left of their own accord.

Aymes could read between the lines, realizing that there was a great deal about the story he was missing. The reason for the institutional hatred of the Oathers certainly wasn't in the records, yet he could tell that the hatred was entirely out of proportion to what had happened, particularly considering the time involved.

Very little of the history he had access to made any sense in context, but what it did generally show was that the Oathers were nearly pathologically inclined to pacifism at sometimes insane cost.

That wasn't what he had seen during the last two encroachments on their territories.

Even those ships they had identified as almost certainly Oather in origin had been armed to the teeth and were willing to use their weapons with little hesitation.

Something changed, he supposed. What had changed was not particularly difficult to work out either.

The Drasin.

Aymes grimaced, thinking about those things. Setting them loose on the galaxy was a sign of hubris that the Oathers of propaganda legend could not have hoped to match.

He had no doubt the decision would inevitably sweep back and bite them all in the nether regions, but that was a worry for another day. His more immediate concern was if the results of setting the Drasin on the Oathers had somehow fundamentally shifted the nature of the people.

It seemed . . . *impossible,* frankly.

However, if he was right, they might have awakened a sleeping beast that the Empire was not expecting.

Aymes watched the battle records play, these thoughts at the front of his mind.

I hope I'm wrong, but I fear I'm not.

He knew he was missing critical information. Something very unexpected was happening, and it had *destroyed* the calculations that Imperial Intelligence had made concerning the Oathers.

Aymes couldn't help but believe that it would all come down to the anomaly. Whatever, whoever, controlled that ship—those ships, now, he supposed—*they* were the wild cards he hadn't been able to calculate on. They were throwing everything to the stellar winds, and for his life and career, Aymes couldn't figure where any of it was going to land.

▶▶▶

AEV *Odysseus*

▶ Master Chief Dixon was not a happy man.

"If I find out who's messing with my decks, I'm going to keelhaul the bastard in a leaky suit," he grumbled as he observed the mess someone had left along the engineering corridor.

Dixon had been hunting down system glitches ever since he came on board the *Odysseus*. It was in many ways his job description, but there was no way in *hell* he was cleaning this up.

He stalked over to the closest security panel and flipped open a channel.

"Ship's services."

"This is the chief," Dixon growled. "I want a cleanup crew. Deck 12, engineering section. Tell them to bring a shovel."

"A shovel, Chief?" The voice on the other side sounded disbelieving.

Dixon didn't blame the man, not really, but it irritated the piss out of him anyway.

"Yes, a Goddamn shovel. It looks like someone raided the commissary and spread food and trash along eighty meters of my Goddamn deck!" he snapped out. He was in no mood to deal with someone not immediately jumping to action.

"Sorry, Chief. I'll dispatch people right away!"

"Good, and tell security I'm coming up," Dixon growled. "I want to see their surveillance, so they better pull those files *now*."

"You got it, Chief."

Dixon closed the channel and turned back to the disaster zone that had been his engineering corridor.

"A slow leak." He nodded to himself. "Don't want them to lose consciousness before they reach the aft gravity bubble."

▶▶▶

▶ Commander Michaels whistled as he made his way to the simulators, walking with a bit of a spring to his step that felt like it had been missing *forever*. He'd already been asked three times if he'd gotten lucky while on leave, and that had just made him laugh.

A night with a lovely lady was a grand thing, but it wasn't what put a spring in his step. He'd gotten his hand on a real flight stick again. *That* was worth whistling about.

Oh, he loved the *'Disseus*. She was a grand old ship. She even handled a lot less like the pig he'd expected her to be the first time the admiral had dropped his new assignment on him. The gravity wells used by the warp drive made her damn near as maneuverable and responsive as a fighter, and he couldn't really argue with the results.

No, he would simply point out that "damn near" wasn't "dead on."

There was something about flying a fighter that got into a man's blood. No inertial nullification, just the counter-mass unit and whether you could take what leaked through. The smaller mass of the fighters let them pull off high-speed maneuvers that made *anything*, even the *Odysseus*, look a bit slow.

But it was the *feel* that affected him, the sensation that he wasn't piloting a fighter so much as had it strapped to his back.

You didn't get that on the *Odysseus*.

They didn't even use a restraint system of any kind on board. Anything that hit them hard enough to disrupt the inertial nullification was going to splatter the entire crew across the bulkheads. There just wasn't any middle ground. Either smooth sailing, or everyone was dead. Not a lot of point in seatbelts.

He looked over the simulators that were evenly spaced along the open deck as he walked in, then nodded and headed to the third one.

"Lieutenant," he greeted the man.

"Commander," Lieutenant Keith Lancaster replied in turn from where he was sitting.

Steph leaned in to check the readouts the other pilot was dealing with. "Level nine? Not bad. How long have you been at it?"

"Almost an hour," Keith told him. "Just trying to master close maneuvering."

Steph nodded. "She's a heavy beast, for all her speed. It's still a lot of mass to move around, if you're trying for precision."

He straightened up, patting the side of the simulator. "Keep at it. I'll review your files later. Don't forget to keep your NICS qualification certified; otherwise you're not sitting in the real hot seat."

"Yes sir. I'm scheduled for my requalification test tomorrow."

"Ace it."

Keith nodded firmly. "Yes sir. Wilco, sir."

Steph walked around the other simulators that were in use, observing and making comments or suggestions as he saw fit. The *Odysseus'* helm was a complicated system, so every pilot on board had to regularly qualify on the current systems as well as the proposed updates being considered for implementation.

This most certainly included the chief helmsman himself, so when he was done checking over everyone else's work, Steph climbed into an empty simulator and loaded the program from the last point he'd left off.

Level Thirty-Three.

His program started hot and heavy, and within a few minutes, Steph was sweating as he maneuvered his virtual *Odysseus* through a series of course changes that pushed his skills with the stick to the max. It didn't take long before he forced himself to relax and settle back in his bolstered seat so he could thumb the NICS needles into place.

The sharp sting caused him to stiffen momentarily, but then it was old home week as Steph relaxed and composed his mind.

Slipping into Zen was a practiced skill for the pilots of the Double A squadron, a mental state that often registered as unconscious to unpracticed observers looking at their EKGs. The simulation smoothed out as Steph continued to work his way up the levels until he hit level fifty and decided that was enough for a warm-up.

He wasn't looking to set a record. He had come to the sims for another reason.

Still connected via NICS, he glanced to the left and thumbed a switch.

"Computer, load Imperial scenario one and play from the beginning."

They'd gathered a lot of data on the Imperial ships during the last encounter and from the wrecks that they and the Priminae had torn through. Most of the basic specifications were similar to Priminae tech, which strongly established the connection between the two cultures, but Imperial material science had taken a different path at some point.

The metal alloy armor they used was more durable than Priminae ceramics but not quite as good at handling laser weaponry. An odd choice, Steph had thought, and an indication that at some point the Imperials had done a lot of fighting with someone who preferred physical weapons. The metal armor would take a much more significant beating from kinetic weapons than the ceramic would. You could punch holes in the armor of the Imperials all day, and they'd just patch them and grin at you while they kept on coming. Priminae ceramic armor was prone to cracking and even shattering when hit just right. Patching that was considerably more difficult.

That same armor the Imperials used made them a little more vulnerable to the *Odysseus'* lasers than the Priminae or even the Drasin were.

Steph was trying to determine just how much of a difference that was going to make in the real world.

Three Imperial cruisers, roughly equivalent to the Heroics, appeared in the simulation at his command. They were arrayed ahead of him in what seemed to be the standard formation for the enemy fleet, accelerating toward him at combat speeds.

Steph felt the nerve tingle buzz through him as he was targeted and slipped the ship to port to evade contact. He, in turn, locked up the lead element of the enemy formation and directed orders to his simulated tactical officer.

"Lead bandit locked in; fire when ready. Executing Maneuver Alpha Break Niner," he said calmly, continuing the slip to port before powering up the gravity wells that provided propulsion to the big ship and plunging into the fight.

CHAPTER 4

Priminae Colony

▶ The *Tetanna* slowed, settling into a planetary synch orbit that kept them resting over the new Priminae colony site.

There wasn't a lot down there yet, of course. Drey Martina had seen the colonial census and hadn't expected much, but for someone used to seeing population centers easily from orbit, the locale was a little stark. One couldn't tell that there had been any changes to the surface, at least not without employing advanced scanners.

"Captain," Helena said, approaching him, "the colonial administrator made contact. They're preparing a landing zone for us to drop off supplies."

"I'm surprised they didn't finish that already," he admitted, not that it bothered him much. They had enough flexibility in their schedule to allow for delays with little issue.

"The administrator was quite apologetic," Helena said. "It seems that they had an unexpected cold front move in, and improving residence thermal insulation took a priority."

Drey tilted his head, then nodded. "Well, I certainly cannot fault them for that. I expect I would have done the same."

"Yes Captain. I expected you to agree," Helena said with a bit of a smile. "At any rate, they should be prepared to receive goods within a couple more hours."

"That's fine," Drey confirmed. "We will break orbit temporarily and use the time to complete system survey updates. Our records are at least eighty cycles old at this point. Likely nothing much has changed. As I recall, there were no predicted impact events in the old survey within at least two hundred cycles, but since we have the time anyway . . ."

"Yes sir. I will relay that to the administrator and have the crew get ready," she confirmed.

"Thank you, Helena."

▶▶▶

▶ The navarch settled at her station, eyes casually skimming the daily take from their scanners.

They'd approached Oather territory with considerably more caution this time, not wanting a repeat of the previous excursion. This time things would be different; she needed to know just what had changed among the Oathers and who—or what—the anomalies were. With a specific mission to accomplish, rather than general data gathering, she could be more certain in her stratagems.

They'd slipped into the comet cloud of a system that had been identified as containing a young world still building infrastructure. Clearly, the Oathers were expanding again after the passing of the Drasin threat. She would see to *that* in good time, but for the moment, she was more interested in the ship perched in orbit of the small colony.

Misrem noted that the mass and configuration specifications matched an Imperial cruiser reasonably closely, aside from the material specifications of their hull armor. Oddly, their hulls did not read as the standard Oather energy defensive ceramics. It didn't read as *anything* she recognized, to be precise.

"Bolah," she said, looking over to where her senior scanner officer was standing. "What do you make of the hull and armor composition?"

The officer scowled. "I have been trying to work that out since we got the scans. The odd part is that it does not match any of the scans from the battle, Navarch. It is like whatever they are using is refracting off part of our scans. Not enough to make them difficult to detect, obviously, but it is playing with our analysis software. I *think* they're using a refractory coating on their standard ceramic armor, but we are going to need to capture samples to be certain."

Misrem let out a slow breath, thoughtfully considering that.

"I will see to it that you get the samples you need," she said after a moment. "Until that time, however, continue to try to break the puzzle from this side of things. I would prefer the most information possible before we engage this time."

"Yes Navarch. I have analysis running even now, though I do not expect anything revelatory from it. This will be a matter of gaining ground by a hair's breadth, I fear, but we *will* gain ground."

"Understood. Thank you," she said, calling up another aspect of the report. "Why have their space-warp specifications been flagged?"

"The report references their wake, Navarch," Bolah told her lightly. "Specifically, when we tried to track their wake back to determine the origin vector, we lost the signal just outside the stellar-abyssal limit. It is almost like they were . . . *sitting* out there for some reason, waiting for something. Either that or they have substantially improved their drive efficiency in the deep abyss."

She checked that information quickly, noting the scanner records, and immediately frowned and reread it in detail. Bolah waited patiently for her to finish without saying a word. Finally, Misrem looked up, perplexed.

"They must have been sitting out there," she admitted. "No one can mask a warp wake that effectively, but *why?*"

Bolah sighed, shaking his head. "That is the question I have not been able to answer. One might almost think they were laying a trap for us, but in that case, why expose themselves? I have not been able to devise a satisfactory explanation."

"More puzzles, more questions," Misrem grumbled, irritated by it all. "It is like these are not the Oathers at all. Something has *changed* them in ways I do not believe is entirely traceable to the Drasin incursion."

"Yes Navarch."

"Very well," she said, "we will continue to—"

A soft alarm cut her off and brought Misrem to her feet as Bolah spun back to his station.

"What is it?"

The scanner officer didn't answer instantly, and it was her turn to wait as patiently as she could manage. When needed, Misrem could be a *very* patient woman.

"The ship is breaking orbit," he said. "Low acceleration, falling behind the planet as it orbits. Course . . . uncertain."

"Watch them," she said, tapping out an order on her station. "All ships, all stations, secure to best stealth. Enemy vessel is on the move."

▶ ▶ ▶

▶ "Stand by for system scan. We will be here a few hours," Drey announced to the ship, "so please refrain from accessing any FTL communications for the duration. Interference will just make our current task more difficult."

Going unspoken was that he had, in fact, locked down the ship's FTL transmission systems. He could have left it at that, of course, but it was just polite to phrase things as a request even if there was no choice in the matter.

"System scan starting, Captain."

"Thank you, Hela," he said, settling into his station and trying to make himself comfortable as he watched the scan details filter back in.

The planets, of course, were the easiest to pick up. They appeared on the *Tetanna*'s new model of the system almost instantly. Not even a blind man could have missed the gravity fields of planetary objects.

Slowly, other things began to fill in, varying with distance and mass as the computer located, tracked, and analyzed all possible vectors.

Asteroid-sized objects close to the ship showed up next, and the compiled list expanded slowly outward toward deep space, beyond the influence of the local sun.

Several hours into the scan, Hela walked over to where Drey was trying not to sleep while on duty. System surveys were among the more important yet incredibly boring parts of the job when you were in fleet.

"Outer system anomaly," she said as she approached, catching his attention.

"What sort?" Drey asked, shifting so he could examine the latest data they had acquired.

"Mostly some odd elements of the comet shield are out of their predicted places."

"Oh."

That was a bit of a letdown. Comet fragments in the extreme outer system were always shifting around and pitching one another out of their orbits. Once in a while, they even collided, causing even greater variations. A system survey could usually predict them fairly well, using a statistical model, but there were always outliers.

"Very well. Focus on the anomalies for a more intensive scan," he ordered. "Try to locate what knocked them out of the predicted paths and determine if any of them are likely to be a threat to the colony."

"Yes Captain."

▶▶▶

▶ Misrem swore as the ship they were surveilling began conducting a system-wide survey. She was glad that she'd had her ships stand down to their best stealth, but it was still going to be a nerve-racking experience as they waited to see if they'd been detected.

In the meantime, however, there was at least one thing they could do.

"Use their scanner energy to improve our system survey," she ordered.

"Yes Navarch."

They'd not been able to do a complete survey themselves, being limited to only passive scans since they didn't want to tip off the Oather colony. Since the ship was being kind enough to send out plenty of reflecting energy and they knew the ship's origin point with certainty, they could use the enemy scans for their own benefit.

Beyond that, all she and her group could do was wait and hope they would remain undetected.

That hope died when, after a few hours of standard scans, her ship was suddenly hit with a high-density, localized scanning beam that set off every alarm on board as it clearly exceeded the vessel's detection threshold.

"Power to all engines!" she yelled. "Get the battle group online and moving!"

"Course, Navarch?"

The ship was beginning to hum around her, coming to life in a way that seemed like it charged her as she walked the command deck over to the navigations station.

"Give me an intercept course for the planet."

"Yes Navarch."

Her second approached. "The planet, Navarch? It is a minor world, of no value to us."

"To us, no," she agreed, "but it might be to that ship. If they are smart, they will run, and we will not be able to catch them. But perhaps we can bring them in close enough to deal with them if we threaten their world."

Her second nodded, understanding. "If I may, then, Navarch?"

She gestured to him, and he turned to the communications and signals station.

"Flood the hyper spectrum with enough energy to prevent them from sending signals out," he ordered.

"Yes Commander."

He turned back. "We will lose at least two ships from our immediate order of battle to maintain this long enough, but if your intent is to eliminate them before they can contact their core worlds . . ."

Misrem smiled tightly. "Indeed. Thank you, Commander."

"Your service, Navarch," he said with a slight bow at the hip.

The ships of the battle group were appearing now on their passive scans as they brought their drives to active status and prepared to move.

"Not quite how I intended to announce our presence," she said, sighing. "But so be it. Take us out."

▶▶▶

▶ "Drive signatures!"

Drey twisted in his seat, eyes widening as Hela's call rolled across the command deck.

"Identification?" he demanded, hoping that they were Priminae or Terran drives.

"None yet, Captain," Hela said with a shake of her head. "They were sitting quiet in the comet shield, sir. I do not believe they are anyone we would know."

He pursed his lips. "Damn. I want our FTL communications back up, now!"

"All hyper frequencies are being flooded with enough energy to disrupt signals, Captain," the signals officer said, turning back. "We will not be able to transmit from within the system."

"Damn them to the eternal abyss," Drey hissed. "Power to all systems, focus our scanners, and get a count on the enemy."

"Yes Captain."

The *Tetanna* hummed as her system potential was brought fully online, with military power being directed to scanners and weapons as the ship prepared herself for a fight.

The bridge, which had been running at a third of normal operational staff, now began to fill with officers running to their stations. Alarms continued to sound.

"Initial count coming in, Captain," Hela said, looking up with a stricken look on her face.

Drey knew that he probably didn't want to know, but he asked anyway. "How bad is it?"

"Forty drive signals now, possibly more," she said. "We read at least ten as cruisers. The others are uncertain."

"Log it all," he ordered. "Give me a course to the edge of the system, best speed."

"Yes Captain."

Drey was well aware that against such a force he had no chance, not even with the added weapons they'd acquired from the Terrans in exchange for the ships they had built to free their world from the Drasin. His duty was clear, and whatever his thoughts, he had to run.

"They are moving, Captain," Hela said. "Dropping in system at high acceleration."

"Intercept course?" he asked, leaning back. They had to know that they couldn't catch him.

"Yes, sir, but not for us. They're heading for the colony world."

Drey froze.

The colony had no defenses. The inhabitants had planned an orbital system, but none of the necessary surface-based installations had been completed yet, so they hadn't brought it. The people below were sitting targets, waiting to be picked off.

He didn't know what to do.

▶ ▶ ▶

▶ "The enemy ship has not yet moved, Navarch."

Misrem was surprised at that. She'd expected the quarry either to head for the planet to cut the Imperials off or, if the commander was remotely intelligent, to have turned and bolted for the other side of the system as quickly as the ship's gravity wells could propel it.

"Stay the course," she said, eyes narrowing.

She had time before she would have to make a choice about whether to try to intercept the Oather vessel or continue to the planet. Both were close enough and along similar vectors that she could alter course quite late with only a minimal loss of time either way.

But she might be missing something.

"Increase system surveillance. Look for any reinforcements they might have," she ordered.

She was likely being paranoid, but her previous experiences in Oather territory had made her wary of a repeat. They hadn't seen any other ships when they arrived, but the atypical hesitance of the Oather ship had made her recall the earlier scans and what they had shown when she tried to track the vessel's entry vector to determine a likely system of origin. For some reason, they had just been sitting out there before making themselves known.

That was bad enough, but if one group had done it, well, then it was *possible* that someone else was out there too.

Her battle group should be enough to deal with anything that might be patrolling a minor colony system like this, but if Misrem detected anything, she would have to try to eliminate any vessels that might report her presence and the composition of her force.

▶▶▶

▶ "Captain," Hela hissed quietly from his side, startling Drey.

He looked at her sharply, eyes wide and face white.

"Your orders, Captain?" she said slowly, her voice pitched low.

He swallowed, nodding as he looked back at the displays that showed the advancing fleet.

"How long until they reach the planet?" he asked numbly.

"At current acceleration, and assuming they use a military power turnover," Hela said, frowning, "no more than eight hours."

He winced.

They were moving *fast*. Coming in from the comet shield and making that sort of time meant that they were going to be moving at least three times light while deep in system, a maneuver that only a military vessel would even consider trying.

The move meant, unfortunately, that there was no chance of any evacuation from the colony.

He could put the *Tetanna* between the ships and the colony, but it would be a futile gesture, and Drey knew it. Running felt wrong, however, which left him with a terrifying quandary that he did not know how to resolve.

"Give me a course to the outer system," he ordered finally, "just outside their interception range."

"Captain?" Hela asked, confused.

"We have to run," he said bitterly, "but we do not have to run out the back while they come in the front. Give me the course I asked for, Commander."

"Yes Captain."

▶▶▶

▶ The battle group was a little over light-speed and a half, their energy screens flaring with almost constant micro impacts. Everything from dust to small rocks to solar winds and everything in between was slamming into the screens with the energy imparted by the battle group closing at speeds that could turn a stray speck of dust into a weapon of mass destruction.

The gravity sink in front of the ships bent and deflected most of the minor debris, but closing speeds in excess of light meant that the energy of the impacts prevented many particles from being pulled entirely into the trough of their gravity wave. Whatever made it through had to be intercepted by the ship's energy screens.

The navarch was well aware that staying too long at speeds like this inside a star system could tear up a ship, but she wanted to put her opponent to the test.

So far, she had to admit, she was a little disappointed.

"Oather ship is moving, Navarch."

"Put their course onscreen," she ordered, leaning forward. *So what sort of captain are you?*

She blinked in mild surprise at the course as it appeared. The captain of the Oather vessel had elected to evade her, clearly, but was doing so by closing as near as possible with her ships.

What is this fool hoping to accomplish? she wondered, tilting her head. "Show me the intercept graphs for each of our ship classes."

As she'd calculated, he was outside the range of her cruisers. Their acceleration curves would bring them within technical range to engage him, but he would have no issue avoiding her lasers. Her destroyers, however, had a little more potential acceleration in them due to the lighter mass of the somewhat smaller ships.

She wouldn't like to pit a destroyer against a cruiser, particularly one like this that had clearly been altered with unknown technical capabilities, but she had twenty of them.

"Redeploy our destroyer screen to intercept," Misrem ordered after a moment's thought. "They are to eliminate the target vessel."

"Yes Navarch."

She considered his opening move for several more moments, trying to determine what the enemy was planning. *Do they just want to get as close a look at us as possible before fleeing the system? Or is there something more at play here?*

▶▶▶

▶ Drey was doing everything he could to avoid shaking. He realized that everything he'd been trained to do, everything he had prepared himself to do, meant *nothing* in the face of reality. It left him cold to the core and physically jumping in place as he tried but failed to control his own body.

He was incredibly grateful that everyone was too busy with their instruments to look at him, because if they did, there was no doubt in his mind that even a passing glance would reveal his terror.

"We are reading a contingent on a divergent vector, Captain," Hela told him. "They . . . they might be able to intercept, sir."

"What?" Drey looked up, surprised. He'd chosen the course because it should have led them quite close but still outside the range of even the fastest cruisers.

"They appear to be a lighter mass configuration," she said. "Half a cruiser's mass, at most."

Drey frowned. *That could do it, but they would have to have equipped those smaller ships with practically the same power generators as a cruiser to give them that kind of acceleration. It's likely they'll have weapons to match a cruiser, but not as many emitters, then.*

He wasn't aware of any designs in Central that would fit what he was seeing, but Drey was fairly confident he could predict the vessels' general capabilities.

"Make sure you get full scans of those ships," he ordered. "Adjust our course to evade them, minimal arc change."

"Yes Captain. Minimal arc change."

"They're testing us," he said. "I don't know what they want to learn, but they're testing us."

▶ ▶ ▶

▶ "Oather vessel has shifted to evade the destroyers, Navarch. However, they are remaining as close as they can while doing so."

Misrem frowned, considering the Oather captain's move.

He is testing me. What does he want to learn?

Her options were clear, and she was certain that she couldn't realistically hope to force a confrontation here. The Oather captain had made it clear that he wasn't going to throw away his ship and life in a futile defense of the colony world, but he wasn't just bolting either. That made her wonder if she couldn't trick him into a foolish stance and, perhaps, at least get a chunk of his ship to claim as her trophy before he managed to escape her grasp.

"Recall the destroyers to their previous course," she ordered.

"Yes Navarch."

The destroyer element shifted course again, matching her cruisers on their path to the planet as she settled back to wait and see what her opponent's next move would be.

It didn't take long to find out.

"The enemy vessel has returned to its previous course."

Misrem smiled very slightly.

Offering me a tempting target, she thought. Moving back, now that he knew that she had ships that could shift to intercept along that vector, was a clear challenge. He was, in effect, making a rather rude gesture at her on his way by.

Arrogant pup.

▶▶▶

▶ *What am I doing?*

Drey couldn't believe the idiocy of his actions. He should have just bolted for the outer system and transitioned back to Colonial Space.

Instead, here he was, playing games with a superior force like some kind of idiot.

There was no way he could inflict any serious damage on the enemy, that was obvious, but some part of him couldn't just run without doing *something.*

"Load the transition cannons," he ordered quietly, then realized no one had heard him. He repeated himself, louder.

"Captain?" Hela looked over at him. "The effectiveness of the cannons against a field warp drive system, to say nothing of the singularity core, has been reported as severely limited."

"I am aware," Drey answered. "Prepare the cannons anyway."

"Yes Captain."

Orders given, Drew turned his focus to the files he had on the weapons the Terrans had invented from their clearly twisted brains. The cannons were an obvious extension of their transition drive technology and had proved incredibly effective against the Drasin during the last days of the invasion of their homeworld.

He had seen the records of those weapons and what they could do, and Drey considered the theory behind them to be almost beyond his imagining. The idea of a weapon system with a potential range of near infinity, with no effective delay between firing the weapon and its contact with the target was terrifying.

But the coherence of the tachyon stream used to transmit the weapons could be compromised by a gravity well. Not surprising, perhaps, but a rather large weakness when dealing with ships that belonged to this Empire or the Priminae and now the Terrans as well. Between the gravity wells used to propel their ships and the singularity cores used to power them, it was a matter of luck and little else if you managed to pick a target that resulted in your weapons landing intact and armed.

There were ways to factor for the effects of a gravity well, however, if you understood the fundamentals of the forces you were playing with.

He calculated quickly, basing his numbers on the core of his own ship. The Empire seemed to use vessels that were derived from the Priminae cruiser design, or, perhaps more likely, both the Empire and the Priminae had access to similar source designs.

For the moment that was a curiosity, one he would like to look into when he had time.

He finished his calculations, then switched his interface over to another section and took command of the fire control system.

"Fire control to my station," Drey announced, just to keep his people from getting too jumpy. "I need accurate targeting data, Hela. Active scans."

"Yes Captain," she said nervously. "Scanning station! Active scans, military narrow band. Locate and vector the enemy ships as close as you can."

"Yes Commander." The scanner officer nodded. "Scanning."

▶▶▶

▶ "Real-time scanning, Navarch. They're acquiring targeting data."

Misrem raised an eyebrow. "At this range? They might as well also fire on the Imperial capital from here."

It would be a minor miracle for a laser to strike one of her ships if fired from such a range, but even if it did, it would have long since been attenuated by range and particulate matter absorbing its energy.

She scowled a little, but elected to take precautions just in case.

"Widen our formation," she ordered.

Spacing her ships out would reduce the chance of a lucky hit even more, and just moving at all would force the enemy to recalculate based on their new vectors. By the time a laser could traverse the range involved, she would make a point of moving again just to be safe.

▶▶▶

▶ Drey's hands were shaking as he entered the last coordinates for his plan, noting that the enemy commander had moved formation. Clearly, they weren't taking any chances, because he doubted he would have bothered in their place. No conventional weapon, not even special atomics, would have any significant effect from the range he was currently facing.

The range *was* dropping incredibly fast, however, so perhaps it was merely good planning on the other's side of things. He didn't know, really.

He wasn't working with a remotely conventional weapon, however, and that meant he had something of an advantage. He hoped.

"Forward cannon . . . firing," Drey announced as he keyed in the final command to execute his orders.

The weapon didn't shake the *Tetanna*'s hull. It didn't report in any noticeable way even, but on command, the vessel fired one of the deadliest weapons in known space.

Drey was already calculating the next shot before the sequence finished.

▶▶▶

▶ The navarch was scowling openly as she looked over the converging vectors. The Oather ship was a long way out and shortly would reach the point at which she no longer would have any chance of intercept, even by dispatching her destroyers at their maximum vector and acceleration. Misrem knew she was still going to take that chance, but was debating the precise timing.

She was about to issue the order when a sharp report of static from the scanning station caused her to glance over.

"What was that?" she asked as she walked to the station.

"Unknown," the scanner officer said, shaking his head. "Burst of noise in the real-time range. It would have been unnoticed because of the enemy scanners in the same range, but it was powerful."

"Origin?"

"Unable to calculate. Just not enough of it to pin down," he admitted.

"Were we just scanned by another ship?" she demanded tensely, her eyes darting around the screens.

"No chance. That was too short, Navarch, and the signature was completely different from a scanner. I think it was a pulsar," the scanner officer said.

That would be an oddity, Misrem thought, *but not impossible*. Still, he was right; she didn't recognize the signal, and it wasn't any sort of detection signature. A natural source was most likely, so for the moment, she decided she would accept that deduction.

"Navarch . . ." The communications officer caught her attention.

"What is it?"

"The *Kin Amen* just registered a radiation leak," the officer told her. "They are shutting down their reactor conduits while they look for the source."

Misrem blinked. "How bad a leak?"

"Three decks were irradiated in an instant. It has to be bad."

She nodded to the communications officer. "Give them permission to drop from formation. I will want a full report later."

"Yes Navarch," he said, turning back to relay the message.

Three decks irradiated.

She shook her head. A nasty leak. She hoped that she didn't lose the whole ship over it. While the *Kin* was only one of her destroyers, any loss on this operation was to be considered a significant blow. They needed every gun they could fly, at least until they'd worked out the nature of the anomalies in this sector of space.

Misrem turned her focus back to the ongoing game she was playing with the Oather captain.

"Dispatch all other destroyers to intercept the Oather ship, maximum acceleration, best possible vector," she ordered tensely.

Your move, Misrem thought as she glared at the rapidly closing dot on the screens.

Whatever the enemy was up to, she would learn it soon enough.

One way or another.

▶▶▶

▶ "Enemy ship is slowing, Captain," Hela announced, looking over at him with some surprise. "It looks intact, but they're no longer accelerating."

He nodded, not looking up.

Drey had been in charge of more than one singularity reactor during his career, not to mention the drive elements that all Priminae and, it seemed, Imperial ships were based on. Knowing how to calculate for gravitic interference was among the most basic skills he'd learned early on. Completely eliminating all the effects of such interference was basically impossible due to a number of variables that he would need access to the enemy computers to properly calculate. But he could do a fair job of ensuring the nuclear shells of the transition cannons at least reintegrated within a few hundred meters of the intended target.

It wouldn't be enough to ensure that any of the bombs would be functional, sadly, but the level of radiation it would spread around the decks of a vessel would throw every alarm imaginable into screaming action and scare the abyss out of the crew in the process. Unfortunately, he wasn't sure it would do much more than that, and while he was pleased it had worked, he'd been hoping for better.

"Captain! The smaller enemy ships have shifted course. They are maneuvering to intercept us," Hela announced, scowling at the screens.

"What is wrong?" he asked, recognizing that she was holding something back.

"They've accelerated more than I would have expected them capable of," she admitted. "I am not certain we can entirely evade them."

"Shift course to evade, best possible vector, full military acceleration," he ordered instantly, without looking at the data.

Only once they had shifted course did he pull the data up to examine it himself. Drey whistled softly as he saw the acceleration curves on the smaller ships. They were considerably higher than he'd projected, which spoke of a significantly higher power-to-mass ratio than he had thought possible. He ran the numbers and grimaced as he came up with the same results Hela had spotted.

There were only nineteen of them now. The one he had targeted was still on a ballistic course with its drive either shut down or running at minimum power. He didn't want to bet, however, that the *Tetanna* could take on nineteen enemy ships, even smaller ones.

Thankfully, they would only be able to get a minimal glancing engagement.

Drey grimaced, irritated at himself, knowing that he'd put his ship in danger because he felt like he had to do *something*. Now he and his crew would have to live with the decision.

You're a damn fool, he thought.

▶▶▶

▶ Navarch Misrem noted the converging tracks with satisfaction, a smile on her lips as she crunched the numbers carefully.

They would have a limited engagement period at extreme range, but for several minutes, the Oather ship *would* indeed be within their range. It would not be enough for a kill with a normal squadron, but with nineteen destroyers all focusing their fire on one target, the odds were much better.

"Adjust our course to back up the destroyer screen," she ordered.

They wouldn't be able to intercept the ship themselves under normal circumstances, but if the destroyers got lucky, she wanted to be there to capitalize on the moment.

The planet, for the moment at least, was set aside.

Either way, Misrem was well aware that she would have plenty of time to decide its fate once this encounter was ended. There was no particular need for the Empire to do anything with it, so a passing bombardment would likely be the simplest solution to any potential witnesses. If the ship escaped, then there would be no need to go after witnesses, but perhaps a show of force and determination would be useful.

The next few hours would tell the tale.

CHAPTER 5

Priminae Core World, Ranquil

▶ Steph wiped his mouth and grimaced in disgust. He picked himself off the floor of his cabin, tossing the unfortunately soiled towel away from him as he walked back into the bathroom he had just left a few seconds—and several dozen light-years—earlier.

Normally he wasn't prone to transition sickness, but this time he hadn't been on duty during the transit and, being worn from his time in the simulator, had been distracted in the . . . shower, he guessed, when the warning sounded. The hiss of the mist shower had masked the warning enough that he had been caught unaware when he was walking across the room to his closet and the ship transited out of Sol space. As it turned out, his stomach didn't much like being chucked halfway across the galaxy without warning.

The vomit on his towel and floor would serve as warning to be more aware of his surroundings the next time, he supposed, as he grabbed a fresh towel and a bottle of mouthwash on his way back to the shower booth.

There has to be a better way to do things, he thought, getting cleaned up again as quickly as he could before drying himself off for a second time. *Being tossed through the deep void like you're going through a shredder and being spaced in the process just ain't dignified.*

The transition drive was, unquestionably an amazing technology—no one could deny that—but Steph didn't know anyone who actually enjoyed the damn thing.

Other than that crazy Canuck, he corrected himself, thinking of a shipmate from the *Odyssey*.

Bermont had been Special Forces, though, so he didn't count anyway. It didn't matter what country they were from; those guys were all touched in the head.

Steph knew that they would be in Ranquil now, and he could feel the slight hum through his feet that everyone swore he was making up, so he knew they were dropping downwell toward the main planet. He flopped on the bed after cleaning up the mess he'd made and briefly hoped that Milla had time to spend at home before they were shipped out again.

It was looking like it would be a long patrol, and no one would be home for some time once they got underway.

He was drifting off when he thought he heard an odd childish giggle in the distance. He shifted, opening his eyes to look around for the source, then shivered before deciding it was just sleep induced. He rolled back over and tried to get back to sleep, this time succeeding without additional auditory imaginings.

▶▶▶

▶ "Commodore, you're up rather late."

Eric half turned as Heath approached from his left side, nodding to the commander.

"I just like to watch the star grow," he said, gesturing to the observation windows.

Heath nodded. "I understand. It's hypnotic, isn't it?"

"And inspiring," he said with a fond smile. "Especially Sol, though I find Earth less comfortable than ever now, so I enjoy watching Sol recede as well."

She looked at him, seemingly intrigued by that response. "Most people look forward to getting home for leave."

Eric shrugged. "I don't know. I love Earth, but I don't think it's been home for me since I was given the *Odyssey*. I *like* it out here."

Heath seemed surprised.

"I know," he said, understanding her look, "but it's what I feel. The black is cleaner, more honest. Every time I go home, I get pulled deeper into politics, and I'm beginning to be afraid that they're going to try to promote me to a desk job on Unity."

He had such disgust in his voice at that prospect that she laughed softly.

"I'm sure you could take a promotional spot instead, if you prefer?" she suggested lightly.

Eric shot his first officer a horrified look. "You are an evil woman, Commander Heath," he told her in no uncertain terms, focusing again on the distant star that was now separated from the rest of the field, beginning to look like a sun as they approached.

"I do try, sir," she said with a smile. "I came to see if you were up, because we were hailed by Admiral Tanner shortly after entering the system. I thought you would like to know."

"Thank you. I'll send a canned reply, then turn in for a couple of hours. Try to be fresh and awake when we arrive."

"Good luck with that, Commodore."

He gave Heath a sidelong look, then rolled his eyes. "Get out of here, Commander, before I do something nasty to punish you . . . like give you a promotion, perhaps?"

"Anything but that." She waved to ward him off, retreating from the deck. "I'll see you in a few hours, then."

"You will at that, Commander," he said as she left.

Eric took another long look at the growing star before he stepped back from the overwatch deck and headed back to his station.

The admiral's greeting was waiting for him, as the commander had said. He tossed in a quick greeting himself and sent it along before closing the system down and getting to his feet. It was well after midnight, ship's time, and they'd be putting into Ranquil orbit close to dawn, local time, as scheduled.

He would grab a little sleep and let third watch handle things without the captain looking over their shoulders.

▶▶▶

▶ The *Odysseus* was a large ship, by any measure.

Built to contain and take advantage of a planetary mass singularity, the ship had odd sweeps and angles that would be out of place in any other design. But for those standing anywhere on the decks, it always felt flat and normal because of those oddities. Gravity was, by design, stable no matter where most people went on the ship despite the relatively steep gradient in the wave design of the singularity's output.

There were, as always, exceptions. Two points on the *Odysseus* were able to maintain zero gravity due to the interaction of the ship's cores, and a handful of other points had varying gravities where the wave interactions of the two cores would interact and either reinforce one another or cancel out.

At the moment, Colonel Deirdre Conner was working out in one of the high-gravity zones. It wasn't recommended procedure. Even a slight increase to gravity could vastly increase the odds of injury, but she and her Marines had quietly staked out their preferred section of the ship—and its one and half times gravity—as their gym.

There were a few other Marines working out as well, which was almost always the case when the *Odysseus* was under way. Her Marine contingent was a battalion equivalent, with five hundred soldiers and their attached support. On a ship the size of the *Odysseus*, that sometimes managed to feel understaffed, but it was five hundred more than was normally assigned to any Blue Navy ship as a matter of general policy.

The Confederation had enough ship problems as it was. Rather than add to the stress of building a new fleet, it had been decided that

Marines would ride with the Black Navy full-time rather than just hitch a lift with a ship when their detachment had an assignment. Much of the time, she felt superfluous to the good and proper running of the ship, something she hated with a passion, so she worked out.

If her Marines were needed, they would *really* be needed. With support several light-years away at any given time, that was the way things ran now.

Conner's job was to ensure that they were ready when needed and, sometimes more importantly, didn't cause too much trouble when they weren't. The second part of that was the harder of the two by far.

She'd taken third shift for herself as of late because she had been trying to track down a problem that had quietly made itself known. Some of her Marines were causing issues during the night, and she wanted to step firmly on that before it got back to the captain.

So far, it was nothing big, but small problems turned into large ones if left unchecked.

One of her Marines marching up to her with a look on his face like he wanted to break open the weapons locker was *not* a sign that she'd been able to check the problem.

"What is it, Gunny?" she asked with a sigh as she grabbed the towel from the machine she'd been using and started to wipe off.

"Colonel. Chief Dixon has two of our men in the brig for, and I quote," the gunny snapped, "'befouling the sanctity of his engineering deck.'"

Conner winced, rubbing her temple gently as she considered that for a moment.

"Did they puke during transit?" she asked, confused. She could see making them clean it up if they had, even making them use their own toothbrushes, though that would be a little extreme to her mind. But the brig was pushing it.

"No Colonel." The gunny shook his head. "Someone scattered slop and scraps from the commissary across the engineering decks. Chief thinks it was two of ours. Since he was talking about keelhauling, I decided I'd best bring this to you immediately."

Conner grumbled as she grabbed her uniform tunic and rolled it on over her workout shirt, sweat be damned.

"If he's got evidence on them, they're going to wish he had keel-hauled them before I got there," she gritted out. "Navy/Marine pranking is one thing, but that is a step too damn far, Gunny."

"Yes ma'am." The gunny fell into step with her as she stalked out of the gym. "However, these two aren't the sort I'd expect to be involved in this sort of thing."

"I don't expect *any* of my Marines to be involved in this sort of thing," she replied, "so we'll see what evidence the chief has first, and it better be good. If it is, those Marines are *off* this ship, Gunny. They can damn well wait on Ranquil for the next ride that has room for a couple of useless tools."

"Yes ma'am."

▶▶▶

▶ Dixon was glowering at the Marines sitting glumly in the small brig space across from him, idly picking at the neck seal on a vacuum, when the colonel marched into the security office with a gunny in tow. For the first time in over twenty minutes, he looked away from the Marines, rising to his feet and coming to attention.

"Colonel." He greeted the stern-faced woman who paused only to glare at the pair of Marines before turning back to him.

"I'm told you have a problem with my Marines," she said simply. "I assume you have them on video?"

It was a safe assumption. The whole ship was monitored, especially the engineering decks, but Dixon grimaced.

"Every camera on the deck went out at the same time," he growled, glaring daggers at the Marines. "Before it happened, we have video of them entering the commissary, however, and you can see the state of their uniforms for yourself."

Conner raised an eyebrow and walked over to look at the two Marines that she now realized were looking quite bedraggled. They were covered in culinary scraps, their tan shipboard BDUs looking like they'd been through a food fight with a particularly skilled fourth-grade class. Her lips curled up involuntarily, and she sneered at them.

"You two better have a good explanation for this, or I'll be considering the chief's suggestion."

The two Marines, who had both snapped to their feet and attention when they saw her, practically started falling over each other as they tried to explain.

"Marines!" the gunny snarled. "You will *desist* talking over one another like *children*, or I will arrange to leave you alone with the master chief for a few minutes with the recorders off. Do you *get me?*"

The two Marines looked over the gunny's shoulder at the master chief, who was glaring openly at them, his arms crossed across his chest.

They shut up.

"Now," the gunny went on, "one at a time."

The two exchanged looks before one, the corporal, stepped forward. "Gunny, Colonel . . . Chief. We really don't know *what* happened, we swear. We were heading in for a coffee before we were due to report to the deck chief to do daily maintenance on gear when Lance Corporal Jan let out a yell and startled me. I turned to see what happened and was hit in the side of the face by . . . well, sirs, ma'am, I don't know what. Next thing we knew, we were hauling ass for cover, with food and scraps raining down around us."

"And you ran all the way to my *engineering* deck?" the master chief asked incredulously.

"I don't think we got that far, Chief, honestly." The corporal exchanged another glance with the lance corporal. "Maybe?"

Conner looked at Dixon. "Is it possible, Chief?"

The master chief looked ready to spit nails, but he nodded slowly. "Possible? Yes ma'am. Likely? No. Still, with the cameras disabled, it means someone knew what they were doing. I don't know how anyone could have rigged anything to spread food and scraps that far, though, Colonel. I'll have a team scour the commissary and see if we can find any evidence to support this . . . story."

"You do that," Connor said firmly, eyes squarely focused on the two Marines. "In the meantime, I'll be taking my Marines. You'll know where to find them if you need them."

The chief did *not* look happy to lose his two guests, but he nodded. "Yes ma'am."

The gunny got behind the two Marines. "Marines! Right face! And march two, three . . .'"

Conner watched the gunny march them out before turning to the chief. "Loop me in on the investigation. Either two of my Marines overstepped their boundaries rather significantly, or someone targeted them for a rather elaborate prank and left them to take the blame. Either way, I want to know, Chief."

"Yes ma'am. Rather curious myself," the master chief said grimly. "Privately, between us, ma'am, I doubt it was them. I checked their files while waiting for the gunny to go get you, and neither one could have taken down our cameras."

She looked at him, mildly amused. "So what was with picking at the seals of the vac suit?"

He shrugged with a bit of a smug look. "Didn't see any downsides to that, really. If they're guilty, I scare the crap out of them. If they're not, I still scare the crap out of them. They *should* be scared of me, ma'am. It's the natural order of things."

Conner shook her head, waving idly as she started to take her leave.

"As you were, Master Chief. Remember to loop me in."

"Aye aye, ma'am."

▶▶▶

▶ The lights rose as first watch approached and the ship's day began.

Eric was drying his hair as he stepped out of his bathroom and noticed the shift. He knew that they'd be arriving in Ranquil orbit in short order, but he'd have more than enough time for a meal and a couple of hot cups of coffee before he started the day properly.

As he got himself dressed, Eric glanced over the ship's logs for the night before. Most of them were the normal and routine matters of running the *Odysseus*, and he skipped over anything color-coded with gray. He'd skim those later, just to be sure, but for the moment, they were of little interest.

The lines in black denoted unexpected maintenance issues, but nothing that would impede normal operations. He skimmed those a little closer, but in general let them go by as well. There were no red lines, which was good because if anything that threatened the ship's safety had happened and no one bothered to wake him, Eric wouldn't be starting his day in a good mood.

The blue line caused him to pause and look a little closer. It seemed like a minor discipline issue, so he would leave the incident to ship's security and the Marines. At some point, he'd make a point of checking with Colonel Conner just to find out what had happened, but conflict was inevitable when you mixed Marines with Navy, even if the Black Navy wasn't fully composed of Navy personnel in the strictest sense.

Being a Marine himself, in spirit if no longer in fact, Eric was well aware of just how far "good-natured" jokes could go before anyone really realized it.

That was the only line of any interest in the log, so he closed the display with a flick of his hand and grabbed his uniform jacket on the way to the door, swinging it on as the door clanked open automatically, then shut behind him with a bang and the thunk of the airlock being sealed.

▶▶▶

▶ "Captain on the bridge!"

"As you were," Eric said to the crew who had stiffened to attention at the announcement. He passed his station and toured the bridge briefly, looking over the status of each station in turn.

"Steph . . ." He came to a stop by the pilot's pit, a sunken section of the deck that lay directly in front of the command station, affording both captain and pilot direct and identical images as the main viewer without putting either in the way of the other.

"Raze," Steph said, nodding to him. "Morning."

"Morning," Eric replied. "Everything in place?"

"Humming like a live wire," Steph replied. "Just like it's supposed to."

Eric looked up to the main screen, which was showing an image of Ranquil. "What's our magnification?"

"Hundred times," Steph answered, without looking up from where he was tinkering with some of the control settings. "We're backing off steady now, decelerating hard. Be in orbit within the hour."

"Thanks," Eric said as he turned toward the signals station. "Anything from the planet?"

"Standard greetings, sir," the duty ensign answered.

"Reciprocated, I assume?"

"Yes sir."

Eric nodded, walking back to his station and settling into place. "Good work."

The ensign glanced over at him and smiled. "Thank you, sir."

Eric didn't bother clarifying that his words had been meant for the whole bridge; the rest of the crew had been with him long enough to know that. He looked over the logs briefly, then opened up his ongoing files to work on while they were waiting for the *Odysseus* to enter Ranquil orbit.

He hadn't gotten too far when the signals ensign looked up sharply. "Signal from the planet, sir."

"To my station," Eric said instantly. He wasn't sure what it was about but knew that Tanner wasn't likely to be so impatient as to be unable to wait an hour.

The admiral appeared on his screen, lines of concern etched deeply in the normally smooth face. The man had aged a lot since Eric had first met him, his diminutive stature belied by the authority he carried.

"What's happened, Admiral?" Eric asked without preamble. Something had to be up for the normally genial man to be as concerned as he was.

"We just lost contact with a new colony, Cap . . . Commodore," the admiral said, pronouncing the unfamiliar title carefully. "I have dispatched a squadron already, but I believed that you would like to know as the last time a system went dark like this it was—"

"The Empire," Eric said softly.

"Yes," Tanner said.

"We will head out immediately and provide backup to your squadron," Eric said. "My regrets for this visit being so short."

"I wish that we would have had a long, peaceable time to converse as well, Commodore," Tanner said wearily. "However, it seems not to be in our fates."

"Fate is another word for surrender, Admiral," Eric said. "I don't believe in either. I'll see you when we get back."

"I will be waiting, Commodore. Good luck. You do believe in that, do you not?"

"The good kind? Of course. It's the bad kind that's a myth, Admiral."

Rael nodded and cut the transmission as Eric rose to his feet.

"Signal the squadron," he ordered. "We've got an Imperial incursion in a Priminae system. Priminae squadron is en route, but I want to be there just in case."

"Aye aye, sir," the signals officer said, sending off the orders.

"Helm, bring us about," Eric ordered. "Best time to the heliopause. New destination system has been sent to your station. Looks like we'll deal with our schedule another time."

"Aye aye, Raze," Steph answered, checking the computer before he started calculating a best time course to the heliopause that would put them on a jump course to the system in his computer. "Approximately three hours to jump, at full cruise."

"Give me full military power," Eric ordered.

"Full military power, aye." Steph recalculated the course. "Forty-two minutes to jump."

▶▶▶

▶ The nine ships of the *Odysseus* Task Force moved swiftly as new orders flew between them. They angled away from Ranquil, their reactors beginning to hum as more and more power was tapped and sent to the warp drives. In tight formation, they accelerated to full military power, a flash of Cerenkov blue marking the point they crossed the speed of light and continued to accelerate out of the system.

Behind them, in a surprisingly small office in the military center of Ranquil, a slight-statured man sighed and wished them well.

A younger Rael Tanner would not have wanted to see the day he wished violence on someone, and yet somehow he couldn't keep the sentiment from his mind as he thought about the system that had gone dark.

In any case, he was no longer that same person. For better or worse, he was the Rael Tanner of today. Admiral of the Priminae fleets, survivor of two Drasin assaults, and . . . a man who had to watch as people he called friends set out to do violence on his behalf.

He did not know how to deal with that.

Perhaps it was better that way.

CHAPTER 6

Priminae Colony Space

▶ Captain Druel Piers rose to his feet as the transition alarms sounded through his vessel, the *Zeu*. He firmly ignored both the urge to vomit and the sound of others not being able to resist it themselves.

"We have entered the target system. All ships have reported in."

He grunted, waving the information away. He didn't need to know that the transition had gone well; that was the assumption. He was more interested in what had gone wrong in system.

"Put the current passives up on the screens."

"Yes Captain," his second answered. "We are still compiling data, but here is what we have scanned so far."

Coming into a new system via the Terran's transition system meant arriving mostly blind. They had some basic long-range scans, particularly for large gravity sources, but only in the immediate region of the arrival point. Beyond that, they were limited to what they started picking up as soon as their scanners and computers completed the transition.

The screens lit up with the expected information. Large signals like the local star, planets, and a few planetoids big enough, or known enough, for the computer to recognize instantly populated the image. More items were filling in quickly as the computer caught up to the change of venue.

"We are picking up a localized emergency signal, Captain. It's highly degraded by the jamming, but it is from the colony," the signals officer announced.

Druel closed his eyes and let out a sigh of relief.

The colony still existed if they were getting an active signal, degraded or not. The emergency signal was an FTL system, so he knew that it was still intact.

"Look for the source of the jamming," he ordered after a moment.

"Yes sir. We're vectoring it, but our group is too close to properly triangulate."

"Spread us out, Pol," he said as he turned to his second in command.

Pol Kinn nodded, issuing the orders to send their task group on diverging vectors so they could get enough parallax on the jamming signal to lock in a central location.

Druel settled in for the long wait. He could achieve instant satisfaction by pulsing the system, but that would just announce his presence to anyone with scanner capacity, and he wasn't sure he wanted to do that just yet. Gravity scanners would inevitably pick up the mass of his task group. It was pretty difficult to miss multiple planetoid-size gravity fields showing up in a system, even if they were as tightly controlled as the ones his ships would be projecting. But unless any opposition actively looked, he and his should have time before the reveal.

On the screens, the system information continued to fill out as the passive scanners worked tirelessly in the background. They now had information that showed the colony was untouched as of seven hours earlier and had a ship resting in orbit.

"Do we have positive confirmation that the ship in orbit is the *Tetanna*?" Druel asked.

"No Captain," his signals officer responded. "It matches in general configuration, but we do not have resolution yet to confirm, and no codes have been received."

"Alright. Keep it up. I want this system mapped as quickly as we can manage with passives," Druel said.

"Yes Captain."

Pol took a step back, leaning over slightly. "I am not seeing any anomalies here, Captain. It looks precisely as expected."

"The jammer is enough of an anomaly for me, Poi," Druel said firmly. "We track it down, we will know what happened, but I don't think there's much question anyway. We have only recorded this sort of jamming once before."

"Yes Captain."

Until the Terran's *Odysseus* Task Force had encountered it in another Priminae system, the sort of jamming they were looking at had been thought impossible. The power required to totally disrupt FTL communications was rather extreme, so he had little doubt that it was from the same source.

Empire.

The word didn't really exist in modern Priminae. One had to dig back into positively *ancient* language variants in order to find it.

Druel had done just that when the Terran report had been presented to him, and the definition of the word had disgusted him. The idea of a body politic that ruled by force of arms and, worse, expanded to impose its will on others?

Vile.

Worse than the Drasin. Those beasts were all instinct, no reason. They were nothing more, or less, than a force of nature, no matter their origin. These . . . *Imperials* . . . were rational, thinking beings. They had no excuses for their actions, no reason that he would accept. They were simply vile, in word and deed.

His thoughts were interrupted by his second in command calling his attention to the board.

"Captain, the *Tetanna* is leaving orbit."

Druel looked up sharply. "Did they spot something? Can we determine what?"

"I do not think they have located anything new." His second shook his head. "Their departure is unhurried, and they appear to be aiming for one of the system's null-gravity points."

Druel looked at the telemetry they were still decoding and scowled in thought. The null-gravity points in a star system were areas the interaction of all the major masses within the system reduced gravity to near zero. There were generally dozens of relatively stable ones, even in a small system, and hundreds or even thousands of more marginal points.

"They must be intending to update their charts," he decided, sighing deeply.

"Yes Captain."

"I wish we were here in time to catch their pulse," he said glumly.

Unfortunately, though they were watching the starship move into position to fire off said pulse, Druel was well aware that the FTL echoes of the pulse would have long since faded. They would not be gaining any details from that source, sadly.

The bridge crew watched as the *Tetanna* slipped into position at one of the more stable null points close to the planet and, presumably, sent out an FTL detection pulse. What they detected from it, Druel could only speculate at this point, but the sudden shift of the ship's armor and shields to combat status and sharp acceleration told the story well enough.

"Find what they saw. Find it now!" he ordered across the bridge.

"Yes sir!"

▶▶▶

▶ "Enemy destroyers entering extreme engagement range, Captain."

Drey nodded at Hela's warning, having expected it for the last few moments.

"Initiate evasive maneuvering," he ordered, grimacing.

Any evasive maneuvers they could take would, to some degree, increase their time in the enemy's engagement envelope since they were already on a least-time evasion course. If they tried to remain on that straight-line course, however, they would massively increase the effectiveness of the enemy's firing opportunities, so it was really just a matter of which would be more dangerous to the *Tetanna*.

Since there were *nineteen* enemy destroyers almost certainly firing even as he considered them, staying still simply wasn't an option. If they realized what he was doing and bracketed him all together, not even the *Tetanna*'s armor would allow her to survive the onslaught.

He looked at the range to target, mentally tallied the time they had before the first of the enemy lasers would intersect their general position, and started counting down in his mind.

Five . . . four . . . three . . .

"Brace for impact," he ordered, gripping his station firmly, though it was probably pointless.

There was no impact, exactly, but a distant rumble could be felt through the deck. A quiet alarm sounded.

"Laser burn through the port side armor, aft," his damage control officer announced. "Breach is sealing; teams responding."

"Did we get a frequency on the pulse?" Drey asked Hela tersely.

"Yes sir."

"Adapt our armor to match," he ordered. "Maintain course and speed."

"Evasive maneuvers?" she asked, shooting him a glance even as she directed the orders through the station.

He shook his head. "No. We have a read on the one that hit us. If they're running a zone firing program, we might get lucky and spent a few seconds getting hit just by him before anyone else realizes we're not dodging anymore. Get the armor adjusted and hold us steady."

"Yes Captain."

▶ ▶ ▶

▶ Navarch Misrem eyed the displays with a feral, hungry look.

Her destroyer screen would be her blaster this time rather than her armor, but she would savor what she could from the encounter all the same.

"Destroyers have bracketed the region the enemy ship can maneuver in," her aide said softly at her side. "The first barrage should have struck by now. We will detect the results in a few more seconds, Navarch."

"Good. Pass my compliments to the captains for their crew," she commanded, "and ensure that they continue firing. I would rather see them burn out their cannons than stop before we are sure the enemy is either dead or beyond our reach."

"At your command, Navarch."

She straightened from the screens and looked at the command personnel for a brief moment. They were all focused on their own tasks, none looking up as her eyes flitted by.

Combat at these extreme ranges was one of the most stressful parts of any commander's or command staff's duty. Mistakes here would have very real consequences, but the time delay tended to make people complacent and more likely to make those mistakes than normal. It was easy to forget that you were dealing with the possibility of a boiling, freezing death when it was encapsulated by the sheer size of the void.

She saw no sign that any of her people were getting too comfortable, so she said nothing before turning her focus back to the battle as it slowly played out.

"First hit, Navarch. We have drawn air from their hull."

She nodded, satisfied. So far, it was going to plan. "Press the assault."

▶▶▶

▶ The *Tetanna* was accelerating for safety at her best military speed, having shrugged off three more direct hits from the same destroyer since the first, her adaptive armor easily deflecting the powerful blasts of energy thanks to the technology acquired from the Terrans.

Drey was sweating each strike as it came in, trying to determine the timing. Figuring out when the enemy was going to adapt to his tactic—or more specifically, lack of same—would be the key to their success or failure here. A lucky strike from lasers might damage the *Tetanna* enough to slow their escape, allowing the cruisers to catch up.

"Evasive maneuvers," he ordered, hating it as he did because the shift in course and speed would extend their engagement time.

"Shifting course," the helm officer responded instantly. The *Tetanna* shifted in a random direction and decreased acceleration to further throw off the enemy's targeting.

Drey curled his lip as he noted that the maneuver had extended their engagement time by almost thirty full minutes.

Computer-aided systems traced laser fire around them, using fluorescing bits of matter in space as the primary method of tracking the beams. He watched beam after beam from the enemy ship pass through their previous space and shook his head in disgust.

Too soon. I overestimated them. Damn it.

A shiver through the ship had him cursing even more as he recognized the damage alarm going up.

"Glancing blow, starboard armor," damage control reported. "No breach. No breach."

"Full military acceleration," Drey ordered. "Least time for the system border."

"Yes Captain. Full military acceleration, least-time course."

The *Tetanna* leapt once more to full power, lasers cutting space into sections around them as they surged away from the pursuers.

▶▶▶

▶ "There, what is that?" Misrem hissed, glowering at the screens.

"That appears to be a refraction signature of one of our lasers," her aide admitted, frowning.

"I know that." She scowled at him. "I mean, how are they doing it? They are being struck time and again, but other than the first blow, that ship is just taking everything we can throw at it."

She slammed a fist down into the arm of her console, then stood up.

"Okay, they have something we are not accounting for." She took a breath, considering the dilemma. "At this range, our lasers aren't attenuated enough for normal armor to repulse them like that. The issue is time, not power, so a strike should be as good as any."

She paused, turning to glare back at the screens for a moment. "Captain!"

"Navarch?" The captain of her flagship half turned from where he was coordinating the ships' efforts in the fight.

"You are still operating a zone offense coverage, correct?" she asked, though if the answer was anything but in the affirmative, she would be shocked.

"Of course, as ordered."

Misrem looked away from him for a moment, muttering to herself. "That strange armor of theirs, we need to capture a sample. I think I know what is going on. Captain, new orders for the destroyers."

"Yes Navarch?"

"Maintain zone offense coverage, but I want no less than *three* destroyers assigned to the same spacial sector."

The captain looked appalled. "Navarch, that will degrade our strike probability by well over threefold—"

"I am aware of that. The orders stand," she said flatly. "Issue them."

He stared for a moment, then nodded slowly. "Yes Navarch."

Misrem turned her focus back to the screens. *Now, let us see if I am right about you.*

▶ ▶ ▶

▶ "There!"

Druel turned, his gaze following the gesture his second was making.

Onscreen, the *Zeu*'s computers showed that they had finally located the enemy. He swore as he saw the numbers.

"It is a war squadron," he muttered with both disgust and some measure of fear.

His own squadron was well outmanned, and while he had confidence that they were more than a match for the enemy ships ton for ton, the enemy had a *lot* more tonnage to play with. That would not work well, but he didn't see many options.

"Continue to focus our computers on their locations," he ordered the scanner station before turning and continuing without pause. "Navigation, I want an intercept course readied as soon as we have sufficient telemetry data to predict their maneuvers."

"Yes Captain," both stations echoed.

Druel turned back to his second in command. "They are moving in system. That means they are going on the offensive. The only question is whether they went for the planet or the *Tetanna*. We are not allowing them to do either, if it is within our power."

"Understood, Captain." She nodded, hesitating. "They significantly outnumber us, Captain. That will reduce the effectiveness of the Terran armor design."

"I know, but I see little option at this point. We will do this," he said firmly. "We have to."

▶▶▶

▶ The *Tetanna* shuddered as strikes came in, most glancing off the adjusted armor but more every passing minute digging deep and coring into the interior of the big ship. Drey grimaced with every report coming back from the damage control teams, men and women who were rushing into the affected decks and trying their best to repair any critical systems the beams had torn up.

They were now on a least-time course with full military power, trying to get out of enemy range, but Drey could see that his ship would have to endure several minutes more of the barrage before they were free.

With the enemy now knowing their course, he had a very difficult decision to make: evasive maneuvers or run for the heliopause without looking back.

Drey snarled when another shudder could be felt through the deck.

"Hold course," he ordered. "Hela, get someone from the reactor core on the comm screen. We need everything they can give us."

"Yes Captain."

He leaned forward at his station, eyes boring into the holographic display of the combat zone. The enemy cruisers were still well out of range; only the smaller and apparently faster ships were able to keep up with the *Tetanna*'s initial speed advantage. Even that would only hold just so long, but there was enough of the enemy to make it difficult, possibly even fatal, for his ship and crew before they could pull clear.

All combat in space was reduced to relatively simple mathematical calculations. The inherent limitations of speed, distance, and inertia— even for vessels with inertial compensation—decided the outcome of most battles before the first laser left its source ship. Uncertainties were a human factor, the unexpected things that people might do in moments of brilliance or stupidity.

Drey just hoped that the brilliance would be on his side and the stupidity on the enemy's.

The likelihood of that, of course, was something he preferred not to delve deeply into.

▶▶▶

▶ "Another hit, Navarch. We are scanning venting atmosphere," her aide said without turning around.

Misrem nodded, satisfied that she had been correct. "Are we still registering the ineffective strikes?"

"Yes . . . ," the aide said hesitantly.

"Run an analysis against the estimated strike times of each ship," she said. "I want to know which of our vessels fired the ineffective beams."

"Uh . . ." Her aide looked confused, but there was really only one possible answer. "Right away, Navarch."

Misrem looked on serenely as she settled back.

At this point, she was confirming what she already knew. Somehow, the enemy armor was able to perfectly adapt to a specific beam frequency. Potent armor indeed, but even the finest Imperial manufacturing had to eliminate variance in the beam generators, so while they all ran within a narrow band, none were identical.

It is still very impressive, she thought grudgingly. *Without it, I expect we would already have cut out their singularity cores and left them adrift, or worse.*

Indeed, even the beams that were penetrating were obviously not doing as much damage as they should, and that was stretching the battle out beyond all reason. Since time favored the enemy in this encounter, Misrem was doing everything she could not to show her frustration. Losing her temper in a fight they were clearly dominating would not go over well with the crew. It was one thing to be angry at a loss, but to be furious during even a weak victory would make her look unstable to the rank and file.

That was not acceptable in the slightest.

A computer tone caused her aide to look down. From the surprise in his posture, Misrem didn't have to ask what he'd seen.

"The ineffective shots all belonged to the same vessel, did they not?" she asked, just a little smugly.

"Uh, yes Navarch. How—"

"Don't concern yourself," Misrem said casually, entering an observation in her log as well as suggestions for new standard combat procedures to be registered with the Empire when they returned. "All ships continue as ordered."

"As you command, Navarch."

▶ ▶ ▶

▶ Druel's lips curled back, revealing his teeth as he watched the telemetry data showing the opening stages of the fight.

They went straight for the planet, leaving the Tetanna *no choice but to engage, at least partially.*

He didn't know the captain of the *Tetanna* personally, but he had a fine reputation and was dedicated to the well-being of the Colonies. Otherwise, he wouldn't have been given the *Tetanna* to command. That there was nothing he could do to save the colony would not have impacted his inevitable decision; Druel could tell from the vectors involved that the man had determined to strike and fade rather than make a suicide run or flee altogether.

The infamous Captain Weston's influence shows its way through, Druel supposed. There was a time when the options considered would have been run for reinforcements or stand and die.

"Helm," Druel called as he crunched the contact numbers and determined that they would likely have *just enough* time to intervene, as long as they didn't waste any of what was available.

"Yes Captain?"

"I want a reciprocal course, best time to intercept the lead elements of the enemy formation," he ordered. "Bring us in *across* the *Tetanna*'s course at a perpendicular angle."

"Yes Captain. I will have the course in just a moment."

"Send it to the squadron and engage with full military power as soon as possible," he said firmly.

"Yes Captain."

Orders issued, Druel watched the situation develop on the displays around him.

It would be an interesting encounter, he decided. He watched the telemetry feeds rapidly filling in details as his ships proceeded quickly into the system, continuing to gather information as quickly as light could reach their scanners.

The *Tetanna* was now making for a standard system exit vector, putting the ship on a converging course with the *Zeu's* task force. Not exactly luck, as the chosen vector would also put the ship on course for the nearest central Priminae colony, which was precisely where the *Zeu* and accompanying vessels had come from, but certainly fortunate enough.

With the *Tetanna* between them, Druel's small task group and the enemy ships were now bearing down on one another. If all was as he devoutly hoped, the enemy was too focused on the *Tetanna* to realize it.

▶▶▶

▶The big ship shuddered again as another biting strike from enemy lasers cored deep through its armor, venting atmosphere to space and emptying lungs and terminating lives in the same blinding moment. Drey wrapped his hands around the edge of his station, knuckles white as he stared doggedly forward at the screens and tried not to think about what had been done to his ship . . . to his ship's *crew*.

Drey was not—had never even *imagined* being—a violent man.

At that moment, however, he wanted nothing more than to bring his ship around and put his primary lasers on target. He could do it too. The warp drive would allow him to accelerate out of the system even facing the wrong way, but the efficiency wasn't as high, and with the range opening up every passing second, getting strikes on target with only one ship firing just didn't warrant the slight loss of acceleration.

There was nothing he could do, and it was eating him inside as he watched people working feverishly around him.

Is this what war is? Waiting to die, killing, or being forced to stand and watch as others did both? How do the Terrans do this?

CHAPTER 7

Imperial Task Group

▶ Misrem couldn't help but lean a little forward in her station as she watched the "battle" underway. Calling it a battle might be a little generous. It was really more of an ambush, and she was mildly impressed that the Oather vessel hadn't simply run from the start or succumbed to idiocy at this point.

The exchange of beams between the fleeing vessel and her own task force had piqued her strategic curiosity, however, and now she was watching each new bit of data with intense interest.

The few Oather strikes that landed on her vessels were doing damage well out of line with their power rating, which told her they had something new in their weapons technology to go with the improved armor that she was almost certain she'd already figured out the basics for.

Some sort of adaptive system, which makes me wonder if the lasers might not also be the same. Misrem made a note in her official log to ensure that if she wasn't able to determine the truth of her deduction, then the next Imperial officer assigned would have a place to begin.

The Oather ship was able to ignore the blasts coming from one of her cruisers with relative impunity, an effect noticeably different from the other destroyers and cruisers maintaining active fire on the fleeing craft. The other ships had significantly improved results, varying a fair degree from vessel to vessel.

She made notes as the data became available and began compiling a set of orders to go out when she felt the time was right.

"New signal!"

Misrem looked up sharply from her calculations, eyes immediately drawn to the long-range display.

"Analysis," she snapped, even as she started skimming the numbers.

"Gravity scans are consistent with Oather cruisers, Navarch," the scanner technician answered instantly. "We are still waiting on light-speed data, however."

"What?" She frowned.

That made little sense. Certainly, the cruisers could have remained unnoticed as they approached until the gravity scanners picked them up, but once her ship had its instruments pointed in the right direction, *something* should have been seen on the passive scanners.

"No explanation, Navarch," the tech said, sounding rather frustrated. "It is like they just *appeared*. We have nothing on them yet, nothing at all."

Were they waiting out there all this time? Misrem wondered, though it made no sense. Why would they light off their gravity drives this late if that were the case?

She got up and walked over to the main display to look at the numbers more closely, scowling openly at data that refused to make sense.

"How did they get that close without us picking up their gravity wave?" she demanded, angry at the lapse. "If someone missed their approach—"

"No Navarch," the tech said instantly, surprising her with the force of his response. "No one missed anything. I ran back the scanners personally, but you can of course confirm for yourself. They had to be out there until just a few moments ago, Navarch."

She glared at him for interrupting until he looked away, but didn't challenge his statement. He knew that she *would* check, and if he had lied to her, she would have his head. No, barring something utterly stupid, he was telling the truth.

She looked back at the display again after a moment, eyes quickly picking apart the data until she had an idea of the size of the approaching force.

They weren't enough to turn the tables, but they would certainly cut into her assembly some if they were willing to stand off.

She could take those losses, however, and still accomplish the mission. In fact, their arrival might well play into her hand if she could make proper use of it.

"How long until we get light-speed data?" she asked softly, eyes drifting along the big display.

"Another few hours, Navarch."

"Precise numbers, please," she snapped as she turned on her heel and stalked back to her station. "To my board. Now."

By the time she was settled back into place, the numbers were there, and she started to evaluate the possibilities.

I can work with this.

▶▶▶

Priminae Vessel Zeu

▶ The task group was rapidly accelerating down the gravity well of the local star. It had been some time since they started their course, and Druel knew that their light-speed signal would reach both the *Tetanna* and the enemy vessels. It was unlikely that either was truly unaware of their approach, of course, but they would soon have better access to raw numbers, if nothing else.

So far, oddly, there was no real sign in the enemy formation that they *had* noticed the task group's approach.

He supposed that there wasn't much they could react to yet, but they hadn't even blinked for an instant.

That does not bode well, Druel supposed darkly. If they were willing to fully commit to an attack on this system, he was all too aware that his small group just didn't have enough strength to stop them. They would follow the *Tetanna*'s example, at the very least, and attempt to strike and fade, tying the enemy up for as long as they could. But if help didn't arrive, then he would eventually be forced to decide between standing and dying or fleeing to fight another day.

Without any real possibility of doing more than buying the inhabitants of the local colony more than a few hours—days at most—there was unfortunately no real decision to be made.

Before it comes to that, however, he thought grimly, *we'll bleed them out as best we can.*

▶▶▶

Tetanna

▶ "Visual confirmation on the incoming ships, Captain. They're Priminae."

Drey slumped slightly, relief flooding him. His ship was bleeding air from practically every deck, with more lancing beams now cutting through the armor regularly. If the ships on approach had been more of the enemy, it would have been the end for the *Tetanna* and her crew.

His only real choice then would have been surrender . . . or a final run to inflict as much damage as he could before they burned him from the void.

Drey was desperately relieved to not have to make that decision.

"Put their course up, and overlay it on ours and the enemy squadron," he ordered.

The three vector arcs were lit up on the large holographic display an instant later, and he examined them closely to try to determine his next best move.

The attackers were steadily falling behind, but it was a slow process. The *Tetanna* had lost some acceleration due to battle damage but was still going to clear enemy fire relatively soon. Once that happened, they would be able to freely exit the system.

With a new squadron in the area, however, the Imperials could possibly withdraw.

Drey didn't expect that. So far, the enemy forces had shown a disturbing lack of interest in the health of their *own* people, which left him with no particular optimism for what they might do to anyone else.

"Maintain optimum escape course," he confirmed after examining the approach vectors. The Priminae squadron had apparently plotted their approach based on the *Tetanna*'s escape course, and he saw no reason to foul whatever plan they had in mind.

Not when it only required that he continue doing what he'd already determined to be his best option.

▶▶▶

Imperial Task Group

▶ "Fire orders," Misrem called out, tapping open her orders. "Dispatch to all ships."

"Aye Navarch. Standing by for dispatch," her aide replied instantly.

She flicked the orders off with a gesture, sending the file out to her aide, who instantly redirected them to the fire control officers of the varying ships she'd designated.

Onscreen, she saw the results of the new orders almost instantly as several vessels shifted their deployment formation slightly. One of the cruisers was instructed to drop back from its position in the formation while two more slipped in to replace it.

She watched as they settled in, then tapped off a timer as they fired under her tactical orders.

"Now we wait," she said, confusing her aide and several others around her.

Misrem didn't bother to explain. She didn't have to. They would follow orders, however confusing they might be, and that was enough.

Seconds passed, crawling in her perception as she mentally counted off the distance between her ships and their prey.

When that timer counted down, nothing happened.

Not on the screens. But Misrem smiled and rose to her feet.

"Cease fire," she ordered. "All ships, cease fire."

"Ma'am?" Her aide looked at her, surprise written on the man's face.

"You did not mishear," Misrem said. "All ships are to cease fire. We have them. No need to destroy our prize."

"Yes Navarch," her aide said, obviously uncertain but following orders.

Misrem didn't bother elucidating him as she began snapping other orders.

"I want a boarding Parasite readied," she said. "Full crew. Orders to follow after they launch."

▶ ▶ ▶

Tetanna

Drey supposed that he should have known things were going too well.

They were *almost* out of range when it happened.

The *Tetanna* had become used to a certain pattern in the enemy blasts. They'd adapted their armor to one of the cruisers, and since they were aware of its firing angle, they could safely ignore the expected blasts from that ship.

When the expected beams arrived bearing not only a different frequency but also twice the density anyone had calculated, all went right to the void in a split instant of time.

The *Tetanna* had twisted in space, the outgassing shock alone throwing her off course, and then lurched—actually *lurched*—enough to throw men and women to the deck. Drey hadn't even thought that was possible.

Alarms screamed around him as he picked himself up. He looked at the displays lit around him, trying to figure out what had happened after it was far too late.

"Acceleration is dead! We're drifting!"

They'll be gaining on us shortly, Drey mentally swore. *We were so close!*

Unfortunately, close did not count.

"Repair teams!" he ordered. "Get our drives back!"

"Captain . . ."

Drey shifted, looking over to where his second was approaching. "What is it?"

"It's quiet."

For a moment, he didn't understand what that meant. Alarms were screaming and could deafen any man, but then Drey realized what the second meant. Behind the screaming of the alarms, the previously steady sound of distant pounding as the lasers cut open the decks and exposed them to explosive decompression . . . *that* sound had stopped.

"They stopped shooting," he whispered. "Why did they stop shooting?"

CHAPTER 8

Priminae Colony Space

▶ "Secure from transition!"

The call echoed across the bridge as Eric gripped the rail in front of him with fingers cracking under tension.

His stomach was stronger than most, but even he had to fight down the urge to vomit. As if he was going to let that happen on his flag deck. A couple of deep breaths, the smell of charcoal filters burning away the last urges to release, and he straightened up to look at the plot.

The system signals were already flooding the *Odysseus'* computers, but only one of the other Heroics and three Rogues were on his screens. The rest must have transitioned farther out than the few seconds of light able to reach the ship's scanners so far.

There's the Boudicca *and her escorts now,* he noted just before the last of the Rogues appeared onscreen.

All accounted for.

He turned his attention to the system. The FTL jamming was evident, making a mess of what they were able to scan in the high-energy tachyon range, but even degraded, they could now pick up traces of the Priminae's local network.

Good to see they're still transmitting, Eric thought. *We might not be too late.*

"See if you can connect to the local network," he ordered, looking over to the comms officer. "With the jamming this intense, there probably won't be much of anything useful on it, but anything we can grab is one more arrow in the quiver."

"Aye Captain."

"In the meantime . . ." Eric thumbed a button on the panel in front of him and linked into the squadron's battle network via laser link. "Rogues, I want you to spread formation and go deep and silent. Shadow the Heroics in; we'll be your shields. Don't show yourselves until you have a kill shot lined up. I don't want to waste any chances here.

"*Boudicca, Bellerophon*," he went on, "give me a delta-wing formation. *Odysseus* will take the spear tip—"

"Captain," the scanner chief called, causing Eric to pause and look up. "System scans are coming through the computers now. We've got indications of high-energy discharges deep in system. Looks like lasers, sir."

"How far in?" Eric asked.

"About two light-hours, sir, and closing the range in our general direction according to vector data."

Eric considered that.

That made sense, as they'd made their approach from the vector to the Priminae Central worlds. Anyone running out of this system would likely be heading in that direction. It also meant the Priminae ships were probably in withdrawal, because he'd have expected the Imperial forces to withdraw toward their own territory.

Assuming he wasn't completely off the mark, at least. A lot of factors might change such a theory, but he'd play it the way he saw it and adjust as he got new information.

"Steph, make our course to intercept the projected vectors of those discharges," Eric ordered. "Full military acceleration."

"Aye aye, Skipper. Full military acceleration," Steph confirmed from where he was running navigation vector calculations. "We'll be underway in two minutes."

Eric didn't bother saying anything more. He knew that the squadron would be moving out in two or less, and that was good enough. The computers were still decoding the raw data coming in from the system and would do so for as long as they let them. There was too much data in a star system for even the *Odysseus* to crunch through in any reasonable time.

He was mostly interested in the area immediately around the high-energy discharges, and that was where the most CPU cycles were dedicated at the moment. Eric also checked to make sure that they weren't completely ignoring the rest of the system. Surprises could come out of the black easily enough.

"I'm seeing multiple laser blooms across . . . thirty seconds, at least?" Eric said to Heath, nodding to the combat map that was slowly taking form. "Has to be a couple dozen ships involved."

"More than that, sir," Heath said without taking her eyes off the floating display. "We're looking at, at least, a full battle squadron going up against . . . I'm not sure, but I'd say a strong squadron."

"Which side is on the shit end, do you suppose?" he asked quietly.

"Do you really need to ask?"

Eric grimaced, but no, he really didn't need to ask.

"Well, they'll know we're here long before we can get close," he decided. "So once the Rogues get nice and deep, I want to announce our presence . . . in style."

"Full system ping?"

Eric gestured with his right hand. "And fly our colors."

Heath tilted her head slightly before nodding in his direction. "That's bold, Skipper," she said. "No fade and strike guerilla games?"

He snorted. "In a Heroic? No, we'll take the lead and leave that to the Rogues. I've said it before, Commander, and I'll probably say it again many times. We are *not* carrier task force. The *Odysseus* and other Heroics are battleships. We're going to fight them like battleships. Run our guns down the enemy's teeth and see how they like the taste of fire."

She nodded slowly. "They're going to have us on numbers, sir."

"They're going to need them."

▶▶▶

▶ As the three Heroic Class slips formed a delta wedge and began warping space downwell, their six accompanying Rogue Class ships fanned out and went dark as their armor shifted to black hole energy absorption settings.

On board the *William H. Bonney*, Captain Sheila McGavin settled into her station and stared at the plot that was forming from her ship's computers instead of from the Heroics' feed. The fighting in system was big and loud enough in terms of energy discharges, and there was no doubt about what was going on. But she was still aching for more intelligence than they were likely to get.

In the last encounter with these bastards, Sheila was well aware that the *Hood* had been *cut in half* by enemy fire. Much of the crew had been evacuated, thankfully, but she'd rather not see her *Bonny* turned to scrap on her first command.

"Helm, I have a vector coming your way," Sheila said. "We're going to come in from under the elliptic. Confirm receipt."

"Receipt confirmed," the helm officer said instantly. "Engage immediately?"

"Might as well. We're already dark. Time to get lost."

"Yes ma'am. New vectors input. Thrusters engaged."

The *Bonny* shuddered a little as they dipped their prow below the plane of the solar wind, going nose-down to the elliptic and accelerating.

"I hope this works," Sheila whispered, low enough that no one would hear her.

She turned her focus to the Heroic vessels she was leaving behind and swore, surprised as they abruptly shifted from their standard colors to the full regalia of the ship's individual colors, the *Odysseus'* blue and silver in the lead.

"Holy hell! The commodore isn't pussyfooting around this time, is he?"

Sheila shook her head, not looking over to her first officer. "It seems not, Grant."

Grant Mitchel whistled as the three ships finished running up their colors and went to full military power, diving downwell. With their lights beaming out as bold as brass, there was no way even a passive scanner could miss their approach, which he supposed was entirely the point.

"What part of *escorts* does Weston not understand?" Mitchel grumbled. "We're supposed to be providing cover for the Heroics, damn it."

"He did this the last time too, from what I understand," Sheila said, sighing. "The commodore doesn't consider the Heroics to need escorts in the traditional sense. He'll run his ships to their strengths, as he sees it. That makes the Heroics the swords and shields of the formation, so that's exactly how he'll use them."

"What does that make us?"

Sheila smiled humorlessly. "The daggers that get stuck in the enemy's backs, Grant. Best send the word down to containment. We're going to want a full load out in the tubes."

Grant winced but nodded. "Aye aye, ma'am."

She didn't blame him as he followed her orders. Those things were nightmares incarnate.

▶▶▶

▶ Eric glanced at the plot. They'd been dropping in system for the better part of twenty minutes now, accelerating all the while. The plot they were scanning showed the fighting had peaked about an hour and a half after arrival, then faded substantially but had not stopped.

He wasn't quite sure what to make of the data, but there were few good reasons for that to have happened. He just hoped that it didn't mean a lot of good people were already dead.

Futile hope.

"Light-speed scans should be picking up the fighting shortly, sir," Commander Heath said, approaching from her station. "You wanted to be advised, sir."

Eric glanced up from the display. "Thank you." He rose to his feet. "Commander, stand by for FTL Pulse."

"Aye Skipper," Heath said, straightening and pivoting. "Scanner! Prep for FTL!"

"Aye aye, ma'am," the scanner tech responded. "Standing by."

Eric stepped into the center of the command deck. "Then light this whole *system* up."

"Pulse out!"

▶▶▶

▶ Tachyons were the bastard children of a universe that despised their very existence. The massless particles were more than merely rare by any definition of the natural universe, and technically it could be argued they didn't exist even when created via technological means. They did *not* exist when measured by time, their existence effectively ending in the same instant it began, but during that Schrodinger's instant, they could be measured to exist in space.

Unlike many Doppler-based scanners, tachyon detection gear didn't measure distance by bounce time, but rather using a parallax method. When individual tachyons bounced off an object, they would briefly light it up to gear capable of detecting the energy pulse. Two, usually more, scanners would register the signal and then compare their findings to determine range to target.

To anyone with detection gear, a tachyon pulse might as well be a stick of dynamite set off across the street. You couldn't miss if you *tried*.

▶▶▶

▶ Misrem was hunched over the tactical station as another rake of laser slashed across the port flanks of her squadron. Damage reports went from a trickle to a flood.

"Move destroyer cohort two to cover our port flank," she ordered, ignoring the distant shudder of air explosively escaping the hull of her ship. "Focus our fire on the lead element of the enemy formation as they pass. I want to cripple as many of them as we can so we can sweep this mess up without tracking these pests across forty light-years to do it."

"Yes Navarch. Destroyer cohort two is moving to seal the breach in our port formation," her tactical commander responded. "We're prioritizing the—"

A warning squeal across the deck snapped Misrem upright as she spun toward the long-range scanners.

"Report!" she barked, already striding in that direction.

"Translight scanning pulse, Navarch. Hold on." The scanner tech frowned and leaned into her work. "We are compiling visual signals now."

"Already?" Misrem asked. "That is impressive timing. How far out are they?"

"Fourteen light centals," the tech responded. "They timed their pulse right to the moment we'd pick them up anyway."

"Professional," Misrem replied. "Show me."

"On display."

She looked up to the large screen, and her face twisted slightly as she recognized the gleaming armor and colors of the lead vessel closing on her ship's location.

"It is them," she said with a hint of wonder to her voice.

It was the anomalies, unless she was very mistaken. Oh, a mistake was possible, given that the Oather vessels appeared to use the same ship design, armor, and various other specifications as the anomalies did, but she could read the confidence in the enemy formation without any trouble at all.

They were spoiling for a fight, unlike the desperation the Oather vessels had shown as they made their moves.

These anomalies were almost . . . *Imperial* in how they thought.

"Recall our destroyer squadrons," she called as she turned from the plot. "I want to reestablish our formation well ahead of their arrival. Disengage the fleeing Oather vessels. Let them go."

"Navarch?" Her second looked at her, clearly surprised. "They are only three of them."

Misrem laughed. "If there are only three of them, I will eat my own sidearm. Increase scanning, all sectors."

▶▶▶

▶ "Translight pulse!"

"Localize it!" Druel ordered, pushing sweat-slicked hair back from his eyes as he pored over the tactical positions of his ships and the enemy's deployment.

He was surprised a moment later to see the Imperial destroyers begin to break off, giving his vessels some breathing room.

What is going—

"It is the *Odysseus*, Captain!"

Druel snorted. *That would explain it.*

He turned from the tactical display. "Her location and vector?"

"Intercept vector, twenty marks out, closing *extremely* fast," the scanner technician answered. "They are pushing their space-warp to the limits, Captain."

"Is it their full squadron?" he asked as he walked across the deck.

"No, sir, only three ships. The *Odysseus*, the *Boudicca*, and the *Bellerophon*."

Odd names, Druel thought, but he put that aside for the moment. "That is their entire squadron, Stel."

"Sir?" Stel Avira, the scanner tech, blinked. "I thought they had a nine-vessel squadron."

"They do. The Terrans run their own class of ships alongside the cruisers," he explained. "They will have gone dark, but they're out there . . . somewhere."

"I am not seeing anything on gravity detection," Stel said doubtfully.

"And you will not. Those ships do not have cores. They run on reactors similar to the *Odyssey*. With the reactive armor the Terrans developed, we will not see them until they fire," Druel said. "Do not concern yourself; we are not the ones they will be targeting."

He turned toward the helm. "Prepare for maneuvering! I want the entire squadron ready to come about in a hundred seconds or less!"

"Captain, we are bleeding atmosphere from every deck," his second said quietly, coming up to him. "So are many, if not most, of our squadron. We need time to run repairs."

"We will run them as we fight," Druel ordered, his face set. "It is one thing for the Terrans to fight our battles with us; it is very much another for them to fight our battles *for us*. Get the squadron back in formation and bring us about."

"Yes Captain."

▶▶▶

▶ The *Tetanna* was adrift, atmosphere bleeding from every deck faster than even her generators could keep up with, when the pulse hit their sensors.

It was ignored at first. Drey had more important things to concern himself with, and if they had more enemy ships targeting them . . . well, there wasn't a lot they could do.

"Get those decks evacuated and sealed," he ordered his damage repair teams. "They're nonessential at this point, and we don't have the atmosphere capacity to waste on them. We can worry about those areas if we live."

"Captain!" his second called from across the command deck. "You should see this."

"If it is more bad news, I don't have time for it," Drey growled.

"I believe it may be good news, Captain."

"Then I *really* don't have time for it. Good news can take care of itself."

"It's the *Odysseus*, Captain. The Terrans are in the system."

▶▶▶

▶ Eric pored over the return signals that were showing him just what they were charging into.

"Well, this is certainly a thing, isn't it?" he asked softly as Commander Heath approached him.

"It is at that, Captain."

They were looking at two mauled squadrons, with the Priminae having clearly gotten the worst of it, but they'd also managed to score some hits of their own. The larger force matched Imperial configurations, though the destroyers were new.

We're going to have to figure out how to fight those things now. Eric sighed.

As if he didn't have enough problems to deal with.

"Enemy destroyers are breaking off their engagement, Capitaine," Milla called from her station, where she was monitoring the tactical situation. "It seems they're drawing back to the main formation."

"I see it, thank you," Eric said. "Well, they seem to be taking *us* seriously, if nothing else."

"I would rather be underestimated, sir," Heath told him dryly.

"Increase in scanning energy from the enemy vectors, Capitaine," Milla went on, as if neither of them had spoken. "I believe they are looking for the Rogues."

"I would also rather the enemy be stupid," Heath added.

"May as well ask for Murphy to not be involved in the battle, Commander," Eric said. "I mean, as long as you're wishing."

"I'm an optimist, Captain," she told him simply, "not a recruit."

Eric chuckled. "Duly noted. Well, we'll leave the Rogues to their business for now, but there's no reason we can't give them a bit of a hand just the same."

"What do you have in mind, sir?" Heath asked, more than a bit wary about the look on her captain's face.

▶▶▶

▶ On the *Bellerophon*, Captain Jason Roberts shook his head slightly, more in exasperation than any real objection, as he read off the orders he'd just received.

Eric Weston was nothing if not an unconventional thinker, but there were times that he would very much prefer to be serving under a far more *conventional* thinker despite the commodore's laundry list of befuddled enemies that lay adrift in his wake. It would certainly be less stressful.

Sadly, that was not meant to be.

The former Army Ranger rose from his bolstered seat and walked out to the middle of the command deck.

"Stand by for combat maneuvering," he ordered. "The commodore has an assignment for us."

The low chuckling coming from the pilot's pit did nothing to calm his apprehensions.

"Lieutenant Commander, if you have anything to share with the rest of the class, now might be the time," Roberts said, earning some surprised snickers of his own as the pilot twitched a little.

"Sorry, Captain," Ray "Burner" Little said from where he was already plugged into the *Belle*'s computers. "Just a nervous habit when I hear that Raze has a job for me."

Roberts sighed. "You and me both, Commander. You and me both. Let's see to it, however, without any more interruptions."

"Aye aye, sir."

"Clear some maneuvering distance from the *Odysseus* and the *Boudicca*," Roberts ordered. "We're going to be taking fire shortly, so let's leave ourselves room to evade as we can. Gunnery station, are you ready?"

"Aye Skipper," Lieutenant Marcia Sanderson responded instantly. "Capacitors primed, cannons locked and loaded, and HVM banks are green across the board."

Roberts nodded slowly.

He rather wished that they had a few pulse torpedo launchers as well, or maybe a few dozen in this case, as much as those things terrified even him. However, they would make do with what they had. It wasn't like a Heroic packed light.

"Lock computers with the *Odysseus* and *Boudicca*," Roberts said, not that he thought it would really matter at this point.

"Computers locked, sir."

"Fire on the commodore's command."

▶ ▶ ▶

▶ "Fire."

Eric's voice was oddly quiet, considering that he had just ordered enough firepower into space to put a serious hurt on a planet.

"HVM banks firing, Capitaine," Milla said from where she was standing watch at the tactical station.

The slight shudders of the launch couldn't quite be felt through the deck of the big ship, but they all imagined they could feel them. Shivers ran up the spines of everyone on deck as the weapons were fired into space via gravitic acceleration rather than the magnetic rail guns the *Odyssey* had once used. As the ten-ton weapons cleared the space-time warp of the ships, solid rocket motors ignited along with powerful CM fields, and the already-fast projectiles accelerated to upper C fractional speed in an instant.

"Time on target firing in T minus ten seconds," Milla said calmly, as though she hadn't just sent the equivalent of several extinction-level kinetic weapons into space. She counted down the last few seconds aloud, then closed her eyes as the computers took over and coordinated the firing of the big lasers with the other two Heroics. "Time on target fire mission, out."

The three big Heroic Class cruisers practically hummed with power as they unleashed their lasers, first in a series of pulsed bursts that lanced out and across the black toward the enemy as they regrouped well beyond the normal minimum effective range considered for such weapons.

"Stand by for maneuvering," Eric ordered. "Heroics begin deceleration on my mark. Make our course and relative speed to the enemy, zero zero zero at ten kilometers. Put us right in their teeth."

"Roger, zero zero zero course and relative velocity to the enemy formation," Steph said from where he was now plugged into the *Odyssey's* computer. "You want a slugging match, Raze, you're gonna get one."

CHAPTER 9

Priminae Colony Space

▶ "Gravity shift, Navarch!" the scanner tech said. "Enemy vessels are maneuvering."

Misrem scowled, tempted to pulse the enemy formation, but she knew that it wouldn't net her much more information or arrive faster than the forthcoming analysis of the gravity shift.

While gravity waves propagated at the speed of light within the normal universe, gravity was a function of a dimensional fracture caused by mass. Scanners sufficiently tuned to that dimensional shift could detect gravity changes well ahead of their normal propagation according to the laws of the normal universe. The process wasn't as precise as visual analysis, to say nothing of more advanced real universe scanners, but it was more than she would need to determine what the enemy commander was up to.

"They are . . . decelerating, Navarch."

Misrem blinked.

That she had not been expecting.

"On what vector?" she asked, her attention now focused on the new arrivals.

It only took a moment before she got her answer.

"They are on an intercept and matching course with us, Navarch."

She could feel the blood run from her face as she considered that, but refused to react until she'd taken a couple of deep breaths.

"Confirm that," she uttered through clenched teeth.

"Confirmed, Navarch. I've run the numbers three times. Confirmed."

She refused to blurt out her thoughts, but the urge to call that an impossibility was very hard to resist. No ship's commander, no squadron commander, would ever put such a small task group into a *slugging match* with a battle squadron. It was insanity. More than that, it was *stupid* insanity.

These anomalies are most certainly insane, the navarch thought, *but nothing I have yet seen would indicate that they are stupid as well.*

"Increase scanning!" she said. "All ships, find their destroyers! They are out there—I know they are. Find them!"

▶▶▶

▶ "They are insane."

Druel snorted at the words his second in command had blurted as the track of the Terran ships became apparent.

"I do not think that you'd find many people who disagree with you on the surface of it," he said. "However, I rather think more is going on here than we're aware of. The Terran Heroics travel with smaller destroyers of their own. Do you see any, Pol?"

The officer looked back at the telemetry data and slowly shook his head. "No. But—"

"But indeed," Druel said thoughtfully. "Even with their six escorts, assuming that they are somewhere waiting to strike, I doubt that the Terran ships could easily survive a face-to-face exchange with a group this size. I would agree, incidentally, that Eric Weston is most insane by any standard I am familiar with. He is not, however, suicidal or stupid."

"But what do we do? We don't know his plans, and it *would* be suicidal for us to rendezvous with the Terrans on *that* course!"

Druel slowly nodded in agreement with his second in command. Whatever strategy the Terrans were putting into action, he was not privy to it nor would he be anytime in the immediate future. Without that information, he could not risk his people so flagrantly for so little apparent gain.

"We will provide cover and support from a more . . . *sane* distance," he said, "and leave the good captain's plan unfettered by our own unknowing interference. We continue as planned."

"Yes Captain."

▶▶▶

▶ "Do we have an identity on the foundering ship?" Eric asked as they waited, the numbers falling with an inexorable advance toward contact.

"It is the *Tetanna*, Capitaine," Milla answered first, drawing his attention. "I decoded her identification while analyzing threat profiles."

"Priminae or Imperial?" he asked, unfamiliar with the name.

"It is of the Colonies," she confirmed. "A new ship, a Heroic by the Terran designation."

That was more or less what he'd been expecting, but Eric winced all the same. He was aware of just how much of a beating a Heroic could take and still remain functional, so seeing the *Tetanna* obviously crippled and bleeding air into the black like it was could almost be described as a physically painful sensation.

"Have SAR crews ready to scramble the second I give the order," Eric said. "We may not have much time to get the people on that hulk, so we can't afford to waste any of it."

"Aye sir," Heath answered. "They're on alert now, but I'll be sure to have them heating up their reactors the second we get in range."

"Good. None of our people, or our allies, go out like that if we can help it," Eric said firmly.

Dying in space was bad enough, but he had nightmares about what happened to the crew of a Priminae cruiser that suffered a core collapse. It was almost funny, he supposed, that he considered them as insane as they considered him for wanting pulse torpedoes installed on the *Odysseus*.

Both were nightmarish ways to go out if anything went wrong, he thought. What you'd already assimilated into your worldview made the horror personal. Being blown up in an antimatter explosion was something he'd come to terms with a long time ago. Sucked into a black hole? Not so much.

"Capitaine," Milla broke into his thoughts, "it is almost time."

Eric looked up at the plot, checking the countdowns that were running, and nodded. "Right you are. Show our broadsides to the enemy and stand by for FTL Pulse!"

"Standing by," the scanner tech answered instantly.

"Coming about," Steph said, twisting the big ship in space while maintaining the warp vector on their previous course.

The *Bellerophon* and *Boudicca* both followed suit, the three ships hurtling sideways through space as their transition cannons were brought fully to bear.

Eric checked the clock, waiting for the right moment.

"Pulse out, one ping only," he ordered finally. "Mark!"

"Pulse out!"

"Targeting solution to the cannons!" Eric snapped.

"Targeting solution updated," Milla responded. "Ready to fire."

"Fire!"

"Fire out," she said as the *Odysseus* opened fire with her t-cannons just a hair ahead of the *Bellerophon* and the *Boudicca* as they did the same.

"Repeat! Repeat!" Eric ordered.

"Pulse out!"

"Fire out."

The three ships again painted the targets with tachyon pulses, then opened fire with the t-cannons.

▶ ▶ ▶

▶ For all their speed, augmented by solid rocket propellant, CM fields, and the initial gravity launch, the kinetic-kill high-velocity missiles (HVMs) were the slowest weapon in the arsenal of a Heroic Class starship.

Crossing the void at just over eighty percent of the speed of light, the ten-ton missiles massed effectively nothing while the CM fields were in operation. With a small sensor package in the nose, HVMs were able to, in theory, track slightly to acquire moving targets but, in practice, they were line-of-sight weapons similar to lasers.

Fired first, the HVMs were almost upon their targets when the lasers of the Heroics overtook them and lanced on ahead. Bending through the warp fields the ships used for propulsion, most of the beams were attenuated or redirected away from their targets.

Some, however, struck true and bored through armor and hull as the HVMs entered terminal guidance and abruptly reversed their CM fields to vastly increase their effective mass just before slamming into their targets.

That was when the transition cannons deposited live nukes on short fuses into the chaos of the situation.

▶ ▶ ▶

▶ The alarms that suddenly tore through her ship, and presumably her entire task force, caused Misrem to bolt upright in recognition.

"Laser strikes across the—"

A boom was felt more than heard, and the deck actually lurched under their feet. Misrem and her people grabbed whatever they could, more shocked than actually thrown around, but still wide-eyed and unsteady.

"That was no laser," she snarled. "What hit us?"

"Kinetic strike," her scanner officer said. "Timed to arrive with the laser—"

"Translight detection!"

Misrem felt like she couldn't get a handle on what was happening. Too much was coming at her all at once. She turned to the scanner officer, a new demand on her lips, just as several screens around the command deck flared white before going dead.

"Now what?!" she thundered, striding across the deck with purpose in every step.

"Nuclear submunitions, Navarch, detonating all through the squadron." The scanner technician stammered out, "They are detonating *inside* our warp fields!"

Misrem blanched white. "How did they get those *things* that close undetected?"

"Unknown. Computers are still analyzing, but they must have been part of the kinetic barrage."

Misrem seethed, considering what that meant. Nuclear devices outside the warp fields were negligible. The radiation and energy release would be entirely attenuated or captured by a ship's warped space. *Inside*, however, they were somewhat more serious. It would take *weeks* to clean out the radiated sections of armor and render the ships safe again.

That was just adding insult to the injury of the kinetic strikes.

The timing, however, was impressive.

These are people who know how to fight, she decided as the scanners rebooted from the flash shutdown caused by the nuclear detonations. "Give me damage reports!"

"We are bleeding air on eight decks, Navarch," her second said, coming up to her. "No laser strikes hit us, but we have at least eight hundred tons of irradiated armor that will now have to be stripped, cleaned, and replaced as soon as we make it back to the Empire. If that takes too long, we will lose fifteen percent of our lower crew to radiation sickness."

Misrem groaned slightly. "And the rest of the squadron?" she asked, almost not wanting to know.

"We lost a destroyer," her second admitted. "It seems that one of the nuclear devices may have detonated inside her hull."

"HOW?"

"Unknown."

"Go on," Misrem waved, suppressing her anger.

"The most damaging at this point were the kinetic strikes," her second continued. "Lasers were attenuated by the warping of space, but the kinetic strikes that hit did so with . . . startling power."

That caught her attention. Misrem looked over. "Show me."

Her second wordlessly handed her the report, tapping a section to highlight it.

Misrem stared for a long moment before looking up. "What did they *fire* at us? Small planetoids?"

"We would have detected that, Navarch. Still analyzing; however, the kinetic vehicles either impacted and were destroyed or are long gone now, so we really are not sure," he answered, shaking his head.

"Who *are* these people?" Misrem asked softly, so as not to attract any attention from the crew around her. "They are *not* Oathers, Jachim."

"No Navarch," her second agreed. "They are not. They use similar technology; however, the more we deal with them, the clearer it is they have either bartered for, or stolen, some of it from the Oathers."

"Bartered," Misrem said. "The Oathers have similar changes in both their technology and their tactics, though they are clearly unused to the potential of it yet. That is not the case with these . . . *anomalies*."

She hissed the last word, thinking of the report given to her by Aymes so long ago. She'd then considered the term to be unnecessarily histrionic in nature. No matter what they were, they were just people. Few were those who truly deserved to be recognized as being truly different.

Even the Oathers and the Empire were not really so different, she was well aware. It was merely a point of philosophy and superstition that had driven the wedge between their ancient ancestors.

At the moment, however, she did not have the time to analyze the differences that were becoming evident.

"How long until they enter our engagement range?"

"At their current vector, Navarch? Very soon."

"Continue reforming our squadron. Have all ships stand ready to fight."

▶▶▶

▶ "Initiate evasive maneuvering in"—Eric paused to check the clock— "four minutes. They're not likely to be too happy with us right now."

Heath managed to maintain her composure, unlike some others around her.

"I can't imagine why not," she said, rather proud at having kept her voice level. "Touchy sort, you suppose?"

Eric smiled thinly, tipping his head in her direction. "I believe I'd bet on it, Commander."

"Then I suppose we had best plan our maneuvers accordingly, yes?"

"I suppose we should, yes."

Combat in deep space was a peculiar sort of thing, Eric mused as they settled in to wait. A petty officer arrived with steaming coffee from the mess. He accepted his with a polite nod and took a sip as he contemplated how very far he'd come and how strange his life was.

As a Marine on the ground, he'd once judged action by minutes of terror, hours of tension, and weeks of monotony. In the air as a Marine aviator, it was seconds of terror, minutes of tension, and weeks of monotony.

Since he'd first taken command of the *Odyssey* and now the *Odysseus*, the ratio of terror to tension and monotony had again changed. Instants of mind-numbing terror happened, but the worst were the *hours* of ever-increasing tension that could just eat away at a man's psyche while he waited for something, anything, to happen.

The weeks of monotony seemed nonnegotiable, no matter what his role.

Must be one of the unwritten rules of the universe, he supposed as he sipped his coffee. The hours of monotony on a job were probably a fixed value, whether you served fast food or your flag and planet. What made jobs really different were the smaller instances of terror and tension.

The ships of the formation shifted casually as the countdown reached the end of four minutes, just in case the enemy had decided to lash out with a retaliation strike. After a few more minutes, however, it was clear that hadn't happened. Eric frowned into his coffee as he considered the implications.

They're not like the Drasin. They're unpredictable, measured, deliberate. That was a bad thing.

A deliberate enemy was rarely stupid or foolish. Sometimes being deliberate would slow you down, make you inflexible in how you respond to situations, but in space combat, you had time to consider your options.

He would have preferred it if they had been rash and unthinking. It would make things easier, if nothing else.

▶▶▶

▶ The bridge of the *Juraj Jánošík* was quiet and dark, her captain intent on the passive telemetry plots they were relying on as the Rogue Class vessel continued its plunge deep into the Priminae star system.

Captain Aleska Stanislaw was a reserved woman by any measure, a trait that had served her well during the end of the Block War when she had been commanding her Blue Navy destroyer in the Arabian Sea. It was one she expected to serve her well now that she had been assigned the first starship to fly the flag of her homeland as well as her world.

She and her fellow Rogues had gone dark on Commodore Weston's orders, spreading a wide formation as they fell inward toward the system primary. Normally this would mean that the available scans of the immediate area around them would be somewhat limited due to the nature of passive scans.

With the power being chucked around by the enemy and the Heroics, however, Aleska found that her *Jánošík* was compiling a detailed set of scans for the system and its current population of skirmishing starships.

The enemy, in particular, was blasting space with enough power to make her cringe. As they got closer, the real danger was the *Jánošík* and her crew absorbing more radiation than was strictly healthy as long as they maintained black hole armor settings.

For the moment, however, the inverse square law protected them both from detection and significant radiation exposure. They had still been forced to close off the outer decks, pulling people into the core of the ship to protect them from cosmic radiation or the occasionally unpredictable solar storm.

"The Heroics have engaged the enemy forces," her scanner officer, Lieutenant Jurgen, said softly.

Everyone was talking quietly, though it was patently pointless to do so. It just felt like something they should do, she supposed. Like a scene on a submarine in the movies.

Aleska smiled at that thought, but when she spoke, she too kept her voice pitched low.

"Thank you, Lieutenant. Do we have information on the results?"

"Some strikes, unknown damages," he admitted. "However it seems to have rather . . . annoyed the enemy, ma'am."

I'll bet it did, she thought, amused. "How so?"

"They've vastly increased the power they're putting into their detection systems," he said. "Most of it is focused along the same vector as the Heroics approach, however."

"Good," she said. "They know we're here, but they think we've deployed ahead of the Heroics, as the Rogues did in the last encounter. We will, unfortunately, be forced to disabuse them of that belief, so let us be certain that we get good value for our money, yes?"

"Yes ma'am."

She reached to one side and tapped an icon on a control screen, calling up an image of the ship's chief almost instantly. He had been waiting for her call.

"Ma'am." The chief nodded politely.

"Are they charged and loaded?" she asked with a glance at another screen.

"Aye," he told her. "And I'll be well pleased to have them on their way, Captain."

"As will I," she assured him. "It will not be long now."

"Can't be too soon," he said gruffly. "Most of us are not as foolish as Doohan."

She couldn't resist rolling her eyes a little at the mention of the Confederate chief engineer of the *Autolycus*. The man had already become something of a legend, especially among the Rogues. Intentionally collapsing antimatter containment on board *his own ship* made the man a hero to a few crazy people, mostly engineers, and the boogeyman to damn near everyone else.

She had heard that Commodore Weston had flat-out refused to allow the man to set foot on the *Odysseus*, though whether it was serious or in jest, Aleska did not know.

"I will let you know the moment we can fire," she assured her own chief. "Thank you."

▶▶▶

▶ Hidden in the near impenetrable depths of the black, the six Rogues were converging quietly on their targets as the much more flamboyant Heroics opened their end of the right with the first thrown blows of what appeared to be little more than a slugging match.

In the silence of space, the screams of rage from the Imperial ships were implied and explicit, though unheard. The power of their scanners testified to that, but without having any idea of an approach vector, there was little chance of their beams hitting one of the approaching Rogues with enough time and focus to cross the detection threshold of the small ships.

The captains of the Rogues agreed about one thing—the enemy panicking was a mixed blessing.

Certainly, it would be *very* bad for any Rogue spotted while still using black hole settings on their armor.

As useful as the extreme stealth setting was, it had drawbacks. The biggest was that it absorbed as much of the energy spectrum as possible, including light, to prevent a bounce-back signal the enemy scanners could detect. This kept the ships hidden, but it also made them vastly more vulnerable to all sorts of radiation, from lasers to cosmic sources, as little of it would be reflected away from the ship and its crew.

Even without the added complexity of flying into battle where lasers and high-intensity scanning radiation were being thrown around at such extremes, just the regular cosmic background radiation and stellar wind would eventually force the Rogues to "resurface." Converting their armor back to a more reflective state was necessary, or they would face long-term radiation sickness among the crew and possibly be forced to put the ship into port for a significant refit to replace contaminated armor sections.

That was the nature of space.

CHAPTER 10

▶ "All ships report in formation, Navarch."

Misrem glanced up, then waved her second in command away with a casual gesture. She was focused on the approaching squadron and was already splitting her attention between what they were doing, what they had done in the last encounter, and where in the *black abyss* those missing destroyers were hiding.

"Keep them moving," she ordered. "The enemy is more than willing to take their shots at extreme range, so I expect more fire density as they close. Standard evasion patterns for the moment."

"Yes Navarch."

She resisted the urge to pace, barely, as she continued to consider the oncoming onslaught. The Oathers were predictable, slow to anger, and not especially good at fighting in general. They weren't cowards by any measure, despite what some in the Empire believed. They simply didn't have the affinity for combat that was common in Imperial circles, and it showed.

Imperial Forces were disciplined. They had to be as serving the empress was a harsh life.

These anomalies, however, were something entirely different.

They were willing to fight with a reckless abandon that was utterly alien to the Oather mentality and clearly had enough discipline. Yet a measure of . . . unpredictability seemed to defy all attempts she made at decoding their actions.

It is almost as if the enemy commander lets his people make their own plans and execute them without oversight.

She pushed that thought away, however, because it was ludicrous to consider. You couldn't coordinate space battles if your individual commanders were all flying around on their own cognizance. No battle network could possibly keep up with the chaos, not over the extreme delays caused by the limitations of FTL communications.

And even if they had managed to compensate for that, she shuddered at the idea of letting some of her captains off their leashes. Incompetence tended to rise to the top in every organization she'd seen, or at least to a level commensurate with its severity. She had far more captains who were decent managers rather than excellent combat commanders, and she doubted it was any different in other established fleet organizations.

No, Misrem expected that they were just dealing with more creative maneuvering and combat formations than the Empire was generally used to encountering. It wouldn't be the first time. Such tactics had been used before with varying degrees of success, but ultimately the Empire always won. Creativity was sometimes useful, it was true, but it didn't trump power, discipline, and numbers—three things the Empire had aplenty.

Now, all she needed to do was *find* those damned destroyers!

▶▶▶

▶ "Maintain fire on lasers," Eric ordered. "All Heroics. Check fire cannons and kinetics."

"Aye sir," Milla responded. "Check fire, kinetic and cannon. Lasers continuing. Maximum continuous rate, sir?"

"That's right, Milla," he confirmed. "Don't burn them out. Just keep the enemy on their toes."

"Aye aye."

Milla was settling into the command structure of a Terran ship, Eric decided idly as he ran the numbers of the closing distance. He'd had some concerns when she was transferred to his command or, rather, when he'd inherited her from the previous commander, the admiral, of the *Odysseus*.

He didn't doubt her competence, but the young woman's some-times startling naïveté made her occasionally seem less intelligent than she was. That, combined with the Priminae's general dislike for con-frontation, wasn't exactly what he looked for in an officer, particularly one in charge of the ship's weapons.

A pacifist in command of enough firepower to fry a planet, with plenty left over to do the moon for an encore. That's oddly more reassuring now that I've put it into words. Eric smiled at the thought, though strictly speaking, he supposed that Milla wasn't quite a pacifist.

The Drasin had burned away a lot of her ideals, he suspected. That made him a little more somber than it should, given that they needed every fighting hand they could lay their hands on at the moment. Honest ideal-ism was something Eric had always admired in almost every form it took. It wasn't something he ascribed to himself, but he recognized its value.

When he heard Milla *swearing* a moment later, Eric pulled his focus from the calculations he was running to see what was wrong. The slight woman was muttering under her breath and practically hammering at the interface as she worked. Something was clearly not going to plan.

"Lieutenant Chans?" Eric asked as mildly as possible.

"Sorry, Capitaine," she said, falling back into her accent more than usual. "The laser systems are over-discharging. I am having difficulty keeping them below critical overheat levels. The control systems are not as responsive as they should be."

"Odd. We haven't had any issues with them before, as far as I know," Eric said, taking a walk over to check. "Is it showing up in any of the other Heroics?"

"No Capitaine. Not yet, at any rate, but the *Odysseus* has seen more combat hours than any, save possibly the *Boudicca* and *Bellerophon*. It is possible that this is a glitch in my software and is only developing now."

"Well, find it and kill it," Eric said. "Then determine if we need to make a fleet-wide patch or if it's unique to us."

"Yes Capitaine. But for now I will have to maintain manual power control," she grumbled, cutting the computer off from the weapons capacitors. "Thankfully, target acquisition is unaffected."

Eric nodded, knowing how much of a loss in efficiency would be involved in calculating and aiming the lasers by hand.

"Very well. As you were," he said, stepping away from the weapons console and back to the center of the bridge, where he could keep an eye on everything as it happened.

Let's hope that's our appearance of Mr. Murphy for this battle, Eric thought, being very careful not to articulate such a sentiment out loud lest he be overheard.

"Steph," he called, "distance and closing rate."

"We're down to a half AU, Skipper," Stephanos answered instantly. "Closing at point three C and decelerating. We're inside their known maximum range now."

"Well, they'll be firing on us soon, then, if they haven't already. Engineering"—he glanced over—"how's our armor diagnostics? No glitches?"

"No sir," the engineering chief responded. "White knight settings holding to the letter of the manual."

Eric didn't respond. He hadn't really expected anything less. The chief would have told him otherwise—that was a given. White knight settings were the best general reflection settings available, but they wouldn't hold up for long to the level of power the enemy would throw at them.

Best we don't give them much to shoot at, then.

"Steph . . ."

"Skipper?" Steph glanced back.

"Make 'em flinch."

"Aye aye." Steph grinned wide, tapping into the squadron network. "Burner, Cardsharp, let's play. Full power to drives, controls to manual. Follow me in."

Eric didn't hear the response over the network, but he could imagine it easily enough. He glanced over to Milla. "Lasers, check fire."

"Aye Captain. Lasers check fire."

Heath looked up. "*Bellerophon* and *Boudicca* report lasers check fire. We are now accelerating into the enemy formation . . . ETA revising . . . ten minutes to point-blank contact . . . eight minute point-blank . . . seven minutes . . . Damn it, Commander, you're redlining *two* point singularities! If I'm to die today, I would prefer that the enemy do the job."

"She can take it," Steph said, without looking up from his task.

"She might be able to, but we're *losing* the *Bellerophon* and the *Boudicca*!" Heath snapped.

"What?" Steph blinked, shifting his focus to check the actual numbers. "Holy *shit*."

Judging from his tone, Eric was glad he couldn't see his friend's face. Something told him that Steph had just blanched.

"What is it, Steph?" he demanded.

"I'm not tapping this much power in my program, sir. I swear I'm not," Steph called back, now working furiously at his console. "Someone give me manual control over power draw!"

"There *is* no manual control over reactor draw, Commander!" Heath left her station, heading for the engineering board. "Chief, what's going on?"

The engineering rating shook his head. "I don't know. We're exceeding the *theoretical* power capacity of our reactor cores. I . . . I don't know where the power is coming from."

"ETA to contact . . . three minutes!" Steph said, calling an update. "We're starting to lose fidelity on our battle network with the *Bo* and *Bell*. We're gonna be on our own in a minute!"

"When the hell did Murphy become a mind reader?" Eric hissed under his breath as he tightly gripped his station to hide his reaction.

"What was that, sir?" Heath looked up in his direction.

Eric took a breath and made himself settle back in his station. "I said there's no going back now. Let's ride with it. Steph, you have the helm. I said make them flinch, Commander. I meant it."

"Aye aye, Raze. You've got it."

Eric got up and walked over to the engineering station. "Commander, you and the chief *find* that problem. Fix it."

They nodded. "Yes sir."

He stared for a moment, then curtly turned and made his way to Milla's station.

"Lieutenant, this is going to be hairy," he said calmly as he leaned in over her shoulder. "I need you to check fire until we're right on top of them, then unload everything we have. That little problem with the laser power levels?"

"Yes sir?"

"Forget it. Burn them out. Clear?"

She swallowed, hard, but nodded.

"Clear sir."

"Then make it happen," he said. "There won't be time for me to issue orders, so fire control is now *yours*, Lieutenant."

"I understand, Capitaine. I will not fail."

"Never crossed my mind," Eric lied blithely as he straightened and walked back to his station. He would now force himself to sit down and do what he could for the coming fight.

Which was, in effect, be useless ballast holding his seat down to the deck.

I want my fighter back.

▶ ▶ ▶

▶ "What the hell are they doing?" Roberts growled as the *Odysseus* began to outpace the *Bellerophon* and *Boudicca* by a significant margin.

"More to the point, sir," his first officer said from his right side, "how the hell are they doing it? We're at full military power, and they're leaving us in the cosmic dust. No way that ship should be that fast, Captain."

"What do we have on the network?" Roberts glanced over.

"Unknown malfunction," the commander answered with a helpless shrug. "That's all they know right now."

"Shit. Who taunted Murphy?" Roberts asked, looking around briefly.

No one seemed willing to cop to that, so he refocused on the task. "Alright, barring new information or orders, we stick with the plan. Make sure the *Bo* is with us and start adjusting our tactics to take advantage of whatever the commodore can do in the meantime."

"Aye Captain."

Roberts scowled at the screens as the *Odysseus* continued to pull away from them, a runaway meteor with the mass of a small planet buried in its hull.

At least they're aimed at the enemy, he ruminated, then winced at the thought.

"Godspeed, Commodore."

▶▶▶

▶ Alarms blared again through the ship, bringing Misrem's attention back to the present from the future conflict she had been trying to map out.

"What now?" she growled, stepping into the center of the command deck.

"Gravity detection has shown that the enemy ships are accelerating again, Navarch."

That was actually a bit of a relief, she thought. *At least they are not suicidally insane.*

"What course?"

"Unchanged."

Of COURSE it's unchanged. Whatever could I be thinking? "Clarify that. They're still on an intercept course?"

"Yes, Navarch, they—one moment," the officer said, staring at his instruments in confusion.

"What is it?"

"The lead element is accelerating away from the squadron, Navarch. Course unchanged, but acceleration is . . ." His eyes widened as he trailed off in surprise.

Misrem, tired of asking what was going on, strode up behind the rating and roughly shoved him aside. "Is it really so hard to—"

She paused, checked the numbers again, and then rechecked them.

"That's impossible," she said. "No ship that size can move like that. It's *impossible.*"

"Navarch, my lady, I'm more worried about where it's moving *to,*" the officer said with a quavering voice, pointing to the vectors that were now showing on an intercept.

No. Misrem had to check her assumptions as she reexamined the vector.

The ship was on a *collision* course with her squadron.

Is this a standard tactic for these lunatics? she wondered, remembering their last encounter, which had left her in a nearly dead ship because she'd assumed no one was insane enough to risk a collision between two vessels carrying singularity cores.

"Break formation," she ordered through gritted teeth. "Get out of the way of those maniacs. Fire as they pass."

"Yes Navarch," the helm officer said, clearly relieved.

She wasn't surprised. He'd been on the bridge the last time too, one of the survivors pulled off when Aymes came for her.

▶▶▶

▶ Druel stared, blinking rapidly as he tried to parse what he was seeing. He couldn't believe it, no matter what the numbers said.

"Are we sure this is not an instrument failure? Ghost echoes showing them in the wrong location?" he asked tentatively, simply because he not only didn't believe what he was seeing, but also didn't *want* to believe it.

It was one thing for the Terrans to have *somehow* modified the drives of their cruisers above the theoretical maximum, assuming one hundred percent efficiency, but for them to be suicidal on *top* of that was . . . incredibly discomforting.

"I have checked the instruments. They are operating correctly, Captain," the scanner chief assured him.

"I was afraid you would say that," Druel said dryly, taking a deep breath. "Very well. Cover their charge."

"Captain?"

Half the command staff looked at him as if *he* were the crazy one.

"From a distance," he clarified. "We are *not* flying into that mess."

They were all visibly relieved, and he sighed.

The Terrans are infecting us all if my crew thought I would be that insane.

▶▶▶

▶ "Launch SAR groups," Eric ordered as the *Odysseus* approached contact in T minus one minute. "Tell them to get as many people clear of the *Tetanna* as possible."

"Aye sir," Heath said, transmitting the order. "SAR groups launching."

Good. At least a few will be off this death ride just in case things go as badly as they might, Eric thought darkly. "Any word on the malfunction?"

"None, sir." Heath continued to check the data feed from engineering. "They aren't even sure it *is* a malfunction at this point."

That made him twist around and give his first officer an odd look. "What do they think it is?"

"Complete unknown phenomenon," Heath told him. "All instrumentation passes diagnostics, and everything they've checked by eye is in perfect condition as well. They're pulling and replacing parts anyway, but it's having no effect."

Great. Eric balled his fists but kept them under the console where they wouldn't be seen. "Tell them to stay on it."

"Aye sir."

He hated this about commanding a ship, especially when something was going wrong. The part where he had to just sit down, let his people do their jobs, and do his very best not to get in their way.

A glance at the telemetry display showed that they were now only seconds to knife range.

As the seconds ticked down, he kept sneaking a look over to where Milla was standing at her station. He wanted to jump in, give her the final orders to fire, but it was in her hands now. She knew her weapons best and, at the speeds they were closing, it was all down to her and Steph's cooperation. They had more access to information than he had; they could make the call. He couldn't, not in the seconds this one would have to be made.

Eric forced himself to sit still and look like a captain.

A sack of potatoes sitting in this chair could literally do my job now, he thought grimly.

"Now, Stephan!" Milla said crisply as her fingers danced over the console in front of her.

"Reversing thrust! Hold on, we're going to be testing the inertial systems!" Steph responded.

Eric felt his stomach flop around in his gut, unsure whether it was from the sudden change in acceleration or from Steph's words. "Testing the inertial systems" was *not* something you wanted to hear when you were on the ship being tested. The phrase "tested to destruction" could ring far too true when one small error could leave the entire crew pasted across the rear bulkheads.

If it happens, at least it'll probably be quick.

CHAPTER 11

▶ Objects that exist within the sidereal universe are defined by their mass in relation to other aspects. The only true exception to that rule was what humans called tachyons, massless particles that technically exist for an instantaneous period that defied measurement.

While ship technologies, such as the CM innovations used in early human starships and the more sophisticated versions of the same integrated into Priminae starships and post-invasion Terran vessels, could affect the way mass interacted with the universe, nothing could be done to render anything—from the smallest photon to the largest construction—truly *massless*.

So when the *Odysseus* barreled into the enemy formation at a significant portion of light-speed, and Stephanos reversed thrust, the change in acceleration didn't amount to much in the limited time before they were right in the midst of the enemy ships.

What it did do, however, was alter the configuration of the *Odysseus'* powerful space-warp generators, specifically putting their positive warp bubble in front of them.

To fly a ship the size of a Heroic efficiently required two specific warps in space-time. The bubble in the direction of travel was a negative bubble, or a hole in space that the ship could fall into. The bubble behind the direction of travel was positive, or a hill that was constantly nudging the ship forward, like a perpetual wave for the vessel to surf.

By throwing the ship's acceleration in the opposing direction of flight, Stephanos started the process of slowing and reversing the ship's direction, but he also created a wall of space-time between the bow of the ship and oncoming fire—a wall powerful enough to bend and attenuate lasers.

A barrage of laser fire met the *Odysseus* as she charged into the midst of the enemy vessels, beams hitting a gravity wave powerful enough to scatter even photons to the black as the warship opened fire in turn.

Knowing the amplitude of their warp field, Milla had prepared her firing equations carefully. The beams that lanced out from the *Odysseus* were not immune to the big ship's warp field, but instead *used* it. They hit the warp field and were turned aside, just as the enemy beams had been, but in doing so were put onto their true vector.

A spider web of beams powerful enough to decimate continents raked enemy vessels and vented their oxygen to the black in a devastating instant of combat. Dozens of the *Odysseus'* own beams were also attenuated and turned away by the enemy warp fields, but far more struck home.

Imperials ships died in fire and ice in seconds.

Then the *Odysseus* was in the middle of the Imperial formation, her flanks open to their guns, and they returned fire.

White knight armor settings reflected away as much as ninety-seven percent of the lazed energy, but these were Imperial lasers. Even Priminae weapons could do significant damage with only three percent power striking true, and the Imperial versions were significantly more powerful.

▶▶▶

▶ "Breaches!" Heath announced from where she was now focused on coordinating damage control. "Decks thirty through fifty, more reports coming in!"

Eric winced. There was nothing for him to say just then, as the ball was in motion, and all the power on Earth could not stop or reverse it. He had a repeater display showing him much of the same intel Heath was receiving, though without the interflow of information that made her job possible. For now, they weren't doing all that bad.

There were a lot of breaches, but they were still shallow, basically just through the armor. That wouldn't last once they started taking a few hits in spots the armor was already damaged and more energy was absorbed than deflected away.

The hum of the *Odysseus'* lasers was now clearly audible, though the distant click of their discharge was still more imagined than real. That meant that they were running well above the rated limit for continuous fire, and Eric just hoped that everything would hold up long enough to see the ship through the fight, one way or the other.

"Stand by!" Steph announced. "We're coming around hard!"

Eric gripped his station tightly despite knowing that, in all truth, it was a useless gesture. If the inertial compensation systems failed at all, they were all paste on the walls. The announcement was more pro forma, he supposed, or more likely, intended for Lieutenant Chans so she could prepare for the new conditions.

The commander spun the ship on a proverbial dime, sweeping her hull behind the shielding positive gravity warp even as he twisted the negative warp about to intersect with an enemy destroyer who hadn't fled *quite* fast enough.

Eric's eyes widened in horror as he watched the enemy ship's armor and hull twist and then buckle under the strain of the *Odysseus'* singularity sink. The smaller ship was being torn apart by the sheer of the artificial gravity well that the *Odysseus* used for propulsion.

"Holy hell!" he blurted in shock. "I didn't think there was enough power in the warp to do that."

"There is not," Milla answered, even as she had her weapons firing at maximum and on automatic now. No human could possibly keep up with the maneuvers that Steph was putting the ship through, let alone fire accurately through the shifting gravity warp. "I have never seen the like, Capitaine."

"We're running juiced for some reason, Raze," Steph said from where he was furiously working the stick controls, his voice bearing the detached tone of someone deep into a NICS interface trance. "Don't know where it's coming from, but figured I'd use it while we could."

"Do it," Eric ordered, ignoring the cold pit that had formed in his gut, climbed up his throat, and threatened to lodge itself there. "Let them have everything we can deliver. HVMs, flush the rest of them. Cannons on the destroyers, fire at will."

"Aye Capitaine," Milla said, keying in the command. "Firing now."

▶ ▶ ▶

▶ HVMs were *far* more vulnerable to gravity warping than lasers, even considering their CM fields. As they launched from the ship via gravitational mass drivers, the heavy weapons were twisted strongly in space as their counter-mass fields powered up, then lanced off in seemingly random directions as the solid fuel cores ignited.

Over the relative short range of the now knife-range engagement, the HVMs didn't have enough time to get up to their full speed, but the increase in hits more than made up for it as the *Odysseus* could hardly miss at the ranges involved.

As the ten-ton HVMs slammed into their targets, the CM field generators reversed polarity just before blowing themselves out and hammered the Imperial ships with an iron rain that punched through advanced armor composites like tissue paper.

In the morass of lasers and missiles exchanging back and forth, the minute tachyon bursts of the t-cannons went entirely unnoticed as the *Odysseus* opened up with all batteries. Unremarked by all except the destroyers they had targeted as the nuclear fire gutted the vessels from within, the higher scanner fidelity allowed the gunners to pick the shots and lob munitions through areas of lesser interference from the singularity cores.

Imperial ships answered by redoubling laser fire, raking the *Odysseus* along its already damaged flanks.

Pikes of light burned deep into the ship as the armor finally failed entirely in large sections of the vessel. Deck after deck vanished, boiling away under the heat of enemy fire.

Then, just seconds after entering the formation, the *Odysseus* erupted out the other side, spewing air and trailing steam and ice as her guts opened to deep space.

▶▶▶

▶ "We're through!"

"Accelerate clear of here," Eric ordered, leaning forward, "and someone get me a full damage report."

"Being compiled now, sir," Heath responded. "It's not good."

"It's going to get worse," Eric said grimly. "We only survived because they figured no one would be stupid or crazy enough to try what we just did."

He glowered at the screens showing damage reports from so many decks of his ship. "That they were right just made it worse. How badly were systems damaged?"

"Fire control is still solid, Capitaine," Milla announced, sounding too calm for Eric's liking.

He looked at her intently for a moment, then surreptitiously checked her biometrics from his station. Everyone on board was tracked, particularly those on the bridge, because any sudden health issues could, and often would, be fatal in deep space.

Her heart was hammering, and he could see her hands tremble from his station, which made him feel better. A person who wasn't completely terrified after what they'd just done was *not* someone he wanted to entrust with weapons control. Similarly, someone who couldn't control their fear would be even worse. Eric knew the power of fear and respected the discipline it took to tame it. He turned his attention to the helm.

"Helm controls, Steph?" he asked.

"We're good, Raze," Steph said in the laconic way he always did when he was in the "zone."

Everyone dealt with fear in different ways. Eric knew that if he checked Steph's biometrics, they'd tell him that the young commander was on the verge of falling asleep. Eric was certain his blood work would tell a different story, though. Most people shook as they were coming off adrenaline, but Steph just seemed to get calmer the more of it pumped through his veins.

"Remember to breathe, Steph," Eric said before moving on. "Comms?"

"We're still up, sir," the communications technician responded.

Wow.

Considering what they'd been hammered by, Eric was honestly stunned that they weren't looking at major system damages.

They'd probably lost massive pieces of most of those systems, but the *Odysseus'* redundancies were taking up the slack and then some. Even so, that they were still combat *functional,* never mind effective, at this point was nothing less than amazing.

"New data coming in, sir," the lieutenant at the scanner station said, sounding more stunned than afraid.

He supposed he could understand that without any problem.

"What is it?"

"The Priminae engaged the enemy as we entered the formation," the young woman said, voice shaking a little.

Probably why we lived through that, Eric supposed. "Understood. What are the *Belle* and the *Bo* doing?"

"Moving to engage from range, sir."

Eric smiled. "Well, they're smarter than us, then."

Steph snorted and a few people tittered nervously, breaking the mood a little as Eric tried to figure out what he was going to do next.

It's always a pain when you survive something you figured was going to kill you, he thought with dark amusement. *You never have a plan to take advantage of your good luck.*

It was both sad and telling, Eric supposed, that he had enough experience with that sort of situation to have begun drawing conclusions from the patterns. Time to do what he always had in the past, only hopefully now with more skill and experience.

Adapt. Improvise. Overcome.

"Steph," he spoke up, "start bringing us about."

"Aye sir," the commander said without hesitation, though Eric could feel incredulous stares from other quarters at the order.

"Now is not the time to look weak," he said for their benefit. "Now is the time to make the enemy think we intended to do what we just did."

"Right," Steph's laconic tones floated back to him. "Better they think we're completely out of our damned minds than that we had a malfunction."

"I'd rather the enemy thought I was insane than mortal," Eric said.

"Mission accomplished on that one hell of a long time ago, Raze."

▶▶▶

 Air and other debris streamed from multiple gaping wounds as the *Odysseus* began to reverse acceleration and come about. Ice crystals left a wake as the big ship passed, glinting in the starlight of the system primary, a beautiful display to mask the horrors within as damage control teams forced their way through compromised bulkheads and sometimes over and through the bodies of the dead to get to the breaches.

"Cut that bulkhead out of the way, or we'll never get a patch team through this mess," Chief Dixon growled, resisting the urge to kick an offending section of wall out of the way.

He probably could have kicked it loose. The weld keeping it on was only barely there, but if he missed his mark even slightly, he could slice his own suit open.

The cutting team brought their portable lasers up and started to make short work of the bulkhead on his orders. The new cutters were a damn sight lighter and more powerful than what they'd had to work with before, but with that power came new dangers, especially as the team got closer to the outer hull and any potentially still active armor.

Scattering one of the old cutters might have ablated a few thou off your suit if you weren't careful, but the power of the new ones could easily cut through suit, flesh, and bone at a fraction of the power. So the chief watched the teams like a hawk, both with his own eyes and the overseer software he had patched into his visor. They were moving quickly but carefully, so he stood back and left them to it.

There weren't as many bodies as one might have thought, he noted with a sense of relief and shame.

In combat, all nonessential crew were pulled back to the inner core of the ship. Out on the rings, the outermost corridors, the only crew who remained were generally fast-response damage control teams, and even they were sheltered and wore heavy suits during general quarters alerts.

That didn't save everybody, unfortunately.

Some just got unlucky, a beam slicing right through the hull where they were stationed. Others were deeper in the ship when a beam burned in and were caught in the explosive decompression, sucked out into the ring decks or into the black itself.

It would be hours, at best, before they got a crew tally and found out if they were missing anyone.

Which we assuredly will be, judging from this mess. Dixon sighed as he surveyed the damage.

He'd never have believed just how deep and *wide* the enemy beams had gone if someone had told him and he hadn't seen it with his own two eyes.

A deep, thudding vibration shook him through the deck, and he glanced over to see that the bulkhead had fallen silently in the near vacuum they were working in.

"Alright, patch crew through the breach! I want atmo back in these decks within the hour, or we'll *never* get this mess cleaned up!"

He followed the crew through as they physically hauled the patch kit over the rubble with them. It had to be carried, as there wasn't enough room to navigate a lift through the mess the enemy beams had torn in the decks. A pain, but the job was the job, he supposed.

They got to the breach, and the cutter team moved to the front again, this time with their lasers tuned low enough to scour the raw armor plating clean and clear out jagged chunks of metal before the patch team took over again. Dixon felt his stomach lurch as he looked out on the endless abyss beyond the hole, but firmly kept his gut in its place. He didn't have time to be sick.

The hull patch was ceramic concrete in an inflatable truss, so they got it into place and put the air to the truss, then just stepped back to watch the whole thing unfold. It went from about three meters square to over four times that and was pushed up against the hole until everything was covered. Uncured, the patch was flexible enough to be molded to the hull. Then they hosed it down with the catalyzing agent and stepped back as the exothermic reaction cured the material, generating tremendous heat in the process, and left a solid piece of ceramic armor. The barrier wasn't thick enough to do much against an enemy weapon, of course, but it was enough to protect the crew from the more common dangers of space.

"Spray in the diffracting foam and seal this hole up," Dixon ordered. "We've got three more breaches on this level before we can put the air back into the system."

It was going to be a long day on the *Odysseus*.

▶▶▶

▶ With damage control teams working on nearly every deck of the wounded ship, Eric was trying to figure out what put them into such a mess in the first place.

His original intent was something more along the lines of a war of maneuvers, using his three cruisers to draw out the enemy forces so that the Rogues could get their licks in. The unexpected supercharging of the *Odysseus*' power plants—*Where the hell had that come from?*—had put an end to that plan in no uncertain terms.

Now he had to figure out what had happened, keep it from happening again (unless they could control it, whatever it was), and try to find a way to get his battle plan back on the rails.

Well, at least the enemy formation is pretty much shot to hell.

Whatever coherence they'd had to begin with was now *gone*, not that he actually blamed the Imperials. A cruiser powered by a pair of planet-massed black holes was *not* something you wanted hammering through your formation, even if they didn't hit anything. The near miss from the *Odysseus*' cores could easily have caused frequency oscillations that, if they hit a sympathetic chord, could have potentially destroyed much of the region.

That actually brought a point of curiosity to Eric's mind. *I wonder why they never weaponized their singularity technology. It's rather terrifying and potentially far more destructive than even antimatter.*

He made a mental note, then shoved it aside. He had more important matters at hand.

"Steph, are we on course?" he asked, frowning at the screens. "It looks . . . odd."

"That's because I'm fighting her, Raze." Steph sounded frustrated. "We're showing strange flux in our warp fields."

"Are we losing stability?" Eric asked.

That would be *bad* news. The gravity generators that molded space-time would be more than capable of disrupting the *Odysseus'* own cores if they lost stability controls. That would end very badly for the crew as well as anyone hoping to travel through this particular part of the star system for the next few decades.

"No sign of that," Steph said. "Honestly, it feels like I'm fighting a current or the jet stream, almost—"

"Someone figure out what the hell is going on with our systems," Eric growled. "We don't have *time* for this right now."

"We have teams on it, Skipper," the engineering chief assured him. "Just no luck yet."

"Tell them to make their own."

"Yes sir."

Eric walked over to the pilot's pit and leaned on the back. "Can you hold it, Steph?"

"No problem," Steph said. "We've flown worse."

Eric nodded, pushing back and pretending he didn't hear Steph's next whispered words as the pilot patted the console in front of him.

"Come on, buddy, hold it together. I know, it's rough, but we can do this. Come on . . ."

CHAPTER 12

▶ Druel stared at the telemetry repeaters in stunned silence.

He wasn't alone. The silence on the command deck was practically oppressive.

"What in the *abyss* was THAT?" he blurted out finally, looking around. "Was that the plan? Tell me someone understood it?"

His communications officer trembled in her seat. "No sir, that wasn't the plan. I'm linked to their battle network now. The *Odysseus* encountered a malfunction."

"What kind of malfunction *boosts* a ship's power output well over the theoretical maximum?" Druel asked.

"They do not know, sir. Everything after that was the crew of the *Odysseus*"—she blinked, cocking her head to one side as she read the data crawl—"playing it by . . . ear? I'm not certain, Captain, but I believe that means they were improvising."

Druel covered his face with both hands and rubbed vigorously for a moment before pushing his hair back and taking a deep breath.

"Just as well we were covering them, then," he said, shaking his head. "Weston has the luck of chaos touched, I swear to the abyss."

"Sir!" the scanner tech blurted out.

"What? What is it now?" Druel dreaded the answer.

"The *Odysseus* . . . they are coming about, sir. They are angling for another attack run."

Words left him for a moment as he stared at the man, then back to the telemetry repeaters where, sure enough, the *Odysseus* was coming about.

"I am almost afraid to ask," Druel said without looking over at the communications officer, "but what does their battle network have to say about this?"

She looked down, startled. "It seems that Captain Weston is intent on making the enemy believe that his previous maneuver was intentional."

Druel groaned.

Of course he does.

"Terrans. If they are all this crazy, the Drasin may have been intended as a mercy."

"Sir?" His second shot him a look as though he couldn't believe what he'd just heard.

"Back them up," Druel ordered. "I want our course changed to match the Terran's vector. Bring us into formation with them. We will take this to the enemy, once and for all."

▶▶▶

▶ The Priminae squadron, also damaged, shifted course and acceleration to rendezvous with the *Odysseus* as the ship continued to accelerate toward the enemy. On the other side of the Imperial formation, the remaining two Heroics continued to close at far less insane rates of acceleration, and, hidden in the dark, their Rogues were preparing to make their own runs.

On the *Juraj Jánošík*, Aleska Stanislaw was not in a much better mental place than her Priminae comrade, though she did have better insight into the commodore's intent.

"Make a note, Commander," she told her first officer "I want every system we have scoured down to the quantum level when this is over. Whatever happened to them may have something to do with Priminae technology, but it might be software as well, and we coded that and then used a variant on the Rogues."

"I'll make a note of it, Skipper," Jurgen nodded, doing just that as they continued to close on the enemy.

The *Odysseus* suddenly going rogue—Aleska winced as she noted the bad pun—had thoroughly overturned their original plans, but the other Heroics were remaining on course and hadn't signalled for any change in stance, so she was going to go terminal on the planned schedule.

"They tore the hell out of that formation, Captain," her pilot said quietly from the helm position. "I thought they were done for."

"They likely would have been if the Priminae had not offered some long-distance support," she said thoughtfully. "Though I expect the biggest factor was that no one on the other side believed that anyone would be so *stupid* as to do what they just did."

People around the deck chuckled softly in agreement.

I would likely require a new pair of trousers had I been in their position, Aleska thought.

The sheer firepower of the Heroic Class was terrifying to behold when let fully loose in what was effectively knife range. Usually when they engaged another force, it was over vast distances, and time and distance mitigated the effect. The recordings they had of the *Odysseus* unloading everything they had right into the face of the enemy would probably become required viewing when they returned home.

An example of what *not* to do, of course, but even that was useful.

"Secure for the assault," she ordered. "They're hurt, but they still outmass and outgun us, so don't let the *Odysseus'* somewhat Pyrrhic success go to your heads. This fight isn't over yet."

▶ ▶ ▶

▶ "Good God, he lived through that," Roberts said, shaking his head.

If pressed, he wouldn't have been able to honestly say if he was feeling relief, awe, or just utter disbelief at his previous captain's sheer stubborn refusal to *die* in situations that would have killed anyone else a dozen times over.

Probably all three, frankly, he supposed.

"Raze is too lucky to die, sir," Lieutenant Commander Little said from the helm.

"Luck inevitably runs out, Commander," Roberts said firmly.

"You try playing the commodore at cards sometime, then come tell me that," Little scoffed. "Wasn't too damn often we flew into combat without owing Raze money. Used to joke that he wouldn't let us die until we settled our bill. It worked for most of us too."

Roberts snorted. "Makes me wonder what god the commodore owes money to, because someone is watching over his dumb ass."

The crew slowly twisted to look at their normally taciturn captain, not quite believing what they'd just heard, but by the time they had done so, he had returned to his normal stoic pose.

"We're approaching terminal turnover," he said. "All systems, final combat check, and sound battle stations."

There was a brief pause before anyone spoke, then instinct, habit, and training kicked in to get them all moving in the same direction again.

"Aye sir. Battle stations. All decks, battle stations."

▶▶▶

▶ The mood on the Imperial flagship was somewhat less jocular, if no less confused.

"How in the *singular abyss* did they survive that?" Misrem thundered, though she knew the answer.

They'd survived because no one, not even herself, believed that they were actually going to do what they did until they'd already done it.

Well, that and the laser support of the Oather squadron, which had caught her open flanks and served to throw more hydrogen into the reactor at the last possible moment.

Her squadron was now mauled, though so were the enemy. Most of them at least, Misrem amended. The two remaining cruisers on attack vectors were still undamaged, and she was certain that enemy destroyers were out there somewhere. She wasn't sure why they hadn't struck her squadron already. She would have used them to weaken her enemies before even *contemplating* a suicide run like that idiot had just accomplished.

She'd been rather tense in the moments following the attack as well, wondering if the fool was softening her up for the destroyers, but nothing had happened.

Misrem almost wished something had.

Try as she might, she had no idea what kind of tactics the anomalous forces were using, and that unknown factor was making her nervous.

"Get the ships back in formation," she ordered. "The remaining cruisers are going to at least come into our engagement zone for a short—"

"Navarch!" the scanner officer yelled.

She snapped around. "What is it?"

"The enemy ship, Navarch. They're coming around for another pass!"

"They're *what*?!"

They were not possibly fit for a fight, Misrem was certain. Even having survived the bizarre assault on her squadron, they were bleeding air at an atrocious rate as they exited the other side, and they *had* to have taken significant casualties and damage.

She strode over to look at the scanner data firsthand.

They are out of their minds, she thought as she saw the telemetry data the station was processing. *What is wrong with these people? You do not do things like this. Combat is no place for abject foolishness.*

"The Oather squadron has shifted course to join them," the nervous scanner tech said, nodding to another section of the screens.

"The insanity has infested even the Oathers," Misrem whispered, not quite believing it.

This was *completely* unlike them.

What did we unleash on the galaxy when we set the Drasin on them? The Oathers should never have reacted like this. They should have surrendered long ago, the few who lived. Every profile we compiled said that. How did we calculate so poorly?

She knew Oather psychology forward and backward, and there was nothing that would explain what she was seeing. The Oathers should be *fleeing*, looking to regroup with a more powerful force, not rallying to the attack.

If this is an example of what we're facing, the Empire may need to direct more than a single fleet to this sector. Much more.

The Oather production capability was something of a mystery, though the Imperial analysts were fairly certain they had the rough numbers locked in. If they were right, Misrem knew that the current Empire forces were potentially in deep trouble based on what she was seeing.

They had more than enough to harry the Oathers to a surrender, based on the available pysch profiles, but those profiles did *not* include a willingness to throw ship after ship into the fight and slug it out until there was nothing but scrap left drifting in space. If they were going to fight to the last ship, Misrem knew that she didn't have enough ships.

She checked the timing on the now-divergent targets her squadron would have to deal with, noting that they were going to be hitting her from both sides at roughly similar times. It was difficult to be precise because many of the vessels in question were still settling into their accelerations.

"I have had enough of this," she said. "These people are complete imbeciles, with far too much power under their control for the comfort of any sane people."

She still had more than enough ships left to take on the forces she was facing, but it would absolutely gut her forces even if she won. Best case, assuming no surprises going forward (an assumption she was no longer willing to make), she'd lose two-thirds of her ships before the last of the enemy vessels were disabled or destroyed.

Unacceptable.

Withdrawal, however, was an even less tolerable option.

How in the abyss did I get into a death fight over a useless Oather system of absolutely no value to the Empire at all? Ridiculous.

"Do we have word from the soldiers dispatched to the enemy ship yet?" she asked, looking over to the communications position.

"They've proceeded through the craft easily and expect to acquire the necessary intelligence in short order."

Misrem nodded. She needed that intelligence to turn the entire fiasco of operations in this sector around. "Good. Bring the squadron around and head for the enemy vessel. Inform them I want them off that ship, *with* the intelligence, by the time we get there."

"Yes Navarch."

An alarm sounded as the squadron started to shift course, catching everyone by surprise.

"What *now*?!" Misrem hissed.

"Enemy destroyer detected, Navarch. Inbound along a negative course relative to our own. They will be in engagement range shortly!"

Misrem groaned inwardly, but there was nothing to do about it.

"Stand by countermeasures, all ships! I want cover for our men on the enemy cruiser, but order them to get off that ship as quickly as they can! Retrieve and secure our expeditionary team, and then we are getting *out* of this insanity."

CHAPTER 13

▶ "Ma'am," the pilot called over his shoulder to the rear of the shuttle as they approached the damaged *Tetanna*, "you should see this."

Colonel Conner unstrapped and made her way to the front, then leaned in between the pilot and copilot. "What is it?"

The pilot pointed ahead of them, where the *Tetanna* was floating in the black, still small but growing quickly now. "See those lights?"

"I see them," she confirmed.

"Didn't detect them until we got close, but those are ships, and they don't scan as Priminae."

"Shit!"

The SAR group had a Marine contingent, which is why she was on board, but they didn't have the numbers to deal with a serious boarding action. She'd grabbed a seat primarily because her Marines weren't going to be doing much otherwise, and this was a chance for her to see them in proper action and evaluate their abilities in a real-world scenario.

Now she was going to get more than she bargained for.

"We're still going to need to get on that ship," she said. "Can you do it, through them?"

"We don't have comms with the crew, but we can deliver teams through the hull breaches," he confirmed. "Some of them are big enough. You'll need to use the portable airlocks to get onto the ship."

"We can do that. Okay, new plan," she said. "You're going to do a combat insertion. Try to find us a place where we can get in without being shot. Once my teams are on board, dust off and orbit the ship. Don't engage the enemy ships if you can avoid it."

"No worries."

A shuttle, even a Marine lander, was not particularly adept at fighting. They could hum a few bars if they had to, but they were too small to have significant armor and too focused on delivering men and gear to have much of a weapons load.

"Just get us on the ship," Conner said. "We'll handle the rest, but if we need dustoff—"

"We'll be waiting, Colonel. Don't you worry about that."

"Good man." She clapped his shoulder once and pushed back, drifting in the null gravity to the rear compartment. "Chief!"

"Colonel?" The chief was instantly up and at attention relative to her, which struck her as slightly funny. Being alert was one thing, but knowing exactly how to twist his body to position relative to hers in zero g so quickly was something else.

"Break out the kit," she ordered. "Someone else beat us to the punch, so odds are looking good that we have hostiles on board."

"Roger, ma'am," the chief said, twisting in space before bellowing, "Marines! Kit up!"

▶▶▶

▶ The Marine shuttles dispatched from the *Odysseus* closed on the *Tetanna*, flying a ballistic trajectory through the last half of their flight path right up until the last possible moment. They fired their thrusters hard as the big ship loomed in front of them, splitting up and hurtling through space toward the damaged cruiser at near insane speeds.

The lead shuttle hit its CM field just enough as they threaded a breach, slowing the last bit and bringing the big bird around within the massive cavity carved by the enemy weapons. The pilot's compartment was now sealed and the Marines were in a vacuum as the rear hatch descended and the squad leapt to the burned-out deck, fanning out to secure it.

Others, including corpsmen, started tossing gear out of the back of the shuttle with little care for neatness, then followed suit themselves.

In all, it took a little under three minutes to unload, disembark, and clear the area so the shuttle could fire its rockets and fly back out the breach for the next to fly in and repeat the process.

On the scorched and scarred deck of the Priminae ship, Conner took charge of her Marines and got them moving before the second shuttle had even started its run. They had work to do.

"Get the portable lock over to that section of the bulkhead." She pointed to a section off to the left that looked relatively unscarred.

With a little luck, it would be clear on the other side, and she could get her Marines moving through the ship more quickly. Until they penetrated deeper into the ship, however, she was well aware that they were likely to run into evacuated sections, making it difficult to navigate at best. Finding a dead end could slow them down fatally if the enemy were close to gaining full control of the vessel.

"Corporal Han." She grabbed one of her comm specialists by the shoulder. "Get me a patch to the ship's communications network. I want to know if anyone is still in charge here or if we are looking at a total loss."

"Yes ma'am." The corporal tossed off a quick salute before grabbing his computer and transceiver gear and heading for a section of the bulkhead with an access panel.

"Chief," Conner called, "we have to assume that we'll need multiple airlocks to gain egress, so get someone to plot out the most likely route to the internal decks. I want a clear path to evacuate the crew, assuming we find them, and ourselves if it comes to that. That means securing the locks as we go, and that's going to cost us Marines we may need forward."

"Yes ma'am. We can rig traps to our IFF signals," the chief offered hesitantly.

She understood that hesitance. The idea of leaving lethal traps at their rear, relying on IFF transponders to let them pass unharmed, was cringe-worthy to say the least. All it would take was enemy signal jamming at an inopportune time, and they'd fall on their own grenades in the most literal and historical way possible.

Unfortunately, she didn't have enough Marines for any other option.

"Do it," Conner ordered. "Directional mines should do the job, Chief."

"Yes ma'am."

While her men got to work, she pulled out a computer and started plotting the best course to engineering and the command deck. Those were the two more critical areas of the ship, and it seemed likely the enemy would be focused on them as well. Both were deep inside the hull, heavily protected by deck after deck of armored ceramic bulkheads, but they were on opposite sides of the primary core, and that was a little bit inconvenient.

Not enough men to split my forces. Command first, or engineering?

She opted for engineering with only a slight hesitation. They needed to know just how much the ship was damaged, and that area would most certainly have access to that information. Command would *probably* have it, but depending on how bad the damage, communication between the two areas might have been cut.

"Colonel!" Corporal Han called over the tac-net. "I'm in. The *Tetanna*'s internal communications seems mostly intact, but their line discipline has gone to hell. There are panicked calls all over every channel, mostly calling for damage control parties, but there's a lot of reports of hostiles too."

"Any near engineering or the command deck?" she asked, linking into his system so she could have a quick look herself.

"Hard to say for sure. It's a mess, like I said," Han answered, "but I'm pretty sure this bunch is from the engineering level. Not sure they're there, though."

"Probably heading that way, if they're not," she decided. "Okay. Keep linked into this, and let me know if anything changes. We're heading for engineering as soon as we've got our teams on deck and the airlock ready."

▶ ▶ ▶

▶ Lasers powerful enough to fluoresce the air they passed through crossed the corridors, creating a lethal net of energy that made everyone on both sides of the fight keep their heads as low as they possibly could while still firing at one another.

Half Centure Leif of her Imperial Majesty's Void Troopers pressed himself against a ceramic bulkhead and shouted orders while firing his own beam pistol back across air slowly filling with smoke. That would attenuate the beams quickly, he knew, but over the ranges they were locked into, it wasn't going to be much of a factor besides significantly raising the internal temperature of the ship.

If they didn't finish this fight soon, that might actually become a problem. He didn't know if the ship's cooling was still online. Beam weapons would quickly heat the ship up to unsustainable levels if cooling was running even slightly below optimum, and he couldn't imagine that anything on the Oather ship was currently running at optimum.

We need to acquire the target and get off this deathtrap before we bake to death.

The initial penetration had gone smoothly. No one was ready for a fight and, once they realized they had one, it had taken the Oathers a stupidly long time to start mounting any sort of resistance. Now that had changed a bit. The resistance was fierce but hardly effective. Few of them seemed to understand their weapons particularly well and fewer had their will in the fight.

That didn't make it *easy* going just the same. Even a halfhearted hand could unleash a laser with the same power as an enthusiastic one, and once those beams started cooking the air, only true fools rushed in.

Fools, or troops on a mission.

"Clear this deck. Bring up the auto-tracking systems," he ordered. "I want to get through to the ship's computer core before the navarch decides to leave us here to cook!"

His men scattered without a word. They knew their tasks and were starting them even before he finished speaking.

Leif was almost disappointed with the nature of the defense they'd encountered, despite the relative ferocity of it. It was a rough defense, easily broken if that were his primary goal, and he would expect shipboard defenders to have weapons more compatible with their particular circumstance.

Popping off combat-level lasers on board your own ship was generally not considered a sane idea. Even assuming you didn't put holes in the hull and let the air out, always a consideration on board a starship, the excess heat would put stress on the ship's radiation systems in remarkably short order.

Leif couldn't decide if the Oathers were suicidal or stupid.

Either way, he supposed it wasn't his problem.

A rapid-fire staccato of explosions startled Leif, causing him to risk his head with a look around the corner just in time to see a large section of the corridor up ahead billowing smoke as it slowly fell away from the hull and slammed into the deck with a resounding thud that he could feel through his feet and armor.

What in the abyss? he wondered, ducking back. "Did we do that?"

"No sir," his lieutenant responded. "All our people are accounted for."

"Well, I doubt the Oathers blew a big hole in their *own* ship," he grumbled. "So what the hell's happened?"

▶ ▶ ▶

▶ "Blow it."

"Yes ma'am," the corporal said as he ducked back around the corner and palmed the detonator for the breaching charges they'd just set. "Charges live! Fire in the hole!"

The damage to the *Tetanna* was such that all the transport tubes were shut down. Practically every deck had taken some level of destruction, cutting off Conner and her Marines from the most direct routes to engineering and the command deck. Trying to go around the damage would have taken time, more than they had, judging from the communications they had been able to tap into.

So Conner had elected to *make* a direct route.

The breaching charges blew out in a rapid fire of explosions that sliced through the ceramic bulkheads of the Priminae ship, cutting a ten-foot wide swath out of the corridor wall as clean as could be managed with explosives. By the time the chunk of ceramic was falling, her Marines were already moving to and then through the breach.

Laser fire fluoresced in the air on the other side, petering out as both Priminae and Imperial soldiers looked in their direction.

"Pop smoke!" Conner ordered the Marines at the front of the charge.

The armored Marines pulled canisters from their belts, thumbing the catch clear of the arming lever, and tossed them into the corridor beyond the breach. The canisters began hissing before they clattered to the deck, glittering white smoke billowing out to fill the corridor as the Marines continued to charge right into the thick of it.

Conner held back, two of her Marines guarding her as she monitored the tactical network.

"First squad, bear right. Enemy at your two o'clock with man-portable lasers. Wax 'em," she ordered, then shifted her attention. "Third squad, corpsmen, cover the Priminae crewmen and get them clear of the smoke. I don't see breathers on any of them."

The laser-attenuating smoke had suspended metal particles that no one should be breathing without respirators. Lung replacement was possible with modern medicine, but not something she'd wish on anyone.

Enemy troops were wearing what looked like full environmental suits, so they'd be spared the health effects of the smoke. Lead poisoning, as the old joke went, was another matter entirely.

Uranium poisoning these days, of course, Conner supposed idly as she continued to monitor the situation.

▶▶▶

▶ Billowing clouds of smoke filling the corridor of a starship was universally a *bad* sign.

Leif didn't know what was going on, but it could *not* be good. What made it even worse was that the smoke appeared to be pouring from thrown objects, so they were apparently *intentionally* filling the breathable air with smoke.

And I believed the use of lasers was a bad idea, he thought grimly as he peered into the approaching wall of glittering smoke billowing slowly toward him.

He could see forms moving around and quickly leveled his laser and fired off a pulse. He was only slightly surprised to see the beam diffract, scattering energy all over the area and diffusing it quickly to nonlethal levels. The temperature in the corridor went up half a degree almost instantly, since the energy had to be turned into something and wasn't being focused anywhere in particular. But the laser certainly lost its immediate lethality at least.

Interesting solution to the problem they're facing, he supposed.

"Close with the enemy," he ordered. "The refractive smoke will impede their lasers as much as—"

Three sharp cracks echoed across the deck. One of his men went down.

"What the abyss was that?" Leif snarled, ducking for cover.

"Projectile weapon, sir!"

That can penetrate our combat armor? That is not in the Oather supply line, according to intelligence!

Leif had heard rumors of another species involved in the region using ships that defied definition by Imperial standards, but no reports existed for people engaging them in combat to this point. Not close infantry combat, at least. If this were the unknown species, his forces might get some of the information they'd been sent after firsthand.

"Bring forward the third cohort," he said. "Did they get the auto-tracking systems up here yet?"

"Yes Centure."

"Good. Set them up here. Hold the enemy forces at this junction while we finish the job," he said. "Make sure they record and transmit everything that happens."

▶▶▶

▶ Corporal Jack Rivers was running on thermal optics as he walked point for first squad through the glittering smoke that served to dissipate laser energy, but even that was spotty at best through the reflecting metal particles that hung suspended in the white smoke.

Everything was shot to hell, in fact. Visibility was effectively nil, thermal was almost as bad and getting worse every time someone fired a laser into the mist, and even the battle network between his closest squadmates was registering speed rates that sounded like something he'd last heard of in history class.

What the hell is a megabit in real-world numbers anyway? he thought, annoyed at the slow updates he was being forced to wait for.

On the other hand, he hadn't been turned to pink mist by a stupidly overpowered antipersonnel laser, so being frustrated was something he could deal with.

His assault rifle was locked to his shoulder as he moved forward, though he didn't bother to use the weapon's optics. They were useless in the current environment and only marginally more effective than his HUD at their best.

He held up his fist. "Hold position. I've got movement."

"Roger," the scratchy response over the network hissed back at him. "Holding."

First squad came to a stop behind him, spreading out to the walls as Rivers took a knee and shifted to his suit's ultrasonic scanners. Only slightly degraded by the smoke, the ultrasonic system was very close range and returned information that sometimes took an expert to make sense of. He wasn't an expert, but Rivers wasn't too worried about specifics either. He just scanned for any Doppler shifts that looked roughly human-sized, trusting that the enemy was in front of him and his allies were behind.

"Target up," he said softly as he stroked the rifle's trigger, sending a burst downrange into the moving target. It dropped in place, like a puppet with strings cut. "Target down."

"Good job, Rivers," the sergeant said. "Do you see any others?"

"Movement on sonics," Rivers answered. "Nothing firm. No line of sight."

"Roger that. Move forward if you think you can."

"Roger, moving forward."

The smoke was thinning, giving him better visibility but also a more vulnerable position. So before he got up, Rivers palmed another grenade.

"Smoke out," he said, flipping the safety catch off the canister and rolling it down the hall.

The canister clattered off the deck, bouncing downrange as the glittering smoke began pouring from it. With his ultrasonic now the primary system showing in his HUD, Rivers got back to his feet and started forward again, the rifle leading the way.

He got about three steps before alarms screamed in his ears. He swore and threw himself to the ground.

"Shit! What the hell was that?" he demanded, rolling for the wall as his armor scanners told him that the ambient temperature had just gone up another degree. "Christ. What just happened?"

"Multiple laser pulses, corporal. Hold position if you can; withdraw if not," the sergeant ordered. "We're trying to determine enemy locations."

"I can chuck a frag over their way, maybe flush him, Sarge," Rivers offered.

There was a brief pause before the sergeant came back.

"Do it."

This time Rivers palmed a round ball from his belt, activating the charge with his suit codes and making sure that the IFF readers were showing green just in case something stupid happened. That feature on the new grenades had saved his life half a dozen times over his short career, usually when one of his own—never himself, of course—screwed up their throw. It also kept the enemy from turning the grenade into a weapon against him in the rare worst-case scenario.

With the explosive detonator primed, Rivers got back to his knees and wound up for the pitch. He flung the grenade on a high and fast arch, aiming to drop it behind his estimation of the enemy position.

Corporal Rivers didn't know why the grenade suddenly detonated only a dozen meters away, at the height of its arch. The concussion washed over him with enough force to have killed an unarmored

Marine. He blinked as his ultrasonic display was rendered to total noise and the armor defaulted back to normal vision.

The shockwave had blown the reflective mist back, and for a second, Rivers could see right downrange to where the enemy had set up some sort of automated turret.

"Oh sh—"

Rivers never finished the sentence as the laser turret opened fire again, and he was boiled away in his armor in the tiny fraction of a second before the suit failed as well. Nothing remained of the corporal but scorch marks on the deck.

▶▶▶

▶ Conner swore under her breath as she received the last few bytes of data from the now-dead corporal, his suit having recorded and transmitted right to the end.

"Pull back! Pull back!" she yelled. "The enemy has moved point defense systems into the corridor."

She could see squad one withdrawing on her HUD overlay, and squad two laying down heavy suppressive fire as they did.

The Imperial ground forces hadn't overly impressed her the last time they'd tangled, but she'd had a decisive advantage that time, and clearly they'd known it. This time, they seemed more than willing to pony up and play for keeps, and if anything, they had at least a small edge on her now. They'd come expecting a fight; she was here on a rescue mission. Her Marines were supposed to be pulling people out of the fire, not laying it down.

"That's one hell of a defense system," the chief noted darkly.

Conner nodded, swapping back to her own HUD view as she stepped forward. "Some sort of auto-tracking turret. The grenade was tracked and killed before it got halfway to the target, right through the smoke. Even with the smoke being thinner up higher, that's more powerful a system than we've seen so far. We could assault that position and take it, but the cost would be high. Not worth it for now. I want this corridor locked down. Bring up proximity mines. They want to deny access, it works both ways. We can secure the primary route to engineering from here."

"Yes ma'am," the chief said, dispatching some of the men to do just that before turning back. "But they have to know that too, Colonel."

She nodded. "Which means they're going for the bridge. Chief, find me a route."

▶▶▶

▶ Drey limped across the command deck, favoring his left side as he leaned heavily on a console and brought up what information he could get.

"Heavy fighting across the inner decks," he said, looking over to the engineering station. "Has the enemy reached engineering yet?"

"No Captain." The engineer shook her head. "I have reports that soldiers from the Terran forces managed to board somehow as well and have begun securing the path to engineering."

Drey wanted to ask how in the abyss the Terrans had gotten on his ship, but he suspected the answer would be "through one of the many holes blown in it by the enemy," and that assumption was good enough for the moment.

"Inform as many of our people as you can and be sure they know to work with the Terrans," he said wearily. "We don't need mistakes allowing enemy forces into the singularity controls."

He had no clue why they would want to access that section. Yes, it was the most vulnerable part of the ship from the interior, but the *Tetanna* was dead in space. The Imperials didn't need to get to the controls unless they wanted to take over the vessel entirely.

That would have made sense if his ship was truly still spaceworthy, but as much as Drey despised admitting it, his *Tetanna* was not.

The command deck was near engineering, of course, which made the position he now held another likely possibility. Certainly, if you wanted access to ship controls *and* the minds of officers in the Colonial Fleet, the command deck was the place to be. He had anticipated that early on and arrayed his primary defenses along that approach, yet the enemy seemed more interested in engineering controls.

Drey glowered at the reports filtering over the display. *What are you looking for?*

▶▶▶

▶ Conner ran down the corridor, two squads of Marines ahead of her, most of the corpsmen assigned to the mission following behind, and a third squad covering the rear.

They were moving quickly, trying to get through the maze of corridors that made up the internal structure of a Priminae cruiser/Heroic Class ship.

The shifting gravity of the local singularities that powered the ship complicated the process, and the extensive battle damage and occasional ambush points the enemy had chosen to exploit made it impossibly frustrating.

They'd lost three more Marines to enemy laser fire, almost lost a few more to friendly laser fire, and she was starting to be concerned about the rising temperature levels.

It was now well over thirty degrees Celsius in the corridors. That wasn't, on its own, too bad of a problem. She'd fought in hotter places on Earth, as had most of her men, but on a starship, that high temperature was *not* a good sign.

The vacuum of space, while quite cold, was not a good conductor of heat. That meant controlling the temperature of a starship was a significant problem at the best of times. And when you had an enemy firing off gigawatt lasers inside your decks, the situation was far from the best of times. It was clear that, whether due to battle damage or overloading, the ship's internal heat dispersion systems were being taxed to failure by the fighting.

If they went out entirely, the heat from the cores would quickly turn the cruiser into an oven that even an armored Marine wouldn't survive in for long.

A burst of laser fire up ahead sent Conner, and everyone around her, diving to the deck as the rapid-fire response from the lead Marines roared through the deck.

"Status report!" she called with her sidearm in her grip, pushing forward as she crawled to the wall.

"Two up, two down," a Marine replied in clipped tones. "One casualty. Indirect contact. Vicker is still alive. Send a corpsman."

"On it!" the closest corpsman said, scrambling to her feet and running forward.

"Pull him back to the evac point," Conner ordered, standing and moving forward as well. "If we need to get out of here, there'll likely be no time to waste later. We'll push on."

"Yes ma'am," the corpsman responded, sliding on her knees by the injured Marine and checked him as best she could through the smoking armor he wore. "I've got vitals, but he's got to cool down. What happened?"

"Laser baked the wall he was standing in front of," a Marine answered without looking back, gesturing across the deck as he watched for enemies ahead. "See for yourself."

Conner and the corpsman looked over and both flinched when they saw a shadow baked into the wall opposite where the strike had impacted.

Jesus, these people have no damn common sense at all! Who uses weapons this powerful on board a ship, of all places?

"Okay, pull him back a bit and see to his armor as best you can," she said. "Then get back to the evac point. Call for a dustoff if you need it. The shuttles have better medical gear."

"Yes ma'am," the corpsman answered as she prepped the armor for movement and signalled a couple of others to help her. "Good luck, ma'am."

With her Marine and the corpsmen out of the area, Conner moved up to where the remaining Marines of first squad were holding up.

"What's it look like?" she asked.

"Honestly, ma'am, I'm not sure," Sergeant Gallows answered her. "We think they're aiming for the bridge, right?"

"Best guess, Sergeant, that's right," she said.

"Then they're being a little half-assed about it, ma'am," the sergeant told her.

"What makes you say that?" Conner asked, frowning under her armor as she called up everything they had on enemy movements.

The sergeant pointed down one corridor at the junction they were occupying. "Best route to the bridge is that way. They went this way." He pointed down the next junction before going on. "Now, it could be they're just turned around a bit. The gravity warping down here makes keeping your orientation difficult."

That much was true, as she was well aware.

The decks of a Heroic Class ship had to warp with the gravity of the cores. That meant that while they seemed straight while you walked them, the floors and bulkheads actually twisted severely in places in order to keep the floor pointed "down." The effect was most pronounced the closer to the cores you got, and both command and engineering were buried deep in the ship for protection.

Getting turned around while navigating the inner decks wasn't merely common—it was expected until one got truly used to the layout.

"The path they chose will get them to the command deck, but it's a fair sight longer, ma'am," the sergeant told her. "Hard to say if they were just unaware or what, though."

She shook her head. "We have to assume they have layout schematics of the general designs. They seem to use similar base designs, so they'd be fully aware of the problem and come in prepared. What else is down that route?"

Her last question was more rhetorical, as Conner was already running her own data search for the route. Practically every vital system was buried as deep in the ship as possible, which meant that everything from environmental control, command, engineering, weapon controls stations . . . They were all dotted around her HUD overlay map of the area.

They could be after anything down here. It's an intel goldmine, if nothing else.

That thought set off a bad feeling that she felt run down her spine.

"Intel," she said softly.

"Pardon, Colonel?"

"Intel, Sergeant. Where's the library core?" she asked, mostly of her own computer.

A yellow dot appeared on her HUD, and Conner instantly shot it off to her Marines.

"Oh shit," the sergeant swore. "You thinking a core dump? What do they have in the computers of this thing?"

"More than we'd like," Conner answered. "I don't know if Earth's location is in there, but it wouldn't shock me either way. Transition drive details won't be there, but the basics will. Weapon schematics, armor specifications . . . Jesus. There's a *lot* in here we'd rather they not have."

"Shit."

CHAPTER 14

▶ "Pulse torpedoes, fire on the mark!" Aleska ordered as the *Juraj Jánošík* bore down on the enemy formation.

"Aye Captain. Mark in twenty seconds . . . Count down to the main display."

Aleska nodded curtly before focusing her attention elsewhere, knowing that they were about to be exposed. Things were going to get a lot more interesting in the coming moments. The countdown to firing had almost completed when a flash of light from one of the displays startled her, and she looked up just in time for someone to scream.

"That was the *Kid*! They got the *Kid*!"

She swore viciously in her head, trying not to let it reach her mouth, but a glance at the data confirmed the announcement. The *William H. Bonney* had been spotted during terminal maneuvers, and there was no way her crew even saw the laser that killed them. With their black hole armor still absorbing all forms of radiation, the laser would have vaporized most of the hull in an instant.

"Reconfigure armor!" she ordered as the countdown ended. The *Jánošík* fired a barrage of antimatter charges into space. "White knight settings! Go to full acceleration, swing us back into formation with the Heroics, link up our defense network!"

More lights showed on the displays, these less shocking as the remaining Rogues opened fire with their own pulse launchers, setting gleaming death loose in the universe.

▶▶▶

▶ The death of the *Kid* shook the crew of the *Bellerophon*, but Roberts refused to show it as he stood his station. Inside, though, his thoughts were a mix of rumbling anger and sorrow, but he had a job to do.

"Rogues have begun firing and shifting back from black hole armor settings!"

"Good," Roberts said. "Flush our HVM banks. All military power to the lasers. Don't baby the tubes. We can refit when we're done."

"Yes sir!"

The *Bellerophon* opened fire, with the *Boudicca* following suit just seconds later. A rain of destruction poured down on the enemy position from multiple quarters as the Terran vessels threw everything they had into the assault.

If there had been atmosphere around them as they fought, the rumble of the weapons would have shaken the world. As it was, all they heard was the distant whine and click of capacitors discharging and the almost imperceptible vibration of the gravity acceleration systems chucking HVMs into the black.

Combat in space was a lonely, quiet experience.

▶▶▶

▶ "Negative matter detected!"

Misrem clenched her fist. "Fire countermeasures!"

"Countermeasures firing!"

Her ship shuddered, something she'd never felt before on the deck of her vessels. Misrem didn't like the sensation.

There was no way around it, however, as the systems had been hurriedly installed and the normal care hadn't been possible either in the short time or because of the nature of the systems themselves.

Actual physical devices launched from the ships of her squadron as she watched, tracking out intercept courses with the incoming negative matter projectiles. Misrem truly hoped this worked. If not, things were about to become rather uncomfortable on her ships in the very near future.

"Countermeasures deploying!"

On the screens, the devices exploded as planned, scattering matter in a cloud just as the negative matter came reeling in. The enemy weapons collided with the clouds of matter the devices deployed, and, in a brilliant flash of light and energy, the two mutually annihilated.

The gambit wasn't perfect. Some enemy weapons slipped through, making Misrem clench her fists as negative matter rained down on her ships, tearing them to shreds. In the brief cataclysmic exchange, she lost another cruiser and two destroyers.

It was far better than it could have been.

And now it was time to return the favor.

"Track and response," she ordered. "Kill those pests. Consign them to the abyss with my regards."

The ships of her squadron responded flawlessly, lasers snapping out, tracking the vessels that had fired on them as they appeared from the shadows like glittering specters arising from the night.

Before their lasers could cross the relatively short range, another set of alarms went off.

"Enemy projectiles inbound, Navarch!"

▶▶▶

▶ Roberts rocked back, shocked by what the scanners were telling him.

He wasn't as surprised by what the enemy had done, actually, as he was that he hadn't thought of doing it first.

They deployed chaff, he noted, jotting down a reminder to look at similar systems for future ships deployed from Earth.

It seemed, according to what he could scan, that they'd really just launched some jerry-rigged explosives packed with plenty of shrapnel. Against a pulse torpedo, that would do the job, if you could get it in front of the weapon. Any sort of matter would self-annihilate with the antimatter in the torpedo, so chaff was effective.

That might render one of our best weapons almost worthless if they can improve their deployment system.

The move was already pretty effective, from what he could tell. They'd blocked well over sixty percent of the incoming weapons, which defanged what remained of the Rogue's arsenal.

"They're firing on the Rogues, Captain," Little said from the pilot's pit. "Permission to provide cover?"

"Granted."

▶▶▶

▶ Aleska held on to her station as the *Jánošík* twisted in space, trying to evade the lasers that had lanced out from the enemy formation.

She knew that even with white knight armor, the Rogues simply didn't have the mass to absorb much of the level of power now being thrown in their direction. They'd taken a glancing blow that had scarred the ship all the way down her port flank, taking out more systems than she wanted to think about just then. Another hit on that section would be the end of the *Jánošík*, and her crew with her.

A flash on the scanners made her wince automatically, as it meant that they'd almost been nailed again; if the enemy was able to adjust, the next time they probably wouldn't get to see the flash. She counted down the seconds, figuring that if they were still alive when she got to thirteen, the enemy hadn't been able to adjust.

At twelve, a shadow eclipsed the local sun, which meant something really big or really *close* had moved in. She checked the main display in time to see the *Bellerophon* put herself between the *Jánošík* and the enemy as a flash of laser light erupted off the big ship's armor.

"The *Bell* took that one for us, Captain!"

"I see it! Helm, sling us around the *Bell*'s negative well," she ordered as she looked over to the weapons station. "Tactical, what do we have left?"

"HVMs are out on the port side, Captain. We're loaded on the starboard, however," the tactical officer told her.

"Helm, you heard him. Favor the port side, show starboard to the enemy," she belted. "Tactical, hammer them when we come around the *Bell*!"

Both stations acknowledged the orders as the *Jánošík* began to move.

"Hold on tight," the pilot called. "I'm going to kill our CM as we drop into the *Bell*'s gravity sink."

He's going to what? Aleska thought, cringing. She didn't say anything aloud, however, because they were already committed. There was a time to second-guess your specialist, but that time was *not* when fractions of seconds counted.

Thrusters flaring, the *Jánošík* turned in space and accelerated into the gravity well that existed ahead of the bigger ship. Using the sink to accelerate hard, the *Jánošík* shuddered as it dived into the gravity trough at full mass until it reached turnover and brought its CM field back to full power.

Shooting out of the gravity well like a Polaris missile from under the sea, the Rogue Class ship slung out from around the *Bellerophon* at high speed and flushed everything they had left in a single barrage of firepower.

At the now almost point-blank ranges, the high-velocity missiles crossed the range in seconds rather than minutes or hours, slamming through the chaff that had stopped the antimatter of the pulse torpedoes and hammering the enemy formation.

Lasers from the *Bellerophon* burned past the *Jánošík* as the smaller ship turned to bring its starboard cannons to bear and opened fire with the last of the nuclear submunitions in its stores.

▶▶▶

▶ "Enemy has engaged with . . . surprising ferocity, Navarch."

Misrem nodded, noting effectively the same thing across her update boards. The ships of the anomalous species, assuming she was right about them, were fighting with a distinctly different set of tactics than the Oathers.

They were more creative, by far, but more importantly, she was seeing a vastly improved level of coordination between them, though that insane death charge seemed to throw other evidence in the face of that conclusion.

They are a strange people, as judged by their fighting prowess at least. She didn't know what to make of them.

The initial contact was more indicative of a barbaric berserker species. Not something one normally saw in a spacefaring culture, to be frank, but not entirely unknown either. The Empire had dealt with at least one species of that nature—well before her day, of course—about a third of the way around the galactic rim from their current position.

They'd been dogged adversaries, but their insistence on personal glory in battle had been *far* more expensive than their culture could maintain over even a slightly elongated campaign. Replacing starships cost time, if nothing else, depending on the nature of a society's economic structure. The investment in time alone was too high to just throw ships away like detritus.

So while she'd been taken aback by the initial berserker assault they'd endured, Misrem would have preferred it to what she was seeing now.

The enemy vessels were fighting in close formation, covering one another and making good use of their individual strengths. That would magnify their effectiveness several times, and the costs to the Empire would be similarly magnified.

They needed better information.

"Tighten our formation. Evacuate anyone we can from the damaged vessels," she ordered, preferring not to leave people behind as a general rule. "All ships are to continue returning fire as we maneuver."

Not every commander in the Empire felt the same, and even she wouldn't hesitate to cut her losses if called for, but trained forces were investments as well.

"Yes Navarch."

"And tell the expedition force that if they are not off that Oather vessel in time to be picked up," she growled, "I will personally order that ship burned to *cinders* with them on board."

The communications technician looked pained, but confirmed the order. "Yes Navarch."

Retrieving crew was all fine and good, but missions had to be accomplished.

▶▶▶

▶ "Dogged bastards," Captain Hyatt growled as her *Boudicca* shifted to cover the Rogue Class destroyers as best she could, laser fire burning between the cruiser and enemy ships.

"Yes ma'am," Commander Jennifer "Cardsharp" Samuels gritted out from where she was locked into the NICS interface in the pilot's pit.

Hyatt could see the commander flinch occasionally and wondered just what she was experiencing. The NICS system wasn't entirely bidirectional. No one was dumb enough to design an interface that let the user feel sensory input as actual pain, limiters be damned, but it did send return data along the nerve endings of the user as part of the control system.

Flashes of light, laser strikes along the hull of the *Boudicca*, and various other stimuli were all part of what allowed the pilot as much real-time information as possible for quick maneuvering decisions.

From what she was told, not being NICS-compatible herself, it could be an incredibly distracting environment to work in. One of the key things pilots and operators were tested on was the ability to focus through an extreme level of information overload while parsing out the vital bits that just couldn't be ignored.

Hyatt shifted her focus back to the fight, noting that the enemy had begun to maneuver to break contact with the squadron.

This was a critical point in the fight, and unfortunately they were going to have to play a lot of it by ear with the *Odysseus* on the other side of the fight and out of real-time contact with the rest of the group.

The smart move was obvious.

Let the enemy break contact and run them out of the system, but ultimately let them go. The *Odysseus* had taken too much damage in their initial mysterious run. With their other losses, the enemy simply had them outmassed and outgunned to a level that made forcing an engagement stupid and suicidal.

Playing the smart move wasn't always the commodore's strong suit, however, so Hyatt wasn't sure how the *Odysseus* would move.

Not that they'd have much choice if Captain Roberts and I made the call before the commodore got close enough to issue orders, she supposed.

The decision would technically be a joint call. She and Roberts were of identical rank, but traditionally he had time in service over her as she had been a blue-water captain until recently, and he had been the XO of the *Odyssey*.

Time in rank meant a lot, but time in service would trump it in this situation, given the significant differences between Blue and Black Navy operations.

Not that she suspected that she and Roberts would be at odds. The captain of the *Bellerophon* was known for solid decisions, taking risks when needed but generally following the book a lot more than his former captain.

▶▶▶

▶ "The enemy is maneuvering to break contact, Captain."

"I see it," Roberts told the officer standing the scanner watch. "Signal the *Bo*. We'll stick with them until they clear the Priminae vessel they disabled earlier. Let's keep them thinking about us and not the people on that ship."

"Aye sir."

Roberts was mildly concerned about the enemy breaking contact so readily, but though they would almost certainly win this fight, he was certain that they knew it would be a Pyrrhic victory at best. He was also sure that they didn't know just how much the loss would hurt the Priminae and Terran forces, which was why they weren't going to press the fight.

If the enemy commander had any idea how limited the Terran "fleet" currently was, they'd press the fight to the bitter end and leave the entire first fleet of Earth's forces smoking in space.

That was why the commodore was so determined to show the flag as constantly as he could, at every possible meeting with the Imperial forces. Make them think they were dealing with a significant force, a group that could throw metal into the masher and come back for more. If they realized how badly they could mangle Terran forces just by eliminating three cruisers and a handful of destroyers, it would change the game in a very bad way for both Earth and the Priminae.

Every trained man, every ton of space-going steel and ceramic, every gun, and every core represented a significant portion of the available forces holding the line here.

No one was sure just how large the Empire was. The interrogations of captured Imperials had been spotty in determining how reliable the intelligence from captured enemy forces was, but the higher-ups believed the Empire was big. Time was the currency Eric Weston had been charged with acquiring, and Jason Roberts was going to ensure his CO accomplished that mission.

"Press the attack harder and target their destroyers. Pick off as many as we can."

"Aye aye, Captain."

▶ ▶ ▶

▶ Beams of destruction nearly on par with the effects of cosmic cataclysmic forces crossed the empty space between the dueling fleets, burning through armor and bulkheads with almost impossible ease. Missiles tore into hulls, ablating in energetic releases that made nuclear weapons look like pop caps as they peeled open ships like overripe fruits.

For all the destruction being flung around, however, the core of both groups was designed with just such a force in mind and could take beating after beating with minimal loss of functionality.

The smaller ships—Rogues and Imperial destroyers—caught in the blasts tended to die in silent fire as they were burned or torn to their component atoms. The larger vessels, however—the cruisers on both sides—waded in and took the beating while dishing plenty of the same from their own weapon systems.

Up close, the fight degenerated into a slugging match between giants wielding great clubs with inelegance only matched by their raw power. Despite the devastating power being exchanged, however, the Imperial squadron reformed mostly intact and began to accelerate away from the closing course the Terran ships had taken.

The *Boudicca* and *Bellerophon* twisted space into pretzels as they too shifted course to follow, their remaining Rogues taking up escort positions as lancing laser fire poured into the Imperials from the other side.

The *Odysseus* and Priminae squadron had finally closed back into engagement range.

▶ ▶ ▶

▶ "Enemy ships are withdrawing from combat, Commodore."

Eric nodded from where he was standing at the captain's station. "I see him, Lieutenant Chans. Thank you."

The scene hadn't changed a lot since they'd blown through the enemy squadron, leaving them somewhat in disarray but incurring a frightful level of damage themselves in the process. The enemy still had more than enough weight of metal to take on both the Terran and Priminae vessels and emerge the victor. The only thing in question would be the final butcher's bill, but it seemed that the enemy estimated that price to be too high to be palatable.

Good, Eric thought grimly.

He was under no illusion that the situation would last. For now, the Imperial forces were trying to determine just what they were up against and what it would cost them to secure it.

Eventually, though, they would finish with their probing missions and advance to taking star systems in earnest. It was inevitable, for that was what an empire did, after all.

All too often, truly successful ones never found an external force to stop their expansion. They just kept taking and taking until the overreach and internal rot finally did them in. That too was ultimately inevitable.

Eric didn't want the Earth to suffer while waiting for that eventual outcome, however, so he was determined to stop this empire dead in space, one way or the other.

"What's the delay on signals to the rest of the squadron?" he asked, glancing over to where the commander was standing her station.

"Just over a minute and closing now, sir," Heath answered. "The *Bell* and the *Bo* have turned to press the engagement, but I think it's mostly a pro forma action. They're not maneuvering as radically as they could."

Eric nodded. "Captain Roberts knows our orders. We're here to make them think twice, not die gloriously and uselessly in the black. Match our profile to his, on a reciprocal approach of course."

"Aye Commodore." She entered the orders and sent them to the helm with a swipe of her fingers. "Their withdrawal course is going to bring them close to the damaged Priminae vessel, *Tetanna.*"

Eric checked the telemetry again and saw that she was right. He hadn't been paying much attention to the ship, as it was effectively out of the conflict for the duration.

"Damn. We have people there."

"Commodore," Milla said, "I believe that they may also have people there."

"What?" Eric looked over, then turned to the scanner station, where the technician was nodding.

"She's right, Skipper," the chief standing watch said. "They've got a couple of their small Parasites tucked in under the *Tetanna*'s hull. We missed them coming through. Probably they were on the other side of the ship and, well, we were distracted."

That was an understatement, Eric supposed, and not one he could really fault.

Still, the situation wasn't great. He hadn't sent *nearly* enough Marines to properly mount a defense of a ship the size of the *Tetanna*. Actually, Eric wasn't certain he *had* enough Marines on board the *Odysseus* for such a mission, though obviously the brass thought differently.

"Okay, best-case scenario, they're looking to pick up their people," he said. "But let's not count on that being their only goal. The Imperials haven't exactly been the most thoughtful sorts in our previous encounters with them in that regard. Run simulations. I want to have options for getting our people out of that mess!"

"Aye Skipper," Heath answered. "We'll get something for you as quickly as we can."

"Copy everything to the *Bell* and the *Bo*," he ordered. "They're closer than we are and have more shuttles and Marines. Most of our people are still trying to run damage control."

"Aye Captain. I'll shoot a heads-up over to them," Heath said. "Get them working on solutions from their end too. It'll probably cut down on delays if they can mount a rescue force entirely from their end."

Eric turned his focus back to the Imperial vessels but was unable to keep from sneaking glances at the stricken *Tetanna* now that he knew the cruiser was back in play.

CHAPTER 15

▶ Conner drew her sidearm as one of the Imperial troopers broke through the line, charging her position, and emptied the magazine before he got within twenty meters. As the armored man tumbled along the deck, she evaluated the situation, dropped the spent magazine, and reloaded.

"Looks like they were heading for the bridge after all," she said with a bit of a scowl.

"Something in your voice makes me think you aren't convinced, Colonel," the sergeant said. He leveled his assault rifle and stepped between the colonel and the line in case anyone else tried a bum's rush. He wished that the colonel wouldn't insist on seeing the situation with her own eyes. That was why they put scanners on enlisted suits, after all.

"Numbers feel light," she admitted, "but they are putting up one hell of a fight."

"You tell me to mount a distraction, Colonel, do you expect me to half-ass it?" the sergeant pointed out dryly.

Conner had to give him that one. Her Marines would do what it took to sell the story she wanted the enemy to buy. Unfortunately, the severe damage the ship had taken was preventing her from confirming most of what she suspected was going on. Internal scanners were spotty, even this deep, as power shorts on other decks had caused massive outages.

"Well," she said finally, "I guess there's only one way to know for sure. Sergeant, get me a squad for a recon mission."

"Rider! Get your ass up here!" the sergeant called instantly.

A corporal ran up. "Yeah Sarge?"

"Colonel has a mission for you, Ramirez, Kensey, and Dow."

The corporal turned to the colonel, saluting quick and dirty. "Colonel, ma'am. Ready and willing."

Conner nodded crisply. "I need eyes on the library core. I have concerns, Corporal. I want them put to rest."

The Marine was silent for a moment, but Conner could see him pulling data over the network as he grabbed whatever he could in relation to the *Tetanna*'s library core. He nodded after a few seconds.

"Yes ma'am, we'll put 'em to bed for you."

"I knew you would, Marine," Conner said as she walked past him, slapping him on the shoulder. "Recon!"

"Oorah!" Rider answered back instantly before running back to his squad.

"Now, we'd best get to the bridge and secure it just in case I'm chasing ghosts, Sergeant," Conner said firmly. "Get everyone ready to move. I want this deck cleared of hostile forces in the next five minutes or, by God, I'll go out there and start shooting the enemy myself. You want that to happen, Sergeant?"

"Ma'am, no ma'am!" The sergeant shook his head.

That was the last thing he wanted to happen. If she got herself killed, he'd have to explain to the commodore just how the hell he managed to lose a full colonel on a damn rescue op. If she survived and actually managed to help, the sergeant would have the very devil of a time keeping the colonel out of trouble in the future.

Best to go see to this personally.

"I'll make it happen, Colonel," he said.

"I suspected you would," Conner replied, trying to hide her amusement over the fervency of the sergeant's promise.

▶▶▶

▶ As Corporal Rider arrived back to where the rest of his squad was holding their position, Private Ramirez looked up questioningly.

"What's up, Rider?" the private asked.

"Mission for the colonel. Get ready to break contact. We're going to do a little recon," Rider answered.

"Sounds fun." The private grinned under his armor, nodding to the next team over. "We've got an op for the colonel. We need to drop back. You guys good?"

"We got this," the man down the line answered, waving them off. "Just give me a second to get my team ready to shore up the hole."

"Take your time," Rider said. "I'm still plotting our route."

That was something easier said than done, Rider quickly realized, even with the access they had to the ship's internal systems. Damage was only the first problem to deal with, with entire decks cut off due to toxic fumes, fires, and hard vacuum. The enemy held key positions between them and the directive's goal, which made the colonel's concerns more real. Possibly worse, multiple potential routes were completely hidden from him because the internal scanners in those sections were damaged or sabotaged.

If he chose one of those routes and was wrong, they'd waste valuable time. On the other hand, the only other viable routes would certainly require a fair amount of fighting, which they were up for. But Rider would rather not risk his team if the mission profile could be done on the down low.

"Okay, I've got a route," he said finally. "We're moving out as soon as we can break contact without getting anyone killed."

"We've got cover, Rider," Private Dow, the squad-designated marksman, told him. "We're good to go."

"Alright, pull back by the numbers. We're heading for the ship's library," Rider said with a grin.

"Are you *shitting* me?" Ramirez asked. "What kind of place is that for Marines in the middle of a firefight?"

"It's the place the colonel has an itch," Rider answered. "If she's wrong, no loss. If not, well, what do you think the enemy might do in a ship's library core?"

Kensey slapped Ramirez across the back of his helmet. "He's got a point, Ram. Let's go make sure no one is talking too loud in the library for the colonel, shall we?"

The recon Marine team broke contact with the enemy as the teams on either side of their position moved in to secure the hole they were leaving. Crawling back until they reached a junction in the ship's corridors, they then scrambled to their feet and broke into a light jog as they began making an end run around the fight.

▶▶▶

▶ The sounds of fighting were starting to get closer to the command deck as Drey made sure that the surrounding crew had been issued hand lasers. He didn't expect the doors to hold for long once the enemy got there, but the command level was reasonably defensible, and he hoped to at least put up a decent accounting of himself before it was all over.

The outcome, unfortunately, was not in question.

Infantry lasers would make short work of any cover they might use within the command deck, so once the enemy decided to cut the defenders out, there was little that Drey or his crew could do. He just hoped that they would be trying to minimize damage, at first at least, which would allow the defenders some chance at extracting a level of justice from their attackers.

"Secure all controls. Lock everything," Drey ordered as he walked around to take cover in front of his station. "Whatever they are seeking, they do *not* find it here."

"Yes Captain!" his second said and ran from station to station to check the work of the other officers.

A hiss in the air caused him to shift his attention to the main entrance of the command deck, where the door was smoking and starting to glow a deep-red color.

"They are cutting through! Get away from the door," Drey ordered, waving people away from where they'd been caught staring at the entrance in horror. "Get to cover! Move!"

The door was ceramic, and it quickly reached a temperature at which any metal in the universe would have begun to slag and drip to the deck below. These doors, however, continued to hold. They didn't melt, they didn't bow, but eventually they did give as the material sublimated directly from solid to gaseous matter when its limits were finally reached.

A blue line cut through the air, striking the far bulkhead of the command deck. Sparks flew from a power relay behind the light plate. Power to half the bridge cut off in an instant, the lights shifting to distributed load sources and dimming to conserve energy.

Drey fired a beam back through the door, the red florescence of his laser like an afterimage on the eyes as it cut through the air and burned out into the hall. He didn't know if he hit anything, but at least he was finally able to *do* something.

Other officers followed his example, the lightning flashes of their lasers igniting the air as they fired. Blue flashes answered their red ones, not particularly well aimed except for the fact that it was almost impossible to miss something of importance when firing into the command deck. Drey felt his stomach twist as he realized that the enemy didn't seem particularly interested in taking any part of his ship intact.

They could have just shot it out from under us from their ships. Why send an invasion group? he wondered bitterly.

He steeled himself for the last defense of his command, thinking briefly about what might have been.

▶ ▶ ▶

▶ Conner felt more than a little useless and nearly as silly as she watched the sergeant lead the clearing of the corridor ahead of them. She'd prefer to be down there herself, frankly, but her NCO was right. Colonels didn't belong in the thick of a firefight. If that happened, you knew that something had gone drastically, horribly bad.

Ah, for the days of being a mere captain, she thought idly as she watched over the fight through the battle network. But she didn't see anywhere she could cut new orders that would substantially improve things. She generally didn't like to interrupt her Marines when they were doing something right or the enemy when he was making a mistake. Two rules by which she attempted to run her command, and to this point in her career, they had both served her well.

She took a knee as laser flashes left the ceiling not far from her position, glowing red and radiating enough heat into the corridor to seriously burn an unarmored human. If they didn't get this situation in hand in short order, much of the ship was going to be temporarily inhospitable to humans due to risk of heatstroke, along with other dangers.

The ship will have to be abandoned if the heat dissipation systems can't be brought back to full operation, she decided. It might take weeks to cool down sufficiently to even begin serious repairs if those systems were entirely disabled, given that they couldn't shut down the cores, which would be continually generating internal heat.

Thankfully, it wasn't going to be *her* problem to work out, Conner decided as the last of the fighting died down under the direction of her NCO's determined maneuvers. She got back to her feet and took note of what the Marines in her command could see before she made her way down to where the sergeant was looking over the mopping-up operation.

"Good work, Sergeant," Conner said as she approached.

"Thank you, Colonel. I'll relay that to the men," the sergeant said crisply, as though his armor wasn't smoking from a near hit.

She noted that the sergeant's armor was reporting that his coolant was redlined and the system in general was reporting potential faults across half its base functions. She let him play it off as nothing important, though, as there was no point in bringing up the issue. The most she could do was order him back to the shuttle evac point, and while she knew that the sergeant wouldn't disobey a direct order, she also doubted he'd ever forgive her or fully trust her again for not trusting *him*.

That said, she wouldn't be letting the damn fool run out front again until his systems had cooled down enough to at least be entirely in the yellow, if not green.

We'll just have to see how he likes directing a fight from the rear, I suppose, she thought with dark amusement.

"Colonel! Sergeant!"

Both turned to see a corporal running in their direction, which struck them as odd because signalling them over the battle network was quicker.

"Calm down, Corporal," Conner ordered firmly. "What is it?"

"Signal over the Primmy ship network," the corporal gasped out. "The bridge is under siege."

"Shit," the sergeant swore, starting toward the other Marines.

Conner put a hand on his shoulder, restraining him with the full force of her armor against his. "Sergeant, calm yourself and remember protocol. Redeploy our forces to center on the ship's bridge, but remain in an advisory role on this one. Your armor is in no shape to take the fight to the enemy."

She could see hesitation and momentary indecision in his body language, even in his armor, but he nodded a couple of seconds later.

"Yes ma'am."

"Then see to it," she ordered. "We have allies waiting for the Confederation Marines. Let's not be late."

▶▶▶

▶ "Deck's sealed, Corporal," Ramirez said, shaking his head. "Hard vacuum on the other side."

"Shit," Rider swore, looking around as he put the overlay of the *Tetanna*'s construction over his HUD, the wireframe of the ship systems appearing in blue, white, red, and yellow as he looked. "Okay, I didn't want to do it this way, but we'll take the power relay access points. That should get us two decks over and bypass the damaged section."

I hope.

The Priminae design for starships was about as straightforward as a lawyer's preferred language, but he was pretty sure he had figured it out. The ship was the same as a Heroic, given that they'd been built in the same shipyard from the same basic plans, so unless the crew had made some significant changes over what he'd studied on the *Odysseus*, he thought he was right.

The team got the access panel popped off the bulkhead and squeezed into the interior section where all the power relays were run. Every cruiser had thousands of miles of relays, and they all had to be serviced to keep them running properly. They went everywhere on board—literally *everywhere*—so if you knew how to navigate the maintenance corridors, which were practically an entire second *ship*, you could move wherever you wanted, unseen in the normal corridors.

The corridors were, however, just a tad tight for a squad of Marines in armor.

"Don't break anything," he growled as he pressed himself as flat as he could and started inching past power relays that were carrying enough energy to turn most of his armor to rapidly expanding molecules.

What that same energy would do to him wasn't something he wanted to think about. There was a reason the access sections were engineers' country, and only fools or Marines would think of using them as a shortcut.

It was painstaking work, but the four Marines made their way across the decks, up and over the evacuated corridor, until they finally got to where Rider was hoping they'd find a relatively undamaged corridor from which they could continue on mission.

"I've got atmo on the other side," Dow confirmed from where he was kneeling.

"Okay, pop it."

▶▶▶

▶ The panel dropping from the ceiling startled the Imperial troops, who rattled on the deck as they spun around looking for the source. It took precious seconds before they realized that the panel had come from above and a pair of already smoking canisters had dropped from the new hole in the ceiling. As the corridor began to fill with glittering thick white smoke, a blur of a form dropped from the hole and landed with an unsubtle thump.

The troopers brought up their infantry lasers in response, the shadow in the smoke rolling to the right just as another form dropped to the deck and rolled left.

The Imperials opened fire first, laser flash blinding everyone as the beams refracted off the cloud and scattered energy in all directions just as the roar of magnetic-accelerated rounds breaking the speed of sound rent the air asunder. Another ripping sound joined with the first as Marine-issue M-45 assault carbines started putting depleted uranium downrange, shredding Imperial armor with the same ease as they would the light armored vehicles they were developed to counter.

The last body hit the ground as the fourth, and last, Marine dropped from the ceiling in a crouch and looked carefully around before straightening up.

The four walked out of the smoke, the glittering vapor sticking to them as they moved and curling around in drifting patterns behind them.

Rider checked the status of his squad's armor, noting that the two "door kickers" were running hot. The smoke had kept the lasers from being lethal, but all that energy still had to go somewhere, and a fair chunk made it into the intended targets all the same.

"Ram, Dow, you two hold back until your armor cools down," he ordered. "I've got point. Kensey, take up the drag position."

The four rearranged their positions without further discussion as Rider walked over to the closest body. He nudged the dead man over with his boot and kicked the laser rifle away from his grip. He then dropped to a crouch to check the gear strapped to the armor, and pulled the Imperial's laser sidearm from its holster and slipped it into his own gear.

"You know they'll never let you keep that, especially when you transfer Earth-side," Ramirez said.

"Word is there're going to be other options pretty soon. I was thinking of applying for a spot on a colony. They're going to want people with military experience just as much as they'll want doctors and engineers."

"Oh yeah? I thought those were just rumors," Ram said as they moved up the corridor, pausing to clear the corners before continuing on. "Seems like they don't have enough ships as is. Who's going to fly people out to the colony worlds?"

Rider nodded. "Government doesn't have enough, but private concerns are also getting in on the act. It's not a problem of a lack of resources; it's more a lack of time and facilities to build military spec hulls. Colony programs don't need those. They can use the old infrastructure—what's left of it after the invasion anyway. Don't forget, once the fleet stops production on Rogues, all those slips are going to be obsolete, Ram. For military purposes, at least."

"Damn," Ramirez said. "Didn't think of that."

"Most people don't. If we can come through this war without getting the planet nuked, or worse—again . . . there are interesting times coming," Rider answered, coming to a stop and holding up his hand. "Hang on. I think we're here."

▶▶▶

▶ Conner could feel her NCO's frustration radiate from him without even *looking* at the man, and she was almost unable to hide her amusement.

"You don't need to be so damn happy about this, Colonel," the sergeant grumbled.

Alright, apparently she was completely *unable* to hide her amusement.

"Just like to see my men get a taste for my frustrations once in a while, Sergeant," she told him as they watched the Marines move into position.

The bridge was under siege, but the enemy was underpowered for the job. That wasn't making her feel any better about the situation, because it meant the enemy had likely shifted their numbers to a more important objective. Since engineering was now secure, Conner had a sinking feeling that she knew precisely what their objective was.

"If you don't like watching other people work for a living, you shouldn't have become an officer, ma'am," the sergeant told her blithely.

He was probably trying to draw a bit of irritation out of her, but if that was his goal, he needed to get up a lot earlier in the morning. She'd heard all the standard jokes about working for a living long before she even joined the Corps. It wasn't even the first time someone had told her as much to her face.

It might be the first time she let that person get away with it, however.

And there was a certain value to letting him get away with it. Conner suspected that the sergeant would prefer having a strip ripped out of his hide to being forced to stand back and watch his men execute an operation without him.

"Keep your mind on the op, Sergeant," she told him with a smug tone. "The men are counting on you, after all."

That effectively ended the conversation, probably more because the forward element of the Marine squads was in position and the operation was about to kick off.

He focused on the men as the last of them slipped into position and reported that they were ready to move.

"Execute," the sergeant ordered after a confirming glance at Conner.

▶▶▶

▶ Sweat beaded on Drey's forehead, the heat from the laser fire having built up enough around him to raise the temperature on the command deck to uncomfortable levels. Nevertheless, he fired a return beam back out the door even as another laser flash left an afterimage on his retina and a flash burn seared the side of his face. He wasn't hit—he'd never have felt that—but something close had just absorbed a lot of energy and was radiating in his direction.

Drey ducked back and shifted away, glancing over to see a console— or what was left of it—smoking from the enemy laser destruction. The remains of his navigation officer were charred and smoking behind the ruins of the machinery.

He grimaced and popped up again to return fire through the door and almost threw himself to the ground as a round of *thunder* rent the air asunder and flashes completely unlike the laser afterimages blinded him. Drey slumped down, wiping at his eyes and blinking furiously as he looked around, trying to get his bearings.

"What was *that*?"

He could hear the call from his second, but couldn't see the other man.

"I do not know," he admitted. "Can you see?"

"Barely. I think I'm bleeding from my ears," the *Tetanna*'s second in command grumbled.

The distant thunder was still shaking the air as Drey's vision returned to him, and he risked another look over his console, now the only cover he had from enemy fire.

No more laser flashes came into the deck, making him hesitant to fire since he had no idea what was going on.

The thunder fell quiet, and he lifted his weapon again, pointing it unsteadily at the doors when a shadow moved against the smoke now slowly drifting in.

"Hello the bridge!" a voice called, louder than he would have expected. "We're Marines from the *Odysseus*! Anyone alive in there?"

Drey blinked in surprise and saw similar looks on the faces around him.

He was almost hesitant to respond, afraid of a trick, but there was nothing else he could do.

"We are alive," he called. *Most of us.*

"I'm coming in, slowly, with my weapon slung. Don't shoot."

Drey swallowed. "Slowly!"

There was a bit of a scraping sound he could barely hear, then a shuffling as a big figure in environmental armor stepped into the open doorway with hands up and in plain sight. Drey recognized the armor from briefings and knew that it was Terran, so he got to his feet.

"Captain?" The armored man looked in his direction.

"That is correct," Drey responded. "I suppose we should thank you for your assistance."

He couldn't help but look around at the devastation and loss of life, even there in the most secure section of the ship, and didn't want to imagine what the rest of the *Tetanna* looked like.

"Yeah, well, I think we can let that remain unsaid," the man in armor said. "The colonel is coming in, sir. She'll brief you on the current situation as best we know it."

Drey nodded slowly, letting his weapon drop until it was pointed at the deck. With his free hand, he wiped the sweat from his burned face, then tried pointlessly to dry it off on his sweat-soaked uniform tunic as another figure appeared and strode in with a purposeful gait.

"Don't bother," the woman told him as he tried again to dry his hand. "Even if I weren't in armor, a little sweat is the last thing I'd worry about, Captain. Are you and yours okay?"

Drey looked around. "Those of us still breathing will likely continue to do so—Colonel, was it? I suppose that is the best one might expect."

"Often is after combat," the woman agreed. "I've called for corpsmen to get your wounded out of here. The heat is . . ."

She shook her head as he nodded in agreement.

"Environmental systems are clearly down on this deck," Drey said. "I don't know how bad the situation is across the ship. Most of our systems were destroyed in the fighting here, so I cannot check."

"Damn. I was hoping you'd be able to tell me about the library core."

Drey looked at her intently. "Why that specifically, Colonel?"

"We secured engineering, and now here, but the bulk of the enemy forces seem to be elsewhere on this level. I was checking the facilities list, and that stood out."

"There is too much information there for them to remove with any portable system," Drey said, holstering his sidearm. "If they have gone for the library core as you believe, then they have specific information in mind. We need to get to a command access station."

He turned and his eyes fell on the smoking ruin of the command deck console.

"Elsewhere," Drey finished with a sigh. "You have engineering secured?"

"We do," the woman said.

"Good; we will go there. It's the closest, and I want to see the status of my ship."

"Marines!" the woman snapped. "Escort the captain to engineering. I'll see to the evacuations here and join you shortly."

"Oorah, ma'am!"

CHAPTER 16

▶ Eric looked at the telemetry plot, his mind running to the possibilities that the tracks left for the immediate future. There were only so many of them, but with almost infinite variation lying between each.

The enemy fleet was on a course to withdraw from the battle, if not the system, but they were closing with the damaged Priminae cruiser. Presumably, they intended to recover the troops they dispatched to the stricken vessel, but given his previous interactions with the Imperials, Eric wasn't prepared to make any assumptions in their favor.

"Press the acceleration, Commander," he ordered Stephanos. "Redline it if you have to, but don't let them get comfortable. I want the Imperials looking over their shoulder every light-second until they're well clear of that ship."

"Aye aye, Raze," Stephanos said, deep in the mental fugue that piloting via NICS required. "Increasing acceleration by two points."

It was probably his imagination, but Eric thought that he could feel more than hear the distant tremor of the *Odysseus'* reactors responding to the demand. A red icon lit on his panel, but Eric ignored the signal. He had expected it earlier, the warning that the reactors were in the redline. He would be looking at a major refit the next time he put the *Odysseus* in for repairs.

Not like there was any doubt about that at this point, he thought.

The *Odysseus* spewed atmosphere from almost every deck despite the efforts of the damage control teams. Depending on how the fight went from this point, the hull might be scrapped and the cores repurposed to another ship. He didn't know what had caused the malfunction that threw them into the fight alone, but Eric cursed the waste it had caused, both in lives and material.

The lights dimming briefly made him look up and around, frowning. Then the lights returned to normal.

"Engineering," he signalled on the comm. "What's going on with the power?"

The chief was on the comm almost before he finished talking. "Don't know, Captain. We're trying to track fluctuations, but they're showing up in odd areas without any apparent cause. As bad as they burned us, we're not showing any problems in the power relays, so I can't figure out why."

"This damn malfunction again," Eric growled.

"Maybe. No way to tell, sir. It's possible, probable even, that we took a hit that caused damage we haven't pinned down yet."

"Just find it. We're still in a fight here, Chief. I need this ship in fighting trim, or we'll all be sucking vacuum before this is over."

"We'll keep her fighting, Skipper. You have my guarantee on that."

"I know you will, Chief. Weston out."

The comm was cut as he looked back to the telemetry and kept a mental tally of the converging numbers. The *Bell* and the *Bo* were leading their Rogues in on a reciprocal course, while the *Odysseus* had been joined by the Priminae task group. Both groups were within the optimal engagement range of the enemy squadron, but the Imperials had arrayed their rear drives to interpose their space-time bulges between them and the Allied guns.

Getting a strike through the space-time warp of a ship drive on full power required accurate knowledge of the warp or a lot of luck. Lasers would be attenuated by many things, including the short wavelength of a ship's gravity generation. Even at close range, anything less than a perfect shot would barely heat the enemy hulls.

Fortunately, the Imperials were dealing with the same problem. While they knew their own warps well enough to put accurate shots through, they would have to be able to calculate the correct deflection through the Allied ship's space-time sinks. Unlike the bulges at the aft of the vessel, a sink was effectively a miniature black hole. Light that entered the event horizon of the sink would, at the very least, be scattered to the universe, assuming it came out at all.

So for the moment, the two forces were in a standoff despite the occasional opening that crews from both groups would take advantage of as they could.

Eric could risk firing with t-cannons or HVMs, perhaps, but the odds against solid hits were still high, and they'd risk potting the Priminae cruiser at the same time. Not a big risk, but it would continue to grow until the Imperials overtook and passed the stricken ship, and Eric didn't think that the vessel could take much more, from the looks of it.

No, for the moment he was going to have to be satisfied with putting on the pressure and keeping the enemy from getting too comfortable.

The dogs are at your heels, he thought. *You may be wolves, but this pack of dogs can bleed you out, even if you get us in the end. So run for the hills. We don't put up with your sort in these parts.*

▶▶▶

▶ "Keep our warp fields interposed, interlock the squadron's fields," Misrem ordered, leaning over the navigation console as her officers worked.

"Yes Navarch," the navigation officer replied. "The enemy squadrons are making the maneuver difficult, however. They are on converging and reciprocal courses, and covering both flanks at once is . . . tricky."

"Just get it done," she ordered firmly. "We need to pick up the boarding crew and determine what they learned before we can make future decisions here."

"Yes Navarch," the man dully repeated.

She straightened up and made her way to the tactical station, ignoring the officer there as she examined the raw data feeding in through their aft scanners.

The enemy strategy was clear enough, and effective, she had to admit. They were intent on making a show of force, establishing that they were not intimidated by her forces despite being clearly outnumbered and outgunned. It might seem to be a laughable stance, but they did have just enough weight of metal to make it clear that even if she were to destroy them entirely, they would wreak more than enough damage to leave her own survival in doubt.

This is not an Oather stratagem, she thought with grudging admiration.

The Oathers would have withdrawn ahead of her forces, gathering their own until they had sufficient power to assure a defeat of her forces. A stand like this was alien to their psychology, and yet here they were. At least *some* of the ships she was dealing with were Oathers—she was certain of that. The enemy had fought according to Oather psychology until the anomalous group arrived with their damnable destroyers.

These people are a threat, Misrem decided firmly. *Not only are they reasonable ship handlers and possess an admirable fighting spirit, but they lead and invite others to follow.*

That leadership was more dangerous than all the ships in the universe, than all the courage, skill, or impressive technology. Leaders could turn the weak into juggernauts of unstoppable power, ready to roll over whatever stood in their path.

Leaders, not merely commanders, could alter the balance of power in the galaxy if left unchecked for too long . . . and Misrem rather *liked* the current balance of power.

Occasional laser blasts slashed across the intervening space between the fighting ships, an almost entirely useless waste of energy as the beams were attenuated by the gravity warping. But enough got through that the damage control board was lit up on her ship and, she suspected, most of the others within her force as well.

"Do we have reports from the boarding crew?" she demanded as she crossed the command deck to the communications station.

"Yes Navarch. They have encountered hard resistance, but not from Oather soldiers, they believe," the communications officer replied. "They are cutting through decks now, attempting to avoid contact while they make for the shuttles."

Misrem grunted, irritated that her warriors were, in effect, running from the enemy.

"Are they outnumbered, then?" she asked.

"Uncertain," the communications officer said. "The centure in charge has elected not to risk finding out in the more difficult fashion while he has vital intelligence."

She couldn't fault the man for that, she supposed. "Can they transmit?"

"Not at the moment, Navarch. The entire ship has been irradiated, both sides have jammers in operation, and the data they grabbed is . . . significant." The officer sighed. "We are barely getting base transit code through as it is. It would take *days* to send the information they grabbed, and they have no way to filter it down to more useful elements while they're under fire."

"Understood."

She didn't like it, but she was well aware of the limitations of transmitting data over significant distances, particularly in a combat zone. The restrictions could change as they closed on the ship, which was happening *fast*, but by that point, the centure and his team would hopefully be able to extract themselves from the stricken vessel and be picked up.

In either case, she hoped they'd retrieved significant intelligence from the enemy library core.

Otherwise, this particular operation would have been rather costly for little gain.

We need better information. I do not like working blind, as we have been, Misrem thought as she watched the distance between her ships and the stricken Oather vessel decrease.

▶▶▶

▶ A glancing beam flash-fried a hundred square meters of the *Bell's* armor, making both Roberts and his pilot cringe almost in unison. That was something of an accomplishment on the captain's part, if any had noted it, given that he wasn't as plugged into the ship as his pilot was.

So far, they'd only taken light damage, however, so Roberts tried to ignore it as he focused on the converging paths of the three distinct squadrons now about to descend on the *Tetanna.*

Don't worry. We're the military, and we're here to help, he thought.

Sure, it wasn't quite as bone-chilling as "We're the government, and we're here to help," but it *had* to be close in his book.

"Commander," Roberts ordered softly, his voice still managing to carry amid the general hubbub of the bridge, "adjust course, starboard . . . three degrees. I want a better angle on the enemy destroyers if we can get it."

"Roger that, Captain," Little responded. "Adjusting course. I might be able to open the firing window a hair if we accelerate by five points as well, sir."

"Make it happen. I want to bleed them, people," Roberts said, looking around. "Every tiny cut adds up. The more they bleed now, the less we bleed later."

"Yes sir."

The crew responded quickly, and he could see them refocus their efforts on the situation with new energy.

He made a notation and sent the basic information along to Hyatt on the *Bo*, as well as to the Rogues. They would already have gotten the maneuvering alert over the squadron battle network, but his notation would ensure that everyone knew *why* they were doing it as well as what they were doing.

The *Odysseus* was now in range for a delayed link to the network, but it would take several seconds for the ship to get the alert and several more before a reply would reach the *Bell*. Organizing fleet movements over ranges of several light-seconds was a pain, and almost impossible without the use of FTL networking, which was the first thing enemy forces took out when they intended to conduct operations within a system.

We're going to have to develop a playbook to deal with that, Roberts supposed.

What exactly that playbook would entail would probably take up the better efforts of most of the current Black Navy's command structure, with input from multiple other organizations, including the Block, no matter how distasteful.

No one wanted a repeat of the Drasin Invasion.

▶▶▶

▶ Chief Dixon was starting to feel like his mind had been blown when the *Odysseus* took the beating she had, leaving him with some sort of permanent mental trauma.

"Please tell me someone else is hearing that," he muttered, twisting around in his firmsuit, trying to locate the source of a sound that he shouldn't have possibly heard.

"I hear it, Chief," one of the engineering mates said, his voice shaky. "I really don't want to be here right now."

The mate wasn't the only one.

Dixon adamantly refused to break and run, but he wanted to be anywhere but on the evacuated deck listening to the sound of a child sobbing.

"When I get my hands on whoever is fucking around, I'm going to rip him a new asshole," the chief snarled, masking his fear with anger.

He'd checked his suit systems, and the sobbing *wasn't* coming over his radio. Given that he and the others were standing in a vacuum, *that* was a major Goddamn problem when considering someone was playing a joke.

He keyed into the tactical channel. "This is Chief Dixon. Get me some Marines out here."

There was a pause before the damage control coordinator on the bridge responded.

"Dispatched, Chief. What's wrong?" Her voice was concerned, not that he blamed her.

"Don't know," he growled. "Either we're all hallucinating down here . . . or there's a little kid crying somewhere on this deck."

"A . . ." The damage control coordinator hesitated. "A kid? Chief, the entire deck you're on is in hard vacuum."

"You think I don't know that?" Dixon snapped. "If there was air, I wouldn't be freaking out so damn much. I've checked my suit. Everything is working, but that sound I'm hearing isn't registering on the pickups."

"Chief, you're in vacuum. If there *was* anything registering on the suit pickups, something would be wrong with the suits." A new voice cut in, one that the chief paled upon recognizing.

"Yes, sir, Skipper." Dixon took a breath, trying not to snap at the commodore. "I can't explain it. It's just . . . we need some backup down here, okay?"

"It's on its way, Chief. Can you locate the source of the sound?" Weston asked seriously.

Dixon sighed, glad that the commodore wasn't talking like he thought they were losing their minds.

"No sir. It seems to be coming from all around," Dixon admitted. "But I'm not the only one hearing it, sir. We're all hearing the crying, and it's really spooking us. I don't mind saying, sir, I wish the lights were working down here right now."

He heard Weston chuckle softly. "I bet. Alright, try to keep calm. The Marines are cycling through the airlock now. They'll be to your position in a minute. Let them find the sound. Just try to get the ship patched as quickly as you can."

"It'd help if you stopped getting us shot, sir," Dixon said, hiding his nerves as best he could as a sweep of lights lit up the corridor a little ways down. "I see the Marines now."

The commodore apparently elected to ignore his sarcasm. "Okay, good. Just hold it together, Chief. You're the one holding *us* together."

"Roger that, sir. Sorry, I'll get on it," Dixon promised.

"Don't worry about it, Chief. I'll leave you to it. Weston out."

The commodore closed the link from his side just as the Marines arrived. They stomped silently up to the repair crew in hardsuit armor as they looked around, their rifles sweeping the halls.

"What's going on, Chief?" the lead Marine asked, his HUD ID showing him to be Lance Corporal Jan.

Dixon frowned, recognizing the name, but it wasn't the time.

"It's that damn—"

The chief was cut off by the sound of a child sobbing again and spun around.

"That. Do you hear that?" he demanded.

The Marines had circled around the repair crew on instinct, guns pointed out. They'd heard the sound, but none of them could find anything.

"What the hell?" Jan swore. "I've got nothing on my suit pickups."

"We're in hard vacuum, Lance Corporal," the chief reminded him. "There's nothing for them to pick up."

"But . . . then . . . what?"

"Now you know the problem, Marine," Dixon said flatly. "Solve it. Good luck. *We* have a ship to repair."

He stomped away, irritated that the vacuum kept his march from sounding more impressive, and hauling his team with him as the Marines stood in the dark, listening to the impossible sound coming from all around them.

"Try not to shoot anybody!" Dixon growled over the comm, knowing that he was just trying to mask how much he was creeped out too. He hated that fact but was unable to stop himself all the same.

If this is a joke, I swear I'm going to actually keelhaul someone.

▶▶▶

▶ Jan looked around nervously, not bothered by the lack of light as his armor HUD had plenty of ways to compensate for that. The strange sounds echoing around the corridors, however, were creepy enough on their own. And the fact that the sounds had no trouble propagating in hard vacuum was wrong on so many damn levels.

"Okay, spread out," he told his squad. "Look for the source of that sound, but *don't* go out of sight of each other. We'll secure each area before we move on, clear?"

The other members of the squad acknowledged and replied with firm "oorahs."

Jan put his own orders into action, carefully clearing the area around him before he moved to check around the bits of debris that had been thrown everywhere when the deck explosively decompressed.

Nothing.

The sounds were intermittent as he and his squad slowly cleared the deck. There didn't seem to be any directionality to the crying, which made a twisted sort of sense, he supposed. Hard to tell what direction it was coming from when there was nothing for it to travel *through*.

The logic didn't relieve him of the creepy feeling that was permeating the area, however.

"Clear," he said finally. "Anyone have anything?"

Negative replies came back immediately from the squad as they also cleared their sections.

"Alright," Jan ordered. "Next section, on me."

The squad formed up as he led the way, moving through the corridor to the next section of the deck, an open lab from the looks of it. He was about to move in when a flash of gold in his peripheral vision caused Jan to pause and turn to his left.

"You see that?" he asked the man at his back.

"See what?"

"I don't know. I caught a flash of something," Jan said. "Hold position while I check it out."

"You got it," the Marine said with a shrug as Jan walked down the corridor to the junction.

It was dark, but the optics in his armor and the augmented HUD rendered that fairly meaningless. Jan could easily see down the length of the corridor in both directions once he reached the junction, and he slowly swept the area without finding any hint of the golden flash he'd spotted.

"Weird. This place is getting to me," Jan said, turning back the way he'd come.

A sobbing sound to his left caused him to turn again and look down the corridor. There was a figure at the end of the hall, wearing something he had to look twice to place. The attire looked like old armor, the sort he'd only seen in museums. It was shiny, what little light there was glinting off the golden surface, but what really spooked him was that the armor didn't cover the figure's whole body like an environmental suit would.

"What the hell?" he whispered, cocking his head to one side. "This has to be a gag, right?"

"Jan?" a Marine private called out. "You okay?"

"Yeah, I . . ." Jan had glanced back for a moment, then froze when he realized that in the time he'd looked away, the figure had vanished. "What the . . . Did anyone else see that?"

"See what?" the private asked from down the hall where the rest of the squad waited at the door to the lab. "You sure you're okay?"

Jan stared down the hall, over the rail of his rifle, as he sought out what he'd seen to no avail. He slowly shook his head. "You know what, I'm not sure any—"

He lowered his rifle as he spoke and started to turn back, only to come face-to-face with the armored figure less than a foot away. Jan felt a chill run down his spine as he looked down into the bleeding eyes of a child staring back at him.

"It hurts . . ."

The low, hissing voice broke him of his frozen terror, and Jan jumped back, a full augmented leap that slammed him into the nearby bulkhead. He screamed and his finger tightened on the trigger of his rifle.

CHAPTER 17

▶ "We're looking at too many to take, boss."

Rider couldn't help but agree as he piggybacked on Dow's suit imagery, looking over the large squad currently occupying the library core area. The suit counted at least thirty troops, with what had to be an officer working quickly at the access node.

"Keep eyes on, Money," he told Dow. "I'm going to try to link up to the battle network, but interference is pretty stiff. Could take a while. Don't get spotted."

"Roger that," the Marine said from where he was crouched against a wall, holding a sensor probe out around the corner.

"You two, keep an eye on him," Rider told the other pair. "Withdraw at the first sign of detection. I don't know what's going on here, but we'll not do any good getting killed for nothing."

Kensey and Ramirez nodded as Rider ducked back and tried to find a signal to the Marines battle network.

The Priminae ships usually didn't put up much in the way of signal interference. In fact, the ships' materials were noted for unusual signal clarity, but the fighting had irradiated large chunks of the ship, the Marines had popped enough laser-attenuating smoke to choke a small town, and the enemy was presumably running some sort of signal jamming on top of it all.

He was able to get into the ship's network, however, due to its frequent repeaters. From there, Rider looked for a repeater node somewhere within range of the colonel. He couldn't find her, unfortunately, but the sergeant was clear as day as he entered the range of the engineering repeater.

"Sarge, Corporal Rider," he signalled.

"Go for NCO, Rider."

"We're outside the library core, Sarge. Large contingent here, outnumbered and outgunned. No way can we take them with what we have at hand. Orders?"

"Hold one. I don't have a link to the colonel. She's on the bridge, heavy damage there. I've dispatched a runner."

"Roger. Holding."

"What's your situation?"

Rider considered briefly before responding. "Nominal. We've not been spotted; we're armed and have cover. We could tear them a new one before they got us, Sarge, but they would get us. There's just no maneuvering room on this heap."

"Roger that. Hold . . . I've got the colonel linked in. Colonel, Rider is on the line."

"Report, Corporal." The colonel's voice was tense, but steady.

Rider did as ordered, laying out the situation as quickly and cleanly as he could.

"Hold your position as long as you can without being compromised," Colonel Conner said. "We're trying to determine what the enemy is looking for. Let them search."

"Roger that, ma'am," Rider answered. He didn't really have much choice, but he wasn't going to say that. "Holding position, remaining linked in. Will update if anything changes."

"Good work, Corporal. Copy any intel you can grab over to the network as you can," Conner ordered. "Everything we can get on them matters now."

"Yes ma'am."

▶▶▶

▶ The sergeant led the way as the Marine escort and the captain of the *Tetanna* strode into the engineering level.

Drey ignored the work going on and headed for the secure library node, where he could not only pull data but also use command-level functions. He quickly put his security level in and called up the data access history.

"They have been inputting specific search terms," he announced. "It seems they knew what they were coming on board for."

"What were they looking for?" the Terran sergeant asked, looking over the captain's shoulder.

"Armor specifications, laser specifications, information on Priminae allies . . ." Drey stoically looked over at the armored face.

"None of that is good, Captain," the sergeant said.

"On that we are in accord," Drey said. "These . . . Imperials have noted that while they have a power advantage on our weapons, the modifications we acquired from you still gave us an edge in terms of combat effectiveness. They are clearly seeking to neutralize that, and they are curious as to where we acquired it."

"What do you have in there about us anyway?"

"Not much, but perhaps too much all the same," Drey said, skimming the search response as he spoke, just to be sure he wasn't forgetting anything. "Your admiral requested that we not record your home world and, while I cannot speak to the records on the core worlds, that request was honored by the fleet. I am sure that there are captains who know the location of your world, but they will not pull it from our computers."

"That's one thing, I suppose. What *is* there, though?" the sergeant pressed.

"Basic information, approximate total population, habitable worlds—or world, in this case. General technological information," Drey said.

"That's bad enough. I need to speak with the colonel," the sergeant said, then paused. "What about drive mechanics?"

"Pardon?"

"The transition drive. Did they search for that?"

Drey looked quickly, a cold rush chilling him despite the heat he was still feeling. It only took seconds to determine, however, that the Imperials had not searched for it, and he sighed in relief.

"No, they did not."

"Good. They may not have noticed us using it yet," the sergeant said. "Can you shut them down from here?"

"Yes, but that won't remove the data they've already acquired if they've been copying it as they searched."

"Alright, hold tight on that. I need to bring the colonel in on this one."

▶ ▶ ▶

▶ Conner swore softly to herself as she examined the intelligence that was currently flying right into enemy hands.

We're definitely looking at a load of intel we do not want the enemy to acquire at this time, she thought. *Or ever.*

She was privy to the commodore's orders from on high, and just the limited intel about Earth alone was a serious blow to the bluffing strategy they were gambling on. Granted, she didn't think that strategy would hold for long, but the longer it did, the better for Earth and, by extension, the Priminae.

They were going to have to cut that font of knowledge right off, and quick, she decided. The question was how to deal with what would happen right afterward.

The enemy would begin to evac along with the intelligence they'd already gathered, which was a strict no-no to her mind. Unfortunately, their remaining forces still strongly outnumbered her Marines, and while the locals were willing to fight, the fewer people flinging giga-watts of heat energy around the already sauna-like starship, the better.

A glance at her own armor showed that she was severely taxing the environmental controls, and she hadn't taken any damage or significant indirect exposure to laser flash. A lot of her Marines were into the redline of their suit's environmental controls, and as hot as the interior of the ship was already, the suit's radiators weren't functioning anywhere near peak.

A prolonged fight would see her lose as many Marines to heatstroke as to enemy fire, to say nothing of what would happen to the unarmored Priminae crewmen still working to keep the *Tetanna* from collapsing under its own weight.

She took a breath, considering her options, but really, they boiled down to just two.

Assault or ambush.

Ambush it is.

"Sergeant," she said over the battle network, "have the captain kill their access, then pull your Marines back to . . . Bravo One Niner and prepare to ambush the enemy as they withdraw."

▶▶▶

▶ Half Centure Leif stood watch, impatiently kicking at the deck with his armored boot while the technical specialists ran their search parameters through the Oather computer, grabbing the details it spat back in response. The closer they got to completing the mission, the more nervous he grew.

Reports from others had ranged from bad to worse, with entire quarter centures going silent off schedule, which didn't bode well for their survival. The Oathers' allies were efficient, brutal, and quick. He found that respectable in an enemy, but he would prefer to do his respecting later, perhaps in a history class talking about how well they'd fought before finally succumbing to the Empire.

Unfortunately, that day wasn't upon them yet, and nothing could be done to speed things along. Grabbing data from a fractal core was, ideally, a dockyard job. Doing it in the field, under fire, was the sort of mission a troop could have nightmares about.

There was simply too much data stored in a core to just grab a copy and run. So he and his troop were holding the area while the searches were completed. They hoped that the enemy would focus their attention on the command and engineering decks rather than the computer core. They'd done similar missions a hundred times in the past, and trained for it a thousand times at least, but now there were too many unknowns.

He wanted to be clear and on his way out of this soon-to-be derelict hulk of a ship.

The technical specialist starting to swear in multiple languages, several of them decidedly non-Imperial in origin, was a *bad* sign.

"What is it?" Leif yelled, gesturing for one of his men to take his place as he fell out of formation and moved over to the computer interface.

"Someone just cut us off. We are finished here," the specialist said, already packing up his gear.

"What? How?" Leif demanded.

"It appears to be a command override," the specialist said, "likely the captain or engineering chief. Either way, this is as far as we can go."

"Very well. It is time to leave, then!"

▶▶▶

▶ "Shit," Dow swore as he pulled back from the corner. "Rider, we've got an issue. They're packing up. We're going to be uncovered here really damn quick."

"Pull back," Rider ordered. "Colonel and the Primmy captain cut their intel feed. We're to keep eyes on until the colonel can get a reaction team to join up with us."

"Better be some reaction team, boss," Dow said as he put away his hand scanner. "These boys are packing heavy, and they look like they mean business."

"So do we, Dow. Drop a couple of disposable scanners and meet at the fallback point."

"Oorah," the private said as he slapped a scanner package on the wall just around the corner. Then he joined two other Marines. They cleared the area as quickly as they could while remaining relatively silent until they were a fair distance down the hall. They broke into a jog as they headed to meet up with Rider.

They planted scanner packs as they moved, trying to cover as much of the area as possible with each one. The mobile systems weren't as good as their armor, but the tech's transceivers served to expand the battle network and increase their battlefield intelligence.

The corporal was waiting for them at the fallback point, as expected, and he joined in the formation as they continued to run.

"We've got information on decks that are closed off and places the enemy still controls," Rider said, sending them copies of the intel. "So we've mapped their likely egress point. Colonel wants them stopped dead, literally if necessary. We're to rejoin third squad and get dug in for a fight."

"We're going to need more than third squad to pull that off, Corporal," Ramirez said as they moved. "They're packing the equivalent of heavy artillery, and the battleground favors their loadout."

"Yeah, I know. We'll figure it out."

▶▶▶

▶ Colonel Conner skidded to a stop near the portable airlock that connected back to where the Marines had made their entry to the ship. There were people already there, cycling gear in from the cold as quickly as the lock would allow.

"Colonel . . ." One of them turned, wearing light Marine aviator's armor. "We've got everything we could strip off the birds and fit through the lock. The last couple of loads will be through in a minute."

"Thank you, Lieutenant," she said. "People will be here to transport it shortly."

"My LEO and I are volunteering to be part of the effort, ma'am."

She looked closer at the man and the tag on his chest. "Lieutenant Hadrian, you're not exactly in field armor, and you're a pilot."

"I'm a Marine aviator, ma'am. Rifleman first, pilot a *distant* second," he said seriously. "Besides, how much will field armor stand up to one of those infantry lasers?"

Conner grimaced under her armor, knowing that the answer to that was not at all. Even a decent glancing hit would cook a Marine in field armor just as well as a man in BDUs. The lieutenant's light aviator's armor would serve as good as anything else short of a field mech.

"Grab a rifle, then, and start hauling crates to the ambush point, Lieutenant," she said. "We've got work to do."

"Oorah, Colonel!"

Conner watched as the young lieutenant reached for a rifle from the stack against the bulkhead and nudged his LEO. The two men picked up a crate of munitions and started off, leaving her shaking her head.

Too gung ho for his own good.

That wasn't something unique to the lieutenant, however, and at the moment, she needed every rifle hand she could get.

▶▶▶

▶ Getting everyone ready to move, along with the equipment they'd brought to interface with the Oather computer, had taken longer than Leif would have preferred, as the enemy had clearly worked out what they were up to and where they were likely working. He got his men in order, put the technical specialists in the middle of the pack, and set them moving.

Their path out of the ship was limited largely by the damage incurred when the Oather vessel had tangled with the navarch's squadron, but also by ominous black spots in their surveillance since the unknown warriors had engaged them. Leif had to assume that those black spots were now in hostile control, and he thus had far fewer paths to pick from.

They'd entered the ship by forcing their way in through the shuttle bays, perpendicular to the majority of the places the enemy forces had been spotted.

They must have come in through one of the hull breaches, he supposed.

That wasn't an uncommon approach, though he was honestly surprised that they hadn't tried the shuttle bays themselves. They had probably spotted the Imperial Parasites loitering near them, or perhaps they'd been unable to communicate with the command crew of the ship. In either case, it didn't matter now.

What did matter was that the enemy lines back to their own ships lay well away from his egress path. With luck, he might be able to silently retreat before they knew what was happening.

Of course, with luck, they'd not have realized what he and his team were doing until it was far too late anyway. Luck was a fickle ally at the best of times and not one to count on in a fight.

"Scouts out front," he ordered. "Watch for ambushes."

A small reconnaissance squad nodded and ran up ahead of the group. Running an ambush in the corridors of a ship would be easy to set up but hard to hide. Unless they planned to completely give the game away from the start, they'd not be able to use that smoke in the opening moments either, so Leif was confident that they could probably get one good clean barrage before the battle got clouded.

With luck, that would end the fight before it got started.

Of course, the enemy was well aware of that as well, so he had to expect that they had a plan for just that event.

That sort of plan and counterplan gave Leif a headache. He preferred a straight-up fight. Open power versus open power, and let the victor be the one left standing. Few were the forces that could match an Imperial group in terms of raw power, and of those that could, numbers made up for a lot of weaknesses.

▶▶▶

▶ "Everything is in place, Colonel," the sergeant said softly as the Marines settled into their positions.

With time to prepare the battlefield, her Marines had torn the panels off the walls to give them room and cover. It would be of limited use against the infantry lasers the Imperials were bringing to the table, but even soft cover was better than hanging bare ass in the open. Conner nodded approvingly as she was carefully situated a short distance from the ambush sight, out of the direct line of fire, by the sergeant.

He'd tried to assign her a pair of Marines for security, but she'd stepped on that in short order. Every hand was needed in the fight, and two guns babysitting her were two guns not firing on the enemy. Her NCO treating her like she was fragile was amusing most of the time, but while she could understand his position, there were limits.

So, instead, she was only tucked into one of the maintenance corridors. The space was cramped and far from ideal, but it was a reasonably secure position from which to observe and direct the fight. Now it was just a matter of time and patience, both of which she suspected they were about to run desperately short of.

They had eyes on the enemy thanks to the recon team and the mobile scanners they'd planted along the likely withdrawal paths. Unfortunately, the Imperials weren't running along like cocky fools.

Their officer had dispatched a recon team of his own that ran well ahead of the main body, which was shortly going to give her a tough decision.

If she didn't take the recon team out, they were going to run into her Marines in their semifortified positions. If they reported that back, that would be bad. If she *did* have the team eliminated before they could happen on her people, which was really the only realistic option Conner could see, then even if they didn't get a message out before they were taken down . . . the main force would almost certainly notice them going black.

Either way, there went the element of surprise.

"Let the recon team get as close as possible," she ordered. "And then take them out."

This is going to get ugly.

▶▶▶

▶ The Imperial scout troop made their way through the corridors ahead of the main force, eyes sharp as they looked for any sign of enemy presence.

The scouts were often a punishment assignment in the Imperial forces, given when a troop screwed up enough to warrant severe punishment yet not enough to warrant execution. Generally, it was bad form to ask what a fellow scout had done to get their position, but secrets still got around.

Kel was in the lead, his infantry laser cradled in his arms. He sought anything that looked out of place as they moved. He didn't like the situation in the least, but it was rare that a scout had any liking for the job. Not the sane ones, at least.

"Hold," he ordered as he noticed something. "We have lost contact with the main contingent."

"Jamming?" one of his men asked.

"Maybe," Kel said cautiously. "There is a lot of radiation here, but we caused a fair amount of it, so it is hard to say."

They paused as he checked his instruments, trying to figure out what was causing the interference while he tried to reconnect for good measure.

"Are these supposed to be here?" a quiet voice asked over the suit comm, causing him to turn to where his second, Tiran, had paused, looking closely at a black boxy shape on the wall.

"Scan it," he ordered.

"Right." Tiran lowered his laser and brought up a powerful scanner to examine the object. "Hmm. No power source to speak of, no volatiles of record. Chemical analysis is curious, but it could be a lot of things."

"Weapon?" Kel asked.

"That would be one of the things," Tiran confirmed. "Not any composition we are familiar with, but the energy potential is significant, though not exceedingly so."

Kel looked at the device, then up and down the corridor as he realized that they'd most likely walked into a kill zone.

"Arms up!" he ordered sharply, bringing his laser up quickly.

His team had just started to react when movement at a junction ahead caught his attention. Kel had started to shift his aim when the dark blurs exploded into flashes of fire and smoke, and he felt hammer blows smashing through his armor.

He went down to his knees, his men falling around him as his laser clattered to the deck. Four figures in dark mottled armor approached from the junction as he slumped, and the world began to fade around him.

I detest being a scout.

▶ ▶ ▶

▶ Corporal Rider kicked the lasers clear of the bodies he was standing over. "Clear."

"Good job," the sergeant said from behind him.

"Recon," Rider said.

"Oorah," his team responded as they secured the area.

"Clear the bodies," the sergeant ordered. "Not much we can do about the blood, but we'll worry about that when it becomes a problem."

Rider nodded and gestured to his team as he bent down and grabbed the armor of the man he was standing over, hefting the man's torso up enough so he could drag him down the corridor.

The sergeant watched the job for a moment, then quickly secured the fallen weapons and followed the team.

One job down, the big one still to go.

▶▶▶

▶ Losing the scout team rarely meant good things, but at least it was a warning that bad things were ahead.

Not that I really needed much warning about that, Leif thought. *If it were truly a surprise, I would not have led with the scout troop.*

"We lost contact with them about a hundred meters along this corridor," he said, checking the last time they'd had a signal from the scouts. "So now we have a decision to make. Bull through or try to go around?"

His second stepped up beside him, looking up the empty corridor and then checking the map they had of the ship's internals.

"Going around will add at least thirty-three percent more time," the second said quietly. "Probably more."

"True," Leif said, considering. "However, if they're prepared to hold the corridor against us, going straight will cost men *and* time. In either case, we lose."

"Not a palatable decision, I admit," his second said.

"We have an alternative, perhaps," Leif said as he examined the map.

The Oather design was similar to Imperial cruisers, though the internal layout wasn't identical. There were nonetheless major consistencies. Both ships were built around a twin core of reactors that warped gravity significantly in the short range of deck to deck. In order to maintain a perpendicular gravity to the deck, the ships had to be constructed in line with the warping of space-time.

The only way to get a straight line was to curve it.

In absolute terms, that meant that while he may not know the layout of the decks in any specific fashion, Leif *did* know where he was and where he had to be as well as the most direct way to get there.

"Cutting lasers," he ordered, pointing at a section of deck. "We will go through here."

"The heat will stress our suit systems in short order, Half Centure," his second warned.

"We will either be clear of this beast before that's a factor, or we'll all be dead. Either way, we are not going to care about the heat," Leif said. "Leave that to the Oathers to worry about."

"On your order, Half Centure." His second saluted, then waved up a fire team and gave them their orders.

"Everyone else, perimeter security."

▶▶▶

▶ Rider shifted nervously, risking a glance around the corner.

"Something's wrong," he said after a moment's thought.

"You mean the fact that we're not dodging lasers right about now?" Dow asked. "Doesn't seem like something to bitch about, Rider."

"Yeah, that's the problem alright," Rider answered easily enough, switching channels on the tactical network. "Hey Sarge, anyone see signs along alternate routes?"

"Negative on that, Rider. Why, you think they're playing games?" the sergeant said.

"Should have been here by now," Rider said decisively. "Something's up."

"Corporal," the colonel's quiet voice cut in, "they're probably just being cautious. They just lost contact with their recon squad. That likely slowed them down."

Rider hesitated, not wanting to cross the colonel, but finally elected to just bull ahead. "Ma'am, my gut says they're up to something that means bad things for us," he said in a quick spew of words.

The sergeant's sharp laughter followed instantly. "That's a given, Corporal. They're the enemy. You'll need to be more specific."

Rider ground his teeth, risking another look down the empty corridor.

Still no sign.

"I can't," he admitted finally. "But something isn't right, ma'am, Sarge. Request to deploy recon."

The silence on the channel was nearly deafening until finally the colonel came back.

"Corporal, there's no cover if you get caught out in the open. You're cooked."

"Roger, ma'am," Rider said. "Won't get caught in the open, ma'am."

Another pause stretched out before her voice came back.

"Deploy recon."

"Oorah, ma'am. Recon deploying," he said over the open channel, nodding to his team. "Let's go."

Breaking cover, Rider led the way. He felt an itch running down his spine, not that the feeling really surprised him. Wandering as he was in the open right toward where every bit of intelligence said the enemy was approaching from tended to make his skin crawl. The itch aside, something was bugging Rider. He didn't think they were approaching.

He didn't know for sure, but he couldn't get the thought out of his head, so he was betting his life on a hunch.

His life, and the lives of his team.

With his three squadmates at his back, the armored recon Marine securely planted the butt of his rifle to his shoulder and broke into a loping jog that ate up ground faster. At the junction he stopped, one hand coming off his rifle, fist in the air to signal the rest to follow suit.

He carefully cleared the corner and shook his head when he found no sign of the enemy down the *next* length of corridor either.

"They pulled a fast one," he said firmly.

Dow crossed the intersection while he covered the corridor, then took up position on the other side before replying, "What kind of fast one could they pull? We have the routes covered. There weren't that many to begin with, not with all the damage this heap took in the fight."

"I don't know what," Rider said, "but they're up to something. Okay, we're moving on."

"Hold on, Rider," Kensey objected. "We'll lose tactical contact with the rest if we stretch out much farther. The radiation from all the fighting has turned this place into a transmission nightmare."

Rider hissed, irritated but knowing Kensey was right.

Their suit comms were good, but there were physical constraints to how much range you could get out of a man-portable system. Ideal circumstances would allow spread spectrum transmitters to punch through a lot and reach out respectable distances. While the Priminae vessel was largely designed to be electromagnetically neutral, the squad was in far from ideal circumstances.

The laser radiation from the fighting on board but, more importantly, from the ship-to-ship combat the vessel had endured had left its mark. Lasers powerful enough to burn through combat armor and slice open warships left a longer-lasting mark as heat and other forms of radiation. The squad was also right on top of the vessel's singularity cores, which were even worse.

"Okay," he decided. "We've got the codes to access the shipboard system. We'll link to that, as it should be able to get a signal back to the others. It's hardlined."

"Assuming it's not been cut anywhere," Kensey said in a tone of grudging agreement.

"You sign up to live forever, Kensey?" Rider asked as he used his suit to link into the ship's communication system.

"Not while you're leading the charge."

"Smartass. Okay, I've got the ship's system. What the hell . . ." Rider trailed off.

"What is it?"

Rider ignored his squadmate for the moment, switching tactical channels again. "Colonel, check the status of the ship's communications relays."

"What am I looking for, Corporal?" Colonel Conner asked a moment later.

"A relay just ahead went dead, ma'am."

"There're a lot of dead relays, Rider," the sergeant cut in. "What's your point?"

"No, Sergeant, the corporal may be on to something," Conner said. "The time stamp is only a few seconds ago. Someone just cut that relay."

"Taking down our communications?" the sergeant asked, sounding confused.

"Not effectively, if that's the idea," Rider answered. "That one is on their side of the ship. We don't have anyone on the other side of it, and they should know that—Colonel!"

"I see it," Conner gritted out. "Another one just went dead."

"Closer to us?" the sergeant asked, still uncertain.

"No, different deck," Rider said. "Ma'am, I think they're—"

"Cutting through the decks," she finished for him. "You were right, Corporal. They were up to something. We're redeploying. I'm pulling everyone back. We'll try and cut them off before they get to the flight deck."

"I'll take my team after them," Rider said.

"Corporal, you won't have any backup," Conner warned.

"Recon, ma'am," he answered simply.

He didn't need to say anything more, in his opinion.

He could hear the hesitation in the silence that stretched between him and the colonel, but finally she came back.

"Godspeed, Marine."

"Oorah, ma'am."

Rider cut the link and simply gestured with two fingers before he brought his rifle back up to his shoulder. His team didn't miss a beat; they'd been waiting and watching for the signal. As one, they broke position and began running down the corridor.

Marine Force Recon.

Celer, Silens, Mortalis.

Swift, Silent, Deadly.

It was time to live up to the words.

CHAPTER 18

▶ Commander Heath sat bolt upright in her seat, catching Eric's attention in his peripheral vision as he was monitoring a laser strike that had come in from the enemy fleet.

"What is it, Commander?" he asked, not looking over.

"We just registered rifle fire on deck thirty-eight," she said, pushing quickly through a set of menus to access the system deeper.

"What?" Eric looked over now. "Thirty-eight? That's where the Marines went in looking for the source of a sound, right?"

"Yes sir. I'm getting reports of an injured Marine now."

"Was he shot?"

"No. He apparently slammed himself into the bulkhead and fired his weapon accidentally." Heath let out a breath. "No other injuries. The rifle IFF kept it from cutting down the team of Marines that went in with him."

Eric winced, glad of course that the Identification Friend or Foe system had functioned as intended, but it should never have come to that.

"What the hell happened?" he asked.

"Reports are confused right now, sir. I'm accessing the Marine's suit recorders."

Eric glanced at the telemetry plot, determining how much time they had before they were likely to be in a hot battle again, and decided it was enough. "Shoot me the link as soon as you can. I want to see this myself."

"Yes sir."

Heath soon sent the link over to his station. Eric quickly queued up the file and played it on his station with the audio turned up. The command station had an isolated audio system that kept most of the sound from leaking out to bother anyone else. He was disappointed when he got through the file.

"What was he hearing?" Eric said. "Obviously something spooked the kid, but *none* of the systems recorded it?"

Heath shook her head from across the aisle at her own station. "No idea, sir. Other Marines confirm that they heard the sounds they were there to investigate, but none of the recorders got a hint of it."

"In a hard vacuum, honestly, I'd have been shocked if they had," Eric said. "Something had to be vibrating the air in their suits directly. Gravity flux, perhaps?"

"We would have picked that up, sir," Heath said firmly, "and if by some chance it happened and we didn't pick it up, the suit mics would have. I'm thinking we need to pull our people and examine their suit air, sir."

"Contaminated suit air? *All* of them?" Eric asked incredulously. "That's a stretch."

"It's the only thing that makes sense based on what I'm seeing."

Eric hissed, but finally nodded. "I want a full screen done on that Marine—hell, on all of them. God, we need to pull the damage control teams too. How long until we can purge the suit air from another set and get a new team in?"

"At least twenty minutes, sir."

"Okay, get it done," Eric ordered, shaking his head. "If this keeps up, the crew is going to start thinking this ship is haunted, and that's not going to end well for anyone."

"Yes sir," Heath said, not specifying whether she was confirming his order or responding to his statement. Honestly, it didn't matter as long as she got to work on pulling the damage control teams and the Marines from the affected decks while getting the suit maintenance units to start purging their systems.

Eric returned to the more urgent tasks, but his mind and eyes kept sneaking back to the strange reports coming from the damage control crews.

If I didn't know any better, I'd . . .

Eric shook that thought from his mind. The last thing he needed to start worrying about now was problems light-years away. There would be a sane explanation.

▶▶▶

▶ "You want us to *what?*"

Dixon was incensed. First, his ship got big damned holes blown in it, then some joker starts creeping everyone out while he's trying to fix the ruptures, and now they want him to pull his team *in?*

"You heard me, Chief. Come in, swap out to a new team. We're worried that you might have picked up a contaminant in your air."

"Commander, my air is fine. We're ten minutes from sealing this deck so we can repressurize," Dixon insisted. "How long will it take to swap a team? A half hour at least?"

"Closer to an hour, Chief," the commander said reluctantly.

"An *hour?* Are you kidding me?" Dixon normally wouldn't argue with a commander. Making a fool of oneself was an officer's prerogative, but here she was talking about leaving his ship with a huge gaping wound in her side for an *extra* hour? No.

"We're purging the air out of the other team's suits. We need to confirm that the O2 is pure, Chief." The commander was sounding irritated.

Good.

"You do that," Dixon said. "We're going to finish this job, *then* we'll come out and swap for another team. Ten minutes won't kill us if whatever it is hasn't already done us in, Commander. We're on a clock. Let us do our job."

"Chief, the Marines have been called out. One of them freaked out and hosed down the deck with his rifle."

"One of them *what*?!" Dixon damn near blew up, forgetting entirely who he was talking to. "We're trying to patch my baby here, and you're telling me one of those idiot leathernecks is putting *more* holes in it?"

"Chief, take a breath. Your blood pressure and heart rate are going through the roof. If you don't calm down, I'm sending in a medic team to pull you out by force," Heath said firmly.

Dixon took a couple of deep breaths, watching his heart rate slow as he forced himself to calm down.

"Better. Yes, the Marines were hallucinating or something and one of them damn near threw himself through a bulkhead to get away from . . . *something*," she said when his bio readings had dropped to more normal levels. "That's why we want your team out of there."

"Look, my guys are hearing things, but no one is freaking out," Dixon growled. *Much.*

"We'd rather it not come to that."

"We could argue about it for another five minutes, Commander, or you could let us finish, and we'll be out in fifteen," Dixon said. "And you'll be able to pressurize this deck, and then we don't have to worry about contaminants in the suit air. How's that sound?"

Heath sighed audibly over the comm channel.

"Chief . . . just get it done," she snapped, a little stronger than she intended. "In the meantime, I'll be sitting here, trying to decide whether you get a commendation or a dressing-down in your next fit rep."

Dixon almost laughed over the comm. "Same thing half the time, Commander. We'll be out of here in fifteen."

"Just keep an eye on your people, Chief. Anyone freaks out, you *all* get the hell out of there," Heath said, "right away and on the double, or I'm coming down there to drag you out. Heath out."

Dixon flipped from the comm channel over to the team channel, listening in to his damage control team as they worked. Everyone seemed calm, aside from being a little creeped out by the strange noises. He couldn't fault them on that. He wasn't all sunshine and roses about the damn sounds himself.

Their vitals were all good, though, well within the expected range for the work they were doing, and better than most had any right to expect. Repairing combat damage in the middle of a fight was dangerous enough; doing so in hard vacuum was enough to get anyone's blood pumping. But so far, his people were handling the task like it was a walk in the park.

He expected no less of course. They were professionals.

Now if only that damn sobbing would stop!

Or, at least, if his "professionals" would stop occasionally joining in. Embarrassing is what it was.

Dixon sighed and got back to work.

▶▶▶

▶ Doctor Rame had been the medical officer under Eric Weston's command since the first voyage of the *Odyssey*, and in that time he'd seen plenty of strange things in his life: the first "alien" ever encountered by humans, truly alien beasties that wanted to *eat* humans, lots of fighting, and all sorts of new and interesting injuries to treat.

In those years, however, he'd not encountered something quite like this.

"No," he said with a shake of his head. "I'm telling you, he's clean. They all are. No hits on the tox panels; everything checks out. You can get whoever you want to look at their suit air, but I'm telling you right now, there's not going to be anything there besides a very slight CO_2 imbalance."

"That could cause problems, Doc," the Marine gunnery sergeant said, shooting a glare over at the Marine who was still laid out on the bed.

"Not in this case. It was well within human tolerances. I only mention it because it was just enough to show up on the tox panel, but nowhere near enough to cause any issues."

"My Marines don't just lose their shit and empty a mag down the halls their buddies are standing in," the gunny said flatly. "Something happened."

"Obviously," Rame said. "We have multiple accounts confirming the sounds, and no one here doubts that *something* happened, Gunnery Sergeant. What I'm saying is that it was *not* medical in nature. Other than the banging he gave himself when he slammed into the bulkhead, Lance Corporal Jan is in perfect health."

"Then what the hell happened down there?" the gunny grumbled, mostly to himself.

Rame rolled his eyes, but elected to respond anyway. "In my experience, if the people involved aren't hallucinating, that generally means that they actually *saw* something, Gunnery Sergeant. Which, I would suggest, means that there is something down there."

The gunny shot him a dark look, but did not say anything as he turned and stormed out, leaving Rame alone with his patient, finally.

The doctor turned back to the toxicology workup he'd done on the Marine's blood, noting that the man probably needed to cut down on his caffeine intake.

Right. That'll happen sometime this century, I'm sure.

▶▶▶

▶ The *Odysseus*, with the Priminae squadron in tow, continued to close on the Imperial Fleet, trading shots as they could, but both sides were mostly marking time as the distance between them closed. Eric was growing irritated with the stalemate, but still did what he could to encourage it to continue while he had teams trying to fix the damage incurred earlier.

The new problems below decks were doing everything but soothing those nerves.

"Damage control team reports the deck has been sealed," Heath reported.

Eric shot a glance over at her. "Good. Get them out of there and put the atmosphere back to that deck."

"Aye sir, they're pulling out now," she said as she tapped in commands. "I'm opening the valves to that deck."

"Slowly now," Eric reminded, still tense. "Don't blow out their repairs."

"I doubt the system can feed that much air at once, sir," Heath said, "and if it can, well, better to find out now than later."

Eric supposed she had a point there.

"Raze, we're close to entering optimal range on these bastards," Steph warned from the pilot's pit. "If they choose to turn on us, it'll get ugly real fast."

Glancing at the telemetry, Eric stood up and walked around to look at the large main screen. His pilot was right, of course. The best defense the *Odysseus* had right now was, ironically, the rear gravity warp of the enemy ships. That same warp was the only thing keeping them from hammering the Imperials as well, of course.

Assuming the Priminae held the line—which was an assumption that Eric wasn't entirely comfortable making despite their actions so far—the best outcome of such a fight was total destruction of the Allied vessels and an effective crippling of the Imperial Fleet.

Not a trade he would prefer to make, if he had a choice.

Sometimes you had to accept a beating, though, just to show the bully that he wouldn't get away with that sort of crap so easily in the future.

God, I hope it doesn't come to that.

"Keep pressing closer," he ordered. "Signal the Priminae ships to follow us in. Stand by all weapons from this point. I want everyone on watch. If they *twitch*, don't wait for orders. Burn every last living one of them you can from the black."

"Aye Skipper." The response was the same from three stations as he walked over to the pit and knelt down.

"When it happens, if it happens, it'll happen fast," he said softly. "Do whatever you can to get our weapons the best shot."

Steph nodded somberly. "You know if they turn on us, we don't stand a chance, right?"

"I know," Eric said. "Keep pressing them anyway. And if they turn, don't bother trying to evade. Remember the Alamo."

"Understood, Skipper."

Eric got back to his feet and returned to the command station, where he slipped into his position and checked the data from Heath's operations. The air pressure on the affected decks were returning to normal, though still not quite high enough for people to breathe, and so far there was no sign of leaks.

"Everything is holding as expected," Heath confirmed, noticing his interest. "We can send people to the affected decks in another few minutes."

"Security teams only," Eric ordered, "and make sure they have environmental suits on, even if they're not relying on them. No one goes onto those decks in the open until we have a repair team check that the patches are holding."

"Aye aye, sir."

▶▶▶

▶ "Weston is out of his *mind*," Pol hissed under his breath, leaning close enough so only the captain could hear him talk.

Druel didn't comment immediately. What could he say to that? His second in command wasn't wrong. Pol was arguably *understating* the situation, but there was little they could do about it.

If they turned and withdrew from the fight, they'd be consigning the *Odysseus* and likely the *Tetanna* to quick deaths. Quite possibly the rest of the Terran forces would die in the resulting firefight as well.

Druel ran his hand back through his hair, unobtrusively pushing the sweat that kept forming on his brow back and wiping it away as best he could. This just wasn't what he had joined the fleet for, and he didn't know if he could continue like this for much longer.

"We knew he viewed fighting differently than our people," he said finally. "He threw his ship against the Drasin with worse odds than he is facing here."

"He used guile and stealth against the Drasin," Pol corrected.

"I would say he is using plenty of guile here as well," Druel said tiredly. "He is giving them a decision. Face us and likely lose far more of their forces than it would be worth to eliminate us, as they would almost certainly be left without sufficient power to do anything but withdraw to their own territory, or withdraw now and save their ships for another battle. It is not a decision I would offer them, but then I do not believe I would have survived what Weston has already proven himself against. It is the best option available to us at this time and, short of miraculous reinforcements arriving from Earth or the Central worlds, I see no other palatable options. Please, correct me if you do."

Silence from Pol was all the answer he needed.

"So then," Druel said after a long moment, "insane or not, we will follow his lead in this. If the universe chooses against Weston this time, he has all but secured at least the safety of this system even in defeat. Do you not see it, Pol? In the worst case, Weston has arranged things such that we fulfill our duty to the planet and the colonists. In best, we even get to enjoy the victory. That's not such a bad thing."

Pol stared at his captain for a long time, his expression also clearly showing doubt about the sanity of the man sitting in the big seat, but he kept his peace this time.

It wasn't for him to question, though, and for that, Pol was grateful. Druel didn't blame him in the least.

Perhaps the only thing worse than dying at the weapons of the Imperials was having the fate of so many others resting on his shoulders.

▶▶▶

▶ Eric was trying his best to keep his focus on the enemy, but the questions he had whirling in his brain about what was going on in his own damn ship plagued him.

The doc says there's nothing wrong with the air, but that many people seeing things just doesn't happen, right?

He'd heard rumors, more than anything, of shared delusions, but didn't know enough about the phenomenon to know if it actually *happened* in the real world.

One of his Marines had freaked out enough to accidentally discharge his weapon, not to mention batter himself unconscious against a bulkhead. That was beyond the pale, and without a medical reason for his actions, Eric didn't much like the Marine's chances for promotion anytime in the near future. He'd personally be looking over the man's record and deciding if he was going to stay on the *Odysseus*, though Eric would hold off on any thought of disciplinary action until they figured out what the *hell* the man had seen down there.

In the meantime, however, there was work to finish and more pressing matters to deal with. The enemy outside simply had to be given his attention. The enemy within would have to wait.

CHAPTER 19

▶ The hole burned through the ceramic bulkhead was big enough to drive a Marine fighting vehicle through, and Rider was trying really hard not to imagine just how much power it would have taken to burn that hole.

Ceramic, as a compound, had several advantages over the steel construction that Terran shipbuilders still preferred. The primary reward was that ceramic had extremely high heat resistance and incredibly low heat transferal. Burning through ceramic plate the way the enemy had took a *lot* of power, far more than it would take to go through the metal decks of one of the Rogues.

Rider found himself peering down the hole and looking around him best he could to see if the enemy had left a rear guard.

"Looks clear," Kensey said.

"Alright, let's go."

Rider jumped first, dropping through the hole and freefalling for a few meters as the slight twist of gravity caught him and swung him into the cambered deck below. He landed in a crouch, catching himself with his free left hand as his right kept his rifle under control.

His team slammed into the deck on either side of him, two with more grace than he managed, and one with distinctly less.

"You okay?" he asked, sparing Kensey a glance as the man picked his face off the deck.

"Fine. That twist was a pain," the Marine grumped, retrieving his rifle from where he'd let it clatter to the deck.

"Suck it up," Rider ordered, getting to his feet and gesturing to the next target. "There's the next hole. Let's move. And Kensey?"

"Yeah?"

"Remember the 'silent' part of the motto next time."

"Screw you, Rider."

The four-man recon team, chuckling softly as they ran, paused only to clear the hole as best they could before dropping through it to the next deck. They led with their rifles, or their boots, depending on which seemed more suitable at the time, and didn't slow any more than they absolutely had to as they pursued the enemy from deck to deck in an attempt to catch up.

"They can't be far ahead now," Rider said firmly. "Cutting through these decks *has* to be slowing them down."

"We better hope so, Rider," Ramirez said. "I don't want to think of the kind of power they have in those lasers just to cut through decks in the first place, let alone what it would take to let them move without slowing."

"Not sure it makes much difference," Dow said as they ran. "Our armor ain't ceramic. We'd be cooked either way."

"Point," Ramirez acceded grumpily.

Rider slowed his pace, his left hand coming up in a fist. They fell silent and slowed as he came to a corner.

"What's up, Rider?" Kensey asked.

"Heat spike up ahead," he answered as they walked to the next hole burned through the deck and paused.

There was no sign of the enemy, but his HUD was scanning a *lot* of heat through the hole.

"They're close. Tighten up on me," he ordered. "We're running a wounded tiger to ground here, and when we catch it, it *will* turn on us. Stay frosty, follow my lead."

"Oorah!"

Rider readied his rifle and stepped out into the air, letting the gravity of the ship's core pull him down through the hole to the next deck.

▶▶▶

▶ "Captain, we have a problem."

Drey resisted the urge to sarcastically reply to the Terran colonel. He was well aware they had trouble. His ship was drifting in space with enemy soldiers running around her decks while the enemy ships closed on them. "Problem" was a very understated way to describe the current situation, but it would be somewhat impolite—not to mention impolitic—to point that out.

"What sort of problem, Colonel?" he asked, looking at Conner's face in the small screen he'd appropriated in engineering to run his ship.

"The enemy is withdrawing from the ship," she said. "They've been burning through decks and seem to be heading for the flight decks."

"While I would rather they didn't cut more holes in my vessel, Colonel," he said with feeling, "frankly, I am just as happy to see them go. There are larger problems than a few enemy soldiers at the moment, and I'm staring at most of them."

He looked up at the scanner plot that showed the rapidly approaching enemy vessels as well as the Allied squadrons chasing determinedly after them. He didn't want to think about what the Imperial vessels could do to his ship, even in passing, before the others could catch up. The fate of a few Imperial soldiers was just not a priority.

"I'm sure that's true, Captain," the colonel said tensely. "However, they acquired information from your core that we would prefer they not escape with. Can you track them from there?"

Drey looked up, snapping his fingers in the direction where some of his command staff were working shoulder to shoulder in cramped space with the engineering teams, trying to get everything operational again.

"Sir?"

"Can we track the Imperials on board?" he asked his second.

"One moment, Captain," the man said, turning to where the scanner tech was working. They exchanged quiet words back and forth before his second turned back.

"Not directly, Captain. We know where they've been. There are heat spikes on our environmental control systems, which almost certainly indicate where they've been firing their weapons, but the security systems have been taken down on most decks."

Drey nodded, turning back to the colonel. "Did you hear that?"

"Yes. We think they're heading for one of your primary flight decks. Do you at least know which one they docked with?"

"That I can tell you," Drey answered. "The Imperial ship overpowered security on deck eight when they arrived. The likelihood is that is still where their ship has docked, since we've received no indications of any move since then."

"Alright, we're heading that way now. Can you spare any security forces?"

Drey nodded. "I'll have everyone I can join up with you, Colonel."

"Thank you, Captain."

"Good luck, Colonel."

▶▶▶

▶ Conner glowered as she closed the comm connection to the captain of the *Tetanna*. Asking for help from ship security was potentially a double-edged blade. The Priminae soldiers, no matter how enthusiastic, were in no way up to the level of her Marines.

Numbers were a real concern, however, and they would only have one shot at this. If they failed, then the enemy would acquire whatever intel they'd managed to download from the *Tetanna's* core. That was not an acceptable outcome, so she was going to risk bringing in the Priminae troops and do her best to keep them from vaping her Marines in the process.

"Sergeant," she ordered. "Double-time, if you will."

"As you say, ma'am." The sergeant turned to the rest of the Marines who were lugging everything they could through the halls of the alien warship. "Marines! Double-step! Move it!"

Conner picked up her own feet, keeping up as she split her focus on the tactical relays she was reading on her HUD. "The captain of the *Tetanna* will be sending troops to reinforce our position, Sergeant. Please don't shoot them when they arrive."

"No ma'am," the Sergeant agreed good-naturedly. "Would be unneighborly, ma'am."

"It would at that, Sergeant."

Getting to the flight deck would have been simplicity itself if the ship had been undamaged. However, with the lifts mostly down and her squad being forced to detour around sealed decks due to battle damage, Conner was sweating who would arrive first. Enemy troops were taking a far more direct route, but they had to stop on each deck to cut their way through. Her Marines had a longer route, no question, but they were making steady progress, and with the captain and engineering crew of the ship providing override access to bulkhead locks, she thought that they might just make it.

If not, she still had one trump card in play.

Recon, oorah Marines.

▶ ▶ ▶

▶ "I've got motion," Rider said as he dropped to one knee and put his left fist up to call the others to a halt in case they weren't listening to him.

The Marines arrayed themselves behind him as he covered behind junk that looked like it had broken free where the Imperials had cut through the deck. Rider pulled an extendable scanner from the forearm of his armor and pushed it out around the cover, observing the scene through his HUD.

"Computer counts fifteen men in sight," he said. "Not sure where the rest are. Must be a rear guard."

"Four against fifteen," Dow pointed out. "Hardly seems fair. Want to offer them a chance to surrender?"

The Marines chuckled, though an undercurrent of nerves was unmistakable to each of them. None would admit that on pain of death, of course, but the four took comfort in the concerns of their comrades all the same. No experienced fighting man wanted the man at his side to be fearless, not most of the time, at least. Insanity had its place, but that place was rarely standing in the line with the sane. Like panic, it was too infectious for comfort.

"Grenades and smokers," Rider said softly, letting his rifle hang on its sling as he slipped a pair of canisters from his armor's straps.

The other three Marines followed his example, each taking an anti-laser and a fragmentation grenade from their armor.

Rider thumbed the activator on both, keeping his hand closed around the two weapons to keep the countdown from starting. He nodded to his team as they did the same, then lifted his thumb and felt the devices rumble softly through his armor. The warning wasn't needed this time; he knew they were live and had no intention of hanging on to them.

Rider pitched his over the cover, letting them clatter down the hall as the others threw theirs as well. Some of the devices banked off the walls and others caromed off the ceiling or deck as they clattered toward their targets.

Before the first smoke went off, the Recon Marines retrieved their rifles from where they had hung them. As the frags detonated, they were already moving.

They charged in right on the cusp of the explosions, their rifles roaring in the confined deck of the starship yet barely audible against the multiple detonations and confused yelling ahead of them. Fragments from the grenades pinged off the Marines' armor, but they ignored them as they closed with weapons blazing. They knew the explosives' lethality fell off quickly with range and were far enough out that their armor could deal with the impact.

It was a well-practiced maneuver, one that often lost men on the aggressors' side to friendly fire as they normally used artillery instead of grenades. Over the centuries, it had many names, from "shock and awe" to "establishing dominance." The Marines just called it "knocking down the door."

Lasers flashed in the smoke. Blind shots or aimed, there was no real way to tell. The Recon Marines knew only one thing—if they saw the light, the enemy had missed. They didn't bother diving for cover as they vanished into the smoke themselves.

HUDs up, the recon team could see vague outlines of the enemy through the glittering smoke. Mostly they relied on ultrasonic returns, almost like sonar on an old submarine, because nothing else would be remotely effective. Heat was largely useless, especially after a couple of laser bursts raised the ambient temperature in the corridor, and visibility was intentionally zero in the smoke. The metallic shards suspended in the smoke, causing the mirroring effect, negated radar returns. Stopping Imperial lasers was considered more important than anything else, which left the team relying on the badly degraded short-range ultrasonics as they fought in whiteout conditions.

Thus, Rider was almost caught by surprise when one of the Imperials charged in his direction, either because the man's own environmental gear had better scanners or due to pure luck. At the last moment, Rider's ultrasonic gear picked up the form charging in his direction, and the Marine ducked under a swing that would have rung his bell but good.

Rider hit the deck in a slide, kicking the Imperial trooper's legs out from under him. As the man landed beside him with a heavy thud, Rider rolled hard over and slammed the butt of his rifle down into the trooper's head. The blow would have killed any unarmored man it struck, but both Rider and his opponent were armored, and in moments, it was clear that they were both well experienced with the dirtier aspects of close-in fighting.

A vicious blow to his groin had the Marine wincing despite the armor he wore. He returned the favor by catching the trooper's head in a clutch and dragging him into his chest as he started whaling on the man with his knees and elbows.

Fighting in augmenting armor was sometimes like trying to box underwater, at least if the other man had armor himself. Their blows were powerful beyond human understanding, but so was their ability to absorb the hits. After a few moments of exchanging blows, both Marine and trooper knew that something would have to give.

To Rider, it felt like they both came to that conclusion at the same time, breaking apart and kicking each other away as they went for their weapons.

Rider swept up to one knee as he wrapped his mitt around the pistol grip of his assault rifle and swept the weapon up from where it had hung on his straps. The rifle roared, a heavy depleted uranium round accelerating down the rails to hypersonic speeds by an EM burst. A flash of light refracted off the antilaser mist around them as the steel jacket of the round ablated almost instantly, vanishing in a burst of flame as it tore through the air between Rider and his opponent.

The DPU slug tore through the environmental armor the Imperial trooper was wearing, exploding inside with the force of a small bomb as the slug broke up and fragmented, dumping the kinetic force remaining in the round directly into the body of its target.

The Imperial trooper hit the bulkhead behind him hard, then slowly slid down as an orange foam splattered out of the newly formed hole in a vain attempt to seal the damage and preserve the trooper within. Rider noted that the man hadn't quite managed to get his hand around the grip of his own weapon in the split second and wondered if that was a sign that the Imperials weren't trained to fight close in the way Marines were or if this one was just slow off the mark.

He didn't have time to ponder such matters. The Recon Marine opened a flag on his armor HUD as he got to his feet, noting in the record that he wanted to review the fight when he had time.

"Sweep the corridor clean," he ordered, not really able to tell how many men were still standing around him, though at least all of his own team were still green on his HUD.

▶▶▶

▶ "What was that?"

Leif half turned, looking down the direction his people had come from, a stony expression on his face, though none around him could see it. He knew the sound of fighting, even if it was not fighting of Imperial tradition.

"We are being followed," he said finally. "Contact the rear guard, see if they took out the attackers."

"And if they did not?" one of his engineers blurted without thinking.

"Then I suppose we will not be able to contact them, will we?" Leif said.

The engineer fell silent, looking quickly away from him. Leif was content to leave it at that. He had more important things to deal with than some idiot speaking out of turn. He looked to where his second was trying to contact the rear guard.

"Anything?" he asked, though he really didn't have to. The body language said it all, even before the man shook his head.

"Nothing, Centure," Deca Corval answered. "Lost all contact just moments after the sounds reached us."

"Well, they are efficient if nothing else," Leif said with forced cheer. "It will be interesting to meet these people on the open field. I wonder whose forces will win the day. Do you also, Corval?"

"Yes Centure," the deca answered dutifully, though a bit sourly.

Leif supposed he didn't blame the man much. Few were those who truly enjoyed engaging competent foes in a fight. Even he would generally prefer to deal with the sorts of fools the Empire normally walked over, but once in a while, it was important to have real blood spilled on the battlefield, or your own forces would eventually turn into those selfsame fools.

A good enemy *defined* a soldier in ways a fool never could.

"Well, let us be on with this," he said, turning his focus to where the cutters were working on the next bulkhead. "Are you almost through?"

"Yes Centure, just a few more seconds."

"Good. We will just leave a little gift behind us, then, to show our pursuers our appreciation," he said with a grin that he rather regretted none of his men could see.

▶▶▶

▶ Colonel Conner examined the corridor carefully as her Marines set up their gear. They had just arrived outside the flight deck, and the ship's systems reported that the interior still had atmosphere. She was only mildly surprised, given the enemy most likely had to cut their way in if not blow one of the locks.

The flight decks on Priminae cruisers were arranged carefully in line with the two cores of the ship to maintain a minimal atmospheric level even if they were exposed to space. The gravity of the cores was enough to hold the air in, for a while at least, in case the ships needed to run extended operations out of the large open decks.

In the long run, it would still bleed off atmosphere, though much of it would probably wind up hugging the exterior of the ship. In theory at least, she'd heard that it was possible to build a bubble of breathable air on the outside of a Priminae cruiser due to the gravity of the cores holding the air in close.

In practice, however, cosmic wind, the ship's acceleration, and other forces would blow the atmosphere away almost as quickly as it could be generated.

"Okay, people." She opened up a link to everyone else across the tactical network and to the open air for the benefit of the *Tetanna*'s security people who'd arrived as they were setting up. "We're going to have to breach the flight deck and take the enemy ship if possible. Expect heavy resistance. It's a safe bet that they won't be rolling out the welcome mat."

A few people chuckled nervously.

"We've not been able to get a good look at the enemy ships to this point, unfortunately," she continued, "and I don't expect this time to be any different."

The Marines nodded. They all knew how casual the Imperials had been so far with self-destruct systems, so none of them wanted to be caught on that deathtrap. Not until the enemy fleet was well out of transmission range, at least, and even then only under protest.

"That's why we want that hulk *away* from the *Tetanna* before they realize we're kicking their ass," she said firmly, eyes falling on one of her Marines. "Lieutenant Hadrian, I'm going to need you and a couple of volunteers to go with our Priminae friends here to ensure that happens. Blow it from the hull if you can, but however you do it, get it away from the ship."

"Yes ma'am." The young officer nodded. "You can count on me."

"No doubt in my mind, Lieutenant," she said firmly, turning to the rest. "We get the easy job. The lieutenant and his team are going to need cover and someone to watch their backs, because the Imperial infiltration team *is* going to be showing up, probably at the worst possible moment. We get to greet them when they get here. Got me?"

"Oorah, ma'am," the Marines all roared, startling the Priminae security people, who quickly shied away from the rest as they looked on with clear discomfort.

Conner just smiled in her armor. They could think her Marines were crazy all they liked. That just made the Marines feel right at home.

CHAPTER 20

▶ The *Odysseus* shuddered as another laser strike burned through her armor, venting atmosphere in an explosive burst of energy.

Eric gripped his seat, trying not to look as pissed off as he actually was at the moment. They'd been exchanging blows with the Imperial forces for the last twenty minutes as the *Odysseus* and their Priminae allies closed the range and pressed in to keep the pressure on the enemy, but it was costing them dearly.

One of the Priminae vessels—he didn't know the name—had been disabled after a blow was deep enough to destabilize the core. They had dropped out of the chase, and from what he could tell over the chatter he was monitoring, they were about to abandon ship as the core was proving impossible to stabilize.

The *Odysseus* herself was bleeding air from more holes in her hull, but not as bad as she had been. The repair crews were rushing from one breach to the next, patching them up faster than the Imperials could put holes in her, but he still felt every hit.

Most of his people were stationed deep inside the powerful vessel, out of the reach of all but the worst strikes, so the only losses had been from the damage control teams. But those were bad enough to make him want to bleed the enemy out with his bare hands.

Worse, those teams were still reporting ghosts and phantom sounds in the evacuated sections of the ship.

He wanted nothing more than to get down there himself and find out what was going on, but nothing would pry him from the command station of his ship during a battle. Ghosts might be from that general vicinity, but they weren't remotely close enough to qualify.

For all that, though, he was starting to get truly worried.

It didn't sound like they were dealing with bad air or any sort of chemical action at this point. Whatever it was, the delusion—if it was a delusion—was too widespread, and nothing showed up on any of the scans the doctor had conducted of the affected personnel.

Normally he'd pull those people, shut down the affected sections, and just ride it out until he could get the ship into a port where a dedicated team could tear the decks down panel by panel to get to the source of the problem. Given that they were in the middle of a *battle*, however, he couldn't lose those people. He needed them doing their jobs if anyone on board was going to make it out of the situation intact.

I miss my old ship, Eric lamented silently.

Even one of the Rogues would be a welcome respite from the slugging match they were engaging in. Go deep and just start picking the enemy off from the black—though Eric had noted that, unfortunately, the Imperials had adapted more quickly than he would have preferred to those tactics.

The use of chaff to disrupt pulse torpedoes had been the obvious solution, true, but the Imperials had implemented it quickly and efficiently after dealing with those weapons on only one occasion.

That did not bode well for the future of the conflict the Earth now found herself in.

A smart, ruthless, and *adaptable* enemy was not what they needed to be dealing with now. In any fair and sane universe, they'd have been due a break after the Drasin, but as he was well aware and as every Marine learned early in their careers, the universe was neither fair nor sane.

A warning light blinked, drawing his attention, and Eric noted that the ship had closed the range to within five light-seconds. Effectively, they were within knife range for their weapons. If the enemy turned on them now, the fight would be as swift as it was brutal.

"How much power are you sitting on, Steph?" he asked suddenly, catching the attention of the entire command crew as they waited to hear what the commodore had in mind.

"In theory, Raze? Got another twenty I can push," Steph answered in that detached voice of a man plugged into the NICS interface to the *Odysseus*. "I can only promise ten, though, maybe twelve. Past that, we might just shake this gal apart."

"Well, when I give the order, shake her apart if it comes to that," Eric said.

Silence settled across the bridge, everyone shooting glances from their stations and displays to the commodore, then over to the pilot, as they waited for the response.

"Roger that, Raze. You want it, you got it." Steph reached out and flipped a few old-style switches that had been retrofitted by the engineering department since the invasion. He'd never been comfortable with the smooth-touch panels, not to the degree that he wanted them wrapped around him. "What's the plan?"

"Blitz on my word," Eric said simply.

A low whistle came from the pilot's pit. "You gonna sell that one to our backup?"

"I'll be happy if they don't shoot us in the back, if I'm being frank," Eric said softly, instantly regretting it. "Commander, do me a favor and strike that from the record, will you?"

"Yes sir."

He nodded gratefully to Heath.

"I'm getting tired. How long have we been at battle stations?" he asked.

"Almost twelve hours, Commodore," Heath said. "It's been a long day."

Twelve hours. Eric groaned.

Twelve hours of tension, punctuated only by minutes of terror, was not a recipe for maintaining one's mental faculties.

He looked around the bridge, noting the stiff, sometimes slumping postures of the men and women surrounding him. They were all on edge, and he knew they could keep going longer if need be, but it would be better to end this as quickly as he could.

Unfortunately, the only out he saw at the moment involved opening a hole and letting the enemy escape. Any other attempt was likely to end only one way, and that was with mass destruction on both sides. That might have been acceptable if Eric thought that he could at least eliminate the enemy entirely, but the numbers just didn't come down on his side.

Worse, the loss of a single ship would probably hurt Earth far more than the loss of this entire squadron would bother the Empire.

"I'm going to signal the others," he said. "We'll blitz them when they move to recover their ship. Keep them busy so they don't have a chance to cut up the *Tetanna*, then try to harry them out of the system. Work your numbers, Steph. It's going to be a nasty furball."

"Been running the vectors for the last hour, Raze," Stephanos answered from the pit. "Knew it was going to come down to this. There was no other option, really."

"Wish there was," Eric said honestly. "Shoot your numbers over to the other ships."

He glanced over at the telemetry and noted that the squadron was close enough now for real-time communications across all the ships. A touch to the panel in front of him linked his station to the other ships in the squadron, the captains of each appearing in a split display in front of him . . . aside from the captain of the *Kid*, he noted silently as they acknowledged his signal.

How many men and women will follow them before this is over?

"Commodore." Jason Roberts nodded curtly to the screen. "Good to see you back in the fight. Any idea what that was all about?"

Eric shook his head, knowing the man was referring to the malfunction. "Not yet. Some odd things happening over here, but we seem to have a handle on it for the moment."

Hyatt raised an eyebrow. "Odd things?"

"Stories for another time," Eric told her. "If we get through this, there are more than a few drinks that will be bought and sold based on what's been going on here. For now, however, we don't really have the time."

His two flag captains agreed quickly.

"So what's the plan, Commodore?" Hyatt asked him.

"We'll blitz them as they move to recover their men, but I want to leave a hole for them to withdraw through."

"Letting them go?" Roberts asked with the barest hint of humor. "That's not the captain I remember."

"These people are not the Drasin," Eric answered honestly. "I'm half hoping they can be taught, but, failing that, I'd rather they not get into the mindset that every fight with us is to the death. Bad precedent to set, a little like shooting lifeboats or parachutes. Don't ever want to be the guy who sets that sort of habit in motion if it can be avoided."

"Understood," Roberts said.

"Besides, if we corner them, they'll have to turn on us," Eric said, sighing. "And we all know how we would fare if that happened."

The captains all nodded soberly from the split display. For all the severe damage they could inflict on the enemy fleet, no one questioned what the ultimate outcome would be. If the gravity fields of the cruisers didn't scramble the t-cannon shells when they reverted to normal space, it would be different; they could just stand off and blow the enemy out of space from twenty light-minutes out.

Without that trump card, however, and with the pulse torpedoes having limited effectiveness, they only had lasers and HVMs. Even on that level, Eric believed that the Terran vessels swung above their weight class, but in the end, numbers still counted.

While traced to many apocryphal sources, the idea that quality versus quantity generally favored quality had some truth to it, but it was also very true that quantity had a quality all its own.

The last thing we want to do here is replay the Eastern Front of World War II, casting ourselves in the role of the Germans.

The enemy had so far shown too little care for its own people *not* to have enough of them to literally burn. No matter how ruthless you were, you didn't self-destruct and murder your own crewmembers unless there were a lot more back home. Trained people were just too valuable, in Eric's estimation, and if anything about the Empire terrified him, it was that they considered those same specialists to be disposable.

It wasn't just a measure of morality—though he refused to discount that—but more one of military practicality. If Earth were to treat her people with anywhere *near* the same disregard, they'd run out of specialists within a year. Even forgetting how hard it would be to recruit properly trained people, which wasn't something to discount, it took *time* to establish those sorts of skills. Earth could only train so many in a year, and the Empire had killed hundreds of their own people with casual disregard.

That spoke either of far more people than Earth had access to, which seemed likely from what he'd seen of the Priminae population, but perhaps also of superior training methods. If they could churn out more people as needed, trained and experienced in their positions, then treating them so casually might make sense in terms of raw numbers.

In either case, Eric didn't want a knockdown, drag-out war with an Empire that had either possibility.

Not until we can find a way to counter them, at least.

▶ ▶ ▶

▶ "Am I cleared for duty?"

Doctor Rame spared the chief an exasperated look but still sighed audibly. "Yes, Chief, you're clear for duty."

"Good. I have work to do. Those damn Imperials are poking more holes in *my* ship."

"Just report any more . . . incidents immediately," Rame said firmly. "While I do not believe you were hallucinating, I want as many data points as I can manage just to be certain."

"If I figure out who's been spooking my teams, I swear I'm going to . . ." Dixon trailed off as a flash of gold flitted by his peripheral vision, and he spun around.

Rame eyed him for a moment as the engineer looked in all directions. "Are you alright, Chief?"

"Fine, fine," Dixon said warily. "Just thought I saw . . ." He closed his eyes. "No. Never mind. I've got work to do."

Rame watched him suspiciously as he left, but let the man go without comment. He waited a couple of beats before he walked over to the intercom and flipped the switch. "Bridge."

It took a moment before a reply came back, but he had time now, so he waited patiently until the commander's voice came back.

"Yes, Doctor?"

"I've finished examining the Marines and damage control team members," he said. "No signs of any chemical or biological agents. Similarly, their blood workups were clean. No excess CO_2 or the like in their system. I find it highly unlikely that they were hallucinating, Commander."

"Where does that leave us?" Heath asked, a hint of bewilderment in her voice.

"I'm afraid, Commander, that isn't my department. I have no idea what they're seeing or hearing. I'm just relatively certain that it isn't all in their heads."

"Relatively certain?"

"Commander, we're on a starship a thousand light-years from Earth engaging an alien empire in combat. 'Relatively' is as good as you're going to get."

Heath exhaled. "Understood, Doctor. Thank you."

"Not at all, Commander. I've cleared the chief and his people for duty, by the way, so I would be expecting them to start logging time shortly."

"Well, I can't say we don't need them," Heath said. "You might want to prep for trouble, by the way, Doctor. The captain has a plan."

"Oh dear."

▶▶▶

▶ Dixon stalked into the ready room, eyes falling on the men and women who were waiting there.

"Well?" he demanded. "What are you waiting for? Suit up!"

They scattered as they headed for their environmental gear, leaving Dixon to follow with a great deal less enthusiasm than he'd pretended. He didn't know what the hell he had been seeing, but whenever he paused for a moment, that flash of gold and something like a child's laughter—or sobbing again—continued to plague him.

Dixon wasn't married, didn't have any kids he was aware of, but he could now say without any doubt people who claim that a child's laughter was a beautiful thing had never heard it while standing on a pitch-black, airless deck in the middle of combat.

Then he saw the flash of gold and resisted the urge to spin around to catch what it was. He knew he wouldn't be fast enough.

Just get to work. Do the job. Forget this bullshit stuff until I can lay my hands around the neck of whoever is pulling this crap. Just get to work, do the job.

That became something of a mantra for him as he suited up, pulling the helmet on but not sealing it as he met up with the rest of the team who'd done much the same.

"Alright, the decks we'll be working on for now have been sealed up, but that doesn't mean they're safe yet. We won't need suit air, but keep a close watch on your pressure gauges. If the atmo starts dropping or you get an oxygen warning, I don't care what you're doing, you stop and seal your helmets. Got it?"

Everyone nodded.

"Let's go."

▶▶▶

▶ The *Odysseus* was executing basic evasion maneuvers, though now that they'd closed to less than five light-seconds, the value of such was growing less by the passing moment.

Beams from the enemy vessels sliced through space, most missing, but the occasional hit scored a shudder through the target as armor was ablated despite the adaptive coating that reduced the effectiveness of energy weapons.

In turn, the *Odysseus* and Allies returned the favor with their own beam weapons and occasional HVM salvos. While the enemy was holding course, tied to their action by circumstance and need, they had successfully interposed and interlocked their gravity bulges at the rear of each vessel into an unpredictable warping of space-time that had the effect of turning aside light itself.

Lasers from the *Odysseus* Task Force and Priminae allies were bent aside, most scattering out to space to be uselessly attenuated against far vaster background energy signatures of the cosmos. A few banked off the unpredictable warpings of space-time, deflecting from one warp to another and then on up the skirt of the retreating warship unlucky to catch the fury of the mind-bending power of the beam.

Unfortunately, even in those cases, the best effect of the Terran-designed adaptive frequency laser was negated as they couldn't hold the beams long enough to find the right absorption frequency.

So the war of maneuver, even if it had occasionally been an unintended and quite insane maneuver, had been reduced to a slugging match between giants.

Eric Weston was not amused.

He had little choice in the matter as the two groups of vessels continued to close on the stricken Priminae warship.

Little choice but to haul back and let loose with another haymaker, hoping to land a hit.

▶▶▶

▶ Chief Dixon looked around as he heard the clicking whine of the *Odysseus* laser capacitors discharging.

It was a distinctive sound, and it was louder than he expected it to be.

"Someone check the insulation panels along the forward capacitance coils," he ordered. "The explosive decompression probably blew a few of them loose, if not right out into space."

Tracking down all the little things that had been blasted around by the windstorm on this deck when the breach occurred would take days, and there was no way to know how much debris was blown right out of the ship when everything decompressed. Dixon suspected that a lot of office supplies were about to go missing, whether they were actually sucked out of the ship or not.

Not that he cared, frankly, but the thought amused him to a certain degree as he walked the corridors along the forward section that housed a fifth of the ship's deep capacitance systems.

While the cores provided an insane level of power, lasers required more power on demand than even they could readily provide in the instant they had to be released. So the capacitance system drew energy off from the cores and, on command, fed them into the lasers in a span of time measured in milliseconds.

Power enough to run the entire Confederation for a day, all dumped into a single instant of hellish energy.

And the *Odysseus* fired dozens of beams every few minutes.

Sometimes the numbers were enough to stagger even Dixon.

He put those thoughts from his mind, however, as he located a few open sections of wall where the insulating panels had been blown clear. Unfortunately, they weren't anywhere to be found in the local area, so he opened a link to the quartermaster's depot.

"Hey, Chief Dixon here. Yeah. We're going to need . . . oh, four, five . . . oh damn it, just send up a palette of insulation panels. The decompression wreaked all holy hell up here, and I don't know where they wound up. Might find them later, I suppose. Right, thanks."

He closed the connection and finished walking the length of the corridor to check down the junctions. The clicking whine was louder as the lasers discharged with regular timing, and Dixon was just glad that everything seemed to still be in fighting trim despite the general havoc that had rained down on the deck.

He was about to go back down to meet the palette he'd called for when an unfortunately familiar sobbing sound sent shivers across his skin, and he slowly turned around.

A hint of motion and a glint of gold caught his eye as something vanished around the corner up ahead.

"The hell?" Dixon grumbled, hating both that someone was messing with him and, more so, that it was *working*. "Oh screw it."

He pulled the sidearm from his hip and started down the hall, following the sound of soft laughter. At the junction, he pressed against the wall before risking a glance around the corner. When he saw nothing, he broke cover and started down the corridor, gun leading the way.

He turned on his open-air comm. "I don't know who's down here, but come out, or I swear I'll fill you full of holes when I find you."

The laughter stopped for a moment, a soft whispery voice drifting back in response to his challenge. "Too late."

"Okay, fuck you, whoever is doing this!" Dixon snarled, gun sweeping ahead of him as he walked. "Just you wait. I will find you, and you'll *wish* I only keelhauled your ass when I do."

The giggling returned in force, but this time behind him.

Dixon spun around, his gun seeking a target.

"Whoa, Chief!"

Barely restraining himself from firing as the Marines approaching dived for the ground, Dixon jerked the weapon up to the ceiling.

"What are you jokers doing here?" he shouted.

"Checking on you, Chief," one of the Marines said from the ground. "Can we get up?"

Dixon stared blankly at them for a moment but didn't say anything as another figure approached around the corner.

"What the hell are you lot doing on the ground?" the gunny yelled, looking down at the men on the deck, his body language screaming disgust.

"Trying not to be ventilated, Gunny."

The gunny looked up at the Chief, then to the pistol in his hand. "What did they do this time, Chief?"

"Hey!"

"Shut up, Marine," the gunny growled, walking through the men on the ground to stand beside the chief. He switched his comm over to a private channel. "You okay, Chief?"

"Yeah." Dixon lowered his weapon, sliding it back into the holster. "Just a little freaked out."

"Same thing?"

Dixon just nodded.

The gunny was silent for a bit. "One of my Marines was so damn spooked, he almost fragged his own team. I don't know what this is about, but we need to figure it out. This can't stand, especially not while the captain is trying to fight this beast."

"You don't need to tell me that, Gunny. Whatever it is, I have a job down here that can't be put off," Dixon said. "I'm not letting some damn spook scare me off."

"Spook, Chief?"

"I don't know what it is. Looks short, can't be five feet tall, wearing some kind of golden armor. Old-school stuff too. I mean like out of the history books old."

"That lines up with what my Marine reported. He said it looked a kid bleeding pretty bad. Something out of a horror movie crossed with a history documentary."

"I don't believe in ghosts," Dixon said unconvincingly, "but if this keeps up, I'm honestly going to start wondering if this ship is haunted."

"You know better than that, Chief. Someone is messing with us," the gunny said firmly. "We figure out who, then we make them wish they were never born."

"I'm right there with you on that," Dixon said with feeling. "Trust me."

The gunny nodded, swapping back to the common channel. "Alright, Chief, I'm going to assign a team to watch your back. I know they can be annoying at times, but I'd like them back without any extra holes in them, okay?"

"I'll do my best."

The Marines shifted and looked at each other as the gunny walked past them.

"If you have to shoot someone, Greg here has been a pain lately," he said over his shoulder with a gesture at a private. "Aim for him."

▶▶▶

▶ With less than five light-seconds between the *Odysseus,* her allies, and the Imperial squadron, the numbers seemed to be falling faster with every passing moment.

Eric found himself leaning forward in his station, eyes on the big display ahead, waiting for the moment. He didn't know quite when it would show itself, but he knew it was coming. The enemy had tied themselves to a vulnerable maneuver, and even though they held the numerical advantage, he knew that they would have to open the formation and slow their acceleration as they prepared to retrieve their ship from the *Tetanna*.

"There," he said suddenly. "Do you see it, Steph?"

"Got it, Raze. It's small," Steph warned.

Eric smiled nastily. "Go for it."

In the pit, Steph matched his smile, though it went unnoticed. Only Eric knew it was there, and he knew it from the trust of long experience working with the younger man.

"Aye aye, Skipper," he said, sinking deeper into the gestalt he felt with the ship through the NIC System. Steph idly opened a fleet-wide comm. "All ships, *Odysseus* is going active. Cover us; we're going in."

Then he pushed the ship's reactors back to the redline and beyond as the general quarters and combat alarms began to sound on every deck.

The *Warrior King* was going into battle one more time.

CHAPTER 21

▶ "Get back!"

Rider snarled as he yanked Dow out of the way by the armor, just as a beam cut through and splashed off the wall behind them.

The Marine looked up from the ground, his faceless helm not showing any emotions, but his body language screaming everything.

"Thanks, boss," Dow gasped as he watched Rider break cover briefly to fire a burst down the corridor.

"Don't mention it," Rider said as he ducked back just ahead of another pair of beams vaping chunks out of the ceramic corridor bulkheads. "Just learn to duck on your own. I won't be here every time."

"Wilco, boss."

Rider let out a breath, noticing that his suit's thermostat was starting to climb despite the cooling tech being turned up as high as it would go. The exterior air was best compared to an oven, and the temperature wasn't getting any lower with the constant barrages of lasers from the defending Imperials.

"Well," he said, "we're pinned down good and tight, but on the flip side, I'd say we've slowed their advance nicely. Hope the colonel can do something with it, because we're going no farther unless something changes."

"Anyone have any smokers left?" Dow asked from where he was crouched.

The Marines all shook their heads.

"No, we blew our last one ten minutes ago," Kensey said. "Down to my last frag too, and my ammo's not much better."

"Same here," Ram spoke up, "and I think my suit is about to cook me. Not feeling too good, Rider."

Rider ducked into the other Marines' armor code, checking the suit telemetry on his own HUD.

"Shit, Ram! You need to pull back. Your armor is about to boil off its coolant, and once that's gone, you're toast in that thing."

"I can hold on a bit longer," Ramirez said stubbornly.

Rider grimaced, but he didn't challenge the other Marine on that, though he didn't really think it was true. They were all about to cook, in fact, and Ram's condition wasn't much worse than his own. He was sweating profusely in the armor, and his own coolant had started to boil a few minutes earlier.

Even so, he had a little while before he would pass out from heatstroke, but not as long as he might need. *We have to get this done.*

A quick look at the rest of the team showed that they were all in the same boat, unsurprisingly. The Marine armor Mark IIV wasn't meant to deal with this sort of prolonged heat. They had additional cooling packs for extreme environments, but no one had thought them necessary for the mission, and they likely would have gotten in the way when traveling through the ship's corridors.

"Well, the longer we can hold this position, the more time the colonel has to drop her surprise on these pricks," he said to the others, "but I'm guessing we've got *maybe* ten minutes before the first of us passes out. Probably less. I figure Kensey is out in three."

"Hey!" he objected amid chuckles from the other three.

"So the question becomes," Rider continued, "how long do we push this? If we all pass out here, we'll likely be dead of heatstroke before anyone finds us."

The Recon Marines looked at each other briefly.

"Fuck it," Dow said. "I'm in to the end."

"Ditto," Ram said simply.

"I ain't passing out first," Kensey said, gripping his weapon.

Rider grinned humorlessly under his helm. "Alright. Last person standing gets to drag the rest back to somewhere cooler—and all his drinks are paid for next time we're home. Deal?"

"Hell yeah," Dow shouted.

"Recon, oorah!" Ramirez said simply.

"Damn right," Rider said, taking a breath. "Recon!"

"Oorah!"

▶▶▶

▶ Half Centure Leif fell back as the volume of fire thickened from the forces they'd pinned down. He thought he and his troop were wearing them down, but now it appeared that reinforcements had arrived to solidify the position.

Well, you are welcome to it. We just want off this hulk.

"Keep them pinned in place," he ordered the men covering the area. "We are almost through to the flight deck."

"Yes Centure," the closest acknowledged instantly, firing another burst of energized photons down the range.

He didn't hit anything, but that wasn't the point. Once they broke through to the flight deck, they just had to hold the corridor for a few minutes at most, then it would be all over.

A call from the laser crews cutting through the bulkhead shifted his focus, and Leif headed over to survey the progress. As he'd expected, they were practically through, though the integrity of the Oather ceramic bulkheads was an annoyance. They didn't transfer heat well, and the energy required to vaporize material was obscene.

The Imperial infantry lasers were up to the task, however, but as they weren't designed to burn continuously, the process took longer than it would have with an industrial cutter. They had to stagger bursts so the material wouldn't cool down between blasts, taking coordination and time.

Coordination was something they had plenty of. Leif had drilled his team constantly since being put in charge, but time was now of the essence.

"We have opened up the hole, Centure," the chief in charge of the cutters told him as he approached. "It will take just a little longer to make the aperture large enough to pass."

"Good work," Leif praised him. "Hurry them along as you can. We are being pressured from the rear now."

"Understood, Centure. I will see it done."

▶▶▶

▶ "Colonel, check this out."

"What is it, Sergeant?" Conner asked, shifting her focus to his feed.

"Check thermal."

Conner flipped over to the thermal filters on the feed and whistled softly.

Ceramic was a poor conductor of heat, so for a section of the bulkhead to be *that* hot meant they were almost through.

"Alright, boys and girls," she said softly over the team channel, "get ready because here they come. Lieutenant, tell me you're making progress. You are about to run out of time."

▶▶▶

▶ Lieutenant Hadrian paused from where he and the rest of his team were working on the security seals on the airlock the Imperials had used to connect to the ship.

"Almost there, Colonel. Keep them off us, and we'll get this done."

The colonel's voice was tense when she responded. "We'll do what we can."

Hadrian turned back to the Marines and the Priminae security troop who were working on cracking the airlock. "Better step it up. We've got company on the way."

"We are almost through," the Priminae security chief said firmly. "Their code is antiquated, but familiar. I'm surprised they're still using these systems. It's clearly based on something we consider a historical curiosity."

"Weak security?" Hadrian asked, a little surprised and more than a little suspicious.

"Oh no. Quite strong," the chief corrected. "Vicious, even. If you make an error while unlocking, the system is designed to retaliate rather violently. That's the weak point, however." The chief hummed lightly. "Aside from moral concerns, using lethal defenses means that you can't employ more complex security. Otherwise, you'll kill more of your own people than any possible enemies. I do not know how it is with you Terrans, but I have never met a crewman who could remember his security code the first time he entered it."

Hadrian tipped his head slightly. "Fair point."

"That should do it, sir," the Priminae crewman said as the heavy lock began to turn.

"Everyone back," the chief ordered, taking a step back himself, just in case someone had made an error.

The lock swung open like nothing more than an old bank vault door as far as Hadrian could determine. Big, heavy metal creaked slowly on an equally big and heavy hinge. He gestured, bringing three Marines forward.

They led with their rifles, clearing through the lock as soon as it opened enough for an armored Marine to pass. The interior was open and clear, and a moment later, the Marines had it secured. The rest followed them in.

"Now is the dangerous part," the security chief confessed, taking a breath as he looked over the last section. "We're inside their . . . what do you call it? A kill perimeter?"

"Close enough," Hadrian said, shivering as he considered the statement.

As a kill box, the airlock was a potentially superb one, to say the least.

"Get it open." He nodded to the far end. "Try not to set it off."

"Right." The Priminae security staff got to work.

They'd already bypassed the security they'd found—pretty standard cameras and microphones, albeit very sophisticated tech versions of those. Less standard were the tremblers, atmospheric scanners, what seemed to be multispectral systems, and a few items that Hadrian didn't really know the names for.

He was just glad to have the Priminae security people working to bypass all of that, because without them, he was quite certain that his squad would have tripped at least half a dozen systems by this point.

Hell, who am I kidding? We'd have tripped all of them and just gambled on using a breaching charge.

Win or lose, the battle would already have been over if he and his Marines had the lead.

That said, Hadrian could be patient.

He tightened his grip on his weapon, the big rifle oversized for his pilot's environmental gear. Unlike the light augmentation armor the rest of the Marines had, Hadrian's kit was designed more for catastrophic loss of pressure while he was strapped to his shuttle. While armored to a degree, the suit was meant to prevent perforations from shrapnel as opposed to enemy fire.

Granted, against the infantry lasers the enemy was intent on firing, that wouldn't make much difference. Man-portable armor, light or heavy, would vaporize all the same under the hellish heat.

His own infantry weapon, the Marine issued M-45, was designed to be held by augmenting armor, however. The chunky weapon felt like a slab of solid steel in his grip, threatening to pull his arms right off the longer he held it, but Hadrian refused to acknowledge the weight as he stood there and waited for the Priminae to do their part.

"We're through," the security chief whispered, stepping aside.

"Go, go, go!" Hadrian hissed, slapping his team on the shoulder as they rushed passed him, then following as he wrenched his rifle up to his shoulder.

He was a Marine, by God. Infantryman first, pilot distant second. Oorah.

▶▶▶

▶ "Here they come," Conner said as the remaining barrier between decks finally turned black, smoking briefly before vanishing in a brief puff of flame.

The first man stepped through almost instantly. The ceramic bulkheads they'd cut through didn't hold the heat for any length of time to force them to wait.

"Check your fire, clear the lines," Conner ordered as she watched the scene from multiple views on her HUD, every Marine's armor feed linked back to her own. "Sergeant, I don't want any friendly fire incidents. Secure the right flank. They're looking a little shaky."

"Roger that, ma'am," the sergeant said as he shifted slightly and dropped off her command comm line to pass on her orders, likely with more profanity.

The flank tightened up, though, so she didn't care what he'd said. It worked.

Three Imperials were through the breach then, another two appearing behind them. They were coming through slower than she'd predicted or even hoped, really. Their commander was pushing them less than she'd expected.

"Signal from the breach, Colonel," the sergeant pointed out, highlighting a separate comm channel.

Conner frowned, but popped it up on her HUD and took a few seconds as she realized that she was looking at the other side of the enemy formation as her recon team engaged them from the rear. They were laying on the fire double thick, and it only took another couple of seconds for her to realize just why.

"Recon team," she said, "disengage from the enemy. Try to make it look like they forced you back. We're in position; you did your job. We'll take it from here."

"Oorah, ma'am," Rider responded. "We weren't sure you'd made it. Disengaging now. You heard the colonel, boys. Start making it look like we're out of ammo."

"That won't be hard," Dow's voice replied, echoing over the command channel through Rider's suit.

Conner could safely say that he wasn't kidding on that front. The munitions report on the four Recon Marines left her surprised that they were still pushing the fight as they had. In the tight but relatively uncovered terrain of the ship's corridors, their options were limited once the guns ran dry. She knew her Marines were game, but you'd have to be out of your Goddamn mind to be crazy enough to try to close to melee range against the infantry lasers the other side was fielding, at least if you didn't have any smokers left.

"Everyone check fire," she ordered again. "Let them through. I want them in the kill box."

Her Marines didn't respond, but they didn't have to. She knew they'd heard her, and the fact that no one was shooting yet was good enough for her anyway. The volume of fire she was observing, and now hearing, from the other side of the enemy formation slowed and began to peter out in uneven bursts and silences.

In a few moments, the deck of the Priminae ship fell silent as her Marines steadied themselves behind the cover they'd been able to grab on the cluttered flight deck. Boxy Priminae shuttles were now sheltering

Marines and Priminae security forces alike as they all waited for the order.

A half dozen Imperials appeared through the breach, then an even dozen.

Conner watched them from the other side via her recon team's armor scanners, counting off how strong the enemy forces were now.

She was surprised to find that they were closer at this point to a real parity of force, despite her low numbers. Granted, she wasn't confident that the Priminae security would really balance the scales as well as their numbers might indicate, but even with that caveat, she was starting to think that they had a real chance.

Rider and his team did good.

Twenty of the Imperial troops were on their side of the breach then, and Conner surreptitiously checked the limited data she had from the other side.

It was time.

"Open fire."

▶▶▶

▶ The fusillade of firepower from the supposedly clear flight deck cut down half a dozen of his men before Leif could blink, the rest scattering for cover to either side as they dived to the ground and rolled or crawled behind whatever they could manage.

They got ahead of us! Damn! The pursuers were just a distraction.

He probably should have been more surprised—or less, he supposed— but it didn't make much difference. He'd royally fouled up, and how he should feel about it didn't make the slightest bit of difference.

"Fire team, secure the breach. Cover the people on the other side," he ordered, striding across the corridor and firing a burst back down the hall in the direction of the team that had pursued his troop, just to keep them from getting any ideas. "Contact the ship. We should be able to punch through any jamming now that we're this close."

Getting control of his people before the ambush turned into a rout was the only thing left to do, and he refused to foul *that* up.

He was surprised that the volume of fire from the rear had dropped off. If he were in charge of that maneuver, he'd push all the harder now.

Why are they not? Leif wondered, confused. He felt like he was missing something, forgetting some important detail, but couldn't work out what it was, and that was driving him to near distraction.

"I have the landing vessel, Centure," a field tech said.

"How is the signal?"

"Strong at this range."

"Good. Check if they are in contact with the squadron."

"Yes Centure."

There was more than one way to win a war, even if the battle was going against you.

▶▶▶

▶ The fluorescing afterimages of laser bursts etched themselves onto the retinas of everyone in the bay as beams crossed paths with bullets. Chaos reigned supreme as the mad minute overtook everyone in the way it usually did.

Marine fire teams covering behind alien shuttles laid down interlocking fields of fire, turning the other end of the bay into a kill box while Imperial troops cut those shuttles apart with return fire that slagged through whatever it hit with near impunity.

In sixty seconds of the open firefight, the bay temperature jumped fifteen degrees, and there was no end in sight as more and more energy was poured into the enclosed environment from both sides.

A scream of metal and scratch of fiber caused a Marine fire team to pull back from cover just as the shuttle they were using collapsed on their position. All but two survived the ensuing retreat under fire to the next cover point, but those two were little more than carbon-scorched embers after a direct hit burned their shadows into the deck.

On the other side of the fight, a hail of depleted uranium rounds ruthlessly chopped through alien battle armor with vicious efficacy, tearing up the men and women within and leaving them to fall in heaps on the deck while their armor struggled valiantly to preserve their life functions.

Laser bursts from the Priminae security forces, though less powerful than their Imperial counterparts, cut the other direction and burned holes through cover that the Marines' weapons couldn't. In the insanity of the exchange, smoke and retina afterimages obscured everyone's vision, computer-aided systems or not, and by the end of the first mad minute, there wasn't a soul on either side who had any idea who was winning or who was losing.

Most of them didn't care, of course, and those who considered it even in passing fully expected to figure victory out by who was the last group standing.

That was the way of battle at times.

CHAPTER 22

▶ The navarch glowered as she tried to split her focus between the task ahead of the group and the enemy plaguing their trail. The enemy squadron had closed the range to the point where any slight error on either of their parts would leave an opening for the other to exploit. A masterful move on the enemy commander's part, assuming he was willing to risk heavy damages or total destruction to in turn cripple her forces—and he had made it quite clear that he was not only willing, but apparently *intent* on doing just that.

Her forces were his only focus, so he could reasonably expect to be safer from any lapse of focus than she could, with her necessarily split attentions. He was inviting her to make a mistake; there was no doubt about it.

Worse, she was about to do just that.

"The enemy vessel's position is almost upon us, Navarch."

"I see it," she rumbled softly to the navigator. "Stand by to initiate capture protocols. I want that ship and those men on board without delay. Am I understood?"

"As you command it, Navarch," her second pledged instantly before turning and snapping the appropriate orders.

Satisfied, Misrem turned her own focus in the opposite direction. She had no doubt that the commander of the task group now pursuing them would make full use of the moment her ships broke the interlocked warp formation, and when he did, things would become very fast, very deadly, very quickly.

She walked over to her tactical officer. "Watch for the enemy to take advantage of our maneuvering shift. They will move quickly. Do not wait for my orders. Engage the enemy as you can."

"As you order, Navarch."

The man looked uneasy with the directive, but she didn't care. He would have to accept the responsibility. If he couldn't, she would find someone who could.

"Breaking formation, Navarch," the navigation officer announced.

Mentally, Misrem started counting down the seconds as the ships under her command began to break and shift to a capture formation.

She was surprised when she barely got a full second over the light-second gap between her vessels and the pursuers when the tactical officer yelped.

"Enemy moving to engage, returning fire!"

They're good. They knew it was coming and were waiting. Impressive.

▶▶▶

▶ "They're breaking formation! Going to full military power. I see a break! Milla, are you with me?"

"I am with you, Stephan. Lasers and remaining missiles firing," Milla answered calmly, her tone not as detached as the pilot's, despite all his excitement, but far more subdued than his.

The *Odysseus* accelerated just ahead of her sister Heroics, the *Bell* and the *Bo* hot on her heels. The trio charged into the enemies' teeth as the formation ahead of them opened up with full lasers at near point-blank range.

"Armor adapting, Captain. They're coming fast, though. I do not believe we'll be able to continue this for long," Milla said immediately.

"We don't need long. Keep firing."

"Aye Capitaine."

The lights dimmed as every laser discharged, pulling power from their reserves, only to come back a moment later as the bridge systems drew directly from the cores.

On the screens, computer-aided simulations showed a crisscrossed cage of photons as the lasers from both the Allies and the Empire lit up the star system.

The *Odysseus* shuddered when lasers burned through the heavy armor of her bow, the attacks blunted by the forward gravity sink as Steph pushed the system to maximum military levels and urged them beyond. His demand for acceleration overruled protocol, best estimation, and common sense.

The pilot felt the *Odysseus* fight him again, but was ready for it this time and compensated instantly. He didn't know what was wrong with the ship he was driving, but now wasn't the time to take any crap from a recalcitrant starship.

"We've a fight to win, you heap," Steph mumbled under his breath. "You're the warrior king, damn it. Act like it."

He didn't know if the *Odysseus* heard him, but after that, Steph managed to wrestle the defiant systems of the immense starship back into playing nice.

"That's more like it. Let's show them what we've got," he whispered, grinning as the lasers fired under Milla's direction sliced through the exposed armor of one of the enemy destroyers, bringing light to the black.

Burning, purifying, righteous light.

▶▶▶

▶ "Hold steady," Aleska ordered, gripping the edge of her station for stability as the *Jánošík* shuddered again.

They hadn't been hit. Even with their armor adapting as fast as the combined gestalt of the Allied ship computers could manage, a direct hit would have done far more than send shakes and shudders through her baby.

They were, however, flying through the gravity wash of three large and pissed-off Heroic Class starships right into the teeth of an enemy fleet. She was counting her blessings, even if the lack of gravity controls meant that the Rogue destroyer was riding like a small ship in high seas.

Too much more of this, Aleska thought, *and I might even get seasick. Space sick? Oh, it hardly matters. It can't be any worse than transition sickness.*

She was grinning, and she knew it, but couldn't quite wipe what she expected was a more than slightly manic look from her face.

"Stand by the torpedoes," she ordered firmly over the creaks and groans of her ship's protesting hull and bulkheads. "I want to be right in their face this time. We'll see how well they handle a point-blank barrage. I'm willing to gamble that their little trick with the chaff won't be quite so effective this time around. If the enemy can learn from their mistakes, never let it be said that we can't match it and then teach them a new lesson."

"Aye aye, Skipper!" the big man standing the tactical watch responded with enthusiasm.

He was in better shape than most of her crew, who were alternating between looking at her and looking at the main telemetry plot with varying degrees of horror. Oh, they were doing their jobs, of course, or she'd lose her grin in short order and introduce them to some *real* horror, but it seemed that their hearts just weren't in it.

"That's the spirit, Lieutenant!" she told the tactical officer. "Hold for my orders. Not until you see the whites of their eyes, yes?"

"Yes ma'am." He matched her grin with one of his own, very nearly as manic.

She almost sighed but managed to maintain her enthusiasm. She would have to have words with the man. When the captain grinned like a maniac, there was a certain gravitas to the moment. When a lieutenant did it, it was really just sort of sad in a creepy way.

He'll learn, she supposed.

"Hold a little longer . . ." She put the thought aside as the ship bucked under her again.

Without the gravity cores of the larger Heroics, Rogue Class ships could get really bucked around in gravity waves. She'd read about some of the events surrounding the *Autolycus'* first voyage, and was surprised in her own way that the crew of that ship had managed with as few blunt-force trauma injuries as they had.

Of course, if *her* chief tried to detonate antimatter on board her ship, she'd feed him to his own reactors and be done with the man.

How Morgan puts up with that lunatic, I have no idea.

▶▶▶

▶ "Blast it, here they come!"

Misrem glanced over to where her second was stealing a look at the display showing the enemy assault from their rear and caught his eye with a glare.

"Pay attention to your own task and leave them to me!" she snapped, pointing to where the damaged Oather vessel was looming in the distance.

At the speed they were moving, they were now only moments from their only opportunity for capturing their boarding craft. If they over-shot, she was now convinced that it would take a clean sweep of every enemy ship in the system before they could come back around and attempt another try.

If they missed because her second was too busy trying to second-guess *her job*, he would have a rather cold reception upon their return to the Empire, assuming she allowed him to live that long.

"Secure all nonessential areas. Bring our people deeper into the ships," she ordered. "They're going to land a few blows before this is over, so let us mitigate the damage."

"Yes Navarch."

She ignored the acknowledgment, walking across to the tactics command officer and leaning in. "Your strikes are surprisingly light, Krin."

"I know." The man looked frustrated. "I do not understand it. We have analyzed the power of their weapons versus our own, and we have an edge, Navarch, but it is not translating into real-world results. We are missing variables, but I cannot be sure what they are."

"We know that they have superior armor," she said, "some reflective system that is more effective than any I have heard of, clearly."

"Perhaps," Krin said, "but that does not cover the whole of the story. Their strikes are landing harder than they should as well. If I didn't have the raw numbers right in front of me, Navarch, I would swear that they held a power advantage on their weapons as well."

She hissed. "Well that makes acquiring better intelligence on our foes even more of a priority. We will have to make certain that we do not miss our chance."

He looked at her seriously. "We must not miss, Navarch. There is too much here we do not understand. Without knowing more, a true Imperial incursion into this region is impossible to recommend."

She nodded reluctantly.

That was a fact she didn't want to acknowledge, but one that she couldn't deny either. Imperial Intelligence would veto a full incursion just based on the lack of solid data on the new species, whoever they were. Without knowing more, the Empire could walk into anything, blindly, and take utterly ruinous casualties in the process.

Personnel, they could lose. There were plenty more available from any number of worlds, but ships had value. They could lose a few, even more than that, but each one was a real and noticeable investment of Imperial resources. Lose enough and even the normally blind senate would start to squawk in outrage, masking most of the outrage as complaints about casualties, of course, but that was just the way of politicians.

"We will not miss," she said firmly.

The Empire would not be stopped, not even slowed, not by her hand.

Yet Misrem knew that it wasn't entirely in her hand. The men on that damaged starship held the key now, and until they passed it along, her options were . . . limited.

▶▶▶

▶ In the small command deck of the boarding ship, Kiosha, the commander of record, paced in a circle, only pausing every few seconds to look over and see if any new information from the boarding team had become available.

The group, led by Half Centure Leif, had encountered heavier resistance than they'd calculated but had so far managed to execute the mission by the numbers. If not for the jamming that both sides were using, the commander was well aware that the mission would likely already be complete, with the vital data having been sent off to the navarch and the fleet withdrawing to regroup and analyze what they'd found.

That, unfortunately, or perhaps fortunately, in a twisted way, had yet to happen.

Fortunately, the commander supposed, because he was under no illusions concerning how valuable his ship was once that data was put on it. At best, the chances were very strong that the fleet would leave them to be captured. At worst, well, detonating the destruct charges on the Parasite this close to an already crippled cruiser was certainly one way to distract an overly sentimental foe.

He was in no hurry to find the answers at the end of it all, but if that was what the Empire demanded of him, then so be it.

In the meantime, however, he was hoping that the centure's team made it back to the ship as planned.

A hero's return, limited though it might be, was far superior to the alternatives.

"Commander!"

The panicked tone in his subordinate's voice did *not* bode well.

"What is it, Nil?" he asked, breaking his circle of pacing and crossing to the communications officer.

"Signal from the centure. They're under assault!"

The commander grimaced. "Unfortunate but hardly a surprise. Can they make it back?"

"Commander, you do not understand. They're under assault on the *flight deck*!"

That was not what he'd expected to hear, not at all. The commander twisted and glowered at the man standing at the security watch station. "You should have warned me that the deck had been taken!"

"There's nothing on my screens, Commander, I swear!" The man's protests sounded hollow to the commander's ears, and he stepped over to glare down at the screens himself.

He froze, noting there really *was* nothing on them.

"How is this possible?" he muttered, looking back up and over to the communication officer. "Can you confirm the centure is right?"

"Their trackers indicate that they're straddling the flight deck and an adjoining space that they burned through," Nil said. "Plus the centure confirmed this himself."

"Blast!" The commander paled, rushing to his own station and slapping his hand down on a communication control. "Security, we may have boarders! Search the ship; eliminate any intruders you find."

▶▶▶

▶ Lieutenant Hadrian tilted his head, frowning under his environmental suit.

"Do you guys hear that?" he asked the closest Marine.

The Marine nodded. "Activity, lots of it. Boots scraping the deck, armor scuffing the bulkheads. I'd say they know we're here."

"Damn!" Hadrian swore. "Oh well, it was good while it lasted. Gird up, boys. Trouble's come looking for us!"

"Already here, LT," a Marine snapped as a door swung open just ahead of him and an Imperial trooper in light armor stepped through the opening with as much a look of surprise on his face as Hadrian felt was probably mirrored on his own.

The closest Marine, thankfully, was less stunned by the sudden turn than his lieutenant and closed the distance in an instant. He slammed the butt of his rifle into the head of the Imperial, sending him thudding into the bulkhead as he leveled his carbine and opened fire through the door.

Hadrian assumed that the Marine could see something he couldn't and shouldered his own rifle, advancing as the others followed suit. The lead Marine dropped to one knee, opening room for Hadrian to fire over his head just as Hadrian arrived at his back to see a small squadron of Imperials finishing a mad scramble for cover.

Apparently, we weren't the only ones to be surprised by the encounter, Hadrian thought as he sighted down the optics of his weapon and opened fire.

Caught in the open, with little to no cover to rush to, the Imperial soldiers were on the short end of a very painful stick, and soon only the echoes of the fight were left rebounding through the hall.

"We have to move," Hadrian said firmly. "If they didn't know we were here before, they do now. Which way to the command deck?"

The Priminae security man nodded down the hall they'd just cleared. "If they build to similar specification as we do, and it seems they do, then it will be that way."

"You heard the man, let's move!"

"Oorah!"

Hadrian caught the confused look shot in his direction by the lightly armored security man and shrugged. "It's a Marine thing."

▶▶▶

▶ The commander of the boarding vessel snarled. Reports were still blank on whether they had boarders of their own, but losing contact with one of their security teams would seem to have stilled any doubt on that point.

He didn't know what the enemy wanted on his ship, though he didn't really need to know. They would try to either sabotage the vessel in the reactor rooms or come for the command center. Those were really the only two targets of value on his ship, and he was sitting on the highest value of the two.

"Issue weapons," he ordered, turning to the security officer standing watch at the back of the deck. "All command officers and all crew in sensitive areas."

"On your order, Commander," the man said stonily.

That acknowledgment was something of a dual-edged sword, the Commander knew. The security man was acceding to his order, certainly, but he was also setting the record as to who had issued it. Usually this was more of a formality, a tradition from older, simpler times.

This time, however, issuing weapons to many of the crew who might not be fully trustworthy, well, it took on a somewhat more sinister meaning.

The commander didn't care. He had more things to concern himself with at the moment, and the reactions of the officers' corps would only matter if they all lived through this.

▶▶▶

▶ Misrem growled as another series of bursts from high-level laser fire cut through one of her destroyers, leaving it drifting in nearly two separate pieces as the enemy continued to charge in. The three ships they'd tentatively identified as belonging to the anomaly species were leading the charge with their own destroyers in tow, while the Oather ships provided cover from the rear guard position.

It was a good strategy, but more important to her, it seemed to confirm the psychological split she had observed and further seemed to correlate the psychological predictions of Imperial Intelligence for the Oathers.

They *were* hesitant to engage, particularly without a strong showing of force on their own side. It was, or seemed to be, this new group that was urging them on, pushing them to be more aggressive.

We will need to deal with these unknowns first, then, and the Oathers will fall as expected once that has been accomplished.

Of course, as her own ships shook with the effect of a high-powered laser strike, Misrem was reminded that would not be so easy to accomplish.

"Shift sub squadrons to cover the main fleet," she ordered. "Focus available fire on the lead cruiser. We can deal with the rest when the lead vessel has been handled. They were the ones insane enough to charge us alone. Likely the others will be broken if the bravest among them is handled neatly."

"On your order, Navarch."

▶▶▶

▶ Beams hotter than the core of a star lanced out from the Imperial Fleet, all targeting the *Odysseus* herself as the big ship led the charge. Refractory displays brilliantly lit up the black as the big ship's armor valiantly worked to deflect the worst of the energy, but more than enough was absorbed to flash away her prow.

Many times more than enough.

The *Odysseus* shuddered in space, plasma plumes erupting from the holes burned through her, but the ship didn't falter this time. It didn't change course, didn't unexpectedly boost ahead.

She continued her charge as intended, implacable into the fire, with the cavalry riding right along behind her.

▶▶▶

▶ "The *Odysseus*, she can't take much more of this, Captain!"

Aleska didn't bother to respond. She could see that for herself. In her old duties, this would be unthinkable. A destroyer, or a hunter submarine might be a better description of her lovely Rogue, didn't use their primary as *cover*. The idea of a sub letting an aircraft carrier take this level of damage while sheltering behind the brute was simply unthinkable.

She held her tongue on the matter, though, both because it was her orders and because she saw no other real possibility.

"Hold," she ordered through clenched teeth. "Just . . . hold."

"Aye Captain," her weapons officer said reluctantly.

Aleska noticed, though he likely did not, that he'd dropped the "Skipper" honorific.

She didn't really blame him. She wasn't feeling much like the skipper right then herself.

The *Odysseus* was taking a horrific beating. Lasers that would have cut her lovely ship in two and then vaporized the remains were burning through decks of ablative armor, penetrating into the areas people worked and lived, wreaking an unholy carnage on the big ship.

It was almost enough to bring tears to her eyes, not that she would have ever come clean about that if it had.

"Captain, *please*." The ship's pilot was hunched over her controls.

Aleska didn't need to see her to know how she felt about things.

"Just a little closer," she said, stony-faced.

To flinch now would be to ruin the commodore's entire plan. And after the sacrifice his *Odysseus* was giving to put this plan into motion, that would be a crime greater than she was willing to contemplate.

The enhanced displays of the Rogue showed every detail, and many more than the human eye could see besides, as lasers struck the vessel. Atmosphere turned to plasma under the heat, escaping in a stream that looked more like something out of stellar cartography anomalies than real life. It was awesome, but more so because she knew the cost.

And then it was there.

The moment.

Aleska lunged forward in her position. "Now! All ahead flank, full military power to the drives!"

The maneuvering alarm sounded as the drives and counter-mass powered up, but if anyone had been foolish enough to be out of place when she gave the order, the siren would give them no time to correct the mistake.

The Rogue fired its reactors, *hard*, and darted out of the shadow of its big sister. Using the drive warp to pull them along faster, the craft curved around the *Odysseus*, spiraling under the laser beams and using the forward drive warp to sling themselves even more quickly and launch themselves into the face of the enemy.

"Ignore the destroyers," Aleska hissed. "I want the cruisers. Flush the tubes, fire *everything*."

Against the backdrop of the *Odysseus* burning in the black, the *Jánošík* was the first destroyer of five to unload everything they had against the enemy at point-blank range.

Starting with the pulse torpedoes.

CHAPTER 23

▶ "Veer to port," Eric ordered over the cheering as they watched the Rogues make their move. "Interpose our undamaged armor to take any further hits. All stations are weapons-free. Empty the tubes, burn out the capacitors, get someone out on the hull to throw *rocks* at them if you can find volunteers."

He paused, considering what he'd just said, then hurriedly cut off Steph, who was turning his head to speak.

"Volunteers *other* than Marines," he corrected firmly. "Navy boys shoot at ships, Steph. Marines shoot at people."

"Yes sir," the pilot said, sounding a little sullen at having had his smartass crack cut off.

Eric moved on. "Signal the *Bell* and the *Bo*. It's on them now."

"They already know, Commodore," Heath said, looking up. "They've begun their attack runs."

Eric glanced over to observe the enhanced telemetry that showed the two big cruisers break on either side of the *Odysseus*, their tremendous beams cutting swaths through the shield of smaller ships the enemy had thrown up around themselves in a last-ditch maneuver to cover their deceleration to rendezvous with the boarding vessel.

Fires were raging in deep space, something not normally considered possible, but in the muck he was looking at, Eric wouldn't have been surprised if there was, for a short time, enough atmosphere now leaking around them to hear someone scream.

He couldn't count how many ships were now burning or breaking up, or some variation of the two. Most impressive, though, was the *Jánošík*'s action. Apparently, Captain Aleska had a burning score to settle with the cruisers and hadn't wasted any of her punch on the small fry.

She'd unloaded her ship's entire compliment of firepower at point-blank range, right into the formation of cruisers to . . . spectacular results.

▶ ▶ ▶

▶ Misrem *almost* screamed as the blinding cores of antimatter tore through her cruiser fleet, ripping huge chunks of her ships into rapidly expanding gasses.

There had been no time to deploy countermeasures against the ships slung around the main cruiser. In the seconds it would have taken to issue the order, the havoc had been wrought.

What infuriated her most of all, however, was that she hadn't seen it coming.

She should have, she told herself. She really should have. In retrospect, the maneuver was obvious, and the fact that the lead ship was willingly taking the focus without any sign of demanding more cover or attempting to break contact should have made that clear.

Unfortunately, she'd underestimated the enemy commander and his people.

Again.

Now the fight would be even more bloody, though the outcome would still be the same. The only difference was that they would be able to mock her from the other side of life, and that irritated her more than it should have.

"Navarch! Problem from the boarding vessel."

She viciously suppressed another desire to scream, turning to look at her second with a glare to match the lasers her ship mounted.

"What sort of problem?" she demanded softly.

He apparently caught her tone, which made him somewhat more intelligent than she had come to believe, and paled.

"They have . . . uh, they have been boarded."

Misrem closed her eyes.

Forget screaming. She wanted to cry.

"They have what?" she asked softly, not believing what she had just heard.

"The commander of the vessel reports enemy forces on his ship."

"That *idiot*," she hissed. "What is the status of the team with the intelligence?"

"Cornered and pinned down just a short distance from the ship."

Misrem honestly wanted to shoot the imbecile just then, but since he was merely delivering news of stupidity, she forcibly restrained herself. The intelligence she wanted—*needed*—was sitting out there, just mere steps from her boarding vessel, and they were telling her that they had been *boarded*?

She took a couple of calming breaths, then issued orders to the defensive line with a few quick gestures to the command computer, hoping that they would not be doing anything stupid . . . er . . . while she was shifting her attention.

"Are we in contact with the boarding team?" she demanded as she strode across the command deck.

Her second swallowed but nodded jerkily. "Half Centure Leif has been in contact. He is attempting to punch a signal through with enough power to upload the captured data."

"Oh, he is? At least someone in that mess is thinking. Can we help him?"

She looked around when her second didn't respond quickly enough, eyes falling on the other officers who were doing poor jobs of pretending not to listen.

"Well? Anyone?"

Obviously hesitant, the engineering technician cleared his throat and received her full attention. He quailed slightly but then rallied as he shook his head.

"No, Navarch. We can overpower a signal from us to them, but that would only be useful if we wanted to send significant data to the half centure. I'm afraid that this is currently in his hands and no other."

Misrem curled her lips. "I was afraid you were going to say that."

▶▶▶

▶ Centure Leif flinched as a pressure wave blasted over him, likely enough to kill him outright were he not wearing armor. As it was, the shockwave was mildly noticeable, and his flinching was purely instinctive from the brief audio overload that had jolted him before his armor cut out the volume to preserve his hearing.

He ducked down on one knee, grabbing the back of the communications technician and pulling him back up from where he had thrown himself in a similar if somewhat exaggerated version of Leif's response to the explosion.

"Keep at it," he shouted at the young man. "I need a high-strength signal relay, and I need it *now!*"

The technician nodded in his suit, and may even have said something, but Leif had already shifted his focus as he saw four of his men retake their positions and pour more energy into the flight deck beyond their position.

"What is the situation?" he demanded as he made his way over to them, head and body as low as he could without submitting himself to the indignity of crawling.

"Think we lost everyone who went in there, Centure," the closest man said. "No contact after that explosion."

Leif was hardly surprised, not when the shockwave on this side of the barrier had been enough to be felt through his armor. The blast must have shredded anyone at its epicenter.

"Hold the breach," he ordered nonetheless, "and remember to cycle men out after a few pulses. Do not let your weapons overheat, not until things are truly desperate."

The closest man snorted slightly as Leif turned away, and he just overheard the man's words.

"What he considers and what I consider to be desperate are two very different things."

▶▶▶

▶ Conner ducked as another burst of lazed energy slagged a chunk of the Priminae shuttle she was covering behind. The enemy had taken it on the nose in the first moments of the ambush, but their position, combined with some admittedly quick action on their commander's part, had shifted the balance back to a stalemate.

For the life of her, unfortunately, Conner couldn't determine who that particular state of affairs would tend to favor, which meant that she couldn't sit on her ass and try to wait them out.

"Great," she grumbled to herself. "Should have waited for them to come through a bit more—Sergeant!"

Just as she yelled, the sergeant materialized behind her and nearly gave Conner a heart attack. She refused to give him the satisfaction of actually jumping, and her helmet hid the open-mouthed look of surprise on her face when she turned to him. She made sure to wait long enough that her voice didn't squawk before she addressed the man.

"What kind of heavy weapons do we have, Sergeant?" Conner asked.

"Not much, ma'am. The mission profile called for rescuing the crew, not hammering them into a pulp."

"What I wouldn't give for a couple of twenty-mil thermobarics right now."

"May as well wish for a tank, ma'am. Those were sure as HELL not on our load out for a rescue op."

That, she reflected, was the pure truth.

"We have to do something to dislodge them, and I'd rather not order a frontal assault, Sergeant."

She didn't need to see his face to know he'd winced at *that* idea—not that she blamed him.

"Right you are, ma'am, would rather avoid that if we can," the sergeant said slowly in response.

Any frontal assault was a pain in the ass if the enemy was dug in, but charging into the teeth of the Imperial's infantry lasers would not make for a fun capper to the day.

"I suppose we could use smoke, ma'am, and soften them up with some of the twenty-mil antipersonnel rounds," he offered. "I doubt the shrapnel would get through their armor for the most part, but it should shake them up a bit."

She nodded slowly, considering that.

The armor the enemy had was one of the key problems, of course. A more lightly armored opponent could be eliminated with ranged grenade fire. Just pop frags through the breach set to detonate right on the other side of the hole and end the entire encounter then and there. Unfortunately, fragmentation against real armor was just a metal rain. Annoying to the enemy, perhaps, but nothing more than that.

"Ma'am!"

Conner glanced across her HUD, noticing a corporal flagging for her attention.

"What is it, Corporal?" she asked, switching to the open tactical channel.

"Security guy here just noticed something," he said. "Sounds like something you'd want to know."

"Well, spill it then, Corporal."

"Yes ma'am, sorry ma'am," he answered nervously. "The man I'm with here, Reid is his name, he's been monitoring the signals bouncing around, trying to crack the Imperial communication."

"Did he?" Conner blinked. That would be useful.

"No ma'am, not yet."

Damn.

"So what did he find that's so interesting, then?" Conner tried not to sound too terse with the young enlisted man.

"Well, ma'am, he can't crack their code yet. It's pretty sophisticated, I guess, but he just found that they opened up a *strong* link to the boarding ship here. Lot of data being sent."

"Shit. Sergeant," Conner hissed, "it would appear we're out of time. Bring up the twenties and the smokers. We'll go with your plan."

"Not sure I want credit for this one, ma'am, but yes ma'am," the sergeant said in reply before he waved to a couple of the heavier weapon teams to set up and get ready.

One way or another, this was going to be over quickly.

▶▶▶

▶ Hadrian swore as the fighting in the cramped corridors of the smaller ship intensified again when the Imperials were reinforced by another group.

How many of them are there on this tin can?

The damn thing wasn't *that* big, but there seemed to be a veritable ants' nest of the enemy here to rile up, and boy were they *riled*.

"Lieutenant."

Hadrian almost jumped as the signal from the colonel broke through and shook him from his thoughts. He jumped over to the command channel as quickly as he could and found himself looking at the tense and sweating face of Colonel Conner on his HUD.

"Yes ma'am?"

"We have a problem," she said. "We're going to try to plug it from this side, but if we can't, then it'll be up to you."

"Yes ma'am. Lay it out for me."

"The enemy is close enough to punch through the jamming now," she said, "and it seems that they've done just that. They're sending a lot of information to the ship you're on. I would rather that intel *not* leave. Understood, Marine?"

"Got you, ma'am," he responded even as he stroked the trigger of his assault carbine, sending a three round burst down the hall and into the soft armor of an Imperial who had gotten too gutsy for his own good. "We're almost to the command level, if the Priminae security team here is right about the layout."

"Good. Go for it, Marine."

"Yes ma'am, going for it, ma'am."

The colonel's transparently floating visage vanished from the HUD, and Hadrian took a moment to figure out the lay of the land before he started barking orders.

"Okay, it's crunch time!" he said. "Buckle up, boys, we need to take command."

▶▶▶

▶ The commander of the boarding ship was sweating as the data began trickling into his computers. He had a decision to make.

With the enemy on board, he had little doubt that the navarch would order him to transmit to her ships, after which she would likely abandon or, more probably, scuttle his vessel on her way by.

He would prefer to avoid that outcome, of course, but he saw few options at the moment.

"How good a signal can we send back to the navarch's vessel?" he asked his comm tech.

The man nervously eyed him a bit before answering. "The navarch's vessel is close enough for a focused beam transmission now."

Well, that answers that, I suppose.

There would be no covering up, no pretending that the jamming was still in effect. In fact, the navarch either did know, or certainly would know shortly, that he had the information from the team in hand.

The commander hesitated, though he knew the final decision's outcome already. Finally, he just nodded. "Establish the connection and prepare the data for transmission."

"Yes Commander."

▶▶▶

▶ "Navarch!"

"What is it?" Misrem demanded as she crossed the deck to the communication console.

"Data connection from the boarding ship is open. They are receiving data from the team still on the ship."

"Excellent."

She didn't say anything more, primarily because it seemed in bad taste to insult people just when they'd done something right, but she was still in a foul mood over her *boarding vessel* having been *boarded*.

Still, if they were able to complete their mission despite that, then so be it.

"Inform me when we have the data in our systems."

"As you order, Navarch."

With that said, she turned her focus back to the fight. Her squadron had taken a beating, but they were returning the favor in their own turn. The enemy had an edge in weapons and armor, but not remotely enough to ultimately grant them victory in this fight. She would prefer not to be the last woman standing amid a pile of ashes, however, and the enemy squadron itself simply wasn't the important part of her mission.

They needed information, information that would allow the Empire to prepare its final response for this region. They would be brought under the empress' flag, or they would die as she had commanded. There were other fates possible. The Empire had a mandate from beyond, and the galaxy was within their dominion.

Anyone who objected was in defiance of the gods.

▶▶▶

▶ Conner looked over the limited supplies they had available. A few canisters of smoke remained, enough fragging twenties for a brief sustained exchange, and so forth. She could have wished for more, of that there was no doubt, but she and her Marines would do the job with what they had.

Improvise, adapt, overcome.

Speaking of improvise . . . She turned to the closest security personnel from the *Tetanna*. "Excuse me. I'm sorry, but I don't know your name or rank."

"I am Ithan, Colonel." The woman responded with her rank first. "Ithan Kolka."

Ithan, Conner thought. If she remembered correctly that was roughly a lieutenant's rank in the Navy. Low officer at any rate, though sometimes it was a little difficult to be sure. The rank systems between the Priminae and the Earth didn't match up perfectly, unsurprisingly.

"Ithan, then," she said, nodding to the hand laser the woman was carrying. "When we use smoke, you won't be able to shoot with that. Do you have any of your gravity projection weapons?"

The woman shook her head. "No. Those were built for ground army only, not issued to fleet."

We're going to need to see that changed, Conner thought grimly.

"Alright," she said. "Once we pop smoke, you need to take cover and just hole up. There's nothing you can do here."

"It's our ship. They are on *our* ship," the young woman insisted fervently. "Our job. My job."

"You don't have the tools for the job, and you'll get in the way of my Marines. I like the courage, but shitcan the attitude right the hell now, Ithan. If you try to help here, you'll die. That's your business, not mine. But if you try, you'll also get my Marines killed, and *that* is my business. You and your people sit this one *out*."

The ithan looked rebellious, but Conner stared her down until she flinched and looked away. Finally, the Priminae security officer nodded with a damn near mutinous expression.

"Very well. I will . . . instruct my people," she said.

"Thank you," Conner said, switching back to her tac channels as she observed the state of her Marines' preparation.

They were pretty much done.

She took a breath. "Okay, Marines, you know what you have to do. Execute."

A second later, all hell broke loose on the flight deck of the crippled Priminae cruiser.

CHAPTER 24

▶ "Data is transmitting now."

The commander of the boarding vessel grunted an acknowledgment, but he was distracted by the sound of fighting that could now be heard through the sealed bulkheads. The enemy was practically on top of them now, and he didn't know how much longer they had before the battle spilled over into the very command center in which they sat.

He gripped his personal laser, his hand sweating around the pommel of the weapon as he looked toward the primary entrance to the deck.

Soon.

"Stay on that signal!" he roared. "No matter what happens, that information reaches the navarch. On your life, do you understand me?"

The technician nodded, scared.

"Yes Commander. On my life."

A sharp bang made them all jump, and the commander twisted around toward the bulkhead that was still ringing with some sort of impact he couldn't even *imagine*.

"Wha—" He was cut off when a second impact destroyed the hinges of the heavy portal that sealed the command deck off and blew the door open, leaving it to hang on a ruined but still half-intact hinge as it creaked loudly.

He started to bring his laser up just as the first figure burst through the breach, pointing some sort of infantry weapon in his general direction. He threw himself aside as a burst of light and noise deafened and blinded him. He fired back, and the deck descended into chaos.

▶▶▶

▶ Lieutenant Hadrian slammed into the wall as he saw a brief flash of laser fire burn an afterimage onto his cornea. It had missed him, or he wouldn't be alive to see the flash, of course, but he could feel the corona of the weapon even through his suit and started sweating in such a way that he couldn't tell if the source of his reaction was heat or fear.

If he lived to tell the tale, Hadrian supposed he would blame it on the heat. Some people might even believe him.

He swung his carbine back around, firing short bursts as his target dived behind a console. Sparks and power arcs erupted as his weapon tore through the instruments, making Hadrian wince. But he refused to hesitate as he tracked his target.

Behind him, his Marines were scrambling through the breached bulkhead, adding their volume of fire to his. Everyone was a fair target in this mess, and they were cutting down Imperials with brutal efficiency just on the assumption that any of them could be armed.

The situation didn't allow for hesitation.

Hadrian twisted, looking around for the Imperial he assumed was an armed officer but had turned out to be harder to track than he'd expected. He brought his weapon down to his hip, tracking his aim through his HUD as he slowly swept the area and began to move forward.

Dimly, Hadrian noticed a Marine take up position on his left, mirroring him as they both began to clear the area.

"Watch it," he said. "There's at least one armed officer left."

"Roger that, Lieutenant."

The command deck of the ship was cramped, with station and consoles jammed in wherever they would fit. It felt like he imagined a submarine would, back over a century ago, and that struck Hadrian as being odd. There was no reason to build a ship this small if you needed so much gear. Size was relative in a spaceship, especially at the technical level of the Priminae or Empire.

Even the Rogues had more room than this ship did, and if the command team was this cramped, Hadrian didn't want to think about how much the crew must have been packed in.

A flicker of motion caught his eye, and Hadrian twisted just in time to see the officer he'd missed earlier appear, his weapon swinging in the general direction of him and the Marine.

"Get down!" Hadrian called as he threw himself into the Marine. Slamming into the power-augmenting armor was rather like trying to body check a brick wall, but this time the wall lost.

As the Marine toppled forward, a laser flash burned into Hadrian's eyes, and a searing heat engulfed his senses before everything went black for the young lieutenant.

▶▶▶

▶ The commander cursed as he saw his beam miss, the target having been pushed clear at the last possible moment. He barely had time to consider the consequences of his action, though, before no less than three of the armor-clad soldiers spun in his direction and opened fire.

Hammer blows seemed to fall upon him, driving him back to the deck as the world exploded around him.

He tried to move, but it seemed like half his body didn't want to respond. He felt like the world had gotten darker and quieter, that everything was somehow farther away than it had been.

With all that he could muster, the commander flipped himself over and used what limbs would follow his orders to drag himself to the cover of the closest console. He didn't feel any pain, just an overwhelming frustration as he was disconnected more and more from his own body.

Grunting with the exertion, but not noticing either, the commander propped himself up enough so that he could see the communications console and confirm that the signal had been sent. A glance was enough to comfort him.

Mission accomplished, Navarch.

He keyed in his own command override and fell back to the ground as the men in the dark armor charged up to him with weapons in hand.

How odd, the commander thought as he looked up at the barrels of the weapons that he knew were so close yet appeared so far away. *I thought dying would hurt more.*

A soft rattle escaped his throat as he slumped in place, his laser falling from limp hands.

▶▶▶

▶ "Target down!" a private called as he kicked the laser away from the officer's limp hand, glancing over his shoulder. "How's the LT?"

"We need to get him to a corpsman, stat!" the Marine kneeling over the fallen lieutenant called back. "Beam missed him, but his light armor couldn't take the flash off the bulkhead. He's burned pretty bad."

"Shit," the private swore, looking around. "What do we do?"

"Take your lieutenant back," the Priminae security chief said as he picked his way through the deck and checked the surroundings.

"We have a mission, sir."

"And we will finish it," the security man said, examining the consoles that were still intact, one by one.

When he reached the console the officer had died behind, however, he paled so much that no one could have missed it.

"What? What is it?"

"It seems that the commander here"—he nodded to the man on the floor—"has disabled safety features on the ship's drives. It will destroy itself quite soon."

"Oh shit. We have to get it away from the ship," the Marine swore, leaning over another console. "Anyone know how to work this thing?"

He was stopped by the security man pulling him back with a surprising strength.

"You have done enough. The *Tetanna* is my ship," the chief said to him with a half smile that made the Marine swallow hard. "Get your lieutenant and go. I will handle this."

"Sir . . . I . . . you—"

"Go," the man said with a tone that was surprisingly firm given how oddly gentle the look in his eyes was.

Then he ignored the Marines, turning to the console and attaching his hacking device to the circuitry. The Marines slowly backed away from him, still uncertain if they should abandon their position on the orders of someone not in their command structure, or even their world, Allied or not.

"You have until I break these codes," the chief said, not looking up. "Then I am blowing us away from the *Tetanna*, whether you are here or not."

The highest-ranking of the Marines left, a corporal, made the call.

"Pick up the LT," he ordered. "We're clearing out."

The Marines did as he said, and he waved them out through the breach, pausing only to look back from the threshold.

"Godspeed, Chief." He nodded to the man standing his last watch.

A nod was all he got in return before the corporal turned and began running down the hall.

▶▶▶

▶ Leif swore when the smoke canisters landed in their midst, spewing their thick white payload into the air, occluding visibility and, far more importantly, laser fire.

"Stand ready," he bellowed. "They will be coming soon!"

"Centure!" the comm officer called. "The signal is degrading!"

"What? No!" Leif snapped. "Do what you must, but do *not* lose that connection!"

The man swallowed but nodded as he turned back to his gear. "I . . . I can perhaps use the ship's power to boost the connection."

"Do it. Do it fast!" Leif yelled, turning to the others. "Protect him to the last. The signal *must* go through."

He couldn't tell what his men had thought of the order as the smoke was now completely enveloping him and them, but it didn't matter. They would do their jobs, or else.

A rapid-fire series of explosions tore around them, smaller than he'd expected from the enemy, but enough to rattle him and his men as chunks of metal rained down and spattered off their armor. It was not particularly damaging, but the effect was incredibly distracting, and he found himself uncertain where he *should* be focusing his attentions.

What are they doing? he wondered briefly. He knew they had better weapons than this. Was there more to the situation than he could see?

He gripped his infantry laser tightly. In the end, it no longer mattered. This would be their last battle of this mission, no matter how it ended.

▶▶▶

▶ Rider glumly checked his magazine, grimacing as he counted the remaining rounds.

"Down to twenty-eight. You guys?"

"Fourteen," Dow answered.

"Got a full thirty-five. I'm good to go," Ram told them with forced cheerfulness.

Kensey inhaled, favoring his left side where the heat of an enemy laser had managed to overload his armor and scorch him despite having actually missed. "I've got twenty-two myself."

"When the colonel makes her move, we'll hit them again," Rider decided. "Ram, swap mags with Kensey. Ken, you're designated marksman for this one."

Ramirez silently ejected his full mag and passed it off to the injured Marine in exchange for the partial, which he slapped into his receiver with practiced ease.

"And the rest of us?" Ram asked calmly.

Rider risked a glance down the hall, noting the smoke billowing around the area. It was being blown around a bit by the frag twenties, but was still covering almost the entire group of Imperial troops.

"We run our ragged asses down there as fast and quiet as we can," he said, "and then we kill them all. Any objections?"

The others looked at each other, only Kensey grimacing as he could barely stand, let alone run, and he hated the idea of watching from the sidelines even if he would also be *shooting*.

Dow and Ram, however, simply replied with two words.

"Recon, oorah!"

▶ ▶ ▶

▶ Leif was tensely waiting for the attack when a blur of motion from the opposite direction caught his attention. He twisted to look through the thinner smoke to the rear and saw three men sprinting toward his position.

"Watch the flank!" he ordered, gesturing wildly to get some of his men to redirect their focus.

Three did, stepping out of the smoke enough to clear their lasers.

A single crack filled the air for each man, and all three went down with a rapidity that made Leif blink.

He could barely see a fourth figure lying on the ground behind the charging men. He'd only seen him due to the flash of his weapon as it fired, and he was impressed despite himself. The skill needed to kill three men with three shots while firing through your own moving comrades spoke of either supreme confidence or complete uncaring toward your own. The fact that he'd struck his targets seemed to indicate the former.

Leif was just about to order more men to cover the flank, but then the volume of fire from the *other* side erupted into a maelstrom of death.

▶▶▶

▶ Rider waited until he'd closed half the distance to the enemy position, trusting Kensey to provide cover. It wasn't until he could hear the barrage from the other side that he took his first shot, letting his computer handle most of the job of firing the weapon.

His rifle began to bark sharply in a steady staccato as the computer took the data from his HUD and calculated angles before instructing the rifle exactly when the right time to speak had come. He still had to aim it himself—the rifle wasn't on a computer-controlled gimbal or the like—but the computer had taken over the duties of the trigger.

Imperials fell from the steady volume of fire he and his team laid in, but through that smoke, there was only so much even a computer could do. More rounds missed than hit. Before they were at the edge of the smoke, he was out of ammo, and he knew that the others had run out seconds earlier.

Rider didn't pause in his stride as he let the weapon clatter to the deck, drawing his sidearm with his right hand, his left sliding the recon-issue Kanto fighting knife.

He grinned as he entered the smoke, thinking about how many people had argued that there was no point equipping a modern Marine with a fighting knife. He had always come down on the other side of that argument.

Time to find out who was right.

The thick white smoke enveloped them, and then they could see nothing but vague, ghostly shapes around them.

▶▶▶

▶ "Move in!" The sergeant's order was hardly needed as the Marines charged the smoke, firing to keep the enemy's head down.

They'd scratched up everything they had left for one last move, and while he knew the colonel wished they had more, they would make do.

Laser flashes could be seen from inside the smoke, and even as attenuated as they were, the infantry weapons of the Empire retained enough power to cook Marine-augmenting armor at such close ranges of engagement.

Three men went down, their armor on fire, and the sergeant grimaced but didn't slow as he replied with his carbine.

"This is where this ends!" he called. "Take them, Marines!"

A carbine firing on his right caught his eye, and the sergeant glanced to one side as he recognized the icon that represented the firer on his HUD.

"Colonel," he said, forcing his voice to be conversational as he kept his attention on the fight, not pausing in his advance. "Would you mind telling me what you think you're doing?"

"I believe that should be obvious, Sergeant," Conner told him, firing more rounds into the smoke.

"Begging your colonel's pardon, ma'am," he said in a genial tone that held a ridge of tension that had nothing to do with the battle, "but are you out of your mind? You're in command, ma'am. Your place is under cover, directing this mess."

They were almost to the smoke then, and the colonel just laughed at him.

"Direct a fight through occlusion smoke, Sergeant? Really?"

She had a point, he supposed, not that he'd ever admit it. As they entered the smoke, all their gear lost resolution at the best. Most stopped working entirely, and in a second, they were blind fighting.

Please don't let any of us frag the colonel, the sergeant thought, moaning as he went about his duties and tried not to think too hard about his superior officer trying to get herself killed.

▶▶▶

▶ Misrem shrieked as she lost another destroyer. The screen that had protected her cruisers was now looking rather ragged, but it had largely done its job.

Other than the initial damage from the enemy destroyer unleashing those insane weapons from point-blank range, most of her heavier vessels were still intact, if bleeding atmosphere badly.

The enemy was in similar shape, something that infuriated her. They had such a deficit in numbers that they should have lost more ships than they had. The enemy armor was fiendishly effective, letting them take fire that would have destroyed any Imperial ship ten times over, but it wouldn't be enough if this fight went to its ultimate conclusion.

The anomalous lead ship was bleeding gasses at rates she doubted were sustainable, even with the twin cores she knew the enemy cruisers shared with her own vessel's design.

Nothing could take that sort of damage for long and keep coming back. Everything had a breaking point, and while the enemy was still more or less in one piece, as her own ships were, her ships were in better shape.

"Navarch!"

"What is it?" She turned to look at the communications officer.

"The boarding vessel has broken away from the enemy ship!"

"What?" She growled now, looking closer. "Did they recover the boarding team?"

"We don't know, Navarch. There's been no contact from them for some time now," the communications tech said. "Last report was that the enemy was—"

He broke off as the icon for the boarding vessel blinked off the screen and, two seconds later, a flash of nuclear fire erupted on their visual scanners.

Misrem was silent for a brief moment before she made her call.

"Break from the fighting," she ordered. "There's nothing left for us here."

▶▶▶

▶ "Commodore, they're breaking away. Maximum acceleration, heading for the outer system," Commander Heath said, sounding surprised. "Do we follow?"

Eric's mouth was dry as he looked at the damage reports just from the *Odysseus* and knew that, while they had taken the brunt of the fighting, it wasn't much better for anyone else. They'd lost two more Rogues and more than one of the Priminae Heroics was likely for the breakers, unless he was mistaken.

The *Odysseus* herself might have a hard time avoiding a similar fate, but Earth couldn't really afford to lose a single ship if it could be avoided.

"No," he ordered. "We're done here. Let them go."

▶▶▶

▶ Two beaten and battered groups of ships broke apart, no longer intent on fighting one another to the last but with the clear promise of more to come.

Where they had been fighting, now only expanding gasses, debris, and bodies marked their passing.

EPILOGUE

▶ Eric Weston's boots crunched on the debris as he stepped over the battlefield and surveyed it with a critical eye.

"This was some heavy fighting, Captain," he said to the Priminae captain at his side.

"It was indeed, Commodore," Drey said tiredly. "I only wish it had not been your people who took the worst of it."

"Don't," Eric said. "Just thank the fallen for their sacrifice. Wishes and could-have-beens do not win anyone—not you or them—respect."

He paused, looking at a body with a knife driven through the center of its chest. He bent over slightly to confirm that, yes, it was actually a Marine Kanto blade.

"Huh," he said mildly, hiding the depths of his emotions as he examined the scene. "I would have sworn that the blade would have shattered before it penetrated combat armor. Live and learn, I suppose. Oorah, Marine."

He shrugged and stepped over the breach and onto the flight deck.

The damage was immense in scale, a level of fighting that he could barely imagine just due to the close-range nature of the conflict combined with the sheer power being tossed around. It was all rather staggering, really.

"Will you be able to repair?" he asked the Priminae captain.

Drey sighed. "We do not know. Reports are still being assembled, but I would be somewhat surprised if we can. The cores may be salvaged, of course. If they had been significantly damaged, we would not be standing here."

Eric barked out a laugh.

There was truth there. Even if the ship *was* still in one piece, he'd not set foot on her if the cores were unstable. Hell, he'd not let any of his ships within ten light-seconds of it, for that matter.

"There's the truth, Captain."

"And your *Odysseus*?" Drey asked.

"I don't know."

"I hope we can both repair," Drey said finally. "These ships have a history now, do they not?"

"They do, Captain, but their honors will never die. Steel rusts, ceramic degrades, but honor is inviolate."

Drey nodded slowly. "Thank you, Commodore, for your words and your visit."

"It was a pleasure, and an honor," Eric said with a hint of a sad smile. "We will see one another again, I think."

"I would like that, I believe."

The two then stood silently as the cleanup around them continued.

▶▶▶

▶ Eric was tired by the time he got back to the bridge of the *Odysseus*, but then he'd been tired when he left it.

"Damage reports to your station, Commodore," Heath said as he entered.

"Thank you, Commander."

He took a seat and called up the reports. It was a long file.

Enemy lasers had destroyed the forward armor to the point that no repair was possible while underway. There just wasn't anything for the expanding foam to stick to. Even chunks of the superstructure had been melted away.

The cores were intact, of course, so that was something.

They'd lost almost a hundred men on the *Odysseus*. The task group's losses numbered well over a thousand. The loss of the *Kid* alone . . .

Eric closed his eyes.

All this, and for what? The enemy still escaped with intelligence that we can't be sure about.

Drey had provided him with the search terms the enemy had used on his database, and it wasn't good.

They'd gone looking for information on the new laser systems, armor design, and, far more importantly in Eric's mind, Earth.

Oh, they hadn't known to look by name or anything of that nature. They'd been looking for information about the Priminae's allies.

Drey had also provided him with the results of those searches, of course, and it also wasn't good. They didn't know how much intelligence had been transmitted—some had certainly not—but some had, and he had to assume the worst.

If they know how weak Earth is, they'll make their move. We're not ready. We need more time. What do we do? We can't hide, not anymore. We can't run . . . I guess . . .

"We fight."

Eric's eyes snapped open as a cry of alarm echoed around the bridge from multiple sources, drawing in the Marine guard stationed outside. Eric surged to his feet as the Marine entered his peripheral vision, pulling his sidearm and aiming it toward the front of the deck.

"Freeze!"

Eric stared with a mix of concern, confusion, and incredulity at the figure who'd caused the sudden commotion.

It was a young boy, he thought, wearing what looked like ancient Grecian or maybe Roman armor. The child's attire consisted of a gilded skirt and bronze breastplate with greaves and bracers hidden under an equally old one-piece helmet with a vertical fringe running front to back.

The boy's face, through the helmet, was beaten and bloodied, and he held an old leaf-bladed sword in his hand.

Eric slowly got up, holding a hand out to bring the Marine to a stop and tell him to hold.

He and the boy stared at one another for a while, Eric trying to decipher what he was seeing while the boy just seemed etched from stone.

Is that . . . pink glitter around his eyes?

More than *anything*, that incongruous detail flummoxed Eric, and he honestly had *no clue* what to make of it. He made himself focus.

"Who are you?" Eric asked with a sinking sensation as he suspected very much what the answer would be. But it was impossible. It couldn't be what he was thinking. They were nowhere *near* a planet, and the only entities he'd ever seen that he could match this boy to were *planet bound*.

The boy looked him evenly in the eyes.

"I'm Odysseus."

Eric slumped back into his seat, alternatively awed and horrified.

"You woke me up."

ABOUT THE AUTHOR

Bestselling Canadian author Evan Currie's imagination knows no limits, and he uses his talent and passion for storytelling to take readers everywhere from ancient Rome to the dark expanses of space. Although he started out dabbling in careers such as computer science and the local lobster industry, Evan quickly determined that writing the kinds of stories he grew up loving was his true life's calling. Beginning with the techno-thriller *Thermals*, Evan has expanded the universe within his mind with acclaimed series such as Warrior's Wings, the Scourwind Legacy, the Hayden War Cycle, and Odyssey One. He delights in pushing the boundaries of technology and culture, exploring the ways in which these forces intertwine and could shape the future of humanity both on Earth and among the stars.